BIRDING WITH BENEFITS

BIRDING WITH BENEFITS

SARAH T. DUBB

G

GALLERY BOOKS

NEW YORK LONDON TORONTO SYDNEY NEW DELHI

Gallery Books
An Imprint of Simon & Schuster, LLC
1230 Avenue of the Americas
New York, NY 10020

This book is a work of fiction. Any references to historical events, real people, or real places are used fictitiously. Other names, characters, places, and events are products of the author's imagination, and any resemblance to actual events or places or persons, living or dead, is entirely coincidental.

First Gallery Books trade paperback edition June 2024

GALLERY BOOKS and colophon are registered trademarks of Simon & Schuster, LLC

Simon & Schuster: Celebrating 100 Years of Publishing in 2024

For information about special discounts for bulk purchases, please contact Simon & Schuster Special Sales at 1-866-506-1949 or business@simonandschuster.com.

The Simon & Schuster Speakers Bureau can bring authors to your live event. For more information or to book an event, contact the Simon & Schuster Speakers Bureau at 1-866-248-3049 or visit our website at www.simonspeakers.com.

Interior design by Hope Herr-Cardillo

Manufactured in the United States of America

10 9 8 7 6 5 4 3 2 1

Library of Congress Cataloging-in-Publication Data

Names: Dubb, Sarah T., author.
Title: Birding with benefits / Sarah T. Dubb.
Description: First Gallery Books trade paperback edition. | New York : Gallery Books, 2024.
Identifiers: LCCN 2023049281 | ISBN 9781668037836 (paperback) | ISBN 9781668037843 (ebook)
Subjects: LCGFT: Romance fiction. | Novels.
Classification: LCC PS3604.U248 B57 2024 | DDC 813/.6—dc23/eng/20231101
LC record available at https://lccn.loc.gov/2023049281

ISBN 978-1-6680-3783-6
ISBN 978-1-6680-3784-3 (ebook)

For all who facilitate discovery, especially:

teachers

library workers

naturalists

and creators of every kind.

CHAPTER 1

Celeste Johanssen had embarked on some rather outlandish activities in the two years since her divorce. She'd done skydiving, vermicomposting, and even a week of sleeping on her back porch every night—but they were nothing compared to her activity on this sunny Saturday morning.

She scanned the park for her date.

Her *fake* date.

He'd been described to her as "a quiet, sweet guy with a beard, straight out of an L.L.Bean catalog" who was in desperate need of help that morning. And if there was anything Celeste loved more than a new adventure, it was helping. She'd even arrived a couple of minutes early—a miracle for her, especially considering she'd stopped for pastries and caffeine.

In their brief texts, full of proper punctuation and capitalization, John had told her he'd be waiting in a gazebo on the southeast side of the popular park, which tracked with the bearded mystery man sitting there now.

"Whoa." She stopped short, catching the pastry box with the bottom of her cup before it tipped all the way off her arm and onto the ground.

"He's the kind of guy who will stop traffic to help a tortoise cross the road, then go home and build you a table," his friend had said of John. The description had seemed absurd at the time, but she saw it now. Thick arms displayed evidence of manual work, and his auburn beard, glinting cinnamon and sugar in the morning sun, gave him a woodsman vibe. His skin had the soft tan of someone who spent a lot of time outside but always wore sunscreen. Large hands cradled a small, worn book tenderly, fingers rubbing at the corner of a page before turning it slowly. The reading glasses parked on the end of his nose didn't hurt the tableau, either. John seemed a man balanced precisely on the edge between hard and soft.

Celeste began a careful walk across the crunching grass, remembering the most important rule of improv, simple words she'd scrawled onto a sticky note to join the others on her bathroom mirror.

Say yes.

People milled around the park, looking curiously up into the trees, as Celeste pondered which was the ex she was coming to deflect. Eight a.m. did seem an odd time for a date, but she'd been out of the dating pool for decades, so what did she know? When there was a new adventure to be had, Celeste rarely asked for details.

John's attention was still on his book as she stepped into the shade of the gazebo, goose bumps appearing along her arms, left bare by her cotton tank dress. In her rush, she hadn't grabbed a jacket, but soon it wouldn't matter. April in Tucson meant chilly mornings and warm, perfect afternoons.

Celeste allowed herself one more long perusal of John, studying her subject in order to throw herself properly into the scene. The glasses and beard combined to give him a real librarian-in-the-wild vibe. If there was a calendar somewhere of ruggedly nerdy men reading, John could be any month of the year. Interesting that this guy, cords of muscle visible on his forearms where his sleeves were pushed up, needed protection from his ex.

Before she could make out its title, he flipped the book closed and stowed it in a backpack at his feet, then removed his glasses and tucked them into a side pocket of his pants. After a double take, he registered Celeste, his bearded jaw dipping as he did a fast sweep of her body, settling on her face as his brows pulled together.

"Hi!" Celeste stepped forward, arms pulled by the weight of the pastry box. She could have just gotten her standard cinnamon swirl, but she hadn't known what John might like, so she'd played it safe by getting one of everything. "John, right? I'm Celeste, I'm here to—"

But her foot wouldn't lift, and her movement stalled. A panicked look down revealed one of her white low-top Converse tangled in the loose laces of the other, and *oh shit*—

The pastry box went first, catching air. John caught the box with his palm, balancing it like a skilled waiter. Celeste's hip hit something warm and soft, keeping her upright.

Hot liquid from each cup sloshed out of the lids, landing on Celeste's wrists and forearms. At her wince, John released her, his jaw going tense.

Celeste shook her head, arms stinging. "Fuck, I'm so sorry." She slammed the drinks onto the concrete table unceremoniously, swiping coffee from her arms. Something rustled in front of her, and then a soft, worn flannel hit her skin, traveling lightly down her right arm, then her left.

"You okay?" John's voice was as low as she'd expected, considering the beard and big shoulders. A smooth baritone.

She nodded silently as their eyes met before he bent to shove his flannel into his backpack.

Laughing too loudly, Celeste shook out her arms. "I'm totally mortified, but physically unharmed. Thank you. I brought coffee. I got yours black but I have creamers in my bag if you need them." Her eyes darted to the table. "And pastries. Way too many pastries." She propped her foot on the bench to retie her laces and secure them with a triple knot. "I'm usually only half this chaotic, I swear. I'm a little nervous. I've never done anything like this before."

"Oh." John cleared his throat with a rumble. "You haven't?"

"No, definitely not." Did he think she made a habit of meeting strangers for a game of pretend romance? "Have you?"

John scrubbed at his beard with one hand as he narrowed his eyes. "Um, yes. Quite a lot."

Intrigued, Celeste waited for more details, but he quietly studied her like the book in his hands minutes before. Chris had warned her that John was quiet, so she decided not to press. As his open palm reached for the coffee, her hip twinged with the memory of his firm catch.

She took a long drag from her cup, letting the hit of caffeine shock the memory out of her system. Cold permeated her dress as she slid onto the concrete bench. "So, Chris explained the situation to me. He said your ex would be here. Have you spotted her yet?"

John squinted. "You mean Breena? I haven't seen her yet. What did Chris say exac—"

"Oh good. We have a little time, then. Should we get to know each other a bit before everything gets started?"

He only looked at her. Maybe if she went first, he'd feel more comfortable opening up. Celeste set her cup down, rolling her head on her neck, settling back into the purpose of her mission. "So, I'm forty-two. I teach language arts at a public middle school. I've got a daughter who's headed to college next year, so I'm staring that empty nest right in the face, and to be honest, I like how it's looking from here." She tapped her fingers along the table, noting that her purple polish from the mom/daughter night she'd imposed on Morgan a couple of weeks before was chipping. "I love to read, I hike a lot, and I'm embarking on a bunch of hobbies right now. That's how I met Chris, actually, at this painting thing the other night."

John's head cocked to one side. "You just met Chris the other night? I thought you two knew each other."

"We do now. He's the best!" She'd had a blast with Chris, painting their little teapots side by side at the sip-and-paint event she'd decided to hit up last minute. She'd gone alone, and while Chris had seemed to be there with someone, he and Celeste had started talking when he saw her copy of *Dune* sticking out of her bag. Before too long she was hearing about Chris's angst at work and his guilt over messing things up for his best friend.

She pried open the pastry box, revealing the jumbled but largely intact goodies, and pulled out a scone before giving the box a push toward John in invitation. "He was really worried about you. Said he'd let you down, mentioned mating snails. I didn't ask for details. It was serendipitous, honestly, because I was supposed to start this yoga class today but the whole series got canceled last minute. Apparently the energy wasn't right." She tore off a small piece of pastry and popped it into her mouth. "So, what about you? Chris said something about woodworking, I think?"

Chris had actually said that John was *really good with wood*, and she'd almost spit out her wine.

"Yeah." John lifted a flaky croissant from the box and moved it from hand to hand. "I make some furniture, smaller stuff. It was a hobby but now it's part-time work. I just lost my office job—"

He'd shifted his glance up as he spoke, easing toward eye contact, but now he paused and focused on something behind Celeste. She followed his gaze to a stunning woman approaching them. Straight black hair framed a golden face and dusted the tops of her shoulders, and toned legs stretched out of khaki shorts.

Celeste turned her attention back to John, whose jaw was tense. "This is her, right? The ex?"

John nodded and opened his mouth, but Celeste put down her drink and scone, sliding her body over until their thighs were pushed together. She visualized the note next to *Say yes* on her mirror at home.

If you're going to do something, do it right.

She would have preferred more time to prepare for this part, including reviewing what level of intimacy he was comfortable with. But since it was showtime already, she went on instinct alone, hoping John was ready to follow her lead.

His body tensed as his chin dipped, his eyes tracing the line where their legs pressed together. She leaned her shoulder into his, reaching a hand out to extract the croissant from his worrying fingers and place it on the table.

"You're hurting the croissant. It didn't do anything wrong. And don't worry, this is what I'm here for, remember?" Celeste straightened her back, smiling big. "I'm sorry we didn't get to chat more before she showed up, but don't worry—I don't bite."

With this, she slid a hand across his lower back, hooking it on the other side of his waist. The move brought their bodies flush from knee to shoulder. John was stocky and hard, a warm wall of muscle that filled her senses with fresh wood and sunshine. As the ex approached, Celeste dropped her other hand to his knee, rubbing a little circle with her thumb over the soft khaki fabric. All part of the act. She was here to show that John was hers.

For the next few minutes, at least.

And then the ex was there, hands on her lovely hips, looking down at John before brushing her eyes briefly past Celeste. "Hey, John."

John seemed to have stopped breathing, so Celeste dug her fingers into his waist, finding some softness. He sucked in a sharp breath and cleared his throat. "Breena, hi."

"Wasn't sure I'd see you here today." Breena's eyes skirted over to Celeste again, lingering on the hand on John's knee, before looking back to him. "But you made it after all. With someone new, it looks like."

More throat clearing, then a rough, almost questioning, "Yeah."

A beat passed in silence, the odd triangle throwing looks back and forth. If John couldn't muster up an introduction, Celeste wouldn't wait. She was here to help, after all.

She gave John's knee a quick squeeze before shooting out an open palm toward Breena. "Hi." Celeste pulled out the voice she'd perfected for the first day of every school year, the voice that said *I'm ready to play nice, but don't try to fuck with me*. "I'm Celeste. John's girlfriend."

CHAPTER 2

When John was ten, he and his dad had been hiking in the Santa Ritas when a monsoon hit. It was one of those microbursts that filled streambeds and washes in an instant, the rainfall so thick that for a few dizzying minutes, John lost all sense of up and down. All he could do was let the sheets of water sluice off his face and wait for the world in front of him to clear.

Some thirty years later, he felt that way again, even as the sunshine glimmered brightly just beyond the shadow of the ramada. The last few swirling minutes were a blur of sensation—Celeste thrusting pastries at him as her earrings swung to her rhythm, then crowding him on the bench, smelling of peppermint. A park full of birdsong, nimble fingers at his waist, the clench of his stomach when Breena approached, and the surprise at how it was eased by the small circles Celeste drew on his knee.

But none of these pieces completed the puzzle. He had no idea what was happening. Only that Breena was puffing out a short "huh" as she stared at Celeste's outstretched hand just long enough for John to think a rebuff was coming. And that Celeste straightened even more against his body and drew in a breath, keeping her arm outstretched until Breena finally met her hand for a shake. And that when Celeste's hand returned to his knee, fingers relaxed, he had the sensation they'd all passed a test of some sort, even though he didn't even know the subject.

Chris was behind this. John's best friend was always loyal and supportive, but he'd been overboard lately, funneling his own professional malaise into jump-starting what he called John's "long-ignored dreams." It was Chris who'd signed them up for the contest, promising John a fresh start. And when he'd had to drop out at the last minute due to ill-timed snail mating, he'd convinced John to "persevere" and had promised him a new partner.

"Don't let this stop you!" Chris had pleaded when he'd broken the news. "I'll find the perfect replacement. Please, this is what you need, just do this for me."

"Girlfriend?" Breena's tight voice yanked John back in the blurry scene as he blinked, trying to bring it all into focus. "I didn't realize you were seeing someone, John." She snapped one set of fingers close to her thigh. "Nice to meet you, Celeste."

Celeste simply hummed in response, turning away from Breena to give John a beaming smile. Her fair skin contrasted with the rich brown of her hair, and a fan of freckles dotted the curves of her cheeks. Laugh lines framed her mouth in a look he could only describe as conspiratorial. He shouldn't have liked it so much, but he found himself smiling back.

Above them, Breena cleared her throat. "So, does this mean you have a partner after all?"

Celeste gave a breezy nod, her brown ponytail swinging in time with her dangling purple beaded earrings as she kept the full force of her attention on John. "Obviously, that answer is yes. Right, babe?"

"Um." John mumbled, scrubbing at his beard. Somewhere

behind him, a Lucy's warbler trilled, its frenetic call a mirror to his quickened heartbeat. Celeste's fingers on his knee switched from the gentle circle to a dig of nails. "Right," he squeaked.

Breena drummed her fingers on her hip, watching Celeste. "Well, you must be good. John doesn't go birding with just anybody. I should know, since we were champs together three years in a row."

Celeste's hand froze on John's knee. Somewhere across the park, a northern mockingbird cycled through a series of high, cheerful songs.

"Birding." She nearly chirped the word, swallowing the last syllable. John registered the loss of heat from her palm as Celeste reached for her cup and took a long sip of her coffee, closing her eyes. She opened her eyes and smiled. "Yes. Birding. I do that."

Breena nodded, but the rapid staccato of her fingers on her hip gave her away. She rarely showed nervousness, but this drumming was one of her tells. He didn't doubt she'd been triumphant when word filtered down that John wouldn't be in the contest this year. Chris had been sure to bring it up when convincing him that his layoff from his steady job was "a sign from the universe" that this could be the breakthrough he needed. "You know, an extra perk is that Breena will see you don't need her," he'd said with a conspiratorial smirk.

And even though John preferred birding for the joy of it over the scramble of the annual contest, he didn't hate the idea of showing Breena what he could do without her.

Not that he'd get a chance. Chris's snails were mating, and whatever had brought Celeste to the park this morning, it clearly wasn't birding.

"Good luck, B," he said as a goodbye, ready to sort things

out with Celeste so he could head home and put in some hours in his shop. It was second best to how he'd planned to spend the morning, but it would do.

Ignoring John's hint that their conversation was over, Breena held her ground and watched Celeste carefully, her nervous tic giving way to a stillness she'd always had in the field. For a moment, it brought John back to when they'd met, both eager wildlife grad students grateful to have a shot at honing their passions, bonding over microscope slides and invasive species studies. And birds.

But that was a long time ago, and Celeste was no specimen for examination. He wasn't sure who she was, but she'd come to help, and it irked him to see her in Breena's sights.

"Well, Breena, we don't want to keep you," Celeste piped up just as John was working up what else to say to get Breena to go. "Please—" She waved a hand in a gesture of such clear dismissal that he forced down a laugh. "Carry on with your morning."

Breena's eyes narrowed, but then she nodded and turned without a word, heading toward a long table set up under a lanky mesquite tree. Celeste unwound herself from John, the crisp breeze whisking away the warmth of her hands. On the bench, their thighs still touched.

She took a long sip from her cup before turning to John, squinting. "I don't really know what's going on, do I?"

He slid away, creating enough space to turn and face her more directly. One of her fingers traced the plastic edges of the drink top. Ridiculously, John felt a phantom touch on his knee. "What exactly did Chris say about meeting me today?"

Celeste pulled on her ponytail, running it through her fingers as she bit her lip. "The truth is, I'd had a glass of wine and was concentrating a lot on my teapot. Chris was going back and forth between telling me all about how guilty he felt for abandoning you and flirting with the painting instructor. But what I gathered was something about snails." She paused, pursing her lips. "Is that right, is it really snails?"

"It's really snails. They're his life's work."

Celeste took the fact in stride. "So whatever was happening with his snails meant he couldn't help you out with something, and he was afraid he'd really left you in a pickle. And I remember that part because I just did *The Tempest* with my students, and that phrase is there—*How camest thou in this pickle?*" She picked up her scone and took a bite, nodding to herself as she chewed. "I may have missed a few details. But then I perked back up when he started talking about your ex, because I'm petty like that. 'Brilliant but cold,' he'd said. And something about cheating with some genius or something. Was *that* really her?"

She motioned to where Breena stood talking to Marisol, a small pitbull of a birder known for playing birdcalls on her phone to throw other people off.

John nodded and sighed, rubbing at his beard. Leave it to Chris to tell Celeste about the stupid genius, but not give her any details about the actual contest.

Celeste whistled. "Wow, she is gorgeous. Sorry about the cheating." She gave his knee a little pat, a far cry from the trail she'd drawn along his kneecap during her surprise performance, not that he expected that again. "And then he says—" She held her finger in the air. "I remember this clearly, he said, 'And his ex will be there on Saturday, and I'd really like her to see John with another partner. This is important to help John move forward.' So that's when I said I could come and help."

Understanding dawned as the pieces clicked together. "And when he said 'partner,' you thought—"

Celeste dropped her face into her hands before looking back up, blushing. "Romantic partner." She pulled at her hair. The hues of brown streaming from her ponytail reminded him of the grain of the black walnut he'd used in a recent project. "But that's not actually what you needed."

John shrugged, almost laughing. If you asked his mother and some of his friends, he was certainly in need of a romantic partner, but he felt otherwise. "No."

"Jesus fucking Christ." Celeste stood, smoothing her dress over slim hips. She was tall, probably only a few inches shorter than John's six feet, and pacing energetically. "I am so embarrassed. Even for me, this is a lot."

"Really, what you did was very kind, and I appreciate your jumping in to help."

The pacing paused as Celeste smirked. "She *did* seem a little off-kilter seeing you with someone new."

The truth of it surprised him. From the beginning of their relationship, everyone had acted like John had won the lottery. Breena was beautiful, brilliant, and a clear rising star in their field. Always networking and looking five years ahead, she was a study in contrasts with John, the quiet guy in the corner with a book in his hands. When John had finally ended things, she'd told him he'd regret it. "I'm special, John," she'd spat. "You think someone like you will find somebody like me again?"

She hadn't had to go into detail about the *someone like you* part, not when she'd made it clear enough over time what somebody like John lacked—ambition, drive, and forward thinking, among other things.

But for someone who'd sworn she'd washed her hands of him, Breena had paid a lot of attention to Celeste, and it hadn't felt terrible. "Yeah," he said quietly. "Though it might be more about the contest thing than the . . ." He motioned between them, suddenly feeling ridiculous. "Other thing."

"Right." She nodded. "The contest. It's something with birds?"

Birds. Finally, something about this morning John could understand. "Every year, the Arizona Ornithological Society organizes a bird-watching contest. People enter in pairs, and the object is to count as many bird species in our region as possible."

Blinking, Celeste cycled through expressions until she settled on a smile. "Wow. A bird-watching contest. That's a thing." Snails, bird-watching, Breena. Nothing seemed to shake this woman. "That sounds fun, but she was kind of intense about it. Is it a big deal?"

He wished it weren't, and yet. "Not in the grand scheme of things, but over the years the event has taken on more significance within the regional birding community." Her brows lifted at the phrase "regional birding community," but he continued. "Winning is a real badge of honor, bragging rights and all that. And this year the winners will be featured in *Arizona Beauty* magazine and get a speaking role at the next Arizona Bird Festival. Chris entered us because—" He cut himself off, not having meant to go into even that many details, which were of no interest to Celeste anyway.

But she leaned in close, bringing a whiff of peppermint with her. "Because?"

Best to get everything out at once. "A lot of people travel here to go birding, and sometimes they want a local expert to help them make sure they can make the most of their time here. I've thought about starting my own business, doing private bird guiding."

She nodded, looking interested. "Amazing, what a cool job. And what's been holding you back?"

Celeste couldn't know her simple question hit an already

battered target, but John winced nonetheless. What was "holding him back" was a regular topic of debate among his family and friends, whether it was his prolonging his stay at home after college, choosing not to pursue a PhD like his peers, settling for an office job in Tucson he'd never loved, or taking too long to pick an item off a restaurant menu.

"Well, most of the established guides in town are experts, and they have the advanced degrees to prove it. I'm not sure I'm qualified."

"You don't have fancy letters after your name?"

He shook his head. "No, I don't. I'd imagined myself going that way, and I did start graduate school, but—" John paused, hearing an echo of Breena's voice in his head. *How could you just drop out? You're embarrassing both of us!* "It didn't work for me," he said simply. "I've always birded as a hobby, but I went in a different direction professionally."

Celeste tented her fingers together between her bouncing thighs. With each bounce, her knee sent a rush of air against his.

"But you're a good . . . birder? Is that what I would call you?"

"Yeah." His eyes caught again on Breena, who'd once graced John with the compliment that if he just applied himself, he'd be one of the most impressive birders in the region. "And yes, I'm okay at it."

But Celeste tapped her cup and shook her head. "I think you're being humble. When she was over here, Breena said something about being three-time champions."

"Yeah." John gnawed on his lip. "But that was together, and now—" Even with Chris, who knew more about snails than birds but was a beast on the trail, Breena would be tough to beat. But with Chris out, and Celeste showing up as the wrong kind of partner, John was clearly out of the contest.

It was probably for the best. He could search for a new job, keep his life simple, and maybe try again next year.

Celeste twisted her fingers in her ponytail to tug on it again. He watched three faint pulses in the side hollow of her neck, just below the swing of her earring. "You said something before about losing your job?"

John directed his gaze at the blue sky over Celeste's shoulder. He hadn't been this close to a woman in a while, and it was throwing his already confused system for a loop. "I managed donation records for the Southern Arizona Land Conservancy, but we merged with another nonprofit, and my job was eliminated in the process."

"So why are you smiling?"

He rubbed his beard to confirm it, then let out a short laugh. "It was good work. All stuff I cared about, but it was hard being at a desk in an office all day. I'd known for a while it wasn't a good fit for me, but it seemed wrong to leave a good job." So he'd stayed. For years.

"In that case, please accept my congratulations for being fired." She gave a serious nod, smiling broadly. "Are you looking for something else?"

He should be. And he meant to start every day, but then instead he sat on his porch and watched the birds, or practiced something new in his workshop. "I have savings to live off for a few months, and I make some income off the woodworking. But Chris thought that with the contest, maybe I could finally—" He stopped and ran a hand through his hair.

Celeste slapped her thighs. "Do the bird thing! You have time to plan, because you're out of work, and the contest win would give you the boost to get new clients, right?"

Celeste was channeling Chris even in his absence. That paint night must have been quite a scene. "That was the idea, but it's really okay that it's not—"

Celeste interrupted him with a wave of her hand. "So obviously you have to do the contest." She leveled her eyes at him. "This is the moment."

John pictured her at the head of a colorful classroom, arms outstretched as she talked enthusiastically about whatever it was middle school language arts teachers talked about. She was probably the kind of teacher who worked to make each kid feel special, the kind who'd find a way to get that quiet boy in the back row to participate.

But he wasn't one of her students. "It's a moot point. You're required to enter as a team, and I don't have a partner."

"We'll find you one," Celeste answered quickly. "Someone who actually knows their stuff." She closed her eyes tightly, but only for a moment. "This is perfect." She hit John's leg. "My friend Layla, she's the science teacher at school. She wore a T-shirt the other day with birds on it. Maybe she knows stuff. I can call her."

"That's nice of you to think of her," John said. "But there's really no time."

"Oh, I'm sure we can make it work." Celeste grabbed her bag off the ground and started riffling through it, muttering to herself. "I'll call and have her check her schedule. When does the contest start? And how long does it go?"

"It lasts six weeks. But it starts—"

Screeching microphone feedback hit them from a nearby ramada. Linda Sanchez, one of his longtime mentors, stepped up onto a picnic table. Her brown skin contrasted with her gray hair, pulled into its signature braid, which trailed over her shoulder and lay across her gray *Natives Bird Best* T-shirt.

"Good morning, everyone." People clustering under trees began coalescing in a semicircle around Linda, who stood straight-backed, beaming out at the crowd. "I am so happy to see you all here this morning. I'm Linda, current president of the Arizona Ornithological Society."

Celeste's hands froze on her phone as she looked back at John. "You're kidding."

Linda continued, "I am thrilled to welcome all of you here today to the kickoff for our annual contest, the Arizona Ornithology Bird Binge!"

Celeste dropped her phone back into her bag, looking inside like it might hold answers. "The contest." She drew her eyes up. He'd thought them a simple brown, but when the light was just right, there was a hint of gold right at the pupil. "The contest your dreams hinge on, that one Chris said I would do with you—it starts right now?"

He took a swig of the coffee she'd brought him. "It starts right now."

CHAPTER 3

BIRD BINGE, DAY 1 OF 42
BIRD COUNT: 0

"Holy shit."

Celeste glanced at the crowd as they convened around the woman who'd just made the announcement. They were armed to the teeth with binoculars and cargo pants. Of course, these weren't just random people at a park early in the morning. This was a community.

A *birding* community. And Celeste had just claimed to be one of them.

She liked birds fine. They chirped and flitted around playfully, or sat stoically on telephone poles, stark against the constant blue of the Arizona sky. And they were . . . everywhere, she realized. Celeste paused the panic alarm in her mind to listen to the subtle background of birdsong all around them.

As if on cue, a drab sparrow landed near her feet and hopped toward the remains of her scone.

A *sparrow*.

It probably had a more official name, but that was all just details. She'd known it on sight.

She was *birding*.

The sparrow grabbed a hefty crumb in its little cone beak and gave Celeste a quick once-over, cocking its head.

A familiar feeling stirred in her belly. The wonderful, buzzing swirl of butterflies that came with new things. The sensation she'd been chasing as she sought out the parts of herself she'd never gotten to know, waiting for something to settle and show itself, to tell her *This is you*.

She leaned forward slowly, careful not to spook her little messenger, and rested her elbows on her knees. "Okay, little guy. Let's do this."

Beside her, John cleared his throat. "Um, excuse me?"

For a man who looked like he could fell a tree with little help, his low voice was blanketed in softness like the rest of him. Rugged and strong but quiet and gentle, and probably disoriented as hell. He'd played along well, all things considered—those things being that Celeste had appeared out of nowhere, pretending to be his girlfriend.

She grabbed his hand as she stood, her fingertips scraping the roughened calluses along his palm. Peter's hands had always been pampered and baby-butt smooth—not that she'd felt much of them in their final years together. Or much of anything from anyone else since.

Which explained why it had felt so good to dive into character in front of Breena, letting her fingers settle into the warm spot at the back of John's neck where his hair held a tiny curl, or explore the ridges of his kneecap through the fabric of his pants. No doubt it was why she swiped her thumb over John's palm now, bumping over each small ridge.

All she needed to do now was switch modes—goodbye fake girlfriend, hello birding partner. And what was she all about now if not reinvention?

John stuttered as she pulled him to the edge of the crowd, directing her attention to the fearless ornithologist on the table. Celeste admired her look—practical clothes, a long gray braid thrown over one shoulder, and a wide-brimmed straw hat.

"You've all received the rule books with your registration, but I'll review the main parts here."

Celeste stepped beside John, their shoulders rubbing. "You have our rule book?"

He gripped her elbow and turned her to face him. "What are you doing?" His voice was raspy, just above a whisper.

"As always," the woman continued from her makeshift stage, "we're doing a total bird species count for the next six weeks. And this year we are throwing in a few new events where you can boost your score even more. We are proud to announce the first ever Bird Brain Trivia Night! It will be in three weeks, so start studying now."

Murmurs went through the crowd at this announcement. Celeste turned back to John, her confidence boosted further. "I'm great at trivia!"

He guided her a few feet away, then dropped her arm and rubbed a hand over his beard. "You're not doing the contest with me."

"I said I would, didn't I? And you don't have any other options. This is important for your whole future."

John opened his mouth, but closed it again, sucking air like a fish.

"Hear me out. My weekends are mostly open because that yoga class was canceled and my daughter goes back and forth to her dad's. I love being outside, and I'm ready to learn." Celeste just knew that *not* doing this bird contest was an unacceptable outcome. "And I have this feeling in my stomach, this excited feeling. It's clichéd as fuck, but I'm in this period of postdivorce self-discovery, and new things make me feel alive. Make me feel—"

Like some new parts of her might be out there, waiting to peek into the sunshine. Like there could be more to her than anyone, even she herself, had seen for a long time.

The tension in his jaw softened, but he shook his head again. "This contest is more than just a morning at the park. Most people involved at my level have years of experience."

The happy buzzing in her stomach went slow and sticky. "You don't want to take me on."

His face fell. "No, it's not that at all. You're—"

"Too much?" Even now, she heard Peter's voice in the words and twinged as they twisted her like a worn-out dishcloth. "I know I can be a lot."

"Enthusiastic," John countered. "And very generous. But this wasn't anything close to what you agreed to do for Chris, and you don't need to go along out of a sense of duty."

"It's not duty, I swear." Celeste knew all about duty—to family, to work—and how it could blanket everything until she couldn't separate what she wanted to do from what she was expected to do. But this birding thing? It was a *want*. It was random, and unexpected, and the Celeste of a few years ago would have shrunk from how her husband might react if she took this plunge.

But this Celeste? She was fucking free, and she wanted to be in this birding contest. She wanted to help this nice bearded guy—out of desire and kindness, *not* duty—and she wanted to bask in the warmth of something brand-new.

So she straightened and let her smile drop, hoping John would take her seriously—if it was possible for him to take her seriously after she'd swept in with pastries and a fake relationship.

"I know it would be a lot for you, dragging me around. But I promise to do my best, and if you'll have me, I want to be your partner."

John's brows tightened as their eyes locked, and Celeste held his gaze. If he thought he could make her doubt her decision with a staring contest, he'd never been in a middle school classroom.

"It's a six-week contest." His tone was serious, but the corners of his mouth tilted up. "It would mean birding every weekend, putting in some miles on trails. Lots of early mornings."

She'd have to move some stuff around in her schedule, but she could do it. "I love trails and early mornings."

The buzzing in her stomach grew to a roar as Celeste watched John's last bit of hesitance give way.

"If you're sure you really want to—"

"Yes!" she squealed, running in place on her toes. John laughed, his cheeks lifting higher than she'd seen them all morning, as his cinnamon beard caught a glint of sunshine. She thrust a hand out, eager to seal their deal.

John's hand closed around hers gently. It was a tease of a touch, and had no right to make Celeste feel so damn curious. The amplified voice behind her rose to a crescendo, and she quickly dropped his hand and turned to listen.

"And so it is with immense excitement and gratitude for your involvement"—the woman swept her arm out toward the assembled birders, and Celeste—"that I declare the Bird Binge officially underway!"

And just like that, the crowd scattered, breaking away in pairs as teammates took off together, heads huddled close.

Everyone was on the move except Celeste and John. Thirty seconds into the contest and she was already behind. She hated being behind.

"What do we do? Everybody is rushing around. I probably need to order a guidebook and some binoculars and maybe those pants with the pockets?" There were a lot of pockets at this park. She turned back to John, ready to follow him into battle. "Why are you just standing there? Did I mention I'm really competitive? How do we win?" When John chuckled, she groaned. "You just told me your future is hanging in the balance here." Celeste's foot drummed a hurried rhythm on the ground. "Teach me birding so we can get started!"

John simply glanced to their left, where a palo verde was in full bloom. Its gray-green trunk and twisting branches snaked their way to a crown of bright yellow papery flowers, the ground around it covered in a buttery confetti of dry petals.

He took some steps toward it, motioning for Celeste to follow. "You were just telling me how much you like learning new things. Don't lose your excitement about it because everybody is running around with their notebooks out."

"I also like winning," she said, pouting.

But his eyes were on the tree, a subtle smile playing on his face. "Ever since I was a kid, watching birds has been about being outside and discovering something. Eventually, you get to know one bird so well that you can identify it easily, or know its song, but it all starts with that initial curiosity. If I do start guiding, that's what I want to convey to people."

Silence sat between them as Celeste watched the tree, letting all the flowers blur together into a cloud of yellow.

John continued, "If you come out of this thinking that birding is about running around with your nose in a guidebook and making lists, I'll be ashamed of myself. Contest or no contest, we're doing this right. We start with discovery, and we go from there."

Start with discovery. She should put it on her mirror.

She nodded to the tree. "So, can we discover a bird in there?"

John scanned each branch. "Yes, but let's not worry about what it is. Worrying about making the identification is going to stop you from really seeing the bird."

"But the list—"

He shook his head. "There's nothing here today we won't see again, I promise. Don't worry about the count today. Just see the bird."

She glanced sideways at him. His broad shoulders were relaxed, his neck forming a smooth, strong line to his jaw. Celeste had guided their bizarre ship all morning, but this was clearly John in his element.

"Okay," he said quietly. "This is a good one to spot. Once you start noticing it, you'll see it all over town."

Her eyes darted along the branches and through the flowers, but she didn't see a thing. She grumbled to herself. She was going to be bad at this.

John chuckled lightly. "You're going too fast. You have to be ready to take your time with this. Birding takes a lot of patience."

"I can be patient," Celeste huffed, crossing her hands over her chest.

He stepped behind her, leaving space between their bodies, and laid his hands gently on her tensed shoulders. "Is this okay?"

She swallowed, the warmth from his breath fanning across her neck. "Sure."

He pushed down on her shoulders, easing the tension out of them. "You want your shoulders and your neck to feel loose, otherwise you'll be hurting in no time. Staring up at trees can put a real strain on this part of your body."

She released her arms at her sides, shaking them out.

"Good." He lifted his hands off her shoulders. "Now settle

your eyes at the base of the tree and move them up the trunk. Do you see where the first branch goes off to the right?"

She nodded, tracing the curve of the branch with her eyes.

"Now follow that branch out." John's voice drifted back into her ear. "Just a couple of feet."

"Mm-hmm."

"And go up a little, into the flowers. You're looking for a small bird, even smaller than a house sparrow. It's mostly gray but it has—"

"Yellow."

Bright yellow on its face, like it had dipped its head into the confetti flower and come out painted. It hopped from side to side on the branch, pausing to poke its tiny beak under its wing every few seconds.

He gave a satisfied hum behind her. "You found it. Don't forget to breathe."

She *was* holding her breath, her heart thudding. And while a tingle had traveled down her spine as the warmth from John's breath hit her ear, most of her body was still and alert.

"What is it?" she whispered, already enamored with the little creature.

He chuckled quietly, the warmth of his body enveloping her. Apparently birding was a whole-body experience. "It's a bird. That's all it is right now."

CHAPTER 4

BIRD BINGE, DAY 1 OF 42
BIRD COUNT: 0

"I thought you'd sworn off love, John."

John stumbled, pulling out of Celeste's minty haze to find Marisol, Breena's longtime friend. She'd spoken loudly enough to get dirty looks from nearby birders, and her eyes settled coolly on Celeste. "But now you're showing up here with a girlfriend."

The last word hung in the air as Celeste stepped out from behind him, their shoulders just barely touching.

Things had moved so quickly after Breena walked away that he'd lost track of that thread, but obviously Breena hadn't. And she'd started spreading the word.

As John hesitated, Marisol sauntered closer and stuck a hand in the air in front of Celeste. "Hi, I'm Marisol."

Celeste's hand was out in an instant, shaking Marisol's with confidence just as she had Breena's earlier. A tug on his hip brought his attention down, where her index finger threaded through the belt loop of his shorts. It was a small move, but possessive, and it tightened his throat.

A few feet away, Breena was watching the scene play out, one hand resting on her hip.

Marisol's eyes narrowed at Celeste. "You're a birder?"

Celeste radiated calm confidence. "Sure am. It's always been a hobby of mine, but John is helping me step up my game." She shot him a glance, the soft affection in her face warming his cheeks. Her eyes flitted over to Breena as she spoke more loudly. "I'm so lucky he's available to partner with me this year."

Breena's jaw stayed firm as they all shared a few quiet seconds. Then something in the sky caught her attention, and Breena stepped forward to tug on Marisol's shoulders. "Let's go, Mari."

Mari grinned and shot a finger gun toward Celeste. "See you on the trails."

Celeste's finger still hung in John's belt loop as the two women walked away. He should have set things straight, but he'd hardly had time. "Listen, about that—"

But another hand tugged on his upper arm. "John!"

Linda pulled him in quickly for a hug. Still hooked into his belt loop, Celeste stumbled forward into his body, pressing briefly into his back. John concentrated on Linda, even as he tracked the soft shape of Celeste as she peeled herself off him.

Linda's braid fell over the shoulder of her *Natives Bird Best* T-shirt as she beamed at John. He'd met Linda over a decade before on one of his first guided walks, and she'd easily taken him under her wing. She'd made sure John stayed with birding even when he cut his academic plans short. And it was her suggestion years later that he try his own hand at guiding that had spurred the idea to start his own business.

Now she turned quickly to Celeste, her smile lifting even higher. "I'm always happy to see John." She leaned in with a wink, speaking loudly while she acted like she was telling a secret. "But I actually came over to meet you. I saw you two earlier. Then Breena confirmed it for me. A new partner in more ways than one, hmm?"

She introduced herself formally to Celeste, exchanging names and shaking hands before relaxing back into her normal posture, giggling and squeezing both of Celeste's shoulders. "Now that our official greeting is out of the way, we can be best friends. I imagine you already know this, but I just have to take a second to tell you what a special man John is."

Celeste's wide eyes caught John's as Linda continued. "He is just one of the kindest, most talented birders—no, *people*. One of the kindest and most talented people you will come across. When my wife was sick last year, John showed up every other day with a pot of soup. And let me tell you, this man can cook. He's just so . . . competent."

John raised a hand, his face warm from far more than the April sun. "Linda, I—"

But she only waved him off, keeping all her attention on Celeste. "I've told him forever that he is gifted, that birding should be his life, and I'm so glad he's here for the contest with you." She reached out and squeezed Celeste's hand once, still beaming. "And I'm sure you've seen his woodworking. It's amazing, of course. John is just so detail-oriented, so incredibly thorough." Linda wiggled her eyebrows and elbowed Celeste in the ribs like they were old friends. "Though I'm sure you've experienced that yourself in a private setting."

Celeste bit down on both lips, her cheeks going pink.

Oh, hell, Linda was trouble. Breena was one thing, but Linda would take this thing and run with it if he didn't cut her off. "Actually, Linda, there's been a misunderstanding. Celeste and I aren't actually—"

"At the *thorough* stage." Celeste burst in. "With each other." Her eyes sliced across John before a smile settled back on her face for Linda. "We're taking it pretty slow, you know. Two old codgers burned by past love and all of that."

"Codgers, please!" Linda threw her head back, giving a little hoot into the sky. "What I wouldn't give to be in my forties again. I was so limber then."

Celeste coughed, but failed to suppress a giggle. Linda joined her, and soon the two women were covering their mouths with their hands, laughing loudly, drawing the ire of nearby birders.

Laughing in the sunshine, Celeste was effervescent. As she fiddled with her dangling earring, it caught and split the light, scattering rainbows across her neck, jaw, and cheek. She had a gift for thinking on her feet, whereas John had always approached life at a measured pace. Deliberate.

Thorough.

Like the way he could slowly twist his fingers into her ponytail and tug until . . .

John caught the thought and lassoed it back. The only *thorough* they'd be was with the birds.

Linda's laughter settled down as she looked around the park again, smiling like a proud parent. She'd worked tirelessly as head of the association to bring new people into the hobby she loved so much, giving impassioned presentations at local high schools, arranging meetups at parks in underserved areas, doing anything she could think of to draw people to the outdoors.

She deserved all the credit in the world, not just for feeding his own passion but for a whole community made brighter. "It's a great showing, Linda. You should be very proud."

The smile on her face could have lit a campfire. "You know what? I really am! Just wait till you both see all the fun we have planned for this contest." She turned back to Celeste. "It was so lovely to meet you. I'm sure we'll have plenty more time to get to know each other. But for now, you two lovebirds better get birding."

Linda engulfed John in a fly-by hug before heading off, smiling and slapping the backs of the closest birding team.

With Linda out of earshot, Celeste gave in to another round of giggles. "I like that woman," she said, wiping a hand across her face. Her smile dropped slightly as she turned fully to John. "And boy, does she like you. And I just totally lied to her."

Her energy shifted as she shook out her hands. "I just imagined her face falling, and how that would feel for you, and I just—acted. I do that sometimes, but between Breena's friend and this, I think I totally snowballed this whole thing."

Celeste paced in a small circle, the park's dry grass crumbling beneath her Converse. She'd held still for a moment to spot the verdin on its green branch, but now she reminded him of the firecrackers he and his brothers used to throw on their front porch, the ones that zipped around in spirals shooting sparks.

"I could have said something, but you were faster than I was."

She frowned, kicking dirt as she went. "I tend to do that. I'm sorry. I keep fucking this all up."

"No." His hand shot out, brushing her upper arm. Celeste skidded to a stop, glancing at where his fingers curled over her small, tight bicep before he thought better of it and dropped his hand. "All you've done is try to help. You haven't messed anything up."

Celeste swept her hand toward the expanse of park, where dozens of birders were going from tree to tree. "Well, thanks to my 'help,' I think all these people believe we're dating. And with the contest, it seems like we'll keep seeing them?"

"Probably." Especially during the Bird Binge, the same people visited all the same best birding spots. And this year's extra events meant even more interaction with the other birders.

"Okay." Celeste nodded, blowing air out of her lips. "Then

maybe we have to keep it up. Through the contest. It doesn't have to be a big deal. We keep up the facade we created, which seems simpler than trying to set the record straight. Then, after we win, you can come up with a breakup story, and we'll part ways."

She fiddled with her fingers as John repeated her words in his head. It was an absurd suggestion, but also surprisingly logical. Coming clean with Breena and Linda, and however many people had already been told the lie, would be humiliating, and a huge distraction from the contest. He'd been through enough interpersonal drama when he and B split the year before, and the last thing he wanted now was for the contest to be overshadowed by gossip about *him*.

John just wanted to bird.

He shook his head, watching Celeste's smile grow. "I can't believe we're even considering this."

"It's absurd, but it also goes with the theme of the morning, right? Unexpected twists."

Her foot tapped on the ground, then she slid it toward his and nudged his foot with hers. Her white canvas shoes were dusted with bronze dirt. "So what's it gonna be, John? Let's pick one so we can get back to some kick-ass birding. Do we set the record straight, or do we carry on?" Celeste waved to the table where her box still sat, surrounded by a group of interested house sparrows. "Either way, I still have some pastries left. Maybe we could munch on them and find another bird."

John looked back at Breena huddled close to Marisol, then at Linda, holding court in front of a small group of novice birders already under her thrall. Kick-ass birding was a much better alternative than spending time setting the record straight.

"Okay."

Celeste caught him in a stare, raising her eyebrows. “Okay, let’s carry on?”

“Yes,” he managed. At some later point in the day, maybe everything that had happened this morning would make sense. “Let’s carry on.”

Celeste tugged on her ponytail. “But we should be totally clear,” she said. “The birding is real, but the dating . . . it’s not, and it can’t be.” She scrunched her face and laughed awkwardly. “I’m not saying you’re interested like that, I’m sure I’m not your type. I’m just establishing that I’m not dating right now, maybe not ever, I don’t know. I’m working some of my own stuff out.”

John didn’t know if he had a type, only that *he* didn’t seem to be what most people were looking for, quiet with his words and sometimes slow to act. His body was mixed up by the intimacy of his interactions with Celeste, but it wasn’t anything a few steady hours in his woodshop couldn’t make him forget. And one glance over at Breena was all the reminder he needed that he, also, was working out some of his own stuff.

“Understood,” he said. “I’m in a similar place, so that’s good to establish.”

“Cool.” Celeste kicked the ground, then laughed. “After all this”—she motioned between them, then at the park at large, filled with eager birders starting their lists—“did I finally just manage to make this totally awkward?”

So often John felt that conversations with people were puzzles he had to solve, sorting out the real meaning. But Celeste seemed unafraid to say what was on her mind, and it loosened something in his chest. Something he usually kept bound up.

“Not awkward, just honest.” Celeste smiled at his words, giving him an odd glow of pride. But behind her, their pastries looked to be in danger. "We better save those baked goods before those house sparrows find a way to open the box."

Whatever tension sat in the air between them evaporated as Celeste clapped her hands. "House sparrow! That's its official name, right?" When he nodded, she headed to the table, turning her head to call back. "One bird down! Isn't this exciting?"

A streak of sun reflected off Celeste's swinging earring just as a bright red vermilion flycatcher flitted over her head. He could have stopped her to point out the bird and add another to their brand-new list, but he resisted. It was only day one, and they had plenty of time.

"Yes," he said, jogging to catch up with her. "This is exciting."

CHAPTER 5

BIRD BINGE, DAY 4 OF 42
BIRD COUNT: 1

"Please, Celeste, stop doing my dishes." Celeste's best friend, Maria, reclined on her couch and covered a yawn with her fist as her newborn baby dozed slack-jawed on her lap.

With a burp cloth over one shoulder and black curls tumbling from her messy bun, Maria radiated the multifaceted frenzied state of early parenthood—contentment, amazement, terror, and fatigue—that Celeste still remembered even after almost eighteen years.

"Not a chance." Celeste turned back to the sink, raising her voice to be heard over the running water. "There are two kinds of people in this world. The kind who show up after you have a baby and pretend that holding and cooing at it is somehow helpful, and the kind who put themselves to use. I'm the latter."

"Ahh, yes, Celeste the ever-helpful." Maria cocked her head. "Available for dishwashing, bird-watching, and even pretend dating."

Celeste snorted and scrubbed at a crusty plate. She'd given Maria a summary of her morning with John a few days before, and her friend had simply listened, then asked Celeste to repeat herself, twice.

"I'm not going to make a habit of fake dating," Celeste argued. "This just happened to be the perfect scenario. I help out a nice guy, stick around to solve a problem I basically created, and have a new experience all at once."

Maria's lips quivered and her eyes closed. From the look on her face, it wasn't clear which made Maria more exhausted—being a new mom or being Celeste's best friend. "I see what's happening here. This is turning into another step in your self-help journey."

"It's not a—" Celeste stirred the chicken soup she'd started on the stove when she'd arrived. "Okay, yes, it is a journey. Though it's less about help and more about—" She waved the spoon in the air. "Discovery. And yes, this thing with John fits in quite nicely."

Maria chuckled. "How so?"

She turned to lean against the edge of the sink, her hands gripping the countertop. "*Be brave*, *Try everything once*, and *Go with the flow*."

"Ah, the bathroom Bible strikes again." Maria didn't bother hiding her eye roll. She had no qualms about letting Celeste know how cheesy she found her Post-it collection, and Celeste actually loved the ribbing, being by now well aware that Maria saved her biggest attitude for the people she loved most.

The "bathroom Bible" had started simply enough—Celeste had heard someone on a home renovation show say, "It's always important to chase your joy." At the time, she'd been six months into her divorce and losing track of why she'd thrown her life and family into chaos. But the simple statement by some stranger on her TV had been so affirming that she'd scribbled *Chase joy* on a neon green Post-it and stuck it on her bathroom mirror.

From there, the collection of notes had grown, sourced from the tags of tea bags, pages of novels, or the passing wisdom of a grocery store clerk. They helped her focus when she woke in the morning and didn't know how to take her first step in the day. Some were specific, actionable items—*Take a walk*, *Drink some water*, *Learn something new*. Others were more abstract—*Say yes*, *Be brave*, *Blossom on your own*. But all of them gave her a little something to go on, grounding her when the big questions—Who am I? What do I want? What now?—echoed so loudly in her brain that she couldn't think straight.

"I just hate Peter for making you feel like you need wisdom from *People* magazine on your mirror to get up in the morning," Maria grumbled. "What a dipshit."

He certainly could be, but it hadn't always been that way. In college, Peter had been drawn to Celeste's silly chaos and willingness to try anything at least once. She was *fun*. And Celeste had thought he shared her sense of adventure. But by the time she'd moved with him for law school, then his first job, the things Peter had once loved about her became the qualities he urged her to tone down. She was too loud at law firm parties, too enthusiastic about Morgan's bedroom murals, too intense about her students' success. By the time Morgan was six, Celeste had developed armor against the word *too*—but her once-shiny edges had already dulled under Peter's small but constant judgment.

Then Morgan was eight, and then twelve, and Celeste and Peter carried on. The long hours of Peter's early lawyer days never slowed, and their family moved again and again, Peter always promising that the next stop would be the one to give him breathing room. Celeste devoted herself to helping Morgan adjust to new places and new friends, and tried to convince herself that she should be grateful to have a husband who was home for dinner most nights and asked their daughter about her day.

And she adjusted, toning herself down in anticipation of Peter's tensed shoulders, resigning herself to a life of midyear moves and half-established friendships, always hoping the next town would bring something different.

But one crisp spring morning when Morgan was fourteen, two years after they settled in Tucson, Peter mentioned a get-together with colleagues that evening. When Celeste asked what time they'd be leaving, Peter coughed, then told her there was no need for her to come. "Maybe," he'd said neutrally, "you could just stay home with Morgan."

Celeste just blinked at Peter a few times and propelled herself outside for a walk, unable in the moment to let his dismissal slide off her back. A true-crime podcast droned in her ears, only half the words registering, when her foot almost came down on a yellow flower growing across her path. Emerging from a shaded crack between the sidewalk and the red brick of a neighbor's wall, its thin stem stretched and bent, seeking the sun.

She crouched, brushing her fingers over the stubby yellow petals, feeling a kinship with this small living thing that simply wanted light, even if it meant contorting its little cells to find a way out of the shadow.

Later, she tried talking to Peter about it. *Really* talking, laying herself as bare as she felt, sobbing as she told him about the flower, desperate to know why her husband never seemed to want her to bloom.

"A flower, Celeste?" was all he managed to say. "You're doing all of this over a *flower*?"

Six months later, she filed for divorce.

And now, almost three years and a lot of dark nights after that fateful walk, she was determined to stand fully in the sun.

"You know I love you, hon." Maria's voice, devoid of its typical snark, jolted Celeste back into the room and the steaming soup that had certainly been properly stirred by now. "And your hobby-hopping is entertaining as hell. I just worry you're chasing something because you're afraid to stand still."

"Standing still is overrated." She put a lid on the soup and turned to Maria with triumph. "Though I did stand still for about two minutes while I saw my first bird with John."

Maria gave a silent golf clap over her sleeping baby. "I'm so proud. These birders won't know what hit them. This John guy is lucky, getting you as a partner *and* a girlfriend."

Celeste smiled as she shook off the insinuation. "It's just when we're around his ex and the other birding people." She didn't love the deception, but she couldn't deny that it was kind of fun, especially when it clearly annoyed John's ex to see him receiving the attention of another woman.

She just needed to forget Linda's joke about how *thorough* John could be in a private setting, and definitely had to stop hearing his hushed voice in her head, talking her through seeing the bird.

"I guess people have been worried about him, so this can get them off his back."

From her short interaction with Linda at the park, Celeste assessed that John's love life was of great concern to his birding community. She could sympathize. It was impossible to have a simple coffee break in the teachers' lounge without the faculty gossip Andrea asking about her dating status. Celeste had heard about Andrea's single cousin more times than she could count.

Celeste's foot started a quick tap on Maria's linoleum floor.

"Oh no." More curls escaped Maria's bun as she shook her head. "I know that look. You're coming up with another one of your harebrained plans."

Celeste held up her hand like a stop sign, grinning. "My plans are not harebrained."

"You will recall I am the person who picked you up halfway

to Mexico because you got up in the morning wondering how far you could walk in a day."

"It was so beautiful that morning, I didn't want to—" Celeste refused to let Maria distract her from her excellent, brilliant, totally un-harebrained plan. "It's perfect. I am so sick of everybody either trying to set me up or giving me those poor-divorced-Celeste doe eyes. What's the harm in bringing John along to a few things and letting people think I'm dating someone like they've all wanted? Then later when I tell them we broke it off, they'll accept that I tried, and leave me in peace like I want."

Maria brushed a pile of laundry off part of the couch, making space for Celeste next to her. "I see your logic, as convoluted as it is. But"—her face softened—"do you think you might be jumping at the opportunity to have something fake to make sure there's no room in your life for something real?"

Celeste settled on the couch and twisted her fingers into the patch of dark hair on Xavier's baby head. Maria meant well, but she didn't get it. "I had something real, for a long time." She sped on before Maria could interrupt. "And I know you'll tell me I could have something better. But I let myself get lost in my marriage, and I'm not risking that again. I want just what I have now. Myself. And Morgan, while she's still here."

If finding herself after Peter had been hard, she had no idea who she'd be without the scratch of Morgan's pencil in her sketchbook on quiet evenings in their kitchen.

Through all the moves and aborted friendships, and the starts and stops of her own plans for her career, there had been Morgan. It was Morgan to whom she had crooned while packing up boxes, telling her babbling daughter about their next adventure, convincing herself out loud that she was living the life she'd always wanted—seeing new things, challenging herself, growing.

But Morgan was her own person now—not Celeste's faithful pal but a young woman in her own right with her own life. She'd be off to college soon, and life was moving on. Wasn't that what Celeste had been longing for? Time and space to know who she really was?

"I'm going to be alone for the first time, ever." She kept her voice cheerful. "I need that space."

Maria opened her mouth, but seemed to think better of whatever argument she was going to try next, and merely shrugged. "You always do what you want, so I won't bother trying to stop you. But if you're going to ask this guy to be your fake boyfriend for people we know, I need a sneak preview. So dish. Is he cute?"

If Maria caught a whiff of Celeste's first impressions of John—broad shoulders and soft flannel, callused hands and wire-rimmed readers—she'd never support the fake aspect of her new relationship. "He's . . . fine-looking. You know, kind of a librarian-meets-lumberjack vibe."

And cinnamon and sugar sprinkled in his beard, inviting a touch. All with a gentleness that radiated softness and safety. Maria gave one strong tap to Celeste's thigh, drawing her out of her thoughts.

She threw her hands in the air. "Fine, he's good-looking. He looks like the kind of guy who would come inside from chopping wood to nestle on the couch and rub your feet while he wears reading glasses and does a crossword puzzle." Wow, that was detailed. Celeste shook the image from her brain. "And you know what? I can be honest about that because there's no interest there. I established right away that all dating was strictly fake, and he is in full agreement."

"A lumberjack librarian? Tell me you'll bring him to David's party. I need to see this for myself."

The costume party Maria threw for her partner's birthday every year was a hit with all their coworkers. She had insisted on attempting to pull it off this year despite having a newborn.

Xavier mewled and squirmed in Maria's arms before a squelching sound in his diaper drew laughs from both women.

"Ah-ha!" Celeste jumped to her feet. "Useful friend to the rescue."

She swooped Xavier out of Maria's arms, cradling his still-tender neck and head, cooing to him as she held him. It seemed only yesterday she'd been looking down at Morgan, bald and wrinkly against her chest.

Celeste pressed her nose softly to Xavier's pudgy one. "Are you the sweetest little baby, Xavi? Auntie Celeste will get you all cleaned up." She turned to Maria. "Where do you keep your diaper stuff?"

Maria sighed, her smile tight, sweeping an arm around the room. Burp cloths and stray items of clothing adorned every piece of furniture. "Your guess is as good as mine."

Undeterred, Celeste spotted a diaper on top of the TV and a pack of wipes half-hidden under the couch. She cleared a space on the floor for Xavi and was wiping his teeny baby butt when she heard a quiet sniff from the couch.

"Maria." She waited until her friend looked at her. "You are doing great. Seriously, great. Look at this baby, he's perfect."

"Celeste, who are we kidding? Look around." Maria waved her arms in the air, her eyes wet. "Look at me!" She motioned to her pajamas, still on at 4 p.m., and stained with spit-up.

Celeste finished cleaning Xavier and adorned him with a new diaper before any errant pee could hit her in the face. "Honey, you had a baby six weeks ago." She scooted on her knees to Maria and placed her hands on her friend's thighs. "You are in a huge transition, and you are literally fucking amazing." She lifted Xavier from the floor, handing him back to Maria. He was squirming and mewling again, nuzzling his nose into his mother's chest.

Celeste rubbed at Maria's knee. "You know what I tell my students. We're all—"

"Works in progress." The women spoke together as Maria swiped a tear off her cheek, laughing.

Celeste smiled. "Exactly. That means facing changes sometimes, but you're growing. You've got this."

Maria sniffed and pulled her pajama top down to feed her baby. "And you can tell me this every day, right?"

"Yes." Celeste nodded, reaching for the laundry on the floor and folding it into neat piles. "Every hour if you need it."

Maria watched her baby nursing, her body relaxing into the couch. After a moment she looked back at Celeste. "Thank you. I'm lucky I have a veteran mom helping me out. Is Morgan excited about going up to NAU next year?"

Celeste folded a washcloth and added it to the clean pile. "She doesn't talk about it much. I've been trying to get her to go through the paperwork, send everything in to confirm, but she keeps putting it off. She's been a little cagey lately."

Celeste knew it was normal for teenagers to withhold information from their parents, even though she and Morgan had long had the kind of easy rapport that didn't always come naturally between parents and their kids. But walking the line between maintaining their relationship and giving Morgan space continued to be a challenge, especially since Morgan spent half of her time at her dad's.

"Is she dating anyone?"

Celeste dropped the onesie in her hands. "Who? Morgan?"

"Yes, Morgan," Maria sighed. "You've sworn off dating, but she hasn't, right?"

"Oh, no." Celeste waved off the idea, standing up to stack the laundry on Maria's dining table nearby. "No, I'd know if she was dating anyone."

Maria snickered. "Right. Because teenagers are known for their transparency."

Celeste paused, absentmindedly stroking a towel. Could Morgan be dating someone without telling Celeste? And did Peter know? And who would it be, and what were they doing? And was it time for another speech about safe sex and—

"Celeste." Maria's free arm was in the air, fingers snapping. "Don't panic. We were all seventeen once, and we survived. If she's with anybody, she'll tell you eventually."

"Right." Celeste fingered the edge of a T-shirt as she folded. "She'll tell me eventually."

Maria patted the space on the couch beside her. "It's going to be fine. Let's start planning your couple's costume for my party. This year's theme is heroes and villains, and I think you could actually look really hot as Harley Quinn. How would John look in spandex?"

CHAPTER 6

BIRD BINGE, DAY 5 OF 42
BIRD COUNT: 1

John squinted through the magnifying glass, clicking his thumb on a manual counter each time he spotted a tiny, muddy-brown baby snail. Even with magnification, they were barely visible, clinging to the walls of the glass tank in the hundreds.

"One hundred twenty-four over here." He pulled himself up from a hunch, stretching out his neck and shoulders.

Chris nodded and typed something into his laptop as he gnawed on a pencil, then pulled it out from between his teeth and tossed it across the room.

"Thanks, man." He leaned back in his seat. Long and lanky, with floppy blond hair that fell over half of his face, Chris looked tired. "Sorry again that I had to cancel our beer and ask you to count snails instead. It fucked up my schedule when they made me change labs, and I had to get these counts done today."

"No problem." Small and square, the new lab in the basement of the university's biology building was cramped. Fluorescent lights buzzed overhead. "Why'd they move you?"

"They said they needed more space for fossils. I'm told it's all in the spirit of cooperation. Though I wasn't feeling entirely cooperative when I had to move five hundred gallons of water containing baby snails from one lab to another." Chris ran a hand across the glass, the closest he could get to petting his precious cargo. "And did anyone from paleontology call and thank me? Or ask me how my threatened species of snails are doing?"

John rubbed his beard and held back a smile. "I'm guessing not."

"No, they did not. They're too busy being loved for studying creatures that died millions of years ago." Chris gazed at the tank. "No one appreciates these little suckers except me."

No one loved snails like Chris. And few scientists in the Southwest knew them as well, either.

"You getting good data?" John asked.

"Yeah. I think we're learning more about the conditions needed to help them reproduce in the lab, and I should be able to get an article about it. I'm getting more pressure to publish."

"Still think tenure is in the cards?"

Chris stood, shaking out his long arms and legs. His thin Metallica T-shirt complemented the swirls and lines of tattoos covering his arms. As always, Chris looked half white corn-fed farm boy, half rock star. "I don't know. I don't even know if I *want* it. This whole thing where I'm supposed to be a great researcher *and* a great teacher, all while getting paid shit—I'm not sure it's for me. You dodged a bullet leaving when you did."

"Dropping out, you mean?" John tried to smooth the edge in his voice that still popped up when he talked about leaving grad school, even a decade later.

Chris waved a hand freely. "Nah, dropping out would have been if you couldn't cut it. You *chose* not to pursue the PhD. You saw earlier than some of us that academia meant a lot less time in the field and a lot more time in places like this."

He motioned to the dreary basement room, letting it make his point for him.

John just shrugged, still tormented by how he'd failed to complete the doctorate he'd set out for, even knowing Chris was right. It had seemed such a natural path for John, but what he'd imagined would be hours outside observing birds had turned into bleary-eyed late nights staring at datasets on his laptop until he couldn't bear it any longer.

Not that everyone had that experience. Despite his reservations about life in academia, Chris had shone in graduate school, and Breena had always been in a class by herself.

"Breena still seems to be thriving here."

Chris blew a raspberry and sank back down in his chair, his eyes still on the tank. "Of course she is, you know Breena. Youngest woman to make tenure in the department, rising star of ornithology, blah blah blah." He flinched, mussing his hair. "Not that I fault her for any of that. We know B is a superstar, and facing way more uphill battles in this field than I ever have. She just makes the rest of us look bad by comparison."

After completing their PhD work, Chris and Breena had both stayed in Tucson to join the faculty at the University of Arizona. And while they'd all been friends for years, Chris's attitude toward Breena had cooled markedly after her breakup with John.

"And while I'm thrilled my snails finally started reproducing, I'm sorry it happened just as the bird contest was starting." Chris looked up from the tank with a smirk. "Though you still haven't thanked me, by the way."

"For which part? Pushing me into doing it this year, dropping out at the last minute, or throwing me into one of the most bizarre mornings of my life?"

"All three." Chris flicked a finger against John's knee. "Not only did I find you a new partner, but I gave you some excitement. I know you like your quiet life sitting in your woodshop all alone, but even you have to admit that Celeste is fun."

John's breath fogged the side of the tank where he was studying the snails. *Fun* wasn't quite the word he would have used. *Overwhelming*, maybe. *Enthusiastic, spirited, earnest*.

And despite all the reasons he shouldn't have been excited to have a total novice as his partner for the contest he was betting his future on, he was looking forward to the next six weeks. Birding with Celeste certainly wouldn't be boring, and he could get great practice guiding.

But that didn't mean he'd let Chris off scot-free for the mess he'd thrown him into. "I'll point out that when you called me that night you told me, and I quote, 'I found you the perfect partner, John. She knows all about birds and she is ready to rock.'"

"Okay," Chris admitted. "I may have overstated the case. I swear she mentioned birds at some point, though I was a little distracted. Our instructor, Sheila, had this little purple streak in her hair that just . . ." He shook his head and hummed low.

John huffed. "I thought you went with Greg."

John had used to work with Greg, and Chris had been begging him to set them up for months. But knowing the flighty way Chris moved through relationships, he'd been wary of doing so until he had finally left his job.

"I did go with Greg. And he was perfectly nice and certainly hot. But, John . . ." Chris sighed, leaning forward with his elbows draped on the torn denim of his jeans. "He started talking about buffel grass right away. And you know I hate invasive species as much as the next wildlife biologist, but it just wasn't what I was looking for on a first date."

"So you flirted with the painting teacher?"

"I did more than flirt with her." Chris stared into space for a moment, biting his lower lip. Then he shook his head and sat up straight. "We're not talking about Sheila, anyway. We're talking about Celeste. And how everything went more perfectly than I could have imagined. The girlfriend thing was a stroke of genius; I'm actually sad I didn't come up with that idea in the first place. I bet Breena almost went feral seeing you with somebody."

She'd been more cold than feral, but John didn't understand either reaction. She'd been the one to make it clear John wasn't enough for her.

"Why did you even tell Celeste about Breena anyway, if you were talking about birding?"

"You know how these things go." Chris waved a hand in the air, moving off his stool to shift some banker's boxers around on a long plastic table. "One thing leads to another, and before long I was getting all worked up again about that stupid genius."

That "stupid genius" had been one of the foremost experts in the world on bird evolution, his books some of the bibles of John's time in grad school with Breena. He'd recognized him from the book jacket when, having driven to Phoenix to surprise Breena at the conference she was attending, he'd found her pushed against the wall of a hotel hallway, being kissed by said stupid genius.

"It was just kissing," Breena had argued later, as if kissing itself wasn't intimate. But the real heartbreak had been the dreamy look in her eyes when she'd talked about how amazing the guy was, how brilliant and accomplished.

She'd never had that look in her eyes for John.

His phone pinged in his pocket. Then pinged again, and again.

Chris chuckled. “Sounds like Mama Maguire is checking in.”

John’s mom did love sending texts, especially ones asking for updates from “all her boys” on the family text thread. But this string of texts wasn’t from his mom.

CELESTE: *Hi.* ✋ *So . . .*

CELESTE: *I had this idea I wanted to run by you.*

CELESTE: *My coworker is always trying to set me up with her dentist cousin.*

CELESTE: *I don’t have anything against dentists. They do important work.* 😬 *But like I told you, I don’t want to date and I’m sick of everyone either trying to set me up or feeling sorry for me.*

He was already feeling less pressure knowing that Linda and other people in his life seemed happy that he was dating again, even if they didn’t know the truth.

The texts kept pouring in.

CELESTE: *So what I’m wondering is . . . will you be my boyfriend?* 🙏

CELESTE: *The fake kind. You know? Just for a couple of social events? Like I’m doing for you?*

CELESTE: 😳😐😎

The telltale dots of a composing message blinked on the screen just before one more message from Celeste popped up.

CELESTE: *I know you're a quieter person than I am, and this might not be up your alley. But I'll do all the heavy lifting with my coworkers. And I'd really appreciate it.*

Chris cleared his throat loudly. "Who's that? And why are you looking like that?"

John shifted his phone out of view. "Like what?"

"That." Chris motioned to his face. "You have a little goofy smile thing going on."

"Oh." He relaxed his face, letting the smile drop. He and Celeste had had a quick text exchange on Sunday, confirming details of their upcoming hike, and he'd had the same reaction. She had a gift for emoji usage.

"It's Celeste." He turned his phone face down on top of the snail tank. "She wants me to go to some things with her. So her coworkers think she's seeing someone."

Chris narrowed his eyes. "Like her boyfriend?"

"Just for a couple of social events, she said." He didn't imagine he could say no, not after she'd made such a huge commitment with the contest. "I owe her, right?"

Chris leveled his sapphire eyes at John. "Yeah, you owe her. But can you handle it, with her people? It's one thing in your own territory—all these birding people know you're pretty quiet and unassuming, and they'll basically take anything you say at face value. With Celeste's coworkers, you might need to sell it a little more."

"Sell it how?"

Chris sighed, running his hand through his hair. "By acting like a typical boyfriend, John. I rarely saw you even touch Breena in public. And that's fine for that to not be your style, but you want Celeste's friends thinking she has a nice new guy, right? Not a statue who grunts in response to questions."

"I don't grunt." The answer itself betrayed him, low and rumbling. He did much prefer his intimacy behind closed doors, where he'd blissfully spend hours showing a woman how he felt about her. But in public, especially in groups, he tended to stay largely inside his own head and keep his hands to himself.

"We're talking hand-holding, pet names, long strokes down the spine," Chris continued, his eyes going a little dreamy. Chris loved to flirt, and John had seen him in action enough times to know he was a pro. "Don't tell her yes if you're just going to show up and act like a piece of cardboard."

John stared at his shoes. "I'm not a piece of cardboard."

Chris approached him, grabbing his face tight in his hands and tipping it up. "Anyone who really knows you understands that, John." Chris dropped his hands and dragged a stool over to sit in front of him. "But if you do this with Celeste, just be ready to step outside your comfort zone a little, so her friends really know what a great catch she got."

John exhaled and grabbed his phone before he could think better of any of it and responded:

Of course, I owe you. We can talk details Saturday.

They were meeting that weekend for their first real birding outing. He'd already assured her that he'd bring along binoculars and a guidebook for her, and she'd sent a string of fireworks emojis when he'd suggested a long trail in the Catalina Mountains, proclaiming it one of her favorites.

Before he could stow his phone back in his pocket, Celeste's replies came flying through.

CELESTE: 😊😉👍

CELESTE: 💥💪💥💪

As he put his phone away he caught Chris watching him closely, smirking. “I really did set a wonderful series of events in motion.”

John just rolled his eyes, unwilling to give his friend any ammunition. No reason for Chris to know how the swing of Celeste’s ponytail had set its own easy rhythm in his mind, or how he’d thought of her the night before as the smell of his peppermint tea filled his small kitchen.

He cleared his throat. “The dating stuff is just a sideshow. We’ll really just be birding. Don’t try to make it more than it is.”

Chris sighed, standing up and stretching his arms over his head. “Sure, buddy. Whatever you say.”

“Christopher.”

Chris stuck out his bottom lip. “Don’t go stern on me, John. You know that’s the only time I find your beard even slightly attractive.” He held out his hands innocently. “All I’m saying is that I think you and Celeste will work well together, and I wish you the best. And you’re welcome.”

John just shook his head. “I didn’t say thank you.”

“But you will, believe me.”

CHAPTER 7

BIRD BINGE, DAY 8 OF 42
BIRD COUNT: 1

Celeste set her alarm thirty minutes early, but a mishap with the French press and a fascinating story on the radio caused a short delay. When she swung into the parking lot at 7:05, John was waiting for her at the trailhead, leaning against a boulder with his head in a book.

He wore cargo pants and a light blue T-shirt that clung to his chest and shoulders, and was pulled even tighter by the brown straps of his backpack. A worn baseball hat shaded his face as his fingers rubbed his beard.

Celeste allowed herself one long exhale to enjoy the view. No harm in looking.

After a count of five, she exited the car and slung her backpack over her shoulder, warmed by the buzz in her sternum that came with new things.

Since seeing that first bird with John's help, the world around her had been altered. Even though her competitive side wanted to learn each name and acquire her own expertise, she gave herself a few days to follow John's advice, and she simply saw birds—outside her kitchen window, bobbing on a leaf of the sunflower growing on her porch, or at the top of an electric pole, scanning the ground below.

Now some sort of hawk was drawing a giant circle in the blue expanse of sky above. John didn't look up until she was almost upon him, and he greeted her with his warm, quiet smile.

He nodded. "Morning."

She clapped. "Let's do this!"

A flurry of wings erupted from a bush behind her.

"Sorry." Celeste adjusted the brim of her ball cap, blushing. "Just excited." She kept her voice low. "Good morning. I'm ready to see some birds, partner. I have some questions, though."

John motioned for her to continue with a nod and the hint of a smile.

"I was rereading the rules last night, and I don't get how we actually prove to anybody what we saw. Like, we're just keeping a list, and then we turn it in. What's to stop us from just making it all up?"

John pushed up from the boulder. "It's an honor system. We all keep our own records."

Oh, these birders were adorable. "An honor system? For the whole contest?"

"That's generally how birding works. If we were to claim to see something totally out of the ordinary for this region or time of year, like a pileated woodpecker, someone would challenge us on it." He laughed lightly. "That's not a bird we would see, of course."

"Obviously." Celeste nodded seriously.

"But if we did see, say, a northern goshawk or another bird that wouldn't typically be seen here but that wouldn't be too out of range, we'd try to get a photo or a recording of the sound or something, as proof."

"That's another thing," she said. "The sound thing. The rules said it counts if we even hear the bird but don't see it. How is that even bird-watching?"

"Think of it as the same as seeing a bird, just with attention to different details. Sorting out the specifics of a call is actually pretty similar to parsing out a visual identification."

As if on cue, a sharp trill pierced the air, followed by a series of looping notes. It sounded like every birdcall ever. Celeste tipped her head up toward the sound. "So you can just hear that and know what it is?"

"To be honest, it's sort of a specialty of mine. Just a result of spending too much time listening."

Celeste watched him rub the back of his neck, his eyes fixed on the ground. She hadn't ever thought that there might be people who specialized in identifying birdcalls, but it seemed to suit John. "How does that become a specialty for someone?"

He didn't answer right away, so she waited. She knew from her time in the classroom that sometimes when someone was quiet, it wasn't because they had nothing to say, just that they needed time to say it. Her strategy was rewarded when John's hazel eyes finally returned to her.

"My mom made us all take piano as kids. I only lasted about four years, but it was enough to learn to read music, to hear one line from another. That's how it works for me with birds, picking out lines of song and almost seeing them on a page. Visualizing them like that as a kid helped me tell them apart, and then it was just way too many hours listening to recognize one from another." His gaze flitted to a tree. "I grew up in Santa Rita, a small town about an hour south of here."

Celeste had been there a few times on day trips with a young Morgan. The one-hour drive saw the landscape change from the gray-greens of the desert to golden grasslands dotted with short, wind-worn trees. "It's beautiful down there."

John's mouth curved up. "Great birds, too. And not much else, so I had a lot of time to listen." Behind Celeste, another bird *pew-pew*ed like a laser gun, and John's smile went higher, rounding his cheeks. "Once when I was birding with Linda, the woman you met the other day, she told me that she loved learning how to pick out songs and calls because it helped her understand the story that was going on around her." As he spoke, John looked from tree to tree, like he was building the story of the air around them. "Who was hungry, who was territorial, who spotted a predator."

When his eyes swept back to Celeste, his lips closed quickly as he swallowed.

"That's beautiful." She was suddenly hungry for details, not just about what the birds were saying but about his piano lessons and everything in between. Details of the life of a man who'd learned to pull stories out of the air. "So we could just sit here and let you listen and you'd be able to add, what, five birds to our list right off the bat?"

"Maybe a few more. But we'll work up to that."

He reached into his pack and pulled out a pair of binoculars, passing them over to Celeste. The weight of them was more than she expected, her arm dipping as she measured the feel of the object in her hand. "This feels like a big moment. Am I officially a birder now?"

Celeste looked from the binoculars back at John to find his eyes trained not on the sky, but on her. "I think you were already one," he said. "Just waiting to be discovered. I saw the way you were looking at the bird the other day. You're a natural."

"A natural at not knowing anything about birds?"

He shook his head, closing up his backpack. "That all comes with time. But it's nothing without the desire to do it."

She shifted the weight of the binoculars from hand to hand, the cold metal warming in her palms. "There's something about realizing that the birds have been here all along, and all I have to do is learn how to pay attention. It's sort of like reading, I think, looking for those little gems in the text, the words and phrases that call out to you, weaving together the story."

John had been turning away as she spoke, but he paused, his eyes settling on her for a moment, setting off a little storm in her chest. "That's right."

His look was as warm as the sunshine on her back, and almost as intense. She was more accustomed to people's eyes glazing over when she started talking about stories, not . . . this. Not understanding. She didn't know where to put the feeling it gave her.

"Anyway." She cleared her throat. Surely a bird would fly by any second. "Thanks for that help the other day, seeing that bird. I don't expect you to do that all the time. I know there's a contest afoot."

"Actually," John said, "that sort of goes along with how I was thinking we could do this. I want you to get more out of this than just making a list. And the other day I just—" He paused, sliding his tongue along his bottom lip as his brow furrowed. "I liked doing that, slowing down and looking at the bird. I think that's maybe the kind of guiding I would want to do. For beginners. And maybe if you were up for it, you could . . . be my first?"

Celeste straightened and smiled at John, who acted as if he was asking for a favor rather than offering one. "I would love that. I could be your practice run."

"We'd still have to speed things up more than I'd like, since we do have to make this list for the contest. Ideally we'd go out a few times and just get to know everything around us before we even worried about making an ID, and that's not going to work in this circumstance. But we can do our best."

"Okay." She nodded eagerly. "That sounds really good. If you don't think it'll mess up the contest stuff for you. I *could* just tag along so we're obeying the team rule and you could see all the birds. I'll even write them down for you."

"Not a chance. We'll do it together. We have almost five more weeks, so I don't think starting a little slow will hurt us. We can fit in a lot of birding in that time, if you're up for it."

Celeste wiggled her eyebrows, grinning. "You bet I am. And who knows, maybe by the end, you'll be tagging along with *me*."

Birding was awesome.

The trail they'd followed wound through the low desert before climbing gradually through a canyon walled in by soaring granite. Celeste loved the muted, dangerous landscape of her adopted home, rich with every hue of brown and green, from the snaking bark of the palo verde trees to the waxy leaves of the jojoba bush.

And all around stood towering saguaros, arms always reaching, spines shining white in the sun.

With John's help, she was adding to their count, scribbling the name of each bird excitedly into her messy spiral-bound notebook on the pages between a grocery list from six months before and the draft of a poem she was working on.

Each time they started slowly, watching the bird and asking simple questions: What is its size and shape? Is it on the ground, in a bush, in a tree? On the top of the tree, against the sky, or among the sparse desert leaves? Those answers led to more questions: How is it behaving? What might it eat? Is it alone, or in a group?

Each bird was its own meditation, and only once all the initial questions had been covered did they look at color and start to determine an identification. Celeste figured John knew them all, but he was patient as they went step by step, until finally he'd help her thumb through his worn bird guide to land on her best guess.

At one stop, she'd seen four birds without even shifting her feet, just letting her eyes drift from plant to plant. John always kept his voice low, his movements slow and deliberate, explaining how she should look to specific parts of each bird to identify it.

"So for this one, you're going to look at the cap, the belly, and the rump." He'd motioned with his chin toward a small gray bird flitting among the yellow flowers of a creosote. Celeste had choked back a giggle as he sighed, shaking his head. "Are you going to laugh every time I say 'rump'?"

"I can't help it, it's such a funny word." She'd taken a steadying breath then, enjoying the curve of John's cheek as he smiled at her. "But I do observe the rump on this bird, and given its coloring and size, I'm going to say it's a . . ." She'd thumbed through the first pages of her new book, which covered the most common birds of the area, until she landed on the right page. "A black-tailed gnatcatcher?"

When he'd nodded, looking actually *proud* of her, that thing in her stomach had twisted again, another sign that birding with John was more complicated than she'd expected. They'd only covered a couple of miles, but the birds weren't the only thing catching Celeste's attention on the trail. When John spotted a bird, it was . . . an experience. His body stilled, nothing moving but the muscles of his neck as he followed the animal's movement. Sometimes he'd draw the binoculars up wordlessly, training them just where he wanted as he slowly used one finger to adjust the focus with a quiet competency that actually made her blush.

She'd taken to doodling all over their bird list in an effort to keep her eyes to herself.

The morning went on like that. Walking, stopping, watching. John was patient but enthusiastic when appropriate, and he had a gift for encouraging Celeste to sort out which bird she was seeing without doing the work for her. In between bird spottings, the two rarely talked, and Celeste found herself appreciating the way John didn't need to fill a silence.

They were at a whopping twenty-seven species spotted that morning alone. Celeste hadn't had a clue as to how many different birds coexisted here until John showed her the distinct differences between a gnatcatcher and a verdin, or a canyon towhee and a curve-billed thrasher.

The trail climbed slowly through the canyon until John and Celeste were directly across from Seven Falls, the trail's namesake. After heavy rains, or when snow was melting off the mountains, a stream ran down the mountainside, gathering in one pool after another. Narrow falls dripped from pool to pool, untold years of erosion creating gathering places for the water out of the smooth gray rocks, each surrounded by tall green reeds and rushes.

A group of hikers sat snacking and lounging in the sun at the base of the lower pond, so Celeste scrambled up some rocks to the pool above. The water reflected the sky in all its glory, bright blue with little wisps of clouds that would disappear in the coming weeks as the spring gave way to summer and its baking heat.

She was already unlacing her hiking boots as John appeared beside her.

"I can't resist," she said, looking up at him. "You coming?"

He shook his head but smiled.

"Suit yourself." She shrugged, both disappointed and relieved that she wouldn't see him in wet clothes. His constant adjustment of his binoculars was about as much as she could take.

Celeste dropped her pack and peeled off her socks, wiggling her toes in the fresh air. If she'd been alone, she'd have stripped to her underwear and bra before getting in, but that seemed over the line on a birding trip, so she opted to stay in her shorts and tank top, knowing they'd dry easily on their way back down the trail.

A toe dipped into the pool told her the water was so cold that a step-by-step submersion was impossible. She glanced back at John, sitting in the sun and opening a granola bar, and almost opted to join him. She could stay dry and have a snack.

But then she remembered the Post-it that had caught her eye that morning. It had been bright pink, with four words scrawled in pen:

When in doubt, jump.

She dove in.

CHAPTER 8

BIRD BINGE, DAY 8 OF 42
BIRD COUNT: 28

Celeste disappeared under the still surface of the pond, then shot up just as quickly, sputtering and gasping for breath.

"Holy shit! This is really fucking cold!" She swept her arms and swam farther into the pool, then swiveled to face John. "I can't even touch the bottom here!" She smiled and moved in an easy breaststroke to the edge, where a small stream of water fell from above, then dipped her head under, letting water splash over her neck and shoulders as she peered at the rocks around her.

Her mouth was moving, but he couldn't hear any sounds. John hadn't known Celeste long, but it didn't seem strange that she'd speak to rocks, or water, or whatever she'd found back near the waterfall. It was only strange that he wished he could hear what she was saying.

After a moment, she swam back to the edge and stood, her dripping body emerging into the sun inch by inch. When she reached up to squeeze the excess water from her ponytail, John watched goose bumps rise along the tight curve of her bicep. The wet fabric of her gray tank top clung to her body, holding tight to the outline of her sports bra and the curves of her small breasts. Her nipples were so tight and hard he'd be able to close his lips around one right through the fabric of her shirt and bra.

Oh, Christ.

John dropped his head into his hands, pressing hard against his closed eyes. Those were not thoughts he should be having about his birding partner. It was one thing to note how easily her muscled legs had conquered the trail all morning, but this was no place for errant fantasies about tracing his fingers along the contours of her rib cage or smoothing over those goose bumps with his tongue. Especially not when she was his first practice client, *and* they'd taken dating off the table.

Her voice came in a laugh from behind him. "Shit, that was cold. But well worth it. Fresh water has always had some kind of special resonance for me, like it helps me reset."

John kept his eyes trained on his backpack as he pulled out his water bottle. He took a long drink, but his throat was still dry and tight.

When he turned back, Celeste was settling on the rocks in the sun, her damp hair wetting the stone in a halo around her head. "I'm just going to let myself dry off a little if that's okay."

"Of course." He leaned back, the smooth white rocks warm from the sun, and removed his hat. Crossing his hands to pillow his head, John closed his eyes, letting the sun hit his face, lighting up his eyes from the inside with the colors of sunset.

He picked out strings of birdsong bouncing around the canyon, mentally checking off the ones they'd spotted already. He'd heard all the birds they'd seen that morning before spying them and could have added them to the count before ever showing them to Celeste. But being with her, going slower and drawing her into what he loved about birding, was a gift he hadn't expected after the chaos of their original meetup. She did a certain amount of skipping along the trail, as he'd expected she would, but when she needed to be still, she was. She paid incredible attention to each bird, asked all the right questions, and seemed truly delighted to be spending the day outside.

He'd thought about guiding for a long time, but had never gone so far as to imagine what it would look and feel like. And if it could be like this—warm sun and smiles and birds everywhere—it might be worth giving it a go.

"They're like time, you know?" Celeste's voice drifted into his ear, dreamy and low. When he cracked his eyes open to peek at her, her hands were running along the rock beneath them, tracing the small, smooth curves that carried water when it rained. "The rocks, I mean. Whenever I'm somewhere like this, where you can just see how water has shaped everything, I feel like touching the rocks is the closest I'll come to touching time itself."

John ran his own fingers along the rock. "My brother, he's always been obsessed with the stars and the vastness of space, but there's so much vastness on Earth."

"Is it just one? Brother?"

"No, I have two—both younger." Still thinking about the rocks, he recalled the way Celeste had seemed to be talking to them by the waterfall. "Did you see something over there? When you were in the water?"

"Oh!" The exclamation drew his eyes open in time to see Celeste prop herself up on her elbows, smiling big. "There were these little frogs back there. Small and gray, and"—she pouted, furrowing her brow and hunching her shoulders before smiling and shaking off the pose—"they had that grumpy look about them, but they were so cute, too. Just lined up in a little crack of the rock, blending in perfectly. Do you know what they were?"

"An army of canyon tree frogs." He raised up on his own elbows, his lips curving up. "It looked like you were talking to them."

She laughed lightly. "Just bringing them greetings from humankind." Celeste lay back down, stretching her arms long over her head.

John did the same, closing his eyes so he wouldn't count the smooth lines of her ribs made visible by her stretch.

After a moment of silence, she spoke up again. "Why'd you call them an army?"

"A group of frogs," he answered. "It's called an army."

She laughed. "Is stuff like that just squeezed into little pockets in your brain?"

His face was warm and relaxed, his body fusing into the stone. Talking about himself didn't come naturally, but it felt easier today, speaking up into the blue. "When I was a kid, I went through a phase of obsessing about what different groups of animals are called. Some are just what you would expect—flocks and herds—but then there are some special ones. A flamboyance of flamingos, or a leap of leopards."

Celeste hummed. "I wonder what a group of my students would be called."

"Did you say it was middle school?"

"Yeah, seventh- and eighth-grade language arts. I bounced around ages for a while after getting my teaching degree, but this is where I like it most. On my best days, I'm energized by the role I can play in their lives, by all the possibilities there."

"And on your worst days?"

"On my worst days, I'm standing at the front of the room just looking at this classroom of adolescents staring back at me like they wish they could be anywhere else."

A silence settled between them for a moment as a western bluebird choo-choo'd from a tree nearby. It wasn't on their list so far, because it had typically already migrated north by this time, but John didn't want to interrupt the conversation with Celeste just yet. Hopefully it would stick around for a few more minutes and they could see it together.

"How about a potential?" he said after a moment. "A potential of middle schoolers."

She curled on her side facing him, one arm under her as a pillow, smiling. "Oh, you're good. I like that." Before John could pull a response from his tightening chest, Celeste rolled onto her back again. "You're sure about this Tuesday? For my work thing?" Her hands fiddled together over her stomach, where the fabric clung to the indent of her belly button.

John put his eyes back on the sky. "Definitely sure." Between bird sightings that morning, Celeste had mentioned a work gathering she had in a few days. It was time for John to follow through with his side of their agreement.

"You know," she said, "for someone who's my occasional boyfriend, I know almost nothing about you. My teacher friends are nosy. I should know some things."

He sat up, rolling out the stiffness in his neck. "There's not too much to tell. Especially after I lost my job. I watch birds, I work in my woodshop, that's basically my life."

He braced himself for a "That's all?" or something of that ilk. Especially to someone as vibrant as Celeste, his simple life must seem rather dull. But she just nodded and sat up, pulling her knees in to her chest. "How long have you been in Tucson?"

"About ten years." John reached down to grab the toes of his hiking boots, relishing the deep stretch in the backs of his thighs. It was hard to believe he'd been settled in Tucson for just over a decade, especially because it had happened almost accidentally. He'd come for graduate school, left briefly, then come back and stayed. When he'd broken things off with Breena, his brother Jared had suggested a move up to Phoenix, but John knew he wouldn't last a month amid all the concrete.

"And where were you before then? Hiking the wilds of South America searching for exotic bird species?"

"Not quite." He would have left it at that, but whether it was the sunshine or just his companion, he felt more amenable to sharing parts of himself than he had in a while. "After college I started graduate school for biology, but some stuff came up at home and I went back for a bit." Said "stuff" had included his mom getting sick, his baby brother routinely being dropped at home in the dead of the night by the local sheriff, his middle brother putting in a couple of years of college ball before being drafted, and his dad struggling to keep the store going between trips to the doctor in Tucson. His parents had sworn he didn't need to come back, but they hadn't presented any alternatives, either.

"Did things turn out okay at home?" Celeste's eyes had narrowed a bit, but she didn't pry for details. And oddly enough, it made John want to give them.

"Yeah, Mom has been cancer-free for fifteen years now. But when I was there I ended up helping a lot with our store and stuck around for a while."

Celeste wiggled her toes in the sun, small specks of sand along her feet shining like glitter. "What kind of store?"

"Maguire Ranch Supply." Just saying the name conjured up the place in his mind—cramped aisles that had served as a playground for a set of brothers growing up in the grasslands while their parents built a business. "I hauled around a lot of bags of feed in those years."

Celeste's huffed laugh caused John's defenses to rise before he could stop them, trained from years of Breena's subtle teasing about his parents' "cute little store." "It probably doesn't sound like much, but running a business like that is a lot of work."

"Oh, I have no doubt about that at all. I was just thinking about how the population of Santa Rita must have enjoyed watching a young John Maguire toss around bags of feed." Her eyes widened as her jaw dropped. "Not that you would have been better-looking then than you are now. There's a lot to be said for maturity, and a little silver in the beard goes a long way." She dropped her face into her hands before peering back up, red-cheeked. "Please just ignore me. My internal filter doesn't always exist. I don't mean to objectify you."

A laugh burst from John's lips as he raised a hand to rub at his beard but stopped midway, suddenly more aware of his facial hair than he'd been a few minutes before.

"It's fine. I remain totally un-objectified." He cleared his throat. "Do you think that's enough background for your friends?"

Celeste blinked before nodding, slipping her socks and boots back onto her bare feet. "Yeah, I think that's good. Now we just need the story about how we met." She stood, throwing her backpack over her shoulders.

John rose and stretched, subtly making a visual pass of her body just long enough to confirm that her tank top was now blessedly dry before grabbing his own pack.

Celeste jumped easily down the rocks to the trail and tipped her face back to him as she spoke. "How about this: We met birding, maybe at some popular birding place like—"

"Rivera Park," he filled in. It was a sure stop for everyone in town.

She nodded. "Rivera Park it is. We met looking at the same bird, and then I asked you out for french fries."

He slowed as he climbed down a boulder. "French fries?"

"French fries are my go-to. Great on any occasion." She turned to him with a wink. "And I'm pretty sure *I'd* be asking *you*, given that you're quiet and I never shut up."

It would take him weeks of hovering at the edges of someone like Celeste before he'd consider making a move, and even then he wouldn't quite know how to pull it off. But he didn't want to let the other part of what she'd said slide by.

"I wouldn't say you never shut up, by the way," he said, walking behind her. "You just share freely. For the record, I like it."

Her feet skidded along the trail, sending a small cloud of dust swirling around her boots. As she twisted her body back to him, a wisp of brown hair fell across her face, and she moved quickly to tuck it behind her ear. Her chest rose and fell with one breath before her lips turned up. "Thank you."

Celeste's eyes drifted up, over John's shoulder and up farther still, into the sky. "Red-tailed hawk," she murmured. They'd seen a few already that day, but he turned regardless, never one to give up a chance to watch a bird. Its pale underside, streaked with gray and copper, flashed in the sunlight as it rode a column of warm air, tipping its wings to spiral down and back up.

Behind him, Celeste's voice was just above a whisper. "Pretty fucking cool."

He couldn't have agreed more.

CHAPTER 9

BIRD BINGE, DAY 11 OF 42
BIRD COUNT: 44

Celeste tightened her waxy shoelaces as the musical clattering of pins rang through the bowling alley. Her phone buzzed on the plastic bucket seat beside her, threatening to shake its way onto the floor.

JOHN: *Just arriving. You here?*

CELESTE: *Sure am. Hope you're ready to bowl.*

Celeste skipped to meet John at the entrance, where she spotted the wide build of his body framed by evening sunlight in the doorway. Yes, he'd do just fine as a dating decoy. "Hey!"

"Hey." John looked past her, seeming wary. "I know I said this via text, but I'd like to repeat my hesitance about this particular duty. When you said you wanted a date at a work thing—"

"I know." She interrupted him with a wave of her hand. "I know, you thought happy hour, something totally typical and boring. But this is okay, right? Who doesn't like bowling?"

"It's not that I don't like it. I'm just not particularly good at it. And I know you like to win."

She did, always. But she'd also calculated that showing off her new boyfriend was worth the risk of losing this round. "Don't worry." She looped her hand easily through his arm.

They'd established some ground rules over text, making sure they were both comfortable with the PDA of their fake dates. Hand-holding, arms around the waist and lower back, and other small touches in the course of interacting were all deemed acceptable.

But the fingers curled over John's ample bicep hadn't received the "fake date" memo. They wanted to squeeze and, dammit, even stroke the curve of his muscle with her thumb.

Before her hands crossed the line, Celeste tugged John across the ugly carpet to get his shoes, unlooping herself from him while he discussed his shoe size with the tattooed woman behind the counter.

Over at lane twelve, everyone was assembled. Her middle school's eighth-grade humanities faculty battled the math and science teachers at this midtown bowling alley once a month; the winners got bragging rights and free donuts in the teachers' lounge the following Monday. Celeste's team had been on a winning streak as of late, but her coworker Arnold had picked this week to marry the man of his dreams in Napa, and while she was very happy for him, it had messed up their numbers. When Andrea had threatened to cancel that night's bowl, Celeste had been pleased to tell them she'd already secured their extra member.

"Wait. A boyfriend?" Andrea's face had squished into its tightest squint when Celeste told her about John. "You're not dating. You've told me that a million times, Celeste. Because you know I really want—"

"To introduce me to your cousin. I know, Andrea," Celeste had told her, pouring bad coffee into her travel mug before the first bell that morning. "Things with John just sort of happened . . ." She'd launched into the story she'd invented, adding further embellishments when they fit, like the breeze in her hair and the call of the bird.

"You met *bird-watching*?" Andrea had sighed and patted Celeste on the back as she turned to head to her art class. "Can't wait to meet him."

And now she was, shaking his hand as Celeste made introductions, suddenly apprehensive about this mixing of worlds she had arranged. Most of her work pals, especially those as dedicated to the bowling rivalry as she was, were loud and rambunctious—harassment and heckling were all fair game. Not exactly John's style.

But then John turned his glance to her, an expansive smile on his face. The harsh neon lights of the bowling alley dulled the red tint in his beard, but they didn't do anything to diminish the handsome cut of his jaw, or the friendly glint in his eyes as he exchanged easy greetings with the teachers.

She slid her fingers into her shiny purple bowling ball. "Okay, everybody, leave my date alone. It's time to bowl."

He hadn't been lying. John was a terrible bowler. When his ball didn't end up in the gutter it lazily knocked into pins at the edges of the lane with the same polite softness he'd used when gathering up a caterpillar from an exposed part of the trail to move it to safety.

But he was a wonderful sport, simply smiling and shrugging through frame after terrible frame, clapping as their teammates racked up pins, and even earning a high five from Andrea when his ball made an unexpected turn at the end of the lane, miraculously taking out eight pins. As others bowled, he listened in on the chatter between Celeste and her friends, following along but not inserting himself. He was attentive and friendly, even if he did spend most of his time consorting with the enemy, talking science shop with Layla about the unit on owl pellets she was doing with her students the following week.

As Andrea stared down the pins before starting her throw, John leaned his shoulder into Celeste and nodded up at the screen that showed their score. "You're a very good bowler."

She answered his lean with one of her own. "Thank you for noticing. I bowled a lot as a kid. My dad and I would wake up early on the weekends, get breakfast, and go bowling while half the town was asleep."

"We didn't have a bowling alley," John said with a small laugh. "Or much of anything, really. Even now, the closest bowling or movies are still sixty miles away."

"That sounds either incredibly peaceful or incredibly boring. What did you guys do for fun?"

John entwined his fingers, stretching his arms in front of him. "I sat outside, collected ants, read a lot. My brother played a lot of baseball and I played some, too. My middle brother, Jake, and I were both well suited for growing up in a small town, I think. It gave Jake a place to shine and me a place to think. It was harder on our little brother, though."

"John, you're up," Andrea called as she strutted back to them. "We're within striking distance of those nerdy bastards, so maybe you could, you know, *not* throw it in the gutter?"

"Come on!" Celeste protested, standing alongside John. "He's doing his best."

John smiled and shook his head as he and Celeste approached the ball feeder. "She's not wrong."

"Oh, please." She put her hand on his back as he bent to get the ball, more to comfort him than to put on a show. His muscles tensed for a moment under her fingers, and he leaned slightly into her touch. She cleared her throat and eyed the lane. "How about this? Let me give you a couple of pointers. I don't think you're a lost cause. You just need to loosen up a little."

John held the ball gingerly as he nodded and walked toward their lane. Celeste stood next to him, shoulder to shoulder.

"The problem you're having, I think, is that you're too gentle. You're putting the ball down like it's a precious egg or something. But it's not gonna break."

She thought back to the John of the week before. Birding John. He was relaxed, at ease on the trail, shoulders loose and arms limber.

But the man before her was wound tight, staring at the bowling lane like it held secrets he'd never learn.

"Okay." She stepped behind him and put a hand on each of his sturdy shoulders, rising to her tiptoes to speak right into his ear. "Pretend you're birding."

He shook beneath her hands as he chuckled.

"I'm serious," she continued. "You're doing this like it's a chore. You need to relax. Have fun. Really be in your body." She squeezed his shoulders, pressing them down. "Just imagine the bowling ball is your pair of binoculars, and all you want to do is point it right at that bird out there." She lifted one arm next to his head, gesturing to the waiting pins.

"And, John"—she ran both palms down his upper arms, tracing the muscles like so many small streams—"you've got strength here." And he really did, hard and smooth under her fingers. "Don't be afraid to use it. Give the ball a little power. I promise no one will get hurt."

She released him and forced a step back, fingers tingling.

He was still for a breath, then took a few determined steps before swinging his arm back, the marbled blue ball glinting in the fluorescents. One foot kicked behind him as he launched the ball across the line. He froze in his follow-through, legs slightly bent, head erect and watching. The ball spun down the lane with more power than his previous throws, straight and true, striking gold at the sweet spot between pins one and three. Only when the ten pins were all down and spinning on their sides did Celeste realize she'd been holding her breath.

CHAPTER 10

BIRD BINGE, DAY 11 OF 42
BIRD COUNT: 44

Things got a little better after his strike, but not much. John was mostly just not as bad as he'd been earlier in the game. But his minor improvement, combined with the practiced skill of Celeste and Andrea, was good enough to edge out the science and math teachers. John gave the losing team an apologetic nod as they unlaced their shoes, then headed to the bathroom before saying goodbye.

He paused on his way out when he heard some voices speaking quietly around the corner.

"I mean, he's cute for sure, but is he that into her?"

The other person clucked and giggled. "Doesn't seem like it. Celeste was all over him trying to teach him bowling—it was so obvious, but he didn't really respond. I almost felt sorry for her."

John closed the bathroom door behind him with a purposeful bang and waited for the scattering of feet before emerging into the hallway. Two of Celeste's coworkers—their teammate Andrea, and Layla, the science teacher—walked away with their heads tilted in close. Layla giggled and glanced at Celeste as they walked past her.

He ran his hand through his hair, swearing silently. His

first outing as her fake date and he'd let her down. Chris had warned him about this. Public displays of affection didn't come naturally to John, and while he'd been comfortable with the little touches from Celeste, he was realizing now he hadn't returned any. Instead of doting on her, he'd given her plenty of space, wanting to be present for her without interfering with her time with her friends. He'd gotten so involved in actually bowling, and watching Celeste at ease with their team, that he'd forgotten the entire reason he was there.

He'd been a bad fake boyfriend.

Guilt tugged at him as Celeste approached, plodding in just her socked feet with her ponytail swinging.

Her eyebrows drew together as she reached him. "What's up?" She gave him a friendly chuck on the shoulder with a loose fist. "You should be reveling in our win right now."

"I think we have a problem." John stepped closer to her and leaned in, keeping his voice low. "I overheard some of your coworkers doubting my devotion as a boyfriend. I don't think I've been selling it well enough. I'm sorry."

Celeste turned around to survey her friends, who were back at the lane packing up their things. "Who was it you heard talking?"

John nodded to the two women. "Andrea and Layla."

"Shit." Celeste groaned and slumped her shoulders. "Layla is the queen bee of the teachers' lounge. If she doesn't believe I'm off the market, no one will, and before I know it I'll be hearing about Andrea's cousin again."

As if on cue, Layla looked up and gave Celeste a small wave and a weak smile.

"It's okay." He tugged her a little toward a vending machine, one of those that promised a soft plush toy to the person who could manage to maneuver the shaky metal claw correctly. She moved willingly, her eyebrows raised, as he shifted her so that her back was against the machine.

Celeste had shown up for him at the park without even knowing him at all. Surely he could help her out here. "Are they watching us?"

Celeste peeked around his chest. "Why?"

Because he was going to prove he was up for the task. No way would John let Celeste leave this bowling alley with her coworkers thinking he was anything less than enamored with her.

He kept some distance between them but kept his eyes locked on hers to make sure she was listening. Some ideas were brewing in his head, but he didn't want to push their ground rules without warning. "We could sell this a little more. But it will mean getting a little closer than we laid out in our texts. Is that okay?"

Celeste's brown eyes glistened as she grinned. "I mean, I don't want to go out with Andrea's cousin. So go for it."

John stepped in close to her as she peered up, biting her lip. He'd bet anything Celeste was the teenager who always chose "dare" when people were playing party games in high school, the ones he'd always skipped out on by taking a walk.

But he wouldn't skip out on Celeste. Instead, he wrapped an arm around her waist and spread his palm on her lower back, feeling her rib cage expand into his hand as she sucked in a breath.

Her eyes were still aimed over his shoulder. "You caught their attention. They're watching us."

He could probably give her a brief kiss on the cheek and be done with it, but Celeste deserved more than that. She deserved for everyone to believe she had a boyfriend who could take his time with her. So he leaned in slowly to lower his face into the curve of her shoulder. The tip of his nose brushed first at the ridge of her collarbone, then up the side of her neck. He slid his nose up to the little notch behind her ear and found the epicenter of the ever-present peppermint, sweet and tangy on her skin.

Celeste tensed under him and gave a shaky exhale.

"This okay?" he asked, keeping his face tipped into her neck.

"Yes." Her voice was barely audible. Her palm spread on his chest. "It's okay."

He was so close his lips brushed her skin as he spoke. "You're wearing smaller earrings tonight." He'd noticed the small blue gems on her earlobes earlier, and now one glinted at him from a breath's space away.

She gave a small laugh. "I don't wear big earrings when I'm bowling. They, um, distract me."

They distracted him, too. One swing of her earrings would probably have sent every ball of his straight into the gutter instead of just most of them. He cleared his throat, trying to sharpen his fuzzy mind.

Beneath him, Celeste whimpered.

"You okay?" he asked. The scent of peppermint was alive on his tongue. "Want me to stop?"

"It's just your beard, it . . . it tickles." Her head shifted as she exhaled. "They're still watching. Should we do something else?"

"Sure. Tell me what you want."

Celeste's breath hitched as her fingers curled, creating a star of pressure points on his chest. Before he could stop them, John's thoughts raced ahead, imagining Celeste's response under different circumstances. Real circumstances.

He had no doubt—she would be open, even greedy.

And with thoughts like that, he couldn't stand this close to her for much longer.

"Maybe move your mouth up," Celeste whispered. "Like

you're saying something, right in my ear." She gave a small giggle. "I'll make a scandalized face."

He followed her instructions, bringing them cheek to cheek. "I should probably actually talk, right? Are they watching that closely?"

"Definitely. We can, um, use this time to talk about birds. Like I've always wondered, what do they do here, in the summer, when it's so hot?"

His lips hovered a millimeter from the curve of her ear. "Well . . ." He closed his eyes, searching his brain for the bird facts that were usually at the forefront. Right now that space was occupied by peppermint and blue gems and the expansion of Celeste's lower back into his palm. "They hide out during the day, sort of like us, and look for water to cool themselves off."

"Sure." She slid her hand up his chest and around the back of his neck until her fingers were playing with the hair at his nape.

John swallowed hard and went deeper in his brain, skimming through the pages of the old textbooks he still reviewed from time to time. "But, um, they also have a behavior called fluttering, to lower their body temperature. It involves . . ." Celeste's short nails drew down his neck, then along the hem of his T-shirt, dipping just slightly below the fabric. "Rapid open-mouth breathing."

The short sentence came out in a rush of breath onto Celeste's ear. She tensed beneath him, her hand freezing on his neck where her fingers lingered below the hem of his T-shirt.

"Oh." Her voice was tight, almost choked. "Really."

"Yes. And then they do a vibrating—"

"You know what?" Her breath fluttered through his hair. "I think I get it. Rapid open-mouth breathing and vibrating."

John drew a breath to steady himself, but the movement only brought their bodies closer, flush from neck to navel. He emptied his lungs quickly to put space back between them, but not before he felt the soft give of Celeste's breasts against his chest.

His brain was muddled, and his body was . . . responsive. He had to extricate himself, and soon. "So," he said through his tight throat. "Do you think they're convinced?"

John pulled his head back just long enough to take in the delicate rounding of Celeste's ear, the glint of her small earring, and something he hadn't noticed before—a little freckle on her neck hidden just behind her earlobe.

This had started happening on their hike. Little observations about her—the way she tipped her face into the sunlight and hummed, or tugged at her ponytail as she asked about birds—tucked themselves away in a Celeste-shaped guidebook in his mind. Its pages held the bounce of her heels as she fiddled with her binoculars, the chipped red polish on her toes when she'd jumped into the mountain pool, the flex of her calves and the kick of her leg when she bowled, and now—the single freckle, just barely peeking into view.

All of John's mental preparation for the role of fake boyfriend had been logistical, like thinking about when and how couples usually held hands. He hadn't prepared for *this*—the sheer, simple comfort of closeness and the joy of intimate discovery. Or the surge of previously dormant energy awake and buzzing against Celeste's pliant body.

Since his breakup, he'd embraced his single status happily. His friends and brothers had urged him to give love another chance, but he knew what a relationship held for him—constant frustration that he wasn't *more*. More talkative, more forthcoming, more motivated. At times he'd suspected Breena saw him as a project, not as a partner.

And he enjoyed being single—John was a man built to spend

time alone—but damn, he'd missed *this*. Missed it so much his hand was gliding up Celeste's back, then closing around her neck. Wanted it so much he scraped his beard against her jaw, pulling a short gasp from her that zipped straight into that book, where he'd study it later.

Needed it so much that if he just lowered his chin, and—

"Okay, lovebirds!" Andrea's singsong voice froze them both, stopping John from completely abandoning their ground rules. "We're outta here! You still coming with me, Celeste? Or did you find something better to do?"

John dropped his hand from Celeste's neck and stepped back just as she unwound her arm from him.

"Um." She blinked three times before looking past him and lifting a stiff arm. "Yeah, coming. Just give me a sec."

She turned back to him with a smile that was big but tight at the edges. "I better go." Celeste dragged her teeth along her lower lip before lowering her voice. "Thanks for that. You were, uh, great." Between them, her fingers tangled together. "Very convincing. Maybe not with the bowling, but with the other stuff for sure."

He released a breath. "All part of the deal, right?"

"Right. Totally." She took one step backward, then another. "See you Saturday, then? Back to birds."

"Right." John looked past Celeste at the sliding doors, opening and closing as people filed out into the dark parking lot. Suddenly he was eager to get home, maybe turn on some music in his shop and get some work done. "Back to birds."

CHAPTER 11

BIRD BINGE, DAY 15 OF 42
BIRD COUNT: 44

Celeste wiped down the kitchen sink and straightened the line of potted plants on her yellow countertop, then dragged her fingers through her hair, still damp from her shower, before yanking it up into a messy bun. Then she wiped down the kitchen sink again.

"Are you seriously still cleaning?"

Her gaze jumped from shining white porcelain to Morgan, eyeing Celeste from the arched doorway. At almost eighteen, Morgan had been taller than Celeste for a few years, her lanky body shown off now in black cutoffs and a red cropped shirt that exposed two inches of her stomach. Morgan's clothes were more revealing than anything Celeste had ever worn, but the girl was comfortable in her own skin.

She exuded a sense of self Celeste had sought most of her life.

Celeste turned and leaned against the counter. "I haven't been cleaning for that long."

Morgan laughed as she riffled through the fridge, pulling out a cold slice of leftover pineapple-and-jalapeño pizza from the night before. Her long, sandy hair, streaked with one bright blue stripe, was pulled into a nest held together by a pencil. "I've never seen the blanket on the couch so precisely folded. What's your deal?"

"I don't have a deal!" Celeste protested. "It just felt like a good time to clean. I was listening to a podcast about the history of grilled cheese sandwiches and I really got in the groove."

It couldn't be John's imminent arrival at her home that had Celeste buzzing around the house like one of those little black-tailed gnatcatchers she'd spotted on their hike. That would be silly. "Did you know that someone paid thousands of dollars once for a grilled cheese that looked like it had an image of the Virgin Mary burned into the bread?"

"Jesus." Morgan snickered.

"Literally," Celeste countered, satisfied by her daughter's full-throated laugh.

Morgan downed the last of the pizza before sitting at the table and picking up the small notebook next to a potted plant. She pulled the pencil out of her bun, letting her hair fall past her shoulders. Since Morgan could hold a pencil, she'd been drawing, and the evidence of her passion was framed all over Celeste's house. A big part of the past year had involved Celeste searching for an affordable college that had a decent art department but where Morgan could also pick up some more practical, and hopefully employable, skills.

Celeste had landed on Northern Arizona University, about four hours from Tucson, as the perfect solution. Far enough from home for Morgan to spread her wings, it still offered in-state tuition, with guaranteed scholarships if Morgan finished the year strong.

But another email reminder about registration had come in that week, and Morgan still hadn't filled anything out. She couldn't even be bothered to browse the course catalog and had shrugged at Celeste's suggestion that they go up to tour the campus together.

"Hon." She lowered herself to sit opposite her daughter, whose eyes darted between the plant and the page of her notebook. "We should really get serious about your NAU paperwork. Could we spend some time on that later? I know it might feel like a lot, but I can help."

Morgan's hand paused, a half-formed leaf under her pencil. "Can't. I'm doing stuff with Em all day."

"Oh." Em and Morgan had been joined at the hip for years, and she couldn't blame Morgan for wanting to squeeze in all their time together before graduation. Soon, she'd pin Morgan down for college prep. And she was wrapped up with John today anyway.

Well, not *wrapped*. The extremely convincing act at the bowling alley had been a necessary departure from their ground rules, but there'd be no further need for actual, physical wrapping. "What are you two up to?"

Morgan shaded the leaf's edge with a series of small hash marks. "We're going to the skate park, then I'm gonna help Em study for their AP chem exam."

"What do you do at the skate park? Just watch?"

Morgan shrugged. "Yeah. Watch. Take pictures. Draw. Em's working on a new move; it's fun watching them."

Celeste had watched the video edits Morgan had made of Em's skating, and some of the moves made her mom heart cringe. "Em wears a helmet when they skate, right?"

Morgan laughed. "Usually. Almost always." She looked up at Celeste, cutting off the coming lecture with a jab of her pencil. "Do not start texting Em statistics about skateboard accidents."

"I wouldn't do that," she lied. Maybe she'd find a pamphlet instead. She could leave it on the table where Morgan and Em were likely to see it.

"I saw a flyer up for your show downtown." Celeste pulled herself from the edge of a safety-while-skateboarding lecture. Every conversation with her daughter was a balancing act. "Are you so excited?"

Morgan just shrugged, but a small smile played on her mouth. She'd been nominated for an end-of-the-year art showcase of graduating seniors from throughout the region, and she'd been putting in hours every week on the pieces she'd use. The event fell on the same night as the final gala for the Bird Binge, so it would take some balancing to get to both. But Celeste often felt like she lived on a tightrope, so she'd manage.

"Do you want to order ramen tonight and plan our outfits for the show?" Celeste asked hopefully. "Never too early to plan a good outfit."

"Can't tonight." Morgan nibbled at her lower lip as she looked up from her drawing. "I'm doing dinner with Dad and Lucy. His girlfriend."

"Oh, right." Morgan had mentioned Lucy before, though Celeste hadn't known she'd achieved full girlfriend status. It hurt to think of losing time with Morgan to someone she didn't even know. "That'll be fun."

Morgan just let out a sigh and worried her tongue into the side of her cheek, then looked back up at Celeste. "You know you can date people too, right, Mom?"

Celeste leaned her elbows on the table. "I know, honey. I just don't want to."

"But why?" Morgan nibbled at her pencil, then returned to her sketch of the plant. "Do you really want to be alone forever?"

Her voice took on a tinge that sounded a lot like pity. Being "alone forever" did seem pretty sad. But that wasn't how Celeste thought of it when she looked ahead, at least to the next few years. She saw independence, not loneliness. A chance to stand in the sunshine and let herself grow.

"I don't expect you to understand, but I'm having fun learning how to be on my own. Your dad and I met when I was barely older than you are now, and my whole life became about his life. I never really had a chance to be just me."

Her daughter's eyes stopped mid-roll. She'd heard it all before, especially when Celeste had been desperate to explain her motivations for seeking a divorce.

Morgan abandoned the sketchbook and stood, rolling the pencil between her long fingers. "Okay, okay. I just don't want to see you cut yourself off, you know, from love."

Celeste rubbed her temples and looked up at her daughter. "Baby, I'm not. I got to experience love with your dad for a lot of years, and now I'm experiencing it with myself." She laughed as Morgan groaned, well aware that her daughter hated sincere-mom mode. "And I can't wait for you to have love someday, when you're ready."

Morgan opened her mouth for a moment, but then stuck the pencil between her teeth as she remade her bun. Celeste watched the easy movements with near adoration—Morgan sweeping up her hair, twisting it, then skewering it with the pencil. This was the same kid who used to draw all over the walls of their small apartment in Lincoln.

Celeste might have resented a lot of those years with Peter and the shadows they'd cast over her. Even now, two years divorced, she'd learned to always be in her bedroom when she called him so she could throw her phone on the bed as soon as she hit *end*. Especially last week, when Peter had told her he'd be away on a work trip for Morgan's art show.

But she would never regret their relationship, not when it

had given her this young woman already halfway out of the kitchen.

"Don't forget to talk to Em about the helmet!" Celeste called after her.

The only answer was a groan, but a few seconds later Morgan's head popped back into the kitchen. "Uh, Mom? There's a guy on the porch. Says he's here for birding?"

Celeste stood quickly, almost knocking down her chair. There should definitely not be bees swarming in her stomach at the knowledge that John was on her porch, even if the last time she'd seen him, he'd caged her against an arcade game. He'd just been acting for her friends. But Celeste couldn't shake the memory of how his hand had spanned the whole width of her back or of how his small, quiet observations had made her feel like something unique and precious.

The dream she'd had last night didn't help, either.

She'd woken that morning to dawn light filling her room and an aching heat between her legs, sensations from a dream just fuzzy at the edges—callused hands mapping her body, a quiet smile scraping against her skin. Sighing and stretching across her mattress, she'd trailed a hand down her stomach, ready to let the residual arousal from her dream get her Saturday off to a good start. But just as her hand moved down, the edges of the dream had come into focus.

John's masterful hands, John's smile, John's—

With a snap, she'd pulled her arm up and plastered it over her comforter, breathing hard and squeezing her eyes shut tight.

She was not going there. *They* were not going there. They had an understanding.

Clearing her throat, she smoothed down the soft cotton of her yoga pants. "I told you his name was John. He's coming today to focus on backyard birding. I invited you to join us, remember?" She figured having Morgan there would be a win-win. Her daughter could learn about birds and also, maybe, make sure Celeste's mind didn't wander while John was adjusting his binoculars. But Morgan hadn't taken the bait.

Which was fine. Celeste was a grown woman who could control inconvenient lusty thoughts about her birding partner. "Did you just leave him out there?"

Morgan shrugged. "Yeah, just while I checked with you." She grinned as her eyebrows lifted. "He was holding a little birdhouse and asked if my mother was home. Very polite. I like the beard."

"Don't start," Celeste warned, knowing just what Morgan was thinking. "He's just here to bird. That's it."

"Okay." Morgan shrugged nonchalantly but maintained her knowing smile, sliding her hands into her back pockets. Teenagers were infuriating. "Well, Em is waiting, so I'm gonna go. Should I leave the birding guy out there?"

"John. His name is John. And you can let him in and tell him I'll be right there, thank you. Have fun and tell Em I'll get in touch later about the helmet."

Morgan left with a tortured groan, leaving Celeste to listen as the front door closed.

A moment later, Celeste found John in the living room, standing at the bookshelf near her front door. His eyes flitted over the spines of her haphazardly shelved books as his thumb swiped along the grain of the little wooden object in his hand, somehow keeping pace with her heartbeat as she replayed her morning again.

After her shocking wake-up call, she'd launched herself into her bathroom and leaned forward to scan the mirror and the myriad of colorful Post-its that crowded it, searching the notes for something to confirm that masturbating to thoughts of her birding partner was a very, very bad idea.

Seek adventure. Not helpful.

Her eyes kept scanning as she started brushing her teeth.

If you can dream it, you can do it.

A spray of toothpaste and spit splattered her mirror as she let out a barking laugh. No, no, no.

Finally, her eyes had settled on a blue Post-it, faded and curled at the edges, one of her very first.

Learn to bloom alone.

Celeste rinsed her mouth and looked at the message again, silently mouthing the words into the mirror.

It hadn't always been easy, but she'd been blooming these past two years. Sometimes it hurt, but when it did she reminded herself of the hours she used to spend rubbing Morgan's aching calves as her muscles grew faster than her body could bear, tears in her eyes from the growing pains. That pain—the pain of stretching, of growth—was better by far than the realization that in her marriage she was growing smaller with each passing month. Worse, Peter had simply accepted her slow disappearance. And so had she.

Morgan might want Celeste to date again, but Celeste knew where that led, and it wasn't a place Celeste planned to go back to anytime soon.

"Good morning." John's honeyed voice carried a hint of a question. "I hope it's okay I came in. Your daughter—"

"Hi!" Her greeting was both late and loud, but she didn't let it stop her. "Of course, yes, Morgan said you were here, and she"—Celeste motioned to the door—"she was just leaving. And now you've met her, so that's good. Or not. I mean, it doesn't really matter, I guess." Wherever Maria was right now, she was rolling her eyes at Celeste. "You brought a birdhouse?"

He blinked, looking down at the delicate structure like it was a surprise. "Oh. Right. I made it for you. It's a design by the ornithological society, a special project to help Lucy's warblers." He palmed the tiny house in one hand to pass it to her.

It wasn't anything fancy. A few small pieces of wood put together in whatever way people put together wooden things, but it was so perfectly formed that Celeste took it gently, like it already held precious eggs inside. She turned it in her hands, admiring each smooth edge and the way the maple-syrup grains spiraled in nature's own design.

"You don't have to take it," John rushed out. "But I was making them to give away at the trivia night and I thought you might like one early. Lucys are cavity nesters, but their natural nesting spots are taken up by invasive species and—"

"John." It was possible he was as awkward as she was. Going past the ground rules at the bowling alley had not been wise. "It's really lovely. Thank you."

She'd have him show her where to put it up once they got outside. Because the longer she held it, the longer she'd be thinking about John's rough, skilled hands delicately cradling these small pieces of wood.

"Birds!" she burst out, almost dropping the birdhouse. "That's why you're here." She turned on her heels before her traitorous body had a chance to word-vomit any more, leading the way through her kitchen and to the back door. "Let's go see some birds."

CHAPTER 12

BIRD BINGE, DAY 15 OF 42
BIRD COUNT: 46

"This is a great idea, you know." Celeste lowered her binoculars to peek at John. When they'd come out an hour before, she'd waited for him to sit before choosing her own spot across the porch. "Backyard birding sessions. People will eat this up."

"We'll see." When John allowed himself to daydream about guiding professionally, he nurtured these little nuggets of ideas. He wanted to eschew the race for the rarest birds and focus on helping people see what was all around them. Most people had no idea how much there was to discover from their own porches. He'd mentioned the idea to Celeste on their hike, and she'd literally leapt with excitement, inviting him to her yard at his earliest convenience.

At the time, it had been simple to say yes. But that was before he'd been transfixed by the water pouring off Celeste's shoulders in the mountains and before he'd sensed her pulse just below his lips in the bowling alley. Some people doled out flirtation easily—Chris could be found entwined with any number of people in the course of a night—but John could count on both hands the number of times he'd been close enough to a woman to memorize the curve of her ear.

And walking through her house today had laid down another layer of intimacy. He'd been in homes that felt like showrooms, arranged more for appearance than use. But this place was clearly Celeste—walls painted eggshell and lavender dotted with framed posters and pencil sketches, potted plants trailing vines down crowded bookshelves, a worn brown couch with pink throw pillows and a colorful quilt folded over the top. Her kitchen was pure sunlight bouncing off yellow counters, with a small round table on which a sketch pad was splayed open, the drawing on the page a mirror of the philodendron spilling its leaves across the table.

She'd seemed nervous when he arrived, and he'd wondered again if going to her home had been a bad idea. But the morning air and a view of the clear sky in her yard had seemed to set both of them at ease. And by the time they'd spotted the first bird in her yard—a white-winged dove flapping to a slow landing on the back wall—John had pulled his brain out of the bowling alley and was able to appreciate the slow glide of Celeste's porch swing. There was still a connection between them, something thin and flashing like a fishing line, but it didn't strain their rapport once they'd started focusing on birding.

"I'm serious, John." Celeste lifted the spiral-bound notebook where she was keeping her list for the contest. "We even saw a couple of new birds out here we didn't see on the hike. I am seriously amazed. I don't think I would have known what I could see from here."

The yard was small, landscaped with rusty rocks and rosy pebbles with two long basins full of brittlebush, sage, and other native plants. Spiky aloes bordered the yard, their stalks dripping with salmon-colored flowers.

"You've got a very bird-friendly space here. Those hummers

love the blooming aloe." They'd added two birds to their list, both hummingbirds. The Anna's, with its stunning pink throat, could be found almost anywhere in town with blooming flowers. But the more elusive broad-billed hummingbird had been a nice surprise, and when John told Celeste he suspected it was likely nesting nearby, she'd clapped her hands like an excited kid.

After picking a spot for the birdhouse, they'd talked about what types of feeders she could put up, and where, and he'd given her a list of the most likely birds to be spotted in her part of town. But mostly, they just sat and watched. Celeste had been studying, evidenced by the dog-eared pages of the guidebook she clutched in her lap, and she was able to identify many of the birds that stopped over in the hour they sat together. Even though many of them were already on their list, Celeste gave each her rapt attention.

They lapsed into an easy silence long enough for John's mind to go comfortably still as he soaked in the sun that reached them under the porch awning. His eyes drifted open at the sound of a gentle hum and he saw Celeste, her arms stretching overhead, the hem of her ribbed tank top inching up just enough to show a finger's width of pale skin. She'd slipped out of her sandals when they'd sat down, and the bare toes of her right foot—toenails a bright green today—drew a lazy *S* up the curve of her left calf.

The line pulled taut. Awareness hummed in John's blood, matching the pitch of Celeste's sigh as she curved her body slowly to one side, then the other, hands clasped above her head.

A sharp series of *pew*s sang out from a tree in a neighbor's yard, and Celeste's eyes jolted open. Her attention on the tree gave him time to squeeze his eyes shut tight.

"That one!" Celeste stood, pointing to the tree. "I hear that one all the time but I can't find it. What is it?"

John reached for his guidebook, but Celeste waved him off. "No, please. No more lessons today, just tell me. I sit out here with my coffee and my binoculars just waiting to see it, but it just shoots its little laser gun over there out of sight."

John laughed, remembering how he'd always thought of *Star Wars* when he heard these birds in the trees outside his house in Santa Rita. "It's a northern cardinal. Do you usually hear the call-and-response?"

Celeste shook her head. "I don't know?"

"Often you'll hear a pair calling to each other. Going back and forth."

Celeste stood quickly and approached him, grinning. The bench glided back as her weight settled on the other side, just as the cardinal's mate answered its call.

"There it is." He kept his voice quiet. "One is still in that tree, but it sounds like the other is across the yard."

Bright *chip*s and *pew*s traveled across the air. John closed his eyes to listen.

"What are they saying?" Celeste asked in a whisper.

He tipped his face back and let the sun heat his cheeks. "I don't know exactly, but they're keeping track of each other as they search for food, making sure no one goes too far."

"I used to do that with Morgan. If we were in a store, she'd hide in the racks of clothes, and I'd call out, 'Moo-oo.' That was my nickname for her." The bench swung back and forth, stirring a small breeze around them. "And she would call back, 'Ma-ma.'"

They listened to the cardinals for a moment. He heard them switch positions, the calls changing direction, and even though his eyes were closed, Celeste's quiet squeal told him she'd spotted their bodies streaking through the yard.

"Tell me what else you hear," she said quietly after a minute. "What else is happening out there?"

When he peeked at her, she was watching him, her feet tucked under her. "It's my yard, after all. Shouldn't I know the story?" Her arm stretched between them and her index finger pushed into his upper arm. But what seemed to have been intended as a teasing poke lingered, until her hand flattened and her palm cupped the curve of his shoulder. Even through the fabric of his T-shirt, heat radiated from Celeste's fingertips as her eyes widened before she snatched her hand away, staring at it for a moment like it had betrayed her.

John cleared his throat and looked back out at the yard. "Sure." His voice was lower than usual, stuck somewhere right in his sternum. "Yeah, okay." Any reason to close his eyes again and loosen the line that had tightened between them in the past few minutes. It would be easier if it was just him, but his inconvenient attraction didn't seem to be one-sided, though he could tell it was unwelcome for Celeste.

Eyes closed, John pushed back his thoughts of the imprint of her palm and listened. If he couldn't concentrate on the birds, there was no point to any of it.

A slow breath brought in the sounds around them, lines of songs and bursts of calls in Celeste's yard and beyond.

"House finch up high, probably on the electrical wire. He's doing a territorial call."

"Are they the ones with the red chests?"

He nodded and hummed. "A northern mockingbird to the east, looking for love. Funny thing about them is that they don't just mimic other birds. Sometimes they'll do frog calls or even car alarms if they've heard them enough."

He listed a few others, his closed eyes still lit from the sun.

Doves—white-winged, Inca, and rock—cooed from places in the yard and beyond, a Gila woodpecker proclaimed its territory from a nearby utility pole, house sparrows chipped from all directions, and a verdin's song, so much bigger than its tiny body, rolled out from the palo verde next door.

"So many creatures living their lives all around us all the time." Celeste's voice was breathy, almost wistful. "So many little stories."

He risked a look in her direction to see her watching a group of sparrows bathing themselves in a patch of dry dust. They kicked it up into their feathers, some even splaying open their wings to flutter them along the ground.

"I was reading about house sparrows the other day." Her eyes didn't leave them as she spoke. "It's like we're not supposed to like them because they're an invasive species, but they're just doing their best. I mean hell, they mate for life, which is more than I can say for myself."

Her brow furrowed as her fingers tangled on her lap, her own joke obviously biting.

"Probably not a fair comparison, as you do have a significantly longer lifespan than a sparrow. They only have to stay in a relationship for two years," he deadpanned. "And the most recent research indicates that they might not actually be that faithful in that time."

Her answering smile filled him with satisfaction. She tucked a lone strand of hair behind her ear and straightened. "Well, when you put it that way, I'm basically a paragon of relationship success."

He couldn't get over how freely she spoke about her life, even the bad parts. It inspired him to keep talking. "I admire you, though. Doing what you needed for yourself, I'm sure it wasn't easy."

It had taken John actually catching Breena in the act with someone else to finally leave a relationship he knew wasn't right. Without that punch in the gut, they might have gone on for years, liking each other less and less each day.

Celeste wasn't watching the sparrows anymore. She was looking at him, eyes wet at the corners and mouth slightly agape. Her head tipped to one side as she reached up to twist her fingers into her bun. "The weird thing is"—she tracked a bird across the sky, but John stayed focused on her—"when I finally left, yeah, I was mad at Peter. Somewhere along the way he seemed to go from loving me to not even really liking me very much, and that left some marks. But the person I was really angry with was myself, for letting it go on for so long. For being so afraid to be alone."

Her fingers tapped a rhythm on the bench between them, and without thinking, John covered her hand with his own, stilling her movement. He shouldn't have touched her, not with this thing between them growing warmer in the sun, but he hated seeing her shrink like this. "I know we haven't known each other for very long, but I would never use the word 'afraid' to describe you."

When Celeste's eyes found his, they locked him in place. Her voice came just above a whisper. "What word would you use?"

Surprising. Effervescent. Enticing. "Brave."

"Oh." The sound fell from her mouth, barely audible. That line between them was thick now, and tight, tugging his gaze to her mouth. Her tongue darted across her lower lip.

Beneath his hand, her wrist twisted, bringing them palm to palm.

For a stretched-out moment in the sun on the swinging bench, he let himself believe it could be easy. He could follow that line to Celeste's waiting mouth and pull her lip between his teeth. They could move to her bedroom and let this seed between them grow and bloom. He'd make her forget that anyone had ever left her feeling unwanted.

But life was more than this moment. Celeste wanted to be on her own, and he wouldn't be responsible for delaying that, especially when he was on a similar road himself.

He stood so quickly the bench rocked back. "I better go." He swiped up his guidebook. "I have some work to do." He'd just gotten an order for a table made from reclaimed wood he'd hauled up from an old barn on his parents' property. A few hours in his shop were exactly what he needed. "Thanks again for letting me try this out."

"Right." Celeste stood, wiping her hands down over her hips, following a path John would trace only in his imagination.

It was best for both of them to ignore this connection. Even if it pulled at him as he walked back through her house, where a streak of sunshine lit up her bookshelf, so burdened it looked on the verge of collapse. Even if it tugged as she smiled from her doorway, her outline in shadow as he turned his head back to say goodbye. Even if it dragged at him all the way to his car and across town to the safety of his workshop.

CHAPTER 13

BIRD BINGE, DAY 19 OF 42
BIRD COUNT: 67

Celeste was kicking bird trivia ass. She tapped her fingers against the black Formica bar table, leaning in close to John so her voice wouldn't carry to any neighboring teams.

"It's the verdin. I'm telling you, it's the verdin. I know this."

The question "Which bird uses the prevailing winds to keep cool?" had her team in hot debate. But she knew from her bedtime reading that the teeny little verdin built its spherical nest with the opening facing the breeze, to cool the inside in the summer heat. She'd marveled at the genius of the act.

"This question is lacking in needed specifics," Chris argued. "Which season? Which winds?"

Chris had been about this helpful the entire night, which was to say not at all. Although he *had* chosen their team name—the Tweethearts—and contributed to the spirit with jovial conversation and the occasional snail joke. Celeste would never have guessed so many snail jokes even existed, but she was headed home with a handful of them to make Morgan cringe.

"I don't suppose you have an opinion, Jared?" John looked to his brother, who was seated across the table from Celeste. He was in town for the night and conveniently rounded out John and Celeste's trivia team. Jared was taller than John, with a leaner build and darker hair. But they shared the same hard jawline, and Jared had the same habit of rubbing his chin while he was thinking, though he was clean-shaven.

He shook his head. "I leave it all in the hands of the experts." He nodded to Celeste and gave her a little wink, which made her stifle a giggle. She'd learned quickly that Jared was naturally magnetic and flirtatious, throwing winks and knowing smiles around easily, including in the direction of Chris, who just batted his eyelashes in return. He had a movie-star bad-boy quality about him, down to the black T-shirt, hooded eyes, and forearm-covering tattoos. But where she'd expected to see a beer or a glass of bourbon in his hand, Jared demurely sipped club soda with lemon.

"We have thirty more seconds to submit the answer," John said. "Celeste sounds sure, and I know she's been studying up. So let's go with that."

Celeste gave a little cheer, then pursed her lips. "But am I right?"

Their team was neck and neck with the Know It Owls and the Chirp-n-Dales. Nearly three weeks of birding with John, mixed with her own drive to study and compete, had brought her into the trivia event pumped and prepared, especially with John at her side. He was patient after the questions were asked, always giving her time to make her guess before confirming his agreement and entering their official answer. But she waited for his confirmation now as she squeezed some lime into her beer and took a long sip.

He was quiet for a second, then shot her a shy smile. "I don't know. Your answer makes a lot of sense, but I don't know for sure."

"Oh my god!" She hit the table, making all the glasses rattle and sing. “You don’t know? And I do?” She looked at the others at her table, ensuring that they witnessed her moment of triumph. “And so the student has become the teacher!”

Laughing, he entered the answer in the handheld device given to each team, and Celeste was quickly proven correct. She hooted in celebration as Jared gave her a high five. Chris provided her with a golf clap from his side of the table.

“We seem to have a tie here between the Tweethearts and team Know It Owls,” announced Brad, the night’s MC. Celeste glanced over to team six’s table, making sure to keep a smile on her face. They’d been battling for first place all night, and Breena and her companions were clearly annoyed by the competition.

“I bet she thinks you carried our team,” Celeste murmured to John, her mouth close to his ear.

He leaned in, his knee knocking into hers under the table as one hand found the curve of her lower back. “But I didn’t. And you know that, and so do I.” A trail of pleasure tracked from his voice to where his thumb absentmindedly rubbed her spine.

Because the birding crowd was all gathered for the contest’s trivia night, John and Celeste were back to playing fake boyfriend and girlfriend, though Jared and Chris both knew the truth. Chris had even mentioned that he was looking forward to “a bit of theater” that evening, and Celeste had wiggled her eyebrows and smirked as she pinched the ticklish spot she’d discovered on John’s waist.

It felt good to touch him. The memories of the way he’d touched her in the bowling alley were still sharp, but it was their time in her yard she couldn’t forget. The quiet intimacy of sitting together, his profound awareness of his surroundings, and the generous observation he’d gifted her.

They’d been close to something on that bench, and she knew

he'd sensed it, too. He'd looked at her mouth with the same kind of focus he used when bird-watching, and it turned her to jelly.

He'd done them both a favor by leaving, and they'd managed to be normal, un-horny birding adults the next day, adding a slew of water birds to their count at a local pond. But her body still buzzed near him, and if she had the opportunity now, as a faithful fake girlfriend, to lean into his touch, she'd take it. Maybe these small touches would be enough for her, and she'd stop craving more.

"Tie, schmie. I wanted to win tonight," she said to John, their foreheads almost touching. "I know we're catching up in the count, but I really wanted these points."

The night's winning team got five extra points added to their final bird count. Given that Celeste was still getting the hang of things almost halfway through the contest, they could use all the extra points they could get.

MC Brad cleared his throat right into the microphone, drawing a few groans from the crowd, but then spoke excitedly. "Luckily, we came prepared, and we have a tiebreaker question. Can we please have two representatives from each team up to the front?"

Jared smiled and motioned to John and Celeste. "I'm sure as hell not going."

Celeste was already halfway there, stepping onto the small makeshift stage as Breena and her teammate Marisol made their way to the front. She gave a little finger wave toward Breena, who just sniffed in response. But Breena's indifference slipped when John joined Celeste onstage, and her eyes narrowed as she watched Celeste reach a hand over to trail a finger down his firm forearm.

"All right, this question is a little different from the others." Brad used his best show-host voice, low and dramatic, and Celeste dropped her hand back to her side. "I believe it might just be what we need to set one team apart. Are we ready?" He paused for dramatic effect. Back at their table, Chris cheered.

"In Emily Dickinson's poem about a hummingbird, known as 'A Route of Evanescence'"—Celeste's heart leapt into her throat as Brad continued—"Dickinson makes a reference to an insect that prospers here in the Sonoran Desert. What is the insect?"

Celeste shot a hand out to John and squeezed his fingers tight in her fist. A few feet away, Breena looked at Brad incredulously. "Brad," she finally said, "seriously? Is this even about *birds*?"

Brad shot a showman's smile at Breena and shrugged. "Clock's ticking."

John leaned close to Celeste, whispering in her ear. "You're about to break my fingers."

She raised her lips to his ear, trying with all her might to be quiet when she wanted to screech. "I know this I know this I know this! I do an Emily Dickinson unit with my students every fucking year, John. I love this one."

She whispered the poem she'd read dozens of times, the shape of the words familiar in her mouth. "'A route of evanescence, with a revolving wheel, a resonance of emerald, a rush of cochineal.'"

John turned to her with a smile that lit up a sunburst just behind her sternum. She nudged his arm and he quickly typed in the answer. She looked to Chris and Jared and gave them a wink and a thumbs-up. Jared winked right back.

"All righty," Brad said as the time ran out. "Let's see who is the most literary among us. Answers, please." The screen above the bar showed their answers—*cochineal* for the Tweethearts and a series of exclamation points and question marks from Breena and Marisol, who apparently weren't such know-it-owls after all.

Holy. Shit. Middle school language arts for the win.

Finally, Brad spoke again. "And the Tweethearts have it! Cochineal, everyone! Most of you may know this tiny bug makes its webs on the pads of the prickly pear and is known for the bright red color that comes from its body—"

But his words barely reached Celeste. She was too busy jumping up and down, squealing with delight.

Yes, it was only a bird trivia contest in a little bar in Tucson, Arizona, a blip on the radar compared with things far more significant in the passage of time.

But it was also her plan in action—learning new things, having new adventures, discovering new facets of herself. It was having fun with new friends, and it was the sweet thrill of victory.

It was seeing John's *whatcha gonna do?* shrug at Breena, and her slack-jawed expression in response. It was the extra points to help get him closer to his dream.

It was the electricity of John's hand in hers, squeezing back, his face lighting up as he laughed at her victory dance.

And it was the adrenaline racing through her body as she put her hand on the side of his face, finally feeling the rough texture of his beard beneath her fingers. His eyes went a little wide as she focused on his mouth, smiling broadly. That morning, like every morning, she'd studied her mirror, scanned the notes for daily wisdom. One rose in her mind now as Jared and Chris cheered from the sidelines, John grinning down at her.

Give in to joy.

So she pulled John's smiling face to hers, and she kissed her fake boyfriend.

CHAPTER 14

BIRD BINGE, DAY 19 OF 42

BIRD COUNT: 67

John hadn't seen it coming. Celeste had been shouting and jumping, shaking her hips and stomping her feet.

But then she'd turned to him and touched his face as her eyes laser-focused on his mouth. And now her fingers were threading into his beard along his jaw, and her lips were pressed against his.

This was like the bowling alley, a show for the crowd. It had to be. Because even if there was a clear spark between them, they weren't fanning it. Celeste wouldn't be *really* kissing him.

They were a fake couple, and a couple would celebrate with an easy kiss. An easy, public, closed-mouth kiss that didn't need to be any more passionate than his awkward, dry lip-lock with Marjorie Coopers under the bleachers after baseball practice when he was fourteen.

But then Chris's distinct whistle cut through the cheers, and Celeste laughed. And as her mouth curved against his, it drew his up like a magnet, until he and Celeste were smiling against each other. Then the hand she held to his face slipped to the back of his neck, and her tongue snaked along his bottom lip, dipping into his mouth.

And then nothing could stop his instinct to stroke his tongue against hers and bring a hand to her jaw. His thumb brushed a small circle just under her ear and she sighed into his mouth, the sound breaking into a thousand pieces and scattering themselves in his body. His tongue moved against hers, tasting lime and laughter, gathering up every little movement and sound she made and answering them all, angling her face to kiss her more deeply.

He sent more treasures into the *Celeste* pages in his brain: the heat of her tongue, the little dimple at the corner of her mouth, the dig of her fingernails into the back of his neck, and the low moan she poured into his mouth when his free hand landed on her hip, the curve of her bone prominent under her cotton dress.

Christ, she felt good. Better than he'd imagined. And he'd done plenty of imagining.

"Um." Brad's voice cut in loudly through the speakers. "Excuse me, you two?"

John froze against her, breathing hard, their lips still touching. He released his grip on Celeste's jaw and stepped back, taking in her flushed, stunned face as her arms dropped quickly to her sides. Her chest rose and fell in sync with his, and she opened her mouth, but Brad pushed them off the short stage, shooing them back to their table.

He took his seat casually, like he hadn't just shared one of the most stunning kisses of his life with Celeste in a room full of people. Jared looked inscrutably at John, his eyebrows drawn together.

Chris, on the other hand, greeted them with enthusiastic applause. "Amazing performance all around, you two! Celeste, you promised theater, and you delivered."

Looking relieved, Celeste blushed and gave a little bow.

"You really know your Emily Dickinson, huh?" Jared said,

pushing his cheek out with his tongue, clearly holding back a smile.

"Yeah." Celeste picked up her beer and brought it to her mouth, but returned it to the table without taking a drink. "If you'll excuse me, I need a little trip to the ladies' room." She didn't wait for a response before making a beeline for the dark hallway of the bar.

John waited a beat for her to be out of hearing distance, then dared a look at Jared and Chris. "I don't suppose we can skip this conversation."

Jared shook his head. "Definitely not."

"The kiss was nothing."

Chris gave a low whistle. "That kiss was not nothing."

"Not even close." Jared threaded his fingers together behind his head. "I pride myself on having good moves, but damn, John. That was a kiss."

"That was a goddamn kiss," Chris echoed.

John drained his beer, wishing it were bottomless. "It was just part of the whole fake-relationship thing. Acting." He looked to Chris. "You're the one who congratulated us on the theater!"

But Chris just shook his head. "I was trying to defuse some tension, my friend. It was thick."

Jared leaned forward on his elbows. "And you're no fucking actor, John. You can't even lie well. Remember when we broke Mom's special vase playing knights and we came up with that whole elaborate story about the gust of wind that came in through the window? When it was time to deliver, what happened?"

John sighed. "I told her everything."

"You told her everything. Because you, big brother, are honest to the core. Which means you certainly don't kiss someone like *that*"—he motioned to the front of the bar—"without meaning it."

John dropped his face into his hands. Of course he'd meant it. How could anyone kiss Celeste without meaning it? She was so eager, so open, so true to herself, it was impossible not to give that back to her and more.

But that didn't mean it was smart.

"Hey." Breena's voice interrupted his thoughts, and he wiped his face blank. "Marisol said I should come say congratulations. So."

John didn't hear any actual congratulations, but nodded anyway, hoping Breena would walk away. "Thanks." He forced a smile.

But she stayed put. "You guys sure did celebrate. Never knew you for a PDA guy."

"Are you working toward a point, Breena?" Jared piped in. He and Breena had playfully sparred during the years she and John had dated, but there was no humor in Jared's voice now. Even though he clearly meant well, the intervention irked John. It didn't matter that John was the oldest, or that he'd put his life on hold to help out at home for years. No one seemed to believe he could take care of himself.

"I'm just a little surprised, I guess," Breena bit back at Jared. "She just doesn't seem like John's type. I mean, she's so—"

"Energetic?" Chris jumped in, cutting a glance at Breena.

"Silly." Breena's shoulders and jaw were tight as she turned back to John. "She just seems really silly for someone like you, John. She's just a little too much, you know?"

Only then did John realize Celeste had returned to their table, stopped short just behind Breena with a stricken look on her face that left no doubt she'd overheard. In a flash, her smile was back as she gave an exaggerated clearing of her throat.

Brave.

Celeste's smile only grew as Breena swiveled to face her, but

John had observed Celeste closely enough—too closely, really—to know it was strained. "I guess I was *too* smart tonight, hmm? Better luck next time." She nodded to the table. "Boys, it's been fun, but I have papers to grade. John, I'll text you about our next, um, date." She swooped up her bag and was gone before he could say a word.

"Whoops," Breena said with a careless shrug.

John watched the door close behind Celeste, already standing to follow her. But first he faced Breena.

"For the record, B, Celeste *is* silly," he said simply. "She's brilliant, too. And compassionate, and an amazing learner. And she sees magic in little things all around her, all the time. However you've decided to label and categorize her in your head, I promise you she's much more than that."

Breena stumbled back a step, her hard expression softening. "John, look, I didn't mean—"

"You did, Breena. You don't do anything by accident. Whatever meaning you're placing on this contest, however badly you want to beat me, leave her out of it."

John didn't give Breena a chance to respond. Tossing some bills on the table, he strode to the door to catch Celeste. He didn't know what he was going to say, but he knew this wasn't how her night should end.

He spotted her down the block, almost to her car. Behind her, bathed in the washed-out light of the one streetlight on the block, the wall was full of color. It was one of John's favorite murals, a desert scene done in the colors of sunrise—pinks and lavenders and sherbet orange—but broken apart into fractals, as if shone through a prism.

She turned when he called her name. With her head slightly tilted to one side, turquoise earrings dangling over a yellow dress,

Celeste blended into the painting, setting the whole thing in motion. Wisps of her light brown hair, pulled free by his fingers moments before, played along her neck.

"Are you okay?" he asked once he reached her. "I'm sorry about Breena, that was—"

"Nothing." She waved a hand in the air. "Honestly, nothing I haven't heard before. Water off the back and all that."

"Celeste—"

"Seriously." She fiddled with the strap of her bag on her shoulder. "Don't even worry about it. Just relish our victory, right?"

A siren screamed in the distance as a group of college students poured out of a diner across the street. Celeste's eyes roamed to her car at the curb, then back to John. "And hey, I'm sorry if I, um . . ." She coughed and shifted on her feet. "In there, I blew past the ground rules. When we, um . . ." She closed her eyes tight like it hurt to say the word. "Kissed."

This was John's cue to say everything was fine, that the kiss didn't mean anything. He could play the whole thing off as the theater Chris had proclaimed it to be.

The problem was, Jared was right. John was honest to a fault, and there wasn't a chance he could pretend that kissing Celeste had been an act.

But as he opened his mouth to try to tell her so, Celeste started to laugh.

CHAPTER 15

BIRD BINGE, DAY 19 OF 42
BIRD COUNT: 67

Celeste was well aware that laughter was a totally inappropriate response to the perfectly nice man staring at her on the sidewalk. Especially after she'd kissed him and basically made a run for it.

Poor John. All he wanted to do was watch birds, and Celeste had burst into his life with her special brand of chaos, dragging him bowling and telling him about her divorce on her porch swing and kissing him in a bar full of people.

Her wrongness for someone as cool and calm as him was so obvious even his ex had felt the need to comment on it.

But that kiss? Nothing had felt wrong about that.

She wiped a hand across her face. "I'm sorry. I laugh when I'm uncomfortable."

John gripped the back of his neck. The move pulled his shirt tight across his chest as it hugged the bulge of his bicep peeking past the hem of his sleeve. "I'm sorry if I took it too far in there, or if I—"

"No!" she shouted, then swore under her breath, searching for some inner calm. But that calm had been incinerated sometime between the thrill of victory and the scrape of John's fingers along the base of her skull as they kissed. Then he'd had to follow her outside to make sure she was okay. He was so kind it was almost rude.

"No, you didn't do anything wrong. I initiated it. You were, um, great." She winced again. "I mean, not great, but not bad, just . . ." Her arms flailed alongside her words. "I'm not doing this right."

It was *just a kiss*. That's what she'd told herself in the bathroom as she stared in the mirror, willing her heart to slow. People kissed each other all the time and went on with their lives. And they'd been in fake-couple mode anyway, flirting innocently all night. It didn't mean anything.

But when she opened her mouth to brush the whole incident aside, she couldn't do it. Not with John, who talked about birds like they were his friends, who'd trusted her know-how all night, who'd sat on her porch swing and called her brave.

She sighed. "Here's the truth. I was excited and I guess really in character and I just did it. Kissed you. But once I . . . once we . . ." Heat flooded her face. She'd shown her daughter how condoms worked when Morgan turned twelve and somehow this was more embarrassing. "Once it, uh, got going, it was really nice."

Nice was a stroll in the park. Kissing John had been a revelation.

Talk about *thorough*. After so many hours of bird-watching with him, Celeste was well aware of the quiet attention John paid to the world around him, always showing care and taking a keen interest in his surroundings. And dammit, he kissed like that, too. Like she was the only thing in the world. Like he could hold her jaw in his hand and study her for hours with just the movement of his lips.

"It was . . . nice for me, too." John's voice was low and soft.

He stepped closer even as his face seemed wary, brows pulled together. "The thing is, I don't usually kiss people casually, but I also know that when we made our arrangement, neither of us was looking for a relationship, so I think we should just be clear that that was—"

"An anomaly," she blurted. "Just a sudden, spontaneous, really good kiss. But it shouldn't happen again." Celeste stepped back, her ass bumping into the wall behind her. "We're adults, right? So it's not a big deal to admit there's a certain . . . chemistry between us." The words were thick and sticky in her throat.

As she struggled to swallow, John's eyes narrowed on her neck before darting back to her face. "Right. That's the mature way to handle it." He rubbed a hand across his jaw. "But if what happened inside makes this uncomfortable for you, we could stop the contest anytime. It's not a big deal."

"No way!" She pushed off the wall, reaching out for his upper arm before she thought better of it, curling her hand just below his shoulder. "Now that we've aired this out, it will be fine. We've probably already worked it out of our systems. Right?"

"Right." John's voice was all gravel, rough and dusty.

"So I should probably go."

"Okay." His nod was almost imperceptible, especially when all her focus was on his mouth, where his tongue slid along his bottom lip.

This was when she should walk away.

But instead of letting go of his arm, her thumb was tracing rainbows across the firm cords of his deltoid. And instead of stepping away from her, John closed his hand over her elbow, his fingers spreading out like a star and closing again, over and over.

Her breathing shrank with each caress of his fingers, until her lungs were aching like the rest of her. John's eyes swept over her face, then down, until his lashes lowered completely. With his eyes closed, his fingers kept their rhythm on Celeste's elbow, stoking her to a place so high she knew she'd have to jump to reach the other side.

She sucked in a breath. "Or."

John's hand froze on her elbow as his eyes opened, pupils barely visible. "Or?"

She tugged on his arm hard, pulling him toward her as questioning eyes swept her face. "Or we make sure it's all worked out, and kiss one more time." She knew that if she didn't kiss him again—alone, on the street, without an audience, on their own terms—she'd never close this short, complicated chapter between them. "Maybe it won't even be good, and we can just relax."

The smile that lifted his lips was new. She'd seen his quiet, thoughtful smiles as his mind worked, and his quirking grin as he took in her excitement about a bird. But this one—just the slightest twitch on one side—was knowing, wicked. "It'll be good, Celeste."

Hell, yes, it would be.

"So we confirm the theory and move on," she said, her breathing shallow. "I don't want to risk the contest with this stuff, especially when your future is riding on it and when we know this won't go anywhere."

After a quiet moment of deliberation, John spoke. "All right, if you think it'll help." His free hand hung suspended between them for the length of his exhale. "One more, then we put this behind us."

A streetcar clanged past them as a stream of giggling women walked by. Everything was fuzzy around the edges, her only point of focus John's thumb ghosting a spiral on her cheek.

"I'm going to kiss you now." John moved in, so close she felt his hot breath on her cheek. "You're sure this is okay?"

"Yeah," she gasped. "Super okay."

He smiled as his hand tightened on her jaw. He slid his lips across hers once, then twice, before teasing hers open with his tongue. They shared a moan, taking it and feeding it back to each other as she tilted her face to reach more of him, threading a hand in his hair.

His hand on her elbow glided up her arm, slipping under the strap of her bag and sending it tumbling to the ground. When his fingers slid over her shoulder and across her collarbone, her nipples pulled tight, aching for touch, but he just dragged his fingers across her throat, then back to her shoulder, leaving a trail of heat. As he sucked her lower lip into his mouth slowly, raking it with his teeth, his hand moved down the side of her body, brushing across her ribs, down her waist, over her hip. He never touched the places where she craved him the most, but his inventory felt filthy nonetheless. All the while, his mouth worked on hers, giving and taking.

And since this one kiss would have to be enough, she'd take all she could get. One hand in John's hair, fingers kneading his scalp, and the other in his beard, then across the width of his neck, then spread on his chest, hard and heaving. She snaked her hand around his waist and pulled, wanting the whole weight of him pinning her, but his hand shot to the wall next to her head, locking him in place as he resisted her tug.

She whined into his mouth, earning a vibrating chuckle against her lips. John scraped his beard against her jaw as his mouth trailed across her cheek. His breath was hot and labored, snaking into her ear and squirming through her veins as his fingers tightened on her hip. "I think I should keep my distance right now."

And holy fuck, that was the last thing she needed to hear. She clenched her hands, wanting to trace the evidence of his desire and feel its weightiness in her palm. Instead, she bit down on her lip until it stung.

His mouth returned to hers. Maybe that made this two kisses, but she didn't care. Whatever it took to capture this need and burn it out, then stow away the ashes. The fingers on her hip dug in hard as his lips made demands of hers—open, wider, more.

This was supposed to close a chapter, but kissing John was raising more questions. Like how his beard would feel between her breasts, and what type of thorough attention he'd pay her with his fingers, and what it would take to unravel him all the way, to hold the power to make John Maguire lose control.

Jesus, if they were going to stop at all, they had to stop now.

Her fingers loosened, then lifted from his body even as they ached to map the entire thing. His kiss lightened but didn't end. Instead he sipped gently at her lips, drawing his hand back up to her chin, swiping a thumb across her cheek. They shared heavy breaths, lips barely touching, before he pulled back.

His gaze held hers, hand still on her face, even as his feet stepped away from her. Finally, he blinked and dropped his hand, bringing it straight up to scrub at his beard. With a sigh, he swiveled and leaned against the wall next to her, slumping against the scattered colors of the mural.

A couple strolled past them on the sidewalk, hands tangled and arms swinging. Celeste flattened her palms against the wall, still warm from the evening sun.

She sought its solidity as the world moved around them, then finally dared to look at John. His eyes were closed, his head tipped back against the bright mural.

It would be so easy to rearrange herself for this man, for a chance to see how else he could make her body sing.

But it was always easy when it started. It was all that came after that posed a danger.

Celeste stepped away from the wall, dragging her attention from John as he opened his eyes. "So, I'll see you Saturday?" She cleared her throat. "Did you, uh, get the email about the photo hunt?"

His answer was more of a grunt than a word. After another moment he tried again. "Um, yeah. The Instagram thing?"

He said "Instagram" like it was a bad word. The organizers had added a social media element to the contest, a list of items to be captured in pictures and posted online. Each item posted on Instagram earned the team that posted it an extra point. Social media obviously wasn't John's forte, but she had a crash course planned that would knock his socks off.

But not his actual socks. All his clothes would stay on, a fact she would both accept and embrace as soon as she got home and tucked away the memory of their time against the wall.

She scooped her bag off the ground. "I was thinking we could just do the photo hunt on Saturday when we were planning to be out anyway."

"Sure." He nodded, still avoiding eye contact.

Celeste pulled her keys out and tapped them against her thigh. "Well, thank you." She blanched. "Not for . . ." She glanced at the wall. "I mean for, just, everything. All your contributions to, uh, the team."

And a kiss that rocked my world and will never happen again.

Their eyes held until he cleared his throat. "You're the one who won it for us, so I should be thanking you, right?"

A laugh squeezed out of her tight throat. "Wonderful point."

And that was the takeaway from the night—a trivia victory, more points for the contest. That was what she'd think about on her drive home, replaying it over and over.

Somehow her fumbling fingers found the button to unlock her car. "See you Saturday, okay?"

She ducked into the car and threw her bag into the backseat, then looked up to find John leaning in, one hand on her car door and the other on the roof. He was backlit by a streetlight, so she couldn't see his face, just the slow expansion of his chest. They spent three of his breaths like this, slow like molasses, until she thought he might come closer and help them both do something very, very stupid.

But then he stepped back. "Drive safe." The door closed, and John walked away, the outline of his body cutting across the colorful blur of the mural.

John Maguire was always in control. And she was counting on it.

CHAPTER 16

BIRD BINGE, DAY 21 OF 42
BIRD COUNT: 67

"You know, when I was a kid, I actually gave the chaperones something to do at these things." Maria crossed her arms over her chest and nodded at the near-empty floor of the middle school gym. Most of the students at the Spring Fling dance were huddled in groups along the walls, scrolling on their phones. "I lost track of how many times Mrs. Sanders had to remind Danny Lopez and me about the six-inch rule while we were dancing."

Flaccid streamers hung from beige walls as a smattering of limp balloons bounced around on the ground—it wasn't the most inspiring setting, but when Maria, just back from parental leave and overseeing the dance in her role as faculty advisor for the student council, had called Celeste in a pinch, she'd agreed to help chaperone.

"All the better," Maria continued, stifling a yawn. She'd made it over the hump of her maternity leave, but Xavi wasn't coming close to sleeping through the night, and even with the eager participation of her partner, Maria was rightfully exhausted. "This gives me more time to grill you about Mr. Birding. Layla will seriously not shut up about him after seeing him dirty-talking to you at the bowling alley."

"I told you, there was no dirty talk. It was strictly about birds." John's very thorough boyfriend demonstration at the bowling alley had served its purpose. Now instead of telling Celeste about her cousin, Andrea just asked about John as she wiggled her eyebrows suggestively.

And her coworkers hadn't seen the kiss at the bar. Or what had come after it.

"Oh my god." Maria's eyes bored into her. "You just went somewhere in your head and you better tell me where it was. Because I do *not* believe it was about birds."

She'd kept her chatter about John to a minimum with Maria, preferring to keep the focus on her friend as she navigated motherhood and returned to work. And if that meant delaying Maria's know-it-all response to some of the developments between Celeste and her birding partner, so much the better.

But when Maria's brows rose—the right just a smidge higher than the left—as her lips fell into a straight line, Celeste knew she could only put her off for so long. Not just anyone could wrangle middle school math students, let alone make them genuinely interested. Maria was magic, and this look was just the tip of the iceberg. Even Celeste shook in her Converse when it was deployed.

"Celeste. Spill."

She stepped closer to Maria, lowering her voice. "It's nothing." If she said it enough, maybe she'd believe it. "We just . . ." She continued after a long exhale. "We had that bird trivia thing the other night, and we won because of an Emily Dickinson question, which was so amazing because it's this poem that—"

"Hon, I don't care about Emily Dickinson. Tell me what you need to tell me."

Celeste sighed and kicked an errant balloon. "We won, and I was excited, so . . . I kissed him."

She closed her eyes tight, waiting for Maria's onslaught, but her friend only hummed. "On the mouth?"

"On the stage."

"Celeste."

It had been worth a try. "Okay, yes, on the mouth."

"With tongue?" Maria's voice pitched up, drawing the attention of a passing group of seventh graders, most of whom were Celeste's students. Maria cleared her throat conspicuously. "Young. With young . . . people there. Ms. Johanssen, at the party you had, were there young people there?"

Most of the students were talking in a tight circle, but Julio from pre-algebra watched Celeste and Maria none too subtly.

"Yes," she mumbled, tipping her head toward Maria. "There were young people."

Maria tapped her foot as she did another scan of the gym. "Very interesting. And what happened after?"

Here we go. Now that Maria had the scent, she'd drag it out of Celeste regardless, so she spilled. Or spilled as much as she could with Julio lingering nearby. "After that party, we tried out one more party. We thought maybe after, we'd be okay not . . . um . . . partying anymore."

Maria coughed, then stalked to the group gathered nearby. "Students, dear ones." She motioned to the empty dance floor. "This is a dance! Go dance. I know most of you are here because Coach Leonetti promised you extra PE credit, and I will tell him to forget about it if I don't see you shaking it out there for at least three songs."

The students gave a few muttered protests, but stuffed their phones back in their pockets and shuffled away.

"Thank God." Maria returned to Celeste's side, then leveled her with another killer look. "Are you telling me that you kissed

John, *with tongue*, and then kissed him again to—" She shook her head. "To get it out of your system?" Celeste guessed Maria wished she were back home with spit-up on her shoulder at this point. At least Celeste made the postpartum phase seem a little easier. "That is not a thing, Celeste. That's not how kissing works. At least not good kissing."

Celeste held her palms up. "In my defense, I don't have a lot of experience with people I'm not married to, so, you know, I don't personally know that kissing someone out of your system doesn't work."

Maria sighed and rolled her eyes. "Okay, then. If this was an experiment, what are the results? Is it out of your system?"

"Yes, it is," she said quickly. So quickly that Maria scoffed.

Maria wanted to know the results of the experiment? It had failed. Instead of being out of her system, John was overwhelming it. Memories of his fingers on her collarbone had kept her up half the night.

But Celeste was more than a bundle of sexual urges. She was a woman living on her own, protecting her sunshine from being lost in shadow. A system-destroying kiss didn't change that. Couldn't change it.

"Just hear me out." Maria's voice had gentled, and she reached for Celeste's hand and gave it a squeeze. "John is nice. He is smart. He is good-looking. Apparently he has some weird talent with birdcalls that you find impressive. And he is such a good kisser that when you even think about it, your face goes to the faraway place. Is it possible you should consider giving this a chance?"

"That's the point, Maria. He is all of those things, and I'm not looking for that. He's all the things I would get all wound up in until I was lost. I'm just coming up for air after ten years of drowning, and I can't go back under. That's why I'm not doing relationships."

"Ever? How long are you going to turn off that part of your life, Celeste?"

Were Maria and Morgan communicating secretly behind her back? Why was a fear of Celeste's being "alone forever" suddenly everyone's concern?

"I don't know. As long as it takes. I have a lot of time to make up for."

And something to prove, if only to herself. She'd admitted to John on her porch that she was angry more at herself than at anyone else, ashamed of the way she'd let herself get twisted up in her marriage, had let parts of herself shrink. If she'd seen that happen to Maria or Morgan, she'd have intervened. She owed herself the same care, didn't she?

"Honestly," Maria answered, "I get that. Relationships aren't always what they're cracked up to be. And you know what you need. But be honest." She lowered her voice to a whisper. "You've got to miss sex. Especially now that you went to a really good *party* with John."

She'd missed sex a lot less before meeting John. Now the thought of it—the very specific, very thorough thought of it with *him*—was too close to the surface of her brain and body for her liking. But that was her problem to deal with, and they'd talked about her long enough. "It's fine. I am fine, I swear. The real question is, do *you* miss sex?"

Unless anything had changed since her last set of texts on the subject, Maria and David hadn't done the deed since Xavi was born.

Maria's eyes narrowed, but she acquiesced. "I'm only letting you change the subject because I need help. And the answer is yes, but no, but— Oh hell, Celeste. I was recently cleared by the doc, but I can't help but think my vagina is ruined."

"It's not ruined; those things bounce back like nobody's business. But if you're not into it, give yourself time."

"That's the problem. I don't have time. My mom gets here from El Paso next month and she's staying for six weeks." From the tone of her voice, Maria could have said "a decade." "I'm grateful for her help, but I . . . I can't have sex with her in the house. So it's now or never."

"Hon, you're thirty-five. You have a baby. Your mom knows that you—"

"I know she knows. But her knowing and her being in the house are different. You don't know what it was like, Cel, growing up with those fucking crucifixes all over the wall." Maria drew a hand through the air, evoking the scene. "Jesus's eyes tracked me across that whole damn house. He hung over my *bed*. Telling my mom I was moving in with David and having a baby without being married was one thing, but I cannot orgasm with that woman in the house. I know. I've tried."

"Understood. So let's get this done." It was time to plan. "What's stopping you now? Are you afraid it's going to hurt?"

"It's not the fear of pain as much as . . ." Maria sighed, a rare look of vulnerability passing across her face. "I'm worried I'm not the same. That I've been rearranged, body and soul, and I'm not the same."

There was a tremor in her voice, so Celeste hooked her hand through Maria's elbow to tug her into a corner of the gym, nodding to another teacher to indicate that they needed a few minutes. Once they were tucked away, she ran both hands down Maria's arms. "Talk to me."

Maria looked past Celeste's shoulder as she spoke quietly.

"I'm middle-aged, Cel. I had a whole life before this, and now half of the conversations with my partner are about what color our kid's poop is." When she finally looked at Celeste, her deep brown eyes were wet. "David and I had a really good sex life before this. Like, really good." Celeste had heard plenty of the stories. "What if that's gone now?" Maria asked. "What if it's one more thing that's rearranged?"

Celeste knew all about rearranging. She'd rearranged herself in her marriage, then rearranged her family's lives with the divorce. Even now, every morning was a meditation in putting her pieces in order, watching the messages on her mirror for a sign. Sometimes she envied her friend, having had a whole life before starting the deep dive into parenthood. Maybe if Celeste had waited longer to become a mother, she wouldn't have lost herself so thoroughly in all the years that had come after.

Celeste couldn't go back—and she wouldn't, really, because all of that had given her Morgan—but she could help her friend. She could help her meet each stage with bravery and vulnerability, always holding on to who she was.

"Sweetheart." She pulled one of Maria's curls, watching it bounce back up toward her chin. "Your life has changed. You have changed. And all any of us can do is keep going forward. But you and David? You two are . . ." She kissed the tips of her fingers. "That's going to change with a baby, but it doesn't have to change for the worse. You guys can do this. You still feel the hots for him?"

Maria nodded and smiled. "Girl, he came home from a run yesterday and, damn. He looks so good sweaty."

"And he still has the hots for you?"

Maria leaned her head conspiratorially. "Yesterday he said my little pajama shorts turned him on and he couldn't wait to fuck me senseless. Whenever I'm ready, of course."

Yep, her best friend had picked a winner. At least one of them would be having great sex soon. "Okay, then here's the plan. Let this next phase of your relationship start. Go home tonight, have a glass of wine, light a candle, and let your man fuck you senseless. It might not be the best sex of your life, but it will be the first sex of this phase of your life, and that's a big deal."

Maria laughed into her hand, then arched an eyebrow at Celeste. "I don't suppose you'll take your own advice? About the—"

"No, and don't even try. John and I are not going there." Although Celeste wasn't opposed to using her vibrator a couple of more times as she let her mind wander there. Strictly to get it out of her system.

"Fine," Maria huffed. "But you're still bringing him to my party, right?"

The infamous costume party for David's birthday was just a few days away, and Maria was still moving toward it at full speed. "You're sure you're up for that? With the baby and your mom coming soon?"

"I'm not sure I'm up for it," Maria answered. "But I'm sure I want to do it. It's like I have to prove to myself I can still do some of the old stuff." She bumped Celeste's hip. "And you didn't answer about John."

Celeste rolled her eyes. "Yes, he'll be there."

"Did you tell him I requested spandex?"

That was the last thing she needed. Maybe she'd suggest he dress as a zombie, thoroughly covered in rags. "We haven't planned our costumes yet, but there will be no spandex."

They should plan their costumes. They should move on from that kiss, when his touch had been innocent but so damn precise she could still feel his fingers on her rib cage.

They were birding the following day, and it would be fine. Nothing like birds to get them back to business.

"Just hear me out about the spandex." Maria's playful voice was a blessed interruption to her thoughts.

She caught her friend with an arm around her shoulder and pulled her into her side. "You're such a pain, and I missed you so much."

Maria laid her head on Celeste's shoulder, wrapping an arm around her waist. "The feeling is mutual."

CHAPTER 17

BIRD BINGE, DAY 22 OF 42
BIRD COUNT: 67

It was going to be a long morning.

Especially if John kept putting on those reading glasses to peer at his phone. They transformed him from an attractive outdoorsman to the buttoned-up lumberjack librarian Celeste wanted to pull apart. But she wouldn't be pulling apart a single thing, because she was totally cool.

Though she did release a long-held breath when he whipped the glasses off and stowed them safely in his front pocket.

He pressed the heels of his hands into his eyes. "So, what's the difference between a story and a post? And why do they both exist?"

If anything could pull her mind out of the gutter, it was this challenge. Celeste possessed over a decade of educational experience and was a two-time nominee for southern Arizona teacher of the year, but this was her greatest test yet.

She was trying to teach John to use Instagram.

"Posts are bigger statements, things you really want to last. A story is for stuff you want to share but doesn't necessarily have the gravity of a post. It will only stay up for a day."

John's brows pulled together tight. This was probably how

she looked when Morgan tried to explain TikTok algorithms. "We'll get there," she assured him. "By the end of today, you'll be ready to take the social media world by storm. Starting with the scavenger hunt." Each item on the list, when posted with the right hashtags, would earn them one point when the contest was done. They had the next three weeks to complete it, but they'd decided to get some done that long morning.

She'd walked him through creating a profile yesterday afternoon, happy to have a reason to make innocent contact in their post-kiss reality. They'd exchanged perfectly harmless, totally flirt-free texts about social media for an hour. She'd even limited herself to using only the thumbs-up emoji to make sure nothing could be misinterpreted. Perfect groundwork laid for a very normal birding expedition at this sprawling urban park.

Tugging the phone from his hand, Celeste perused the blank profile page for *John M*.

"I thought you were going to make this a business account? Use the name of your guiding company?"

"I don't have a name for that yet," he grumbled. "And it's not the right time to launch it now anyway, with the contest underway."

"What about . . . Walks for Warblers?" Celeste said. "Or Hikes with Hummingbirds?" She loved alliteration. She had done a whole unit on it for her students in the fall. Her free fingers tapped her knee as she waved John's phone in the air, imagining the possibilities. "Trails for Titmice? Is the plural of 'titmouse' actually 'titmice'? Or 'titmouses'? But maybe you don't want 'tit' in the name of your business."

"Celeste."

"Or we forget the alliteration and make the branding all about you. John Maguire, master craftsman, birder extraordinaire."

"I'm not sure—"

"Yes, I can see it!" She could take some photos of him for his profile, maybe even some with those reading glasses. Clients would probably line up just to take a walk with him.

John spoke so honestly and beautifully about birds, trees, bugs, everything. If he could convey even a fraction of that in a post, he'd have potential clients eating out of his hand.

Maybe even some nice, bird-interested woman who wasn't carrying a marriage's worth of baggage. John deserved that when he was ready—a satisfying relationship with someone who could see the full complexity behind the quiet package, and tap into the deepest, sweetest parts of him.

Someone who would do more for him than try to kiss him out of her system.

But she was getting ahead of herself. "Getting these photos up there for the contest will be your first step. Then we can go over the best birding hashtags and the latest trends and—"

"Celeste. Stop, please." A pained groan rumbled from his throat. "This isn't how I want to do this. I just want to go birding."

She patted his knee, just once. "But this *is* about birding, John. This is how people do it now. Have you even looked at the Bird Binge hashtag?" Celeste checked it nightly, tracking how other teams were doing, though no one gave away much about their numbers. These birders were cagey.

Celeste typed *#birdbinge* into John's Instagram search bar. The grid of results showed birders of all ilks smiling in selfies for the camera, and plenty of photos of birds on their own.

"Look? See!" She waved the phone between them. "People can post pictures of the birds they see, and—" Her voice caught in her throat as one picture caught her eye. It was Breena, smiling big at the camera, her cheek pressed against a very familiar cinnamon beard.

Celeste tapped the photo and read the caption.

#ThrowbackThursday to the first year I won the Bird Binge. I came in hot and I'm only getting hotter. Watch out, newbies, and stay in your lane! #BirdBinge

Only a slice of John's face had made it into Breena's post, but Celeste studied it nonetheless, marking the small difference between John then and the one beside her. The small lines around his hazel eyes were more pronounced now, and there was a little more sugar threaded through his beard.

"What the hell?" he muttered, pulling the phone from her hand. "That's me!"

"Uh, yeah, the beard kinda gives it away." Celeste chuckled. "Nice touch leaving you in just enough to be obvious. I believe she is goading you, John. Throwing down the gauntlet about the contest."

He stared at the picture for another moment as one hand scrubbed at his beard. "No, she knows how I am with social media stuff. She knows I'd never see this without someone showing it to me." He tapped the phone, flinching when his movement made the picture take up the whole screen, then quickly made the whole thing go black. "It's more likely she's goading *you*."

"Oh." *Watch out, newbies, and stay in your lane*. "Of course." Somewhere between her first hike with John and her arrival at the park that morning, she'd stopped thinking of herself as a newbie. She studied, she watched, she *knew* stuff. Hell, she'd made the Tweethearts champions.

But most of all, John didn't treat her like a newbie or like someone holding him back. He treated her like an equal.

“Stay in my lane,” she muttered, pushing her sneaker into the dry grass. “Like I even see the lane markings—please. I go where I want.”

She shouldn’t have been thrilled by the laugh that shook John beside her, or the way the low vibration of it hit her right in the gut. Not when this morning in the park was all about moving past their kiss. But her body was not getting the message.

She grabbed his upper arm and pulled them both up, congratulating herself for letting go of him quickly. “Okay. You don’t want to be a social media influencer, I get it. That’s a battle for another day. But today you’ve got to at least take these pictures and post them. We cannot let Breena go unanswered.”

John’s eyes narrowed at her, but a smile still pushed up his cheeks. “You’re a little scary when you get competitive, you know that?”

“You don’t know the half of it.” She pulled her own phone out to consult the scavenger hunt list. “Morgan won’t even do puzzles with me anymore. Now, where do we start?”

Some of the items had been easy: native plants John and Celeste identified and photographed quickly, and a few common birds captured in flight. Other things on the list required a little more creativity, but even though John swore he only saw an oblong blob where Celeste saw a flamingo, he’d agreed to take the photo for “a cloud that looks like a bird.”

And through all of it, Celeste had kept an entirely respectable distance from John. And if she’d heard him clear his throat when she’d bent over to admire a wildflower on the ground, it was only because the air that day was particularly dry.

Because John was cool, too. So there was no way he'd be checking out her ass.

"Okay," Celeste said, assessing what they had left. "We probably have time to get one more today." Given Breena's post, she knew just which one it should be. "Team selfie with a bird?"

John's eyes narrowed as a smile drifted over his lips. "Is this you goading back?"

"Me?" She flattened a palm against her chest. "I would never. I just want to support the ornithological society by posting as many pictures as we can."

"Right. So let's find a bird and get our selfie. How hard can that be?"

Very hard, it turned out. An Abert's towhee scraped in the dirt for seeds beneath a saltbush, but when Celeste crooked her finger at John and dipped into a low squat in front of the bird, it quickly departed. Same with a lesser goldfinch, which drank weightlessly from a pink penstemon flower until John's boot crunched a stick into the ground.

After a few more thwarted attempts, Celeste was sneaking up on a bush full of chattering sparrows when John's hand brushed her shoulder, lifting off so fast his touch was only a breeze. When she turned, he was pointing to a nearby palo verde, where a white-winged dove sat peacefully on a sloppy nest of twigs.

Celeste kept her voice quiet. "Okay, I think this is our chance." She motioned for his phone, confident she had more experience taking selfies than he did. She fiddled with the camera app before stretching her arm out in front of them. "I put it on photo burst so it'll take a whole bunch of pictures in a row, to make sure we get a good one."

She scooted closer to him, then closer still, until their shoulders pushed together and they were mirrored on his phone screen. He must have been working early in his shop, because his smell was all sawdust and fresh pine.

If she could caption that smell, it would say *Eat Your Heart Out, Breena*.

Thinking purely of needling Breena, she nestled even closer to John, keeping the dove in the frame just over his shoulder.

She took in a slow, steady breath. "Ready?"

But just after she pressed the button, a woodpecker called from the air above them, and Celeste couldn't help tipping her head back to watch it pass. She loved the way they streaked across the sky, dipping down between the beats of their wings.

When it disappeared from view, she looked back at the phone. They were smiling together on the screen, cheeks almost touching. The striations of John's eyes matched the greens and browns of the tree behind them.

The dove cooed and shifted on her nest, and he turned to look. When his head shifted, Celeste's did as well, but she didn't look as far back as the bird. Instead, her eyes snagged on the cut of John's jaw, his beard shining in the sunlight, and the tan skin of his neck just below. Her tongue swiped along her bottom lip, wondering how he would taste, right there.

She stepped away, sending John tumbling into the empty space she'd left. He righted himself, clearing his throat. "Did we, uh, get one?"

She tugged at her ponytail. *Cool, cool, just be cool*. Finally, she nodded. "The phone took a bunch of pictures, so we must have, right?"

John stood behind her, far enough that she could hear his breathing but not feel it as he looked over her shoulder. She scrolled through the burst of photos. Several were of them getting into position, then a few of them looking at the camera without smiles. Celeste swiped through pictures quickly, but her hand froze when one image took over the screen.

In the picture, Celeste was looking up into the sky, her neck stretched. And John was looking right at her, his gaze clearly focused on her mouth. His lids were low, lips pulled in tight between his teeth.

Behind her, his breathing stopped.

Celeste's thumb hovered over the photo, her heart straining against her sternum. But she managed to keep her hand steady, and when she finally swiped again, she took them through a group of photos of the two of them smiling with the nesting dove in the background. She lingered on each image, slowing her breathing.

But the pictures changed again as she scrolled forward, each frame another still in a slow-motion movie. First, their smiles at the camera. Then a change behind them, the bird shifting its body. Then John turning to look, bit by bit.

In the last photo of the burst, Celeste's eyes were on John, her expression wearing every thought she'd had about him since their encounter on the wall. Every gasped memory, every brush of her hand against her own skin as she thought of him, every filthy item on the list of things she'd do to him given one more chance. Everything she'd tied up and locked away to come to the park this morning, utterly cool.

Light-headed, she teetered back, but was caught by the hot spread of John's palm across her back. He steadied her on her feet as she fumbled with his phone, almost dropping it in her attempts to turn off the screen, then shoved it into his hands before taking a few steps back. "We got some great ones in the middle there. You can figure out the posting later. I bet Chris would be awesome at that stuff, right? You probably don't need my help."

John blinked, then nodded and slipped his phone into his pocket. "Yeah, he would probably love that."

"Okay." She nodded, then nodded again.

"Okay."

They opened their mouths at the same time.

"So I—"

"I should probably—"

"I've got papers to grade."

John nodded. "Stuff to do in my workshop."

She nodded back. "You gotta work that wood."

Celeste simply let her jaw hang open. And the morning had started out with such promise. She was ready to race-walk to her car when she remembered Maria's party. Maria's stupid, wonderful, obligatory party to which she'd promised to bring John as her fake date.

"Um. Maria's party is this Sunday," she blurted. "And you said you'd go, but I know that was before—" *Before you declined to grind your erection on me the other night?* That would not be the cool thing to say. "I could just tell people you're busy or something, that you couldn't come after all."

"Is that what you'd prefer? To go alone?"

"No." She answered honestly. But it wasn't because she craved his company, because that would be very uncool of her. "Andrea will pounce at the first opportunity of seeing me alone, and Maria will be busy and it's good to have an ally at these things. If you're okay still coming, that would be really great."

He kicked the ground. "Then yeah, I'm happy to still come along."

"Cool." And just like that, she realized what the problem had been all morning, beyond John's reading glasses.

They'd pretended their kissing hadn't happened, instead

of addressing it head-on like cool, mature adults. They were dancing around something they could just lay out in the open.

"And about last time . . ." She worked to dislodge the frog wedged in her throat. "I think it really worked like a charm. I don't know about you, but I'm basically over the whole thing." Not her most convincing performance, but this was a fake-it-till-you-make-it moment.

John just nodded. When he spoke, his voice was flat. "Same. I'm just happy to concentrate on the contest."

"Cool." Celeste took a backward step toward the parking lot, catching her foot on a rock and swinging her arms for balance. "I'll text you the details of the party, and we'll figure out our costumes."

She'd meant to plan their costumes long ago, but somewhere between jumping into a mountain pond, learning how to identify a Lucy's warbler, listening to birds in her backyard with John, and . . . doing other things she really needed to stop thinking about, the whole thing had slipped her mind.

He was backing away too, hands in his pockets. "Yeah, absolutely. Sounds good."

"Cool!" she said way too loudly, curling the notebook in her hand until her fingers ached. "Okay. See ya. Bye."

John was already halfway across the park when she realized she'd failed to delete the evidence from his phone that she was, in fact, not cool at all.

CHAPTER 18

BIRD BINGE, DAY 23 OF 42
BIRD COUNT: 82

That was a goddamn kiss.

John slid the measuring tape down the pine board and drew a quick mark with his pencil before stowing it between his teeth. He pulled the orange handle of the chop saw down quickly, easily shearing off a four-inch piece of wood before sliding it toward the end of the table, where it piled up with others its size.

Or we make sure it's all worked out, and kiss one more time.

He repeated the routine. Measure, mark, cut.

Violins swelled through his shop. Classical today. Not what he usually listened to while using power tools, but he'd hoped it would help calm his mind. That, and the steady rhythm of his work.

Measure, mark, cut.

A rush of cochineal.

He'd been nine when he discovered the thick patch of prickly pear cactus a short walk from his house. Santa Rita was mostly grassland country, but the desert was always eager to claim hot, sandy slopes. That's where John had found the clusters of cochineal, tiny bugs that live and reproduce on the pads of prickly pear. Unlikely insects to end up in an Emily Dickinson poem, except for the precious store of bright red carminic acid in their bodies, making the perfect red dye, a color so precious that the Aztec emperor Montezuma himself had levied a tax on the stuff. Young John had settled for gathering the bugs up in a Tupperware container and taking them home, where he'd mashed them into a scarlet dye for his mother's fancy dinner napkins.

She'd shrieked when she found them drying outside, and he'd confessed immediately.

You're no fucking actor, John.

Measure, mark, cut.

He pushed another piece down the table, sending it careening into the dozens already grouped at the end.

How many pieces of wood would he have to cut to grind out the memory of Celeste's mouth on his? To winnow himself back down to the uncomplicated state he'd been in that early morning at the park, before her earrings swung into his life?

At the rate he was going, he'd have to build a thousand bird feeders.

The feeders were the first items John had sold after starting as a woodworker. He'd begun small, making simple, boxy bird feeders to hang outside his house for the sparrows and finches and the occasional winter songbird. But as his skills grew, the feeders became more intricate. He used them to try new methods, both functional and experimental. After he brought a few down to his parents, he received a call from a childhood friend who ran a small store in their hometown, wanting to sell his birdhouses. From there he'd branched out to shops in Tucson but had resisted Jared's attempts to set up an Etsy shop for him.

Bird feeders, bookshelves, an occasional long dining table—John had small but steady work, and was developing a reputation for his attention to detail.

But he was nowhere near having enough business to sustain himself long term. And even if he did, it wasn't what he wanted. Yes, the worn bench in his woodshop was preferable to the creaking office chair at the offices for the Southern Arizona Land Conservancy. And there were significantly fewer spreadsheets. But drawing more of his income from woodworking would require hours upon hours inside, hunched over his worktable. He'd rather be outside, staring up at trees and clear blue skies.

But the path from *here* to *there* was still blurred. It was that first step that was always hardest for John to bring into focus, his mind preferring to sit in consideration, turning over every possibility. Often the world acted on him to make him move—like his mother's diagnosis his first semester of grad school, or when Breena locked lips with the stupid genius. It wasn't that he never wanted to move on his own, but that his pace didn't seem to fit with the world around him. Somewhere there had to be a middle ground between the stagnancy Breena accused him of and the unending climb she created for herself.

Eventually he'd understood the truth about Breena and him—Breena saw him as a block of unfinished wood, like the ones scattered on the floor of his shop now. Full of potential but in need of crafting.

But no matter how much she had urged him to share more of himself out loud, or how many times she'd told him he could *do* so much more, he'd stayed mostly as he was. And in the end, no matter how many cuts she made, it wasn't enough. For her, or maybe anyone.

John Maguire, master craftsman, birder extraordinaire.

And now the voices around him included Celeste's. She buzzed with an energy that would make a hummingbird tired, thrown into his life and into the contest, brainstorming business names and putting him on Instagram.

Celeste wasn't Breena, not by a long shot. Where Breena chose cynicism, Celeste chose hope. But both possessed an air of movement that could leave John disoriented, being women inclined to push while he sat still. But John didn't feel disappointment from Celeste, at least not yet. Only faith, and excitement.

A faith that was as effortless to her as it was overwhelming to him. His hesitations about launching his own business—with no credentials, no professional experience, zero knowledge of social media—were simply obstacles to be run at headlong. She was competitive, yes, but he could tell she wanted to win this contest for him.

It's not a big deal to admit there's a certain . . . chemistry between us.

Measure, mark, cut.

Whatever was happening between them was way more than chemistry. It was biology—as ever-present as breath and skin. A basic need that made him forget everything but the shape of her ribs beneath his fingers, the hot exchange of sounds, her peppermint pulse as she leaned against a wall bursting with color.

I'm basically over the whole thing.

The hell she was. They'd agreed to move on after their "one more kiss," and they'd each played their parts valiantly. She'd obviously tried to make herself unappealing at the park, dressed in a loose T-shirt without her signature earrings, but his hands had already memorized her shape, and his body had surged at the sight of her bare earlobe, ripe for the plucking.

Anything she was trying to hide was given away in that picture. The one he'd studied so many times since that, if his skills had gone beyond woodworking, he could have sketched in every last detail—the swirling knot on the tree behind them, the fluff of the dove on the branch, and Celeste's open mouth, lush and perfect, just like it would be if she laid her lips against his neck.

He pulled a new ten-foot board from the floor and slapped it on the table.

Measure, mark, cut.

But even if Celeste wasn't actually over it, it was clear she wanted to be. She was unequivocal when she chatted about the coming months, about adjusting to life at home without Morgan, living fully alone for the first time in her life.

When Celeste had opened up about her marriage, he'd been surprised to see her shrink, and he'd seen it again in the bar. Something Breena had said had hit its mark, despite Celeste's insistence that it was water off her back. There were wounds there he guessed most people never spotted, and it wasn't for him to ask Celeste to expose them if she wasn't ready.

John's hand froze on the saw handle. He'd rarely found a problem he couldn't sort out in his woodshop. But damn, the memory of Celeste's moan on his lips had him scrambled.

He flipped off the saw's power switch and pushed open the door of the shop, welcoming the sun on his face and rolling his head on his shoulders as the birdsong around him filled his mind. He'd bought a small place on the edge of the city with just enough space around his house for a few native trees and shrubs. A worn wicker chair on the porch served as his personal coffee, reading, and birding spot, though now he felt too restless to sit. Instead, he listened, and tracked the birds—a group of house sparrows in the jojoba bush to his right, a Lucy's warbler flitting through the branches of a mesquite, and a couple of screeching cactus wrens arguing in front of a cholla.

The sun was rising high in the sky, heating the desert floor.

This afternoon they'd be making their final appearance for Celeste's middle school crowd, going as a pair to the costume party.

That was why he'd woken with the sun and taken his coffee straight to his woodshop. He just needed to clear his head, so he could show up for Celeste and be what she needed. It was time to focus on the goals at hand—for Celeste, a new hobby and a fresh start to her personal life without harassment from her well-meaning coworkers. And for John, a strong—no, the strongest—showing in the contest, the last push toward what could be.

Nineteen more days, and his life would be back to normal. No more peppermint, no more scrambled brain, no more fantasies about that ponytail wrapped around his fingers.

John turned and reentered his shop. He still had a couple of hours before the party.

Measure, mark, cut.

CHAPTER 19

BIRD BINGE, DAY 23 OF 42
BIRD COUNT: 82

"Just please ignore anything Maria says or does, okay?"

Celeste paused with her hand on the doorknob. She was in a white tunic fashioned from a sheet, her usual ponytail twisted into an elegant braid. Sprigs of gray-green leaves sprang from her plait—she'd arrived a few minutes late after stopping to pull some twigs from an olive tree in her neighborhood.

Unfortunately for John's resolve to banish non-birding thoughts of Celeste from his brain, she looked magnificent. The white of the fabric played off the subtle tan of her skin, and the hairstyle left her long neck completely exposed.

He tore his eyes off her skin and tugged at the pleather jacket she'd shoved into his arms on the porch after thumbs-upping the rest of his getup: khaki pants, wrinkled button-down, and a brown fedora he'd borrowed from Chris. "What are you expecting?"

"She's just excited to meet you. Probably too excited. Layla and Andrea really talked you up after bowling, and . . ." Celeste looked down and fiddled with the rope around her waist, leaving John to guess at whether Celeste had told Maria about the kiss.

Celeste cleared her throat and looked back at the door. "Anyway, you ready?" She took a breath, turned, and opened the door, revealing a large, open-plan living room and kitchen, half-full of people in all sorts of costumes. More than one superhero stood chatting, drink in hand, but John's view of the room was quickly obscured by a woman with bronze skin and thick black curls. She was in all red, with yellow and red wristbands and a Wonder Woman tiara on her head. Her hands went straight to her hips as she assessed first Celeste, then John, from head to toe and back again.

"Heroes and villains, honey." This was directed at Celeste, who adjusted one of the olive twigs in her braid. "Where's the spandex?" Her eyes drifted back to John, and she smiled. "Hmm, the man himself. I'm Maria."

He accepted the hand she offered for a shake and gave a nod in greeting. Maria stared openly at him for a minute, her eyes making another pass of his body.

Celeste cleared her throat. "How you doing, babe? Feeling okay about the party?"

Maria sighed, her shoulders slumping for just an instant before she straightened back up. "Yeah, it's fun so far. Not like the other years, because I'm an exhausted shell of myself, but glad we're doing it. Just do not go in my bedroom, because it holds every piece of laundry in the house right now." She picked at the shoulder of Celeste's tunic. "And you are . . . ?"

Celeste gave a small spin, sending the fabric flaring at her knees. "An incredible heroine, of course—Hypatia of Alexandria! I'm surprised you don't know about her," Celeste said seriously. "She was a mathematician, you know, just like you. *And* an astronomer and philosopher. One of the great women thinkers of ancient Greece. She was a pagan who tried to remain neutral as tensions rose between Christians, Jews, and pagans, but eventually she was torn apart and dragged through the city."

John chuckled. Celeste had sent him several links about

Hypatia, but she seemed especially intrigued by her cause of death. "Some also consider her the last head librarian at the Library of Alexandria," he chimed in.

Maria grinned. "Well, we love librarians around here. Especially the outdoorsy kind." Something passed between the two women John couldn't understand before Maria cleared her throat and looked back at John. "Waiting to see how Celeste warps the party theme is always a thrill. Last year was the eighties, and she came as an entry in the *Oxford English Dictionary*."

"Which was published in eighteen eighty-four," Celeste said earnestly. "You never specified the century."

Maria invited them all the way inside as she narrowed her eyes at John. "I'm almost afraid to ask who you are."

Celeste swept her long arm up and down in front of John. "Give it a minute. Take in the whole look."

John squirmed as both women stared at him, forcing himself to keep his chin up. He'd done his best to look the part, even wrinkling his button-down before putting it on. Finally, he cleared his throat. "Just imagine me with a whip."

Maria's eyes went wide. "Oh, I don't think I will." After another moment, she turned to Celeste with a raised eyebrow. "If you're a hero, he's supposed to be a villain. That's how the whole thing works."

"Indiana Jones was one hundred percent a villain," Celeste said emphatically. "I watched this whole set of videos about it the other night. Think about it. The guy is plundering Indigenous sites all over the world and stealing their stuff!"

"But he was a professor!" someone holding a Captain America shield interrupted. "Didn't he work for a museum?"

"The history of museum acquisitions in the West is very closely tied to imperialism," John rebutted. "Most museum collections are fairly problematic."

That earned a smack on his shoulder from Celeste. "Exactly! Problematic is right; listen to my date."

When he'd suggested his villain costume, Celeste had responded with an outrageous stream of excited emojis, making him oddly proud. They'd texted consistently since their photo hunt in the park, planning costumes and chitchatting with remarkable ease. She'd congratulated him on getting the contest photos up on his Instagram profile, complete with the correct tags, and he'd recommended some resources for a unit she was planning on literature set in southern Arizona. And while every notification on his phone made his breath hitch, texting seemed safe. Distant.

But now she was right next to him, lecturing Captain America about the military-industrial complex while her fingers toyed with her belt. He flexed his hands at his sides, imagining the twist of rope in his palm.

He was saved by the appearance of a white man with spiky blond hair and a baby held tight to his chest in a woven purple wrap. One hand rubbed circles on the baby's back as the man wedged himself next to Maria. "Babe, I cannot find the little croissant things." His mouth lifted into a smile at the sight of Celeste. "Hey, Cel. Glad you're here. But I need Maria. I really can't find—"

"The croissant things, I get it." Celeste smiled and brushed the top of the baby's head with her fingers.

Maria nodded toward the party in progress. "Go forth, you two. Drinks are in the cooler by the couch. Andrea and Layla are already here, and some other folks from school, too. Games start in a few minutes!"

She wrapped a hand around her partner's waist and laid a soft kiss on the baby's head as they went to find the croissant things.

Celeste tugged at her hair as she looked across the room. "Okay, I guess we should—" She motioned toward the crowd, where John recognized a few of her coworkers from the bowling alley. Andrea was moving toward them fast, an ankle-length fur coat swishing around her legs. Celeste kept her eyes on John, looking uncertain. They hadn't discussed their ground rules again since enthusiastically breaking them.

His fingers brushed hers as he leaned in closer. "Boyfriend reporting for duty?"

Celeste's teeth closed over her bottom lip as she avoided eye contact. But as Andrea paraded toward them, her fingers tangled with his.

Soon Andrea was upon them, primping a black-and-white wig. "Well, if it isn't two of my favorite bowlers. So nice to see you again, John."

"Nice costume, Andrea," Celeste said. "Is Bridgette here, too?"

Andrea beamed toward a willowy figure near a bookshelf, sporting a headband of furry black-and-white dog ears and a lot of polka-dotted spandex. "Doesn't she look amazing? Our costumes were her idea. And you two look . . . cute, even if I don't know what you are."

John tipped his fedora. He'd watched a couple of YouTube clips to get the gesture just right. "I'm Indiana Jones. Celeste is Hypatia, an ancient Greek scholar."

Andrea rubbed at the faux fur along her collar. "Oh. Okay." She shrugged. "You guys should have come in a couples' costume! You know, Batman and Poison Ivy or something. Since you didn't have to come alone like last year, Celeste."

Celeste stiffened at John's side, her fingers flinching in his hand.

"Didn't Hy—" Andrea paused, frowning.

John spoke up. "Hypatia."

She nodded. "Right. Didn't Hypatia have a special Grecian guy?"

Celeste shook her head. "As a matter of fact, she didn't. Hypatia was celibate."

This seemed to shut Andrea up for a moment before she blew out a loud breath. "Oh god, can you imagine?" She leaned in close to Celeste but winked at John. "Good thing you don't have to worry about that, girl."

Andrea moved on to greet someone else, but Celeste's fingers stayed curled over John's knuckles. "Jesus, that woman. She and Bridgette are like a salt-and-pepper set, always matching. Apparently they're 'couple goals'"—she used air quotes on the last words—"but no thanks. If I ever need a reminder of why I'm single, I just think about how Andrea won't even make plans without checking Bridgette's calendar."

Celeste pushed her shoulder into his. "The celibacy line gave her a shock, though. Though you think that was true? Like, sure, she was a scholar and never married, but would a smart-ass woman like that let convention control her? I bet if she wanted sex, she got it."

John had been trying hard as hell to not put *Celeste* and *sex* in the same sentence, even in his thoughts. Hearing the word from her mouth was the dangerous slide of a key into a lock, threatening to open the store of fantasies he'd been trying to shut down.

Her thumb swiped across his knuckles once, twice.

Their eyes caught. Celeste's free hand rose quickly to fiddle with her braid, her lower lip drawn between her teeth. Her lips parted as her gaze lowered to his mouth.

"Attention all heroes and villains!" Maria's shout broke John out of the fantasy. Celeste dropped his hand as Maria claimed everyone's attention.

"If everyone will please head outside, we will let the games begin!"

CHAPTER 20

BIRD BINGE, DAY 23 OF 42
BIRD COUNT: 82

Celeste hadn't been sure how John would handle the "games" portion of Maria's annual party, but just like at bowling, he threw himself into it with quiet good cheer. Maria loved putting adults through their paces with children's games—she joked that it kept them all humble. There had already been a crab-crawl race and a game of Simon Says (with consolation vodka shots offered to the losers), and now they were back inside for hide-and-seek, with Maria as supervisor and Arnold as the first seeker.

As Maria shouted, "On your marks, get set—go!" people all around them scattered, the lazy ones jumping behind the couch while the more competitive guests left to investigate other areas of the house.

Celeste shooed John. "Go! It's each person for themselves!"

John just laughed and looked around the room, rubbing his beard. Every time he touched that thing, she wanted her hands to follow.

She couldn't get to hiding fast enough.

She really should have stuck to the plan she'd developed at home while braiding her hair in the mirror. *Know your limits*, the lime-green Post-it warned her. She knew it was wise to keep the PDA stuff to a minimum, telling herself they'd made enough of a point at the bowling alley. No need to poke the wasp's nest of sexual tension.

But when Andrea had descended on them and John's fingers had brushed hers, she'd taken his hand.

Why would she make such a blatantly stupid move, knowing how it would send electricity through her body?

Because she'd wanted to. Just like she'd wanted to feel his shoulder next to hers at the picnic table. Especially after he'd taken off his coat and rolled his shirtsleeves up, those woodworking forearms on display in the sunshine of Maria's yard.

Her eyes were tracing the vein just above his wrist when an olive twig fell from her hair. He picked it up gently and angled it back into her braid, his other thumb rubbing a small circle on her neck as he worked.

Celeste was a caretaker. She enjoyed helping people, advising them, coaching them. Parenting Morgan was the greatest joy and accomplishment of her life. Long before their divorce, when Celeste and Peter had moved more side by side than together, she'd stopped expecting that kind of care from him. They had been partners, often unequally, in their home and co-parents to their daughter, but she'd taken care of herself.

And most of the time, that suited her fine. But would it be so bad if she leaned into John's gentle acts of caring during the party? Andrea and other coworkers were there, after all, preventing any one-on-one time that could prove dangerous to her stay-single plan.

She made her way toward the end of the house that held Maria's bedroom and Xavi's nursery. Maria was standing in front of her bedroom door, arms crossed to prevent entry into the den of dirty laundry. When Celeste stopped in front of the hall closet, Maria waved her on, blowing her a little kiss.

She opened the closet door just enough to slip in and shut it behind her. But instead of the old coats Celeste knew Maria kept here, Celeste stepped right into a warm body, her face brushing against a rough beard. She groped about in the darkness, her hands landing on wide forearms, rigid beneath her fingers.

Exactly what she'd been hiding from.

"Jesus!" Her back was against the closed door, and her front was very, very close to John. He smelled like a goddamn pine tree, the kind she used to stick her face in at Christmastime even if it meant getting poked. John moved away from her slightly, making the closet contents rustle, but his sudden absence sent her off-balance, and she stumbled into him.

Her hands pressed hard into his chest, registering the smooth buttons of his shirt. "What are you doing here?"

He held her shoulders, steadying her. "I'm hiding. Isn't that the point?" His whisper went straight into her ear.

She swallowed hard and stepped back, gaining the small fraction of space she could, and whispered, "It's fine." She twisted one arm behind her, searching for the doorknob. "I'll find another spot. Just . . ." She tried to turn, but her hip ran into his, and his fingers on her shoulders tightened. "Just let me turn around."

They each shifted a bit, and she managed to turn, but it hardly improved the situation. Now his chest was hovering just behind her back, warmth radiating from him. God, how she wanted to lean back into the solid wall of his chest.

But she leaned forward and grasped the doorknob instead, starting to turn it. John's arm shot around her and covered her hand. "Wait. Listen."

Thudding steps made their way toward the closet from outside. Celeste had never thrown a game and she wouldn't now, cramped closet be damned. She froze as the steps approached the door and then moved on.

John's palm was warm on her hand, his arm pressed to hers from wrist to shoulder. Even in the dark, she pinched her eyes closed tight, willing her hand to *turn the damn doorknob*.

But the doorknob didn't turn. And John's hand stayed over hers.

Celeste's senses slowed, the air around them thick like honey. The point beneath her sternum was tight and hot, and fuck, so was the spot between her legs.

Finally, John drew in a breath and spoke quietly, his voice strained. "I think it's safe out there."

Unlike in here, he didn't say. But he didn't have to. His fingers still over hers said it all. They asked her a question.

"I know," she whispered. But she didn't move. And that was her answer.

Behind her, his breath stirred just over her neck. "Peppermint." She could barely hear him. "You always smell like peppermint."

She swallowed, then let out a slow breath.

"Yes," she said shakily. His small observations were always undoing her. "It's essential oil. I always put a drop . . ."

"Right here." His fingers touched her pulse point, his touch confident and firm. "I know." He hovered so close behind her she could hear his intake of breath whistle through his teeth. "I've noticed."

The hand on her neck stayed steady on her skin like the one covering hers over the doorknob. She tilted her head to the side, exposing more of herself to his touch.

She was being stupid, reckless. But she was also squeezed into a dark closet with an attractive, intriguing, *kind* man. And he was touching her like he'd been studying her so thoroughly that he could find her in the dark without hesitation, knowing exactly where his hands would land.

His fingers slid from her racing pulse down her neck, leaving a trail of goose bumps in their wake as he murmured into her ear. "I shouldn't be doing this." The simmer in his voice slithered straight down her body, filling her with power.

Celeste struggled past the knot in her throat to make sure John heard her, the hitch in her voice demonstrating her need. "Do it anyway."

He groaned as his palm curved over her shoulder, then ran back up her neck. His fingers slid into her hair, pulling her braid tight. The warmth of his breath shifted from her hair, past her ear, lower, hovering just over her exposed neck.

Then there was a brush of lips and a breeze of hot air. Her sigh ended in a whimper as his free hand wrapped around her waist from behind and his mouth opened against her neck. He scraped her skin with a drag of his teeth before she felt the hot, wet swipe of his tongue, seeking out the same spot where he'd pressed his fingers, tasting her pulse.

She raised both arms and flattened her palms against the door. John's hand stayed on her neck as his fingers and mouth worked in tandem—his thumb tracing lines across her skin that his lips would follow. His motions were excruciatingly, deliciously slow. Her nipples were tight and sore, puckering with need as she clenched her thighs together, desperate to relieve some of the pressure building in her body.

His mouth left her neck, leaving her bereft until his lips closed on her ear, nipping and licking down its curve. A sharp tug on her earring made her moan against the door.

Celeste brought her fist to her mouth, biting her knuckle as John gently slipped the earring out of her ear. He could have pulled off all her clothes for how naked she felt. He closed his lips around her earlobe with a low, pained moan, and her head sagged back against his shoulder. His teeth tugged, sending a jolt that turned the ache between her legs into a rioting scream, and her hips pushed back instinctively, seeking contact.

She found it in the form of his erection, rigid against the slope of her lower back. She circled her hips, grinding into him, his lips releasing her ear just long enough for him to utter a drawn-out, guttural "Fuck."

She'd never heard the word from his lips before. Hearing it now, husky in the pitch dark, the honey-thickness of arousal in her brain spun it into something sharp and needy. "John," she whimpered.

He gripped her hips hard, then spun her around to face him. The bumping and sliding that had been awkward when she entered the closet took on a heightened eroticism that had her legs shaking. Once her back was against the door, John stepped all the way into her, crowding her, his cock pressing into the ridge of her hip. Their breathing, heavy, in sync, thundered in the darkness, and his hand cupped Celeste's jaw.

Her body screamed with need, begging for the relief of his tongue in her mouth and his knee pressed between her thighs. But her brain screamed back, and wouldn't be silenced.

This really wasn't a good idea.

But she wanted this. She *needed* this. And dammit, didn't she deserve it? She and John were on the same wavelength about not wanting a relationship. Maybe they were also on the same wavelength about what they *did* want.

They just needed a plan. She was great at plans.

So even though her body was clear about what it wanted, Celeste let her brain take over.

"Wait."

CHAPTER 21

BIRD BINGE, DAY 23 OF 42
BIRD COUNT: 82

Wait.

Celeste's voice was quiet and rough, but the word was clear as a bell.

John tipped his hips back, panicked he'd gone too far, too fast. Having her body pressed to his in the closet had been too much, that sweet peppermint calling to him from the softest spot behind her ear, beckoning him like a siren.

But now he waited, his mouth hovering just above hers. Celeste's breathing was fast and shallow, her ribs expanding and contracting against him. Even as close as he was to her, he couldn't make out her face in the total darkness of the closet.

He shuffled a foot back, ready to give her more room, but a tug on his shirt kept him close. She turned her face into his hand, pressing a slow, wet kiss to the middle of his palm.

"I want this. With you." Her whisper vibrated against his hand. "But I can't have a relationship. I'm not—" She sighed, pulling at him again until his body was pushed against hers.

Being close to her was intoxicating. Immersive in every way—her scent, her breath, her lips moving against his palm. He was dizzy with it, wanting only to encircle her wrists with his hands and slide them up over her head, returning his mouth to her neck to give her anything she wanted.

"I know," he managed. They were stuck, wanting and not wanting the same things.

Her lips opened on the pad of his palm, followed by the scrape of her teeth. In the dark, it was all sensation, and his body was burning. But he held himself still, waiting for her to tell him what she wanted.

"I don't want a relationship. And I love birding with you. But whatever is happening here—I don't think it will work to keep denying it." She sighed and dropped her arms to her sides. He took the cue to do the same, stepping back and letting darkness fall between them, their breathing still fast. "When I was a kid," she continued quietly, "I used to love to scoot across the carpet in our living room with my socks on. I'd scrape my feet along, building up that static charge as I got closer to touching the doorknob on the other end of the room."

Despite the tension between them, John laughed. That was a perfectly Celeste thing to do.

"That's how I feel lately, with you. Like there's this charge building up." She lowered her forehead against John's chest. "It was stupid to think one more kiss would help. It just made everything worse. I don't know how to go back. I thought I could put it aside, but . . ."

Her head lifted from his chest, and even in the dark he could sense her looking at him. "Do you know what I'm talking about? Is it that way for you?"

She sounded unsure, as if he hadn't just pinned her against the closet door. "You know it is."

He dropped Celeste's earring into his pocket and ran both hands down her arms. "Are you saying you don't want to do the contest anymore?" He'd gone over the countdown in his head a hundred times in his woodshop. Nineteen more days of the contest. Nineteen more days with Celeste, and he was counting on them. He wanted them.

But he also wanted *her*, and that made things complicated.

"No," she rushed out. "I want to do the contest. But now that this . . . charge between us is out in the open, how do we keep going? It might be a little hard to bird like this."

It was hard to *think* like this, the taste of her neck still alive on his tongue.

After a moment, she took a breath and laid her hands on his chest. "I think we can manage it. But we need a plan. I don't have experience with casual sex, but it's a thing people do. Like, friends with benefits is a thing?"

John didn't have much experience with casual sex either. He found he needed a connection with someone to really enjoy himself in bed, where he treated sex as both a good time and an exploration, a give-and-take that required trust.

But he had trust with Celeste. Somehow, despite the outward difference in their personalities, they'd been easy with each other almost from the start.

Maybe it didn't need to be as complicated as he feared. "Yeah, people do it," he said. "I haven't been in that situation myself, but I'd be open to trying it with you. If that's what you're offering."

If he could touch her again, he'd be open to almost anything.

"You know me." Celeste slid a hand up his chest, fingers threading into his beard. "I'm always up for trying new things." She brushed her lips across his Adam's apple as her fingers moved to the back of his neck, working their way into his hair. "We could be birders with benefits till the contest ends. That way we can keep birding, but we also . . . release the charge a bit."

"'Birders with benefits'?" He choked out a laugh as her fingers tightened in his hair. Only Celeste would come up with that. "We could do that."

"Just till the end of the contest. Then we can each keep going on our path of self-fulfillment."

Nineteen more days.

There were dozens of reasons why he should say no and get them out of that closet. The first among them was his lack of proof that he could do a casual thing with anyone, let alone Celeste. Nothing about her called for half measures.

But wasn't he the one always going on about discovery? How could he say no when the thing he so desperately wanted to explore was literally within his reach?

And would he ever sleep again without knowing the shape of Celeste's breast in his palm?

He guided her back against the door. "Okay. Yes."

"Thank the goddess," she moaned. "I'm about to combust. Are we able to start the benefits thing right now? Because—"

He caught her words in his mouth, holding her face with both hands. Immediately, her mouth was open, asking him for what she needed. She was sweet and warm, moaning greedily into his mouth as she gripped his hair, hard.

Their kiss inside the bar had been eye-opening, but muddled by surprise and confusion. The one outside had been a confession, but had felt like an ending.

But this kiss, dark and needy—this kiss was a beginning, a delicious relief. It was rounding the corner of a trail, knowing the view was just around the bend. It was the charge between them, building to near combustion.

It was a current, warm and steady, running between them and heating them both.

He held her face tight between his hands, angling her to him as her arm reached around his waist and pulled him closer, until their chests were pressed hard against each other.

"Touch me," she groaned against his mouth before pushing her mouth against his again, swiping her tongue along his bottom lip and drawing it between her teeth.

John dropped his hand from her face long enough to find one of her hands, placing it over where he gripped her hip. "Show me where."

She dragged his hand up her body, cupping it around her breast. Her nipple was hard through the thin fabric of her makeshift tunic.

When he flicked the nipple with his thumb, she yelped into his mouth, "Oh fuck, yes," so he enclosed it between his thumb and forefinger, listening to Celeste pant. He craved all the knowledge he could gather about her body and what she wanted. His fingers tightened around her taut nipple, squeezing it while rolling over it with his thumb. "Tell me when."

She hissed in a breath and bucked against him, wrapping a leg around his hip. He pinched harder, then harder still, until she moaned, "There. Right there."

He crushed her mouth with another kiss as he played with her, letting up with his fingers before pinching again. He rubbed his beard against her chin and dragged his lips along her neck. "So much I want to explore."

Celeste pushed her hips into him with a moan, all but riding his thigh. "Exploring is good. We should definitely do that."

Muffled background sounds drifted through the closet door, a chorus of voices like someone had been found hiding. "The exploring I want to do requires more space, and definitely more light." He needed to look at her and add each inch of her exposed skin to the guidebook in his mind.

She scraped her nails along his neck, then down his arms, leaning in for a kiss. She pulled back, speaking just against his lips. "So maybe you should invite me home with you tonight. That's the prime benefit of our arrangement, right? Open exploration."

"Tonight." Tonight she could be spread on his bed. Tonight he could hear what sounds she made when they weren't in the middle of a party. "Yes, tonight, I—" He groaned, biting back a curse. "I can't."

"You can't?"

John leaned forward to catch the lip he knew was jutting out from an exaggerated frown, encircling her waist in his arms. "I promised Linda I would go over some numbers for the gala." She'd even promised to make John his favorite veggie chili. "She's been working with some local businesses for donations and—"

She caught him off guard with a kiss, this one slow and gentle. "Contest Linda? Your birding mentor? You gotta go."

He did, dammit. He really did. "Tomorrow? I'm free tomorrow night." His fingers wrapped around the rope at her waist, tugging it gently like he'd wanted to do all night.

She sighed and arched her back, sliding herself over his leg again. He was desperate to know if she could orgasm this way, his hands on the curves of her ass as he helped her set a rhythm.

"Tomorrow's no good." She untucked his shirt and snaked her slender fingers up his chest. "I'm going up to Phoenix for a special training. I've got a sub for two days, so I booked myself a hotel room. I had this idea that I'd treat myself. But now—"

He kissed her cheek, her jawbone, the side of her mouth. "Treat yourself. You deserve that."

She sighed and stretched her neck, giving John space to work his mouth down her jaw. "I love being in hotel rooms alone. I turn the AC down really low and take a long bath and then stretch out on the hotel sheets."

"Jesus." That was a vision John would hold on to. Celeste, flushed from her bath, with goose bumps rising on her skin, stretched out, maybe even thinking of *him*.

She was breathing heavily, moving against his leg with a mission. "But when I'm back, we'll figure out our schedules. Because I really want to—"

"So do I," he assured her, finding her mouth again. Celeste grew more frantic, whimpering his name against his neck. He explored lines of her ribs, the hard dip of her sternum between her breasts, the soft skin of her inner wrist, which he pulled up to his mouth for a long suck.

A groan issued from deep within her as she moved faster on his thigh. Christ, she was responsive, moving faster like she might be close to coming, just like this.

Then there was a small, metallic click, and the world came pouring in as Celeste tumbled backward into the hall.

"Jesus, Andrea, I told you not to—" Maria shook her head at Andrea but broke into a grin of her own when she looked at Celeste, who was smoothing down her tunic before adjusting her braid, which had strands sticking out in every direction. Her face was flushed, her lips wet and swollen, one earlobe bare.

She was breathtaking.

"Looks like I found the last two hiders." Andrea smirked at Celeste. "I knew you wouldn't be in character enough for that celibacy stuff."

CHAPTER 22

BIRD BINGE, DAY 24 OF 42
BIRD COUNT: 82

Chris sailed down the paint aisle on the back of an orange shopping cart, grinning like a schoolboy.

Yes, John had been right to come. A bull in a china shop had nothing on Chris in a Home Depot.

And the outing was a needed change from John's backyard, where he'd been sitting for much of the afternoon, listening to a cactus wren and drafting texts to Celeste. He'd tried to put in some hours in his shop that morning, but the wood had just slipped from his fingers as he thought about the day before—crushed against Celeste's pliant body in the closet, finally letting the spark between them burn.

Even better was the memory of how she'd laughed off Andrea's joke upon their discovery, then given John a wink as she ducked into the hallway bathroom. She'd emerged a minute later wearing her signature ponytail and carrying a handful of olive twigs that she'd slipped into his pocket, murmuring with a smile about how he'd messed up her hair "beyond repair." He couldn't manage to be sorry about it.

They'd returned to the party then, energy humming between them as they stood hip to hip in the late afternoon sun of Maria's backyard, trading small touches and nudges as they chatted with Celeste's coworkers. When it was time for him to leave, Celeste had walked him out, then pushed him against his car for a hungry kiss before folding him into the driver's seat with a playful slap on the ass and a promise to reconnect when she was back from Phoenix.

"Johnny! My shining knight." Chris hopped off the back of the cart and half jogged down the aisle. "You didn't have to come all this way."

John only laughed. "I know a cry for help when I hear one."

Chris's string of texts to John had been a collection of vague diagrams drawn on napkins, inquiries about how much wood he should buy, and, most alarmingly, which brand of staple gun he'd recommend. John had texted back a quick *I'll be right there* and headed for his car.

His best friend was brilliant, but shouldn't be allowed within thirty feet of a staple gun.

"I needed to get out of the house anyway," John answered, the phone in his pocket heavy with all the unsent texts he'd drafted to Celeste. If there was a balance somewhere between *I had fun yesterday* and *You're intoxicating. I can't stop thinking about touching you again*, he hadn't yet found it.

"It could be that I need a little help," Chris admitted. "And I figured if I called you from inside your church, you'd be more likely to come, and I could lay eyes on you. You're a hard man to catch lately, John Maguire. It's all birds, all the time."

John raised his brows at the accusation. "You're referring to the bird-watching contest you signed up for and then abandoned?"

Chris clutched at his heart. "Touché, my friend. The pain is of my own making." His thin fingers rapped against the cart handle. "And how is my replacement doing? Is she keeping up with you?"

John nodded, counting on his beard to cover the heat flooding his cheeks. "She's a fast learner. You saw that at trivia night."

"Ah yes, the trivia night. When the Tweethearts kicked ass and you shared a jaw-dropping kiss onstage and then"—Chris tapped on his chin—"how did you put it? 'Cleared the air' outside afterward?"

"Yup." He hadn't loved lying to Chris and Jared about kissing Celeste outside the bar, but he couldn't exactly tell the truth either. He'd never hear the end of it, and at the time he'd been trying to quarantine any lingering thoughts about kissing her more. "Anyway. What were those plans you sent me? I couldn't even tell if you were working in feet or inches."

"Inches." Chris dug into his messenger bag for the napkin, pulling it taut between them. "I'm making screens for a series of watershed water quality assessments with a team of my students. You know, to catch the larvae and other little buggers."

One indicator of water quality was what lived and reproduced within the streams of the watershed. Healthy snails needed healthy water, so a lot of Chris's university teaching revolved around watershed ecology. When he could, John still enjoyed putting on waders and joining him, though Chris's time in the field had dwindled in proportion to his attempts to secure tenure through serving on committees and taking on a bigger teaching load.

"I thought you had these?" He took the "plans" from Chris. Somehow Chris's depiction made a simple rectangular frame with a screen look like the Eiffel Tower. "I've seen you use them before."

"Oh, I did, Jonathan." Which had never been John's name, but

Chris didn't care. "But they were lost in my office move, and if I requisition more they'll arrive just in time for my grandchildren to take one more look at this abused planet."

"Got it." He passed the napkin back to Chris. "Should be simple enough." A few one-by-twos and some metal mesh were really all he needed. They could assemble it all in John's shop. It would be a welcome distraction.

He strode down the aisle, Chris kicking the cart beside him. "Sooooo," his friend said. "Back to the birding contest. You and Celeste must be spending a lot of time together?"

Chris was clearly a dog with a bone on this topic, and John wasn't sure how to shake him off. "That is in the nature of the contest." They made a left at the washing machines, where Chris reached out and touched every shining knob as they passed. "She's in Phoenix for a teaching thing, but we'll be back to birding this week."

"But you're doing more than birding, right?" Chris turned the cart to face John, leaning both elbows on the handle. A black sweatband held back his usually floppy hair, leaving blue eyes—and his hallmark mischievous sparkle—clear for John to observe. "What about the rest?"

"The rest?" John choked, rubbing a hand on his beard. Did Chris somehow have intel about Maria's party, and how John and Celeste had stumbled out of the closet together, ruffled and near orgasmic?

"Yeah, the rest." Chris narrowed his eyes. "You know, the whole *I'll be your fake boyfriend and you be my fake girlfriend thing*? How's that going?"

"Oh, fine." John brushed past him to turn into the tool aisle, half hoping the shiny blades would distract Chris from this line of questioning. He knew he couldn't evade him forever, but he was only just wrapping his own thoughts around the arrangement with Celeste. And putting the last few days into words was like looking at a photograph of a beautiful landscape, like that blooming palo verde where he and Celeste had seen their first bird together, and trying to render it with children's crayons.

His strategy worked, as Chris picked up a hand drill and waved it around with a grin, pretend-drilling a few screws into the air, buzzing sound and all. "Damn, this stuff is so sexy. If I had a woodshop like yours, I'd be bringing people there all the time to let them handle my tools."

John had never thought of his shop as remotely seductive. Efficient, yes, and a refuge he'd created for himself after Breena moved out. She'd always wanted to convert their covered carport into a home office, and had rolled her eyes at John's ideas to turn it into a woodshop, arguing that his "hobby" distracted him from bigger things.

John usually stepped into new things the way he inched his way into cold water, but the minute Breena had driven away for good, he'd gotten to work. Brushing aside his shock that the years of their lives spent together fit neatly in the back of her car, he'd started drawing up plans.

So he'd never had a woman in his shop. Hell, he hadn't had a woman except his mother in his home since that day.

John opened a carpentry app on his phone and traded it for Chris's drill before taking over the cart. It was best if Chris's hands were occupied when they walked past the Sawzalls. "Work out how much we'll need for how many screens you want. We'll be using one-by-twos, and they come in eight-foot planks."

"One-by-two, eight-foot plank. I got this." Chris chewed at his lip and typed into the phone as he followed John like a baby duckling, humming Coldplay.

But when John arrived at the lumber aisle, he'd lost Chris. He backtracked quickly, assuming Chris was playing with the circular saws. Even without power, he could probably do some damage. But when he found him, Chris was just staring at John's phone.

"Uh." Chris wiped a hand across his face, an uncharacteristic blush on his cheeks. "I think maybe I wasn't supposed to see this." His mouth kicked into a grin before he steadied it back into a flat line. "It's from your strictly fake girlfriend birding partner."

Heart suddenly thumping hard, John took the phone.

CELESTE: *Training done. In my hotel room after my bath. Would it be uncouth to say I'm on the bed all alone, wishing you were here?*

Wow.

Next to him, Chris cleared his throat. "John?" He waved a hand between John's face and the text he couldn't seem to look away from. "Jonathan, my good man, would you care to explain?"

John re-stowed his phone and slowly exhaled. "It's private."

Chris barked a laugh. "No shit, Sherlock. Luckily for me, we don't do private. Remember when I spent that weekend with a Pilates instructor and told you about every position we—"

John cut him off with a look. "I never asked for those details." Though parts of Chris's narration had been very educational, especially since John had only slept with a handful of people. "And I've never given you mine."

"That's because you were with Breena, who was my friend at the time, so I didn't want to know all her kinks." A nearby employee cleared their throat, and Chris lowered his voice, just barely. "And since then you've been a monk. So pardon me if I want the juicy deets." He rubbed his hands together. "So you two are dating? This is amazing! Literally better than I could have imagined."

"No," John answered before Chris could start planning the wedding. "It's . . . casual."

Chris's playful smile dropped. "But you don't—"

"Do casual," he finished for him with a sigh. "I know I haven't before, but I am now. There's an attraction there, and we're exploring it."

He'd never done no-strings-attached sex, but that didn't mean it wasn't possible. Since he'd lost his job, he was breathing a little deeper, shedding the parts of his life he no longer needed and enjoying the space it created. Now he had the opportunity to experience something with a vibrant woman who turned on his body *and* his brain. And he could explore it without the larger complications of combining lives and careers and all the things that had ruined the spark he'd once had with Breena.

Chris picked up a box of screws, turning it over in his hands like it might hold the secrets to John's behavior. "You're exploring it. *Casually*."

"Yes, casually." How many times would they trade that word? "Just while we finish the contest."

Chris tossed the box back on the shelf and leaned down with a groan, cupping his knees with his hands before popping up. "I'm trying to be cool here. But what the hell? You're saying you and Celeste are fuck buddies, but only till the Bird Binge is done? Did I wake up in the other timeline?" He looked down at his worn Pantera shirt, tugging it away from his chest. "In this reality, am I the quiet, steadfast one who takes six months to even ask a woman out, and *you're* the one who falls into bed after two drinks?"

"I'm not falling into—" John pushed his hands over his eyes, taking a breath. "True, this isn't how I've done things in the past, but that doesn't mean I can't now." He pulled Chris to the side to make space for a woman pushing a cart holding a toddler and a hibiscus. "I know that after everything with Breena you've felt like you need to take care of me. But I'm okay. This thing with Celeste isn't something for you to worry about."

Chris made a goofy face at the toddler before turning back to John. "First, I will always want to take care of you. That's just the friend deal we have. It's why you came to Home Depot to save me from myself." His twinkling eyes grew serious. "I'm all for you getting your groove on. But are you really going to be cool with it ending in a few weeks? I can tell by the way you talk about her that you really like Celeste."

"Of course I like Celeste." "Like" was insufficient, but he pulled his thoughts back from that maze. "And I don't know how I'll feel then, but is that a reason to hold back now?"

It had been thrilling to just follow his instincts in that closet and touch Celeste as he'd been dreaming about, letting their energy whisk them downstream. It was a current he wanted to follow, even if he couldn't see where it would lead them.

"And aren't people always telling me to go for things? To move faster?" John continued, knowing even as he spoke that he was justifying his actions to himself as much as to Chris, assuring himself the arrangement with Celeste wasn't out of bounds for him, simply something he didn't have a guidebook for. "It's happening, and I'm going to enjoy it. Can we leave it at that?"

Chris studied him, arms across his chest. "Fair enough. If

you want to give this a go, more power to you. I want you and Celeste to go at it like bees if that's what you want."

Chris loved to bring up the sex lives of bees, the males of whom could mate for fourteen hours straight in breeding season. If only his snails were so prolific.

"But if that's the case, you better reply to her, because there is nothing worse than leaving a sext on 'read.'"

John motioned to the towering shelves, stacks of lumber, and buzzing fluorescent lights. "I can't respond to her from here!"

Chris followed his gaze, smiling. "Honestly, this place is kind of your fantasy land, buddy. Sexy talk should be easy here."

John grumbled toward the floor. Just once he wished he had more of his friend's experience, especially when it came to sending texts like *this*.

Chris must have read his expression, because his lower lip jutted out. "Oh, sweet boy, you've never sexted, have you? It's perfect for you. You can take a minute deliberating about what you want to say."

John could do that. He was great at deliberating, and he'd try it as soon as he got home.

"But don't make the poor woman wait," Chris said, reading John like a book. "She's on her hotel bed. She knows you saw her message. All you need to do is write what's on your mind. Just tell her what you're thinking." He pulled him in for a quick hug, then held him by the shoulders. "My boy, so grown up. Now go send your first sext."

Which was how John ended up leaning against a display of paint samples, all hues of orange, with his phone open to more texts from Celeste.

CELESTE: *I hope that was okay . . .*

CELESTE: *I know you saw it! Did you run away, or are you waiting for more?*

CELESTE: *Shit, was that too much?*

CELESTE: *Joooohhhnnnnn, put me out of my misery.*

He owed Chris a thank-you for the push.

JOHN: *Sorry. Didn't mean to leave you hanging. It was definitely okay.*

JOHN: *I'm just out of the house right now, so I couldn't respond right away.*

He watched his phone, hoping for a response.

CELESTE: *Okay, cooooool. I was stressed for a minute that I'd crossed a line.*

CELESTE: *Where are you?*

JOHN: *Home Depot with Chris. He needs some help getting supplies, and I was afraid he'd hurt himself.*

CELESTE: 😂 *You're a good friend. Go tend to him, I'll keep myself busy.*

His imagination immediately went wild picturing what *sort* of busy. But when wood clattered one aisle over, he knew his time was short.

Just tell her what you're thinking, Chris had said.

JOHN: *I have to run before Chris hurts himself, and then we'll be working on a project for the rest of the evening.*

He took a deep breath and kept typing.

JOHN: *I hope you can enjoy your hotel room tonight, because you deserve it. If you need something to think about, you could imagine I'm there, sliding my hands up your thighs as I push them apart. I'm so eager to touch you and find out what it takes to make you come. I know you were close in the closet, and all I can think about is getting you the rest of the way there.*

He blinked at his own words, letting that current carry him as he hit *send*. Later, after he'd built the screens with Chris, when he was blessedly alone, he'd check his phone. Maybe she'd respond with a string of shocked emojis, or maybe not at all. Or maybe she'd tell him what she was thinking about, too.

CHAPTER 23

BIRD BINGE, DAY 26 OF 42
BIRD COUNT: 82

"Mom, please remind me again why we're doing this. And hand me the glue."

"We're doing this," Celeste said for the fourth time, "to add some whimsy to the shelves in my classroom." She passed the small bottle of glue to Morgan, who sat on the floor on the other side of the coffee table, struggling to keep hold of the world's smallest flowers. "My students are so drawn into social media and everything, I'm just trying to bring a little magic to reading. And that starts with the book nooks. I saw an amazing TikTok about it last week."

"Since when are you on TikTok?" Morgan scoffed, peering at the flowers.

"Since I decided I want to know what my students are talking about, that's when." She worked on finishing off a small decorative line along the edge of her creation. This had looked much easier online, but she was muddling through.

When she finished, she turned her nook proudly toward Morgan. It was as tall as a typical hardcover book, and maybe twice as wide, with a hollow space in the middle where Celeste had added the miniature facade of a creepy house, complete with eerie shapes in the window. Tiny bats hung from fishing line around the house, and tombstones stood in tiny lines on the ground. This nook would be displayed between books in the horror section of her classroom library, while Morgan's fairy world—if it was ever finished—would adorn the fantasy shelf. Celeste hoped the novelty would draw her students to the shelves, where they just might find a book they liked.

Their school had a library, but Celeste found a particular joy in curating her own shelves in her classroom. Students were free to borrow a book or take one to keep or pass on. She wasn't keeping track.

"And you've recruited my child labor because?" Morgan blew a raspberry as she slipped the little flowers into her nook, nestling them next to a toadstool she'd fashioned out of clay. She'd been griping the whole time, but her work was as beautiful as Celeste had known it would be—detailed and whimsical.

"Because," she answered, toying with miniature tufts of moss on the table, "we set this night aside as mother-daughter bonding night, because I love you and I miss you because you're never home."

"Mm-hmm." Morgan hummed and glanced up from her nook suspiciously. She'd begrudgingly agreed to the night in with Celeste, softening a little when she was promised Chinese takeout and Sandra Bullock rom-coms after the nook work was complete. But she must have suspected that Celeste had a hidden agenda up her sleeve, because there was a tension she wasn't quite letting go of.

And she wasn't wrong.

Morgan was affixing a minuscule butterfly to her fairy world when Celeste's phone buzzed on the table. Her daughter paused to pick it up and pass it over, but Celeste just waved her off. "Just ignore it. Mom-daughter night needs no interruption."

She needed to focus on Morgan tonight and make a plan for her move up to Flagstaff for college. That meant not getting distracted by any texts from John. Especially not the teasing, dirty ones they'd exchanged at intervals throughout the past two days, both of them growing a little bolder each time. She'd gotten herself off in her hotel room to that first shocker he'd sent her, imagining his hands on her. Then she'd had a plastic cup of wine from the room's minibar and texted John to tell him about it.

And he'd told her he was doing the same.

It had been near impossible to let him drive away that night at Maria's, but she was glad now for this little window, a time when they could both adjust to the new sexual aspect of their partnership and get comfortable communicating about it. She'd been with a couple of people since her divorce—"wiping the slate," in Maria's words—but nothing that bore repeating. It was difficult to develop the kind of connection with someone she needed for great sex while also avoiding a more serious commitment.

Yes, knowing their exploration had an end date made her stomach hurt a little, but that was just another sign that it was necessary. Because John, as unassuming as he was, was the kind of person she could see herself bending and rearranging for, altering the plans she'd been making to grow on her own. She couldn't fall into a trap, as comfortable and enticing as it might be, of letting her connection to another person dial her own happiness up and down.

Which was why, despite the growing need to see what John was hiding under those cargo pants, Celeste had stuck to her planned date with Morgan. And why, when her phone buzzed again on the table, she shoved it under one of the couch cushions.

Celeste pushed her nook to the side. "So, hon."

Morgan groaned. “Here we go.”

Celeste gripped her knees. “Well, it’s time to buckle down and get all this stuff sorted out for the fall. I’ve been trying not to bug you, but we’re running up against these deadlines for all the paperwork, especially if you want to give any preferences for roommate stuff.”

Morgan glanced up at Celeste before returning her attention to the placement of a tiny butterfly. “Actually, I did want to talk to you about that.”

“Great!” Celeste just barely stopped herself from clapping. This was progress. “We have a lot to cover. I know moving away can seem really scary, but you’re going to be fine, I promise you.”

“I’m not *scared*.” Celeste could hear the eye roll. Morgan sat back on her heels, pulling her long hair through her hands and over one shoulder. “I just wonder if . . .” She worried at her lip with her teeth, then shook her head. “All that gen-ed stuff at NAU—I’m not that interested in it. Like I have to take psychology and math, stuff I don’t even care about. I already did that for four years. It’s a waste.”

Morgan did well in her classes, but always more out of duty than passion. But Celeste knew college could be different. “Oh, sweetie, it won’t be a waste, believe me. There is so much to learn, it’s just going to blow your mind.”

“Not everybody is a school person—”

“There’s a whole world out there waiting for you to learn about it, Moo. I wonder what books you’ll read in your freshman English class. Maybe I could get a copy and read along—”

“Mom.” Morgan’s voice was sharp. “You know it’s me going, not you, right?”

This had long been a pressure point between them. Celeste was a learner, always ready to jump into a new hobby or dive into a book on a new subject. But that time of her life when she should have been free to explore all the world had to offer had been consumed by her relationship with Peter.

Was transferring some of her enthusiasm to her daughter the worst thing she could do?

She just wanted to see Morgan spread her wings and grab life by the horns, to show the world what she was made of. And she hoped she'd have a bachelor's degree and a job when it was all over.

"This is my life we're talking about," Morgan continued. "And maybe I should have a say."

"Of course you have a say," Celeste shot back. "I've always supported you as you pursued the stuff you wanted to do. And you can keep doing that stuff up at college, even the art."

"'Even the art'? Thanks, Mom, that's generous."

"What I mean is"—Celeste drew in a breath—"the art department will be lucky to have you, and meanwhile you can explore what else you might enjoy doing."

Morgan stayed silent, tugging at her hair again and holding the butterfly in place long enough for the glue to set. She sucked her lips between her teeth and let them out with a smack. "Great talk." She stood, rolling out her neck and bouncing for a minute on her feet in her plaid pajamas. "As fun as this has been, I think I'm just gonna work on the pieces for the show. I'm not that hungry."

Celeste jumped up, brushing fake moss flakes from her T-shirt and yoga pants. She'd managed to get them from mother-daughter bonding to Morgan's storming out of the room in ten minutes flat. It had to be a record.

Given Morgan's own helping of Celeste's stubborn personality and tendency to retreat to Peter's house if pressed, the peace Celeste had once felt with her daughter seemed now more like a delicate cease-fire. One she'd apparently thrown a grenade into by mentioning a few college forms.

But there was still time, at least a little of it. So Celeste tucked the topic away for another night. "No way," she said, forcing some humor into her tone. "You can't leave me with all that eggplant tofu to eat. And I have to repay you for your labor."

Morgan paused at the turn of the hallway.

Celeste wouldn't give her the chance to back out. "I'll clean up and bring the food out and you pick the movie. Is it a *Miss Congeniality* or *While You Were Sleeping* kind of night?"

Morgan sighed and returned, plopping on the couch. "Definitely *While You Were Sleeping*. I like watching you swoon over Bill Pullman. You seem to have a thing for nerds."

"I do not," she argued, cleaning off the table. But if one particular man rose to mind, reading glasses poised on his nose as he studied a bird book, she'd never tell.

CHAPTER 24

BIRD BINGE, DAY 27 OF 42
BIRD COUNT: 82

John finished his last cut and slid the board down his table before powering off his circular saw and removing his industrial-grade earmuffs, letting the screaming voice of Zack de la Rocha surround him. He often worked in silence, listening to the birdsong filtering through the open windows of his shop, but whenever he used power tools he cranked music through the speakers Jared had installed for him last year.

He was just standing to stretch when he registered a voice behind him, raised enough to cut through the music. "Well, maybe you need to try harder, Peter! This is a big deal for her."

When John turned, he caught the flare of Celeste's hem as she paced past the open doorway of his shop. "Thank you. I'll have her arrange it with you. Yeah. Bye."

Her back was to him, framed in the fading sunshine filling the doorway, and John watched as she dropped her phone into her bag and rolled her shoulders. When he shut off the music, she turned, her brows knitted together. But she dropped the expression quickly when she saw him, replacing it with a broad smile. She leaned into the doorframe in a gray dress that left her arms bare, her hair pulled up into a bun. "Hey."

"Hey. You okay?"

She looked away, then back into her bag. "Yeah, just"—her smile fell a fraction—"Morgan's dad is going to be out of town for her art show, the one the night of the gala. Anyway, I suggested he FaceTime that night, you know, to be there. And he thinks it's *overboard*." She fiddled with her bun, pulling a few strands loose. "Which is basically his other name for me. I'm always overboard."

She stepped all the way inside, clearing her throat. "Let's not worry about that, though." She dropped her bag near her feet. It was big enough to hold a few essentials, and John hoped it meant she intended to stay the night.

"So, this is the famous woodshop." She eyed the tools hanging on the walls, her tongue rubbing along her teeth. Her body relaxed as she made a slow lap of his shop, and John's throat tightened as she ran a finger along one of his long metal worktables.

"You look like a kid in a candy store."

"I guess I like new stuff." She wiggled an eyebrow. "You know me."

She picked up his smallest hand planer as the industrial fan whirred, moving the hair at the nape of her neck and sending the hem of her dress dancing around her knees.

She turned with the tool in her hand. "What's this one?"

"It's a planer. It's used for—" He scooted his bench in front of a clear work area and motioned her over. "Come here, I'll show you."

John grabbed a few pieces of scrap white pine from the pile in the corner and put them on the table. She sat on the bench with the tool still in her hand.

"This is used to take off thin layers of wood. You can use it to size a board, or in basic shape-carving. Can I see it?"

He demonstrated how to slide the planer against the wood,

peeling off a small layer of pine and letting it flutter to the floor. When he handed it back to her, he made sure to let his fingers brush her knuckles. She smiled before pulling the tool out of his hand.

Clearing his throat, he picked up his half-inch straight chisel, an almost exact copy of the first hand tool he'd ever used, stuck in his Christmas stocking when he was eleven. For years, all John had done with it was idly carve at pieces of wood found on the ground outside. But after college, eager for an outlet during the stress of graduate school, he'd remembered the calming effect of the chisel in his hand and had sought out an experienced woodworker in Tucson, ready to learn. Once he landed back home in Santa Rita, he'd slowly filled his parents' old barn with tools.

"This is a chisel. It can make more precise cuts in the wood." He left it on the table as Celeste practiced planing wood off the block he'd put there for her, smiling as she worked.

She scooted forward on the bench, leaving a scant few inches behind the curve of her ass. "Join me? There's plenty of room. Maybe you can teach me something." Celeste peered over her shoulder at him like a dare.

He straddled Celeste's back, settling into the small space behind her, his legs spread on either side of her hips. She shifted enough to face him sideways, biting her lower lip. "Hi."

"Hi." He took one of her loose strands of hair, threading it through his fingers.

"Is it weird"—Celeste licked her lips—"um, seeing each other after the stuff . . ." She swallowed, and he didn't bother pretending he wasn't watching the movement of her throat. "After the stuff we were texting?"

If there was anything John hadn't expected this evening, it was this—*shy* Celeste. She'd been everything *but* shy in the past couple of days, texting him about how she'd touched herself thinking of him and about the way she planned to fuck him when they saw each other next.

Had her cheeks flushed a rosy pink like this as she typed out those messages? Or as she read the ones he wrote in response?

"It's not weird for me," he said. He'd enjoyed the opportunity to express himself to her, and had loved learning more about what she liked to do to herself. "But it doesn't mean anything has to happen today, if you're not feeling it."

"I'm definitely feeling it." Their eyes caught for a moment before she turned back to the worktable. "So, whatcha gonna teach me, John?"

He slid his arms around her, holding the chisel in one hand and grabbing a block of wood in the other. With the way they were sitting, he couldn't hide the effect she had on him.

"So," he choked out, "we'll just get you used to using this tool with some simple, basic cuts." He demonstrated a mortise cut and carved out a small sliver of wood. "Your turn."

She carved a few shaky lines into the wood, leaning forward eagerly to observe her work. "This is so cool," she said. "Maybe sometime you could help me make something? Like that cute birdhouse you gave me, or maybe something Morgan can take with her up to college."

"I'd love to." His eyes stayed on her hands as she turned the chisel over in her palm, rubbing her thumb along the smooth wooden handle.

She hummed and squirmed against him, trapping his now obvious erection between her tailbone and his abdomen, then chuckled as John inhaled sharply. She opened her mouth but closed it again, shaking her head.

He whispered into her ear. "Go ahead. You think I don't

know you've been dying to make wood jokes since the day we met? There's no way you can resist, given . . . everything."

"You mean"—she pushed into him again, earning a groan—"given all the wood in this shop right now?" She leaned her head back on John's shoulder. "It is hard to resist, now that I feel the wood you're working with."

Her position left her neck exposed for him, and he took advantage, running his nose just under her ear and reveling in her gasp. "I know that's not all you've got."

She sighed as he brushed his lips against her neck. "I had a lot stored up." Her voice was breathy. "About how good you must be at working your wood, and how I'd like to see if I could . . ." John swiped his tongue across her skin. Celeste moaned, giving him one of the sounds he craved from her, alive in the air of his shop. ". . . handle it. If I could handle your wood."

John stroked down her arms and covered Celeste's hands with his. Her clenched fists released the chisel, giving him space to massage her soft palms with his thumbs. "Is that it? I expected a longer list."

"I had a longer list." Celeste slipped her hands from his and raised her arms to entwine her fingers behind his neck. The view it created for John—the small rise of her breasts accentuated by her slightly arched back, her rapid breathing, and the spread of her legs where they pushed up against his own—was otherworldly. "I can't seem to remember any of them."

For a moment it was just their breathing and the soft sounds of the world outside the open door. The moment held the potential of a flock of starlings just before a murmuration, their energy about to be unlocked.

"John," she whispered. "Please."

He gripped her hips tight in his hands, pulling her against

him as he ground into her, breathing hard into her ear. Her answering moan urged him on, and soon his hands were on her thighs, fingers twisting in the hem of her dress, drawing it up.

"You can take it off." Her breathing was heavy. "Please. Take it. Off."

John lowered his mouth to the curve of her neck, grazing his teeth across her skin, then lifted the dress up, Celeste arching up off the bench to help. It was over her hips, then exposing her belly button, her ribs, her simple black bra, the ridge of her collarbone. She released her hands, stretching them overhead as he pulled the dress up and over her.

"Drop it." She sighed, interlacing her fingers behind his neck again. "It can get dirty. Just touch me again."

John abandoned the dress to the wood shavings on the floor, promising himself he'd get it later and send it through his dryer. But even as he planned it, his hands were back on her, tracing each line of her rib cage before covering her breasts with his hands, tracing her hard nipples through her bra. He dipped each hand into the fabric, seeking the warmth of the puckered skin, first brushing lightly with his thumbs before capturing each for a hard pinch.

He drew her bare earlobe into his mouth before grazing it with his teeth. "No earrings tonight?"

"Wanted you to be able to—" He closed his teeth on her again, drawing a gasp from her, then a small laugh. "Yep. That." She continued to move against him, pushing herself back into him in a slow rhythm. "In those texts, you said you wanted to hear me come. You gonna make that happen?"

"No." He reached for one of her hands and pulled it to her thigh. "You're going to make it happen."

"You want me to—" She turned to face him with the rose

blush back on her cheeks. But then she was spreading her legs wider, throwing them over his knees and hooking his calves with her ankles.

His hand stayed over hers as it moved across the dipping crease where the thigh ended, finally cupping her over her black underwear as they both moaned. He took their hands up and under her waistband.

Once there, Celeste wasted no time. A low groan vibrated through her throat as her middle finger cut through her curls.

"Jesus, Celeste." He scooted back to put a slice of air between them, afraid the slightest pressure would have him coming against her back.

As her finger moved, his did too, just a shadow over hers as she drew small circles over herself, then switched to long, slow strokes. He noted each movement and its reaction—how the circles made her shudder and the strokes made her sigh. All as her sounds grew more desperate, her breathing coming in a staccato beat of gasps.

"Help me." Her hips were moving against their hands now, her head thrown back on his shoulder.

"How?"

"Inside me. Fingers inside me?"

It was a question he was happy to answer, dipping his hand lower and sliding one, then two fingers inside Celeste. Her body welcomed him, luscious and tight, and she wasted no time in moving against his hand, taking what she needed.

Their hands bumped and knocked as she rode his fingers, arching her back and rocking her hips to get more of him. Beneath his wrist he felt her switch from long strokes against her clit to short flicks.

"Oh god." Her face turned into his neck. "Oh god, oh god."

John had lain awake at night wondering how Celeste sounded as she came. And now, her legs trembling over his as he curled the fingers inside her, his other hand holding tight to one of her nipples, he was finally making this discovery.

She was silent. Her needy moans and little pleas were subsumed by an intake of breath that held as she tightened around his fingers. It reminded John of leaping off a rock into a local swimming hole when he was younger—that sweet moment of suspension in the air when his body paused between up and down. He held Celeste there until she sighed and melted against him.

Slowing kissing her neck, John withdrew his hand, smoothing it across her stomach as he wrapped an arm around her waist. Outside, the evening sky had given way to the navy blue of early night, the shop now lit only by a single work lamp.

He was still hard behind her, but he wasn't in any hurry. They'd get there when they got there.

"Wow," she whispered, unhooking her ankles. "Thanks." After a moment, she stood on shaky legs, turning to stand between his thighs. She was a vision—face flushed, mouth open, with one long drip of sweat trailing down the valley between her breasts. One strap of her bra fell down her shoulder, exposing a hint of pink that made John's mouth water.

He forced his gaze back to her face. "You did the work."

"It was a team effort," she said with a smile. "I guess we're good at more than birding."

Celeste threaded her fingers through his hair, tugging just enough to tip his face up to hers. "Maybe we should see what else we're good at. You want to tell me where your bedroom is and give me a five-minute head start to freshen up a little?"

He pointed to the door that attached his workshop to the rest of the house, walking her through how to find the bathroom and his room.

When he stood, he left no space between them. Being this close to her without apology, without the nagging voice in his head that *they shouldn't*, was a liberation. He cupped her smiling cheek in his hand and lowered his mouth to hers, finally allowing them a kiss. It was slow and shallow to start, but then Celeste's fingers slipped beneath his T-shirt as her teeth scraped his bottom lip, and he pulled back before they got carried away. Not that he hadn't fantasized about bending her over in his woodshop, but definitely not for their first time together.

Hands on her shoulders, he pointed her toward the door. "I'm giving you five minutes and not a second longer."

CHAPTER 25

BIRD BINGE, DAY 27 OF 42

BIRD COUNT: 82

John had a glorious bed.

The decor of his room was as simple as Celeste expected—a few framed nature photos and a lot of books. Big windows with an unobstructed view of desert and sky, now dark and deep.

But his bed, yowza. It was the kind of four-poster wooden frame she'd dreamed about as a kid, except that every post was different. One was topped with a pineapple, though somewhat crudely carved. Another featured a smooth, polished knob. The third was a pine cone, which looked so realistic it could have come straight from the forest floor. And finally, a bird—small, with tucked-in wings and its head just barely cocked to the side. She couldn't ID it without colors, but the shape and size were all sparrow.

As her fingers rubbed at the ridges of feathers, Celeste realized she was about out of time for what she'd come in here to do, so she hurriedly unclipped her bra and pulled off her underwear, leaving them both on John's dresser. Pulling her hair out of her bun and combing through it with her fingers, Celeste took one look at her naked body in the mirror over John's dresser. Yes, she was forty-two, and her body showed both the ups and downs that came with midlife. Her lower abdomen was striped with stretch marks, and her ass wasn't as tight as it had been a decade before. But she was also stronger than she'd ever been, and feeling at home in her skin.

A skin John had seemed to take quite a liking to.

"Wow."

He filled the doorway, wearing just his shorts, staring at her blatantly. It was a bold look for such an unassuming man, but she was learning that this was John. Often quiet, but confident when it counted. And very, very competent.

The strong curve of his shoulders gave way to the expanse of his chest, covered in a brush of hair lighter and curlier than that on his head. Rather than narrowing at the waist, his body stayed wide, going straight down to his hips, where a little ridge of bone emerged above the fabric of his shorts.

"Wow yourself." She cleared her throat and walked to one corner of the bed, smoothing her hand over the rounded post. "This bed is incredible."

"Thank you." He closed the distance between them in a few strides.

Her throat tightened. "Did you make it?"

John nodded as he brought a hand to clasp the back of her neck. "Yes. The frame was simple enough, and I used the posts as a practice project. I'm happy to tell you all about it, but maybe not right now."

She laughed and wound her arms around his neck as their mouths met. Celeste explored John's bare chest, fingers sifting through the dusting of hair and trailing along his collarbone while one hand worked on unbuttoning his shorts. John pushed her hair aside to reach her neck with his mouth.

After kicking his shorts away, John eased Celeste onto the bed, coasting a hand up her thigh. He crawled over her and leaned down for a series of short, gentle kisses before rubbing his beard along her cheek. “This still good? You doing okay?”

“Yeah.” She sighed as his hand cupped one of her breasts, teasing her nipple lightly. “I’m really good. You?”

“Really good.” His words were spoken just above her nipple, which he then drew into his mouth, making her groan and buck beneath him. He bathed both tight nipples with attention until she was writhing under him.

He chuckled against her skin and rose to look at her. “I’ve been dreaming about having my mouth on you, going down on you. Would that be okay?”

She’d known this was coming. As their texts had grown more explicit, he’d said he wanted to *taste* her. The thought made her wet, had helped get her over the edge as she used her fingers and imagined his tongue, but now he really wanted to do it, and she . . . Well, she wasn’t sure.

John’s brows pulled together at her silence. “If you don’t want that, it’s okay. That’s why I asked.”

Celeste’s gaze hovered over his shoulder for a second as her hand idly brushed up and down his spine. She met his eyes again. “I don’t know,” she finally said. “The times Peter used to do it, I just had a hard time getting out of my head.” He’d had a way of acting like he was doing her a favor, and she was too busy trying to be grateful to ever really relax. “I always felt like I was supposed to react a certain way, and then I’d just sort of want it to end, so I’d . . . you know.”

John rolled to the side, leaning on his elbow. “Fake it?”

“Yeah,” she admitted. “And I think Peter could tell I wasn’t enthusiastic, so he gave up, and over time we just kind of stopped doing that."

John dropped a hand on her hip, stroking gently. "I get that. No pressure from me. I just want you to feel good."

"Do you think I'd like it, though?" She snaked one finger up his chest. "If you were the one doing it?"

His eyes darkened, all the intensity she'd seen him have out on the trail now focused on her. "I do think we have a knack for . . . discovery."

That word shouldn't have been so sexy, but it sent heat straight between her legs.

She'd let Peter hold her back from enough discovery over the years.

"I want to try again. I want to try with you."

His eyebrows lifted, and so did his smile. "You sure?"

"Yes." She nodded, getting more excited by the second. "I just might not come, and I don't want you to feel bad about that."

The hand he'd been resting on her hip moved down, slipping between her legs. She'd enjoyed touching herself for him in his woodshop, but finally feeling his finger on the tingling nub of her clit was ecstasy. She bit her lip and groaned, rolling her hips into him.

He slid his middle finger up and down long and slow, just like she'd done earlier, then drew small, tight circles on her. "Think I can make you come like this?"

"Definitely." And it wouldn't take long.

He lifted his fingers and gave her a long slow kiss, then rolled her to her back and settled his mouth near her ear. "So we have a backup plan."

Celeste laughed and shoved at his shoulder as John rubbed his chin on her neck and jaw before pushing up to look at her.

"You're going to feel my beard on your thighs, and my lips on your skin, and then I'm going to spread you open with my fingers and put my mouth on you. Okay?"

She nodded wordlessly, stunned and turned on by his easy rapport. He was as straightforward about oral sex as he was about identifying a bird, and it was oddly hot. He placed a kiss on her shoulder. "I'm counting on your feedback. Anything you're not loving, just tap my shoulder. And anything you like, tug on my hair. Okay?"

She nodded again. "Okay."

John smiled before starting the journey down her body, stopping to draw one nipple and then another back into his mouth. This time, he used his teeth, nipping at her until she was breathing hard and threading her hands through his hair. Then he was giving a slow kiss to her belly button before scraping his teeth over her hip bone.

Her hands went to her breasts, teasing them, keeping her touch light.

John looked up and gave her a little hum of approval. "You doing okay?"

Her lids were heavy, and she smiled. "I'm good. I like . . . watching you."

He stretched out for a pillow, which he bent in half, then slid under her hips. She was clearly in the hands of an expert.

He glanced back to her. "Keep watching."

Never taking his eyes from hers, John put his hands gently on Celeste's knees and pushed them apart. "Remember the system."

He bent low over her and rubbed his beard against her inner thigh. She groaned and gripped his hair, giving a hard tug. He answered with his teeth on her skin, biting her gently before tracing the same spot with his tongue.

John used his thumbs to dip into the soft brown curls between her legs and open her up for him. She started to tense, but before she could get too far into her head, he put his mouth on her for a long, slow kiss, using his lips and tongue just as he had on her mouth. He moved slowly and deliberately, like he was savoring his first taste of her.

He came up gasping. "Christ, you taste amazing. You're like earth and air. Something elemental."

He lowered his head and kissed her again, harder this time. Then he slowed, tracing his tongue along the edges of her, flicking at her opened lips. It felt . . . interesting, but she started picturing her anatomy and what exactly he was—

She tapped his shoulder.

He looked up with a smile. "Good, yes, just like that, Celeste. I'm listening."

He returned to his work, sliding his tongue lower, so that it teased her entrance. She tapped again.

Undeterred, he drew back his mouth and released a long, hot breath, blowing right over her clit.

She gave his hair a hard tug.

He laughed against her, making her yelp and squirm. "You like that, huh?" He kissed her inner thighs as he spoke.

Then he returned his mouth to her, giving her a long, slow lick, dipping past her entrance but continuing until he reached her begging clit, where he swirled his tongue in a small circle.

He closed his lips around her clit and sucked, moving his tongue against her as he did. She bucked in his mouth and both of her hands were in his hair, pulling. It was soft and hard all at once, a sensation she couldn't find words for, just gasps and whimpers.

He worked her some more, switching the direction of his

tongue and changing the pressure of his lips. She couldn't tell exactly what he was doing or where, but it felt amazing. Hot and warm and wet and safe.

Tug, tug, tug.

But then John's mouth was gone, and he was shifting up, smiling down at her, his cock brushing against her thigh through his boxers.

"Why did you stop?" She didn't disguise the shaky need in her voice. "You were doing really, really well."

He smiled. "I'll keep going in just a second." He caressed her cheek. "But we need to be clear on something first. Do you know how many birdcalls I have stored up in this lockbox?" He tapped at his head.

She shook her head with a laugh. "A lot?"

"Hundreds. And you know what other sounds are stored up there now?"

She only looked at him with a smirk and shook her head, wanting to hear him say it.

"The sounds you make when you come." He bent closer to her. "I know them now." He tapped his head again. "I know the way you breathe when you're close, the way you whimper, and the gorgeous throaty moans you let out when you're almost there. And I know that when you come, you're silent, just gasping for air as your body rides it out."

She grasped his neck and pulled his mouth to hers. She tasted herself on his tongue, and it *was* elemental, even beautiful somehow. She licked her tongue all around the edge of his lips.

John drew back and looked at her seriously. "So no faking, okay? It won't work anyway, because I know your sounds. I'll go as long as you want, or I'll stop anytime and get you there another way."

"I promise," Celeste whispered. "No faking."

He gave her one more kiss before moving back into position and setting his mouth to her with fervor and confidence. Earlier he had created a map of her pleasure, and he was following it now with his tongue. Lick, twirl, suck, lick, twirl, suck, over and over again until her brain was only *yes* and *fuck* and *so good*.

He sucked on her hard, groaning into her body, the vibrations from his mouth going right to her hot, needy center.

Everything was alive in her, climbing toward the same destination. Her hands left his hair and gripped the blanket beneath her as his tongue moved relentlessly, settling into the pattern that was bringing her higher and higher, the fierce pleasure pulsing from her clit all over her body, building up the charge. She was almost there.

Almost there, but then her thoughts flooded in. She was pushing too hard against his mouth, thrashing too much, being too loud. Too shameless, too needy. She bit her lip and held her breath, trying hard to push the thoughts aside.

John's hands found hers where they gripped the blanket, easing out her fists, entwining his fingers with hers. His tongue moved hard against her even as his thumbs stroked gently against her knuckles, soothing her.

She slowed her breathing, letting herself feel his hands around her, his thumb rubbing in the rhythm he was setting with his tongue. The burning edge returned, climbing again, just within reach.

She'd never come on a man's mouth, but she could now, she *would* now, if she let herself.

Say yes.

And she let go. He sucked hard on her once more and her body filled with light, blinding and sharp, throwing spots across her vision. She arched and gasped, mouth open, body rocking. His hands held her steady, his mouth never breaking contact as she hit her peak.

Then he was bathing her inner thigh in slow, sweet kisses, pulling her back to earth.

But she wasn't ready to land.

"More." She let go of his hands, reaching for her own breasts. "More."

John groaned against her thigh and lifted himself enough to look at her. "That's a word I like to hear. Tell me what you want."

"Your mouth." She panted, squeezing her nipples, keeping her climax near the surface, just barely dipping down from her peak. "And your hands, together."

Before she could worry about whether she'd asked for too much, John bent back down and blew a hot breath where two of his fingers were entering her slowly. The slightest touch from him had her moaning, and when his fingers inside of her curled, he pulled more sounds from her.

She was barely down from coming the first time and climbing back up fast.

"Yes, so good," she moaned. She loved knowing how her words egged him on, how much he craved her feedback. His mouth sucked at her, his tongue twirling as his fingers curled onto her G-spot, and she was almost there again, shaking beneath his mouth.

And when she got there, it was more than the moment of John's fingers and mouth playing her perfectly. It was the release of years of accepting *good enough* and *just fine* when she wanted *more*. It was the freedom of spreading her legs and asking for just what she wanted. It was the power of turning *too much* into *perfectly right*.

She hovered in that mindless state, blissed out and slack, as John slipped the pillow from under her hips, placing kisses along her lower abdomen and rib cage, then her neck.

"Celeste." His voice brought her back to earth. "Are you okay? You're . . ."

She opened her eyes to John at last. His brow was tight and wrinkled, his lip worried between his teeth.

"You're crying," he continued.

Her hand shot to her cheek, which was wet, with tears still flowing.

"Oh god." She covered her face, turning away from John, horrified. What a way to thank a man for two mind-blowing orgasms. She had no way to explain herself, except that giving herself up so fully had been phenomenal. Healing and comforting in a way she hadn't experienced sex in a very long time. Tears welled out of her eyes and dripped down her cheeks.

"I'm sorry. I don't know what's wrong with me. That was so amazing. I guess it was a little overwhelming." She curled into a ball. "I'm so embarrassed."

"Hey." His hand ran down her back, then his weight shifted and a blanket was folded over her. He curled around her from behind, the blanket now between their bodies. "I'm honored." He placed a small kiss on her earlobe. "And for the record, Peter was an idiot if he couldn't recognize when his wife was faking an orgasm. He should have been paying more attention. It's a gift to see you like that."

A gift. John said these things so simply, like he was pointing out an ash-throated flycatcher on a tree branch.

She stretched out beneath the covers. "That was a very nice discovery. Give me a few minutes to recover and I'll repay the favor."

"No rush." She felt him settle his head on the pillow behind her. An arm wrapped tight around her body. "Can you stay the night?"

"Mmm." Celeste rubbed her cheek against his hand, the borders of her thoughts going fuzzy. Sleeping in John's glorious bed sounded absolutely delicious, but they had more to do first. "I'm not going to sleep now, though. Just taking a break."

"Just in case, should I set an alarm for the morning? It's a school night."

She shook her head slowly back and forth. His pillows were nice. *He* was nice. "I wake up with the sun. Not going to sleep, though."

The last thing she heard was John's low laugh.

CHAPTER 26

BIRD BINGE, DAY 28 OF 42
BIRD COUNT: 82

The trilling song of a curve-billed thrasher wound through the cracked window of John's bathroom as he shut off the water and grabbed a towel. Goose bumps covered his skin, a by-product of the cold shower he'd taken as an alternative to waking a sprawled and sleeping Celeste with his roving hands.

She'd given him so much the night before—her trust, her vulnerability, her sounds and taste. So his plan was to tiptoe through his bedroom to the kitchen, where he'd brew her a strong cup of coffee before she woke and headed out to teach for the day. And hope they could get together soon to continue their explorations.

He opened the bathroom door quietly, careful not to wake her.

The mattress still held her imprint, and the sheets were bundled at the foot of the bed, but the lithe, naked woman who'd been there when he slipped into the shower was markedly absent. He hadn't expected anything grand this morning, but he would have loved to give her a cup of coffee.

John whipped his towel off with a sigh, tossing it over the pineapple-topped bedpost Celeste had admired the night before.

"Well." Celeste's voice came from behind him. He turned to see her leaning into the doorway of his bedroom, the hem of a yellow T-shirt landing at the tops of her thighs. "Good morning to me." Her eyes roamed up his body, slowing as she perused below his waist. But when she reached his face, her brows tightened. "What's wrong?"

She stepped fully into the room, glancing at the bed, then at John. "Did you think I left?"

He reached for his towel rather than deny it.

"Come on, John, give me more credit than that."

He shrugged, chest opening with relief. "I haven't done casual before, and I didn't know—"

She was right in front of him now. "We can be casual and kind at the same time, right?" A finger snaked down his chest, to the towel he was fumbling to wrap back around his waist. "You were *very* kind to me last night." She tugged, sending the towel to the floor.

Her hands flattened against his chest, then rubbed around to his back, then his ass, where she gripped firmly, humming. "I just went to the other bathroom to freshen up. I brought this shirt over to wear just for you."

The shirt was butter yellow, with a simple sketch of a dove in the middle, and the words *Don't Talk to Me, I'm Birding* arched across the top.

"Very nice." He stepped close again, curling a hand around her thigh and sliding up, finding her bare hip.

With a hand around his neck, Celeste pulled his face to hers, wasting no time before drawing his bottom lip between her teeth. Her hand wrapped tight around his erection, and the kiss went deeper, harder. John groaned into her mouth as her hand, as confident and greedy as he'd known it would be, pulled him with the perfect amount of pressure.

"Do you need to go to work?" The words were mumbled

against her mouth, and she took them with her tongue, returning them in a long sigh.

"No, I don't."

"But it's—"

Friday. And Celeste was dropping to her knees, her face turned up in a smile. "I called in sick."

"Oh."

Her hand was still on him as her lips opened, tongue slipping out to brush his cock. After one long, hot lick, she sat back on her heels, her eyes on him like shafts of hot sun. "I'd like to taste *you* now, John, if that's okay."

He nodded mutely, vaguely aware of a ruckus of birdsong just outside his open bedroom window. Celeste glanced up as she scraped her nails along his thighs. "Tell me what you hear."

Her hand found his cock again, so his word came out a choked half groan. "Wha—"

She loosened her hold. "I want you to hold my hair and tell me about the birds you hear while I suck you."

"Celeste, Christ." He ached with need, wishing she'd squeeze him tighter, desperate for the wetness of her mouth. One hand twisted into her hair, pulling it into a ponytail in his fist. "I can't think about birds right now."

"Please." She licked him once, flattening her tongue along his length. "Your brain turns me on."

His laugh stopped in his throat as her lips closed on him, running up and down. He was lost in sensation—heat and moisture, the pull of her lips and the tangle of her tongue. And then it was gone.

"The birds, John."

He tugged her hair just enough to tilt her face to his. "You can't be serious."

Her eyebrows arched, lips turned up mischievously. "You bet your nice wood I'm serious."

After a hard swallow, John began to speak. He told her about the sparrows chattering in the jojoba bush outside as Celeste took him fully in her mouth, moaning around him. He groaned out the names of others—the phainopepla seeking a mate, a Lucy's warbler singing brightly, a house finch begging its parents for food—as Celeste gripped the base of his cock tightly, teasing the head with her tongue until he was shuddering, pulling tight on her hair. This only seemed to encourage her, and when she leaned in, tugging him all the way into her throat, John's brain went white, the engulfing heat of her mouth short-circuiting the last bit of his rational thought.

When she released him, Celeste chuckled, gazing up with hooded eyes and wet, swollen lips. "Lost your train of thought?"

She opened her mouth to take him again, but John pulled her up and whipped off her birding T-shirt. They met in a hungry kiss as he gripped her hips and walked them to the bed. When her thighs hit the mattress she lifted herself up, pulling him down to her and wrapping her legs around his hips.

"We still doing good?" His voice was all sandpaper.

She nodded, biting her lower lip. "Still really good."

"And you feel okay not using a condom?"

After they'd broken the sex ice with their texts, Celeste had emailed him her latest STI testing results and he'd reciprocated, grateful he'd gone in after his breakup with Breena, just in case. Then Celeste had texted him that she had an IUD and—through a series of creative and increasingly lewd emojis—suggested they could forgo condoms if they were both comfortable doing so.

"I definitely feel okay about that if you do." Her fingers scraped down his back and cupped his ass, pulling tight against her so that they rocked together. "Fuck," she groaned. "John, please."

He backed his hips up, bringing the tip of his erection right where he wanted it. Her body welcomed him, hot and soft and wet. John entered her slowly, letting out a long, slow breath to steady himself.

He settled deep inside her, then pushed a little more, groaning. "Oh shit."

Celeste gave a light laugh under him. "I love making you use bad words."

She rotated her hips, a smirk on her face as her body closed around him like a glove, tight around his cock as he pulled back slowly, almost all the way, and moved back into her with the same deliberate speed. She bit her lower lip and groaned, the smirk on her lips sliding into something needier, until her mouth was covered with his as he kissed her, slow and deep like his thrusts.

When they both came up for air she smiled against his mouth. The feel of her upturned lips against his was a sensation John wanted to feel again and again.

"God," she sighed. "Sex is good. It's been a while."

He chuckled against her mouth, sliding into her again, holding himself up with one arm while a hand traced the curve of her jaw. "For me too." A deep moan rumbled in his throat. "Worth the wait."

Celeste's body, curving into him with every slow thrust, spoke to the animal in him, the one that had been observing this woman for weeks as she took up more and more of his sexual imagination. He bent low again to sweep his tongue across her pulse point, measuring her excitement.

Celeste yanked him closer, pulling him into her as her hips

moved greedily beneath him. But he kept his pace. When she gave a frustrated sigh, he pulled back to look at her pouting lips.

The pinch of her eyebrows made him laugh, which only made her lips pucker more. "You'd better not be laughing at me during sex." Her lips quivered like she was holding back a smile of her own.

John shook his head, running his hand across her mouth to dip a finger between her lips, where her tongue deftly swirled around his knuckle. He shuddered and pulled out of her again, pausing when their bodies were just barely joined. She whimpered and pulled at him, but he stayed put and laid a kiss on her forehead. "I wondered if you'd do this like you do everything else."

"Which is?"

"Eagerly," he said, driving into her again, a little harder this time. "Enthusiastically." She writhed under him, and he put his mouth near her ear, pausing to bite her earlobe. "You feel so good." But he kept his movements slow, pulled all the way out of her after each thrust, as he felt her body grow more restless under him.

"John," she growled, "I need—"

"I know," he assured her. "I can tell you won't hold anything back. But let's start my way."

"What's your way?"

The fingers of one hand traced along the ridge of her hip, then pressed her hip firmly into his bed to slow her movements. "What do you think?"

She squirmed beneath his grip, but smiled. "Hmm. Thorough?"

John scooped his arm under the curve of her knee, holding her even more open for him. Lines of bright sun slanted through the windows across her body.

He shifted, angling them across the bed. "Hold on to the post."

She stretched her arms up, her eyes gone molten. The position pulled the skin along her ribs taut and accentuated the rise of her breasts and tight, puckered nipples. Her fingers curled around the base of the bedpost, gripping the wood he'd spent hours crafting. God, it was worth the work if it gave him this moment.

He set a steady rhythm, slow enough to give his body the time it needed to learn about hers, time to settle deep into her with each thrust, to feel how each adjustment of his hips brought them both closer to falling over and apart together.

He explored her gently, one hand skimming over her hard nipples until she was whimpering again and rotating her hips against his. He closed his eyes and bit his lip hard, holding on to his control.

"You ready to come?" John choked out as he settled deep into her again.

"Always ready," she gasped.

"I want to watch you. Will you show me again?"

Her hand slipped into the tight space between their bodies as John's hungry eyes followed their path. She was stunning, with one hand gripping the bedpost and the other taking herself to the edge.

"Yes, Celeste. Fuck." She shuddered under him when he spoke. "Make yourself come for me."

Her hand moved fast between them, and he lifted to give her space, to watch her fingers slide against her slick clit, hard with arousal, the same dusky pink color as her nipples. He already couldn't wait to get her in his mouth again.

His speed picked up, and he cried out when her fingers brushed the sides of his cock as he slid in and out of her. She pressed at herself with the heel of her hand, freeing her fingers to caress him with each thrust as her breathing came in shallow bursts. His fingers found one of her nipples, squeezing just hard enough to draw out a long, throaty moan.

Her orgasm pulsed tight around him as her jaw dropped open in a silent scream. He pushed deep inside her and took a long, steadying breath as she rode it out.

Then she uttered the word that was quickly becoming his very favorite.

"More."

She let go of the post, gripping John's neck and pulling him down for a hard kiss. When she let go she was breathing fast. "My way now. I want you behind me."

He groaned, pulling out quickly. She flipped onto her stomach and angled her ass toward him, her forearms flat on his mattress, as she turned her head to watch him with intensity.

She was so beautiful in her boldness, so sexy in her need. He stroked himself, still wet from her, as he let himself take in the view.

She pouted out her lower lip. "I believe I was promised a hard fuck."

He laughed and gripped her waist, alive with the discovery that sex could be as fun as it was mind-blowing. Celeste's jaw dropped open as he entered her again. Holy hell, she felt amazing.

"You good?" he ground out, moving slowly.

She nodded and dropped her head to her forearms. "I'm so good." She sighed. "You don't have to be gentle with me."

His hand on her back followed the path of her spine, slipping over her neck before fisting her hair in a strong grip. "I know."

The sound she made next—a moaning laugh, her pleasure clear in all its forms—detonated in John's chest, and he thrust hard. "Tell me if it's too much."

She pushed herself back against him, moaning. "I promise, John. I'll tell you."

John gave her hair one more tug before holding tight to her hips, pulling her to him, thrusting into her all the way. She yelped and ground her hips against him, urging him on, until the room was filled with the sounds of their unified breathing and the slap of skin.

He moved a hand around her waist, slipping it down between her legs, but she batted his hand away. "Just wanna feel you," she gasped. "No distractions."

He gripped her hip and let go of all restraint, trusting Celeste would tell him if it was too much. But as she moaned and arched her back into him, he knew she could take it. Then he was lost, thrusting hard, each sharp intake of her breath getting him closer, until his orgasm rocketed through him.

Celeste purred as she ground her hips back, prolonging his release and pulling a long moan from his throat. He kept his hips flush with her ass as his fingers sought out the spot to make her come. She sighed and groaned and squirmed against him, panting into the mattress until she was muttering his name again and again and shaking around him.

With a long sigh, Celeste pulled away from him and collapsed onto her stomach, a lazy grin on her face. John laid kisses along her spine before lowering himself with satisfaction beside her.

After a moment, she propped herself up, smiling at him. "You're good at sex."

He laughed as he brushed a stray hair off her face. "You're not so bad yourself."

Lines of sunlight fell across her neck as she smiled. "Any chance you can take the day off with me?"

"Happy to. That's a real perk of being unemployed."

Celeste smoothed a hand across his chest. "You're not unemployed. You're self-employed. And soon to be even more so. But if you want, today we could play hooky from everything else and do some birding." Her grin went silly. "And some other stuff."

His mouth met hers for a slow, relaxed kiss, one that spoke of an entire day with nothing on the agenda but two of his favorite activities. Especially when he was doing them with her.

"A day of birding and other stuff sounds absolutely perfect."

CHAPTER 27

BIRD BINGE, DAY 33 OF 42
BIRD COUNT: 101

"Think very carefully before you answer, John. There's a lot hanging in the balance." Chris smirked at Celeste, his blond hair glinting in the sunlight, before returning his attention to the trail. Celeste laughed, hitching her pack higher on her shoulders.

"He doesn't need to think carefully." She turned and gave John a wink. "The answer is obvious."

Behind her, John smiled as he met the brisk pace Chris was setting. They were all skidding down a steep incline on the gravelly trail, descending from a flat patch of desert into a lush riparian ciénega bordered by billowing willows whose branches swayed slowly in the early evening air.

Bounding down the last few feet, Celeste landed in the sandy wash bed that would lead them to the shallow, shaded creek, just dribbling with water in early May. She knelt, swinging her pack to the front to pull out her water bottle. John joined her, squatting so close that his knee brushed against hers.

The simple contact sent a jolt right through Celeste's body, and she knew by the twitch of John's mouth that it did the same to him. They'd been birding with benefits for just a few days, but they'd squeezed in as much alone time as they could. If she had to walk away from their arrangement when the contest ended in nine days—and she definitely did, as she'd reminded herself in the mirror just that morning—she was going to wring all the great sex out of the remaining time that she could.

Which was why she'd set her alarm that morning to arrive at John's house before work. They'd planned to make coffee and go for a short birding walk, but had somehow ended up in his bedroom instead. He'd scandalized Celeste by positioning himself under her, urging her to ride his face before he pulled her body down to slide inside her. He'd even used some bad words.

Celeste took a long swig of water and looked up to find John's eyes focused on her throat. Later, when they were alone, he would whisper to her about this moment—how her shorts showed off the muscles of her thighs, or how the little trickle of sweat dripping down the side of her neck made him hungry for her. He was always making these observations and tucking them away, only to feed them back to her generously as his hands showered her with attention.

"So, John, what's your final answer?" Chris was putting away his own water, taking his next few steps down the trail that would get them to the creek. "Would I have been as good at the birding stuff as Celeste has turned out to be? If you had to really choose between us—just for the contest, of course—who would it be?"

John just shook his head and stood, brushing off his thighs. "You dropped out, Chris. So it's really no choice at all." He started down the trail as Chris sighed, waving a hand in the air. Even for hiking, Chris wore a Black Sabbath T-shirt with a rip down the back that let some of his ink peek out, but he was in running shorts instead of the usual skinny jeans Celeste had seen him in before.

"But if I hadn't dropped out, I'd be as good as Celeste, right? I'm a wildlife biologist, for crying out loud, even if I do focus on mollusks." He looked at Celeste as he blew a raspberry. "I mean, I know I introduced you to Celeste, and I continue to take total credit for that, but I didn't know she'd be some kind of birding prodigy. Now I'm just jealous. You were supposed to end up with a partner that was fine, but not as good as me."

Celeste caught up to Chris and gave him a pat on the back. "Sorry, dude, I'm just the best. Aren't I, John?"

"Not answering!" he called back. Celeste and Chris giggled as they trudged through the wash until they reached the shade of the willows. The wide streambed was green with moss, the narrow belt of water trickling slowly between gray rocks. Chris had been asking to come along on one of their birding outings, and she was happy that he could join them. He had a special way of radiating good cheer, even as he complained about the trials of academia or pouted about being jealous of Celeste. And his presence kept them focused on adding to their bird count instead of getting distracted.

Not that getting distracted with John wasn't a treat in itself. But they still had a contest to win. And their numbers were going up slowly. They'd seen almost all the easy birds, which John assured her everyone would have on their list. Now every outing was with fingers crossed that they would spot something rare—a migrating bird that had never left, a bird slightly out of range, or something more skittish around people. This evening they were hoping to spot a yellow-billed cuckoo, a threatened species that was usually seen only in tiny swaths throughout the region.

"You know"—Chris looked at her meaningfully, blue eyes bright—"the cuckoo is known for laying its eggs in the nests of other birds, but in reality most cuckoos do raise their own young."

Celeste raised her eyebrows. "Studying up, huh? It's almost like somebody wants to impress his bird guide. I'm gonna take a wild guess and say you were always the kid sitting in the front row, always turning in the extra credit?"

John turned back to them with a nod. "Definitely."

"What can I say, I like to shine." Chris jogged a few steps to catch up to John, who was keeping a steady pace on the small trail even as his eyes stayed up, scanning the trees. Chris leaned in and said something to him quietly, making John laugh.

In their times out birding, she and John had run into other birders he knew, and he was always kind and friendly. But he had a different ease with Chris, who had a clear, gentle affection for John that she didn't often see expressed between men. On paper, the two of them would seem to be opposites—Chris was vibrant and exuberant, craving attention and affirmation, while John was quiet and contemplative, sharing words only when necessary. But together, they worked.

She supposed that, on paper, she and John weren't a great match either. She was loud where he was quiet, an open book where he was private. And yet when they were together—on the trail, reading on his couch, or in bed—there was an easy fit, like that satisfying click when a puzzle piece snapped into the right spot.

The thought tightened her throat. Puzzle pieces stayed in one place. They didn't grow, they didn't change, they didn't get to move around the puzzle to see what the other side of the table was like. She'd snapped herself into place years ago and was just now wiggling free.

So why was she so tempted to take this small bubble she and John had together and blow more life into it, to see if it might stretch beyond the parameters they'd set?

It might not feel like it now, but she'd be ready to walk away when the whole thing was over. The final awards banquet of the contest was the same night as Morgan's art show, so the timing was perfect to draw her focus back to where it belonged. Anytime Celeste tried to push her daughter to follow through with her college paperwork—or tried to talk to her about anything at all lately—Morgan simply begged off, claiming she needed to work on her gallery pieces or darting out the door to meet Em. After the show, Celeste could help get her back on track. Plan out their summer together and prepare for Morgan to leave the nest.

She wouldn't have time to miss John anyway.

John turned back toward her, his mouth curving in a smile as Chris talked. When she caught up to them, John leaned into her ear.

"You good?"

Celeste had been caught up in the what-ifs and what-could-bes instead of being there, in the subtle evening light under a swaying willow, looking for a bird.

She nodded as John cocked his head to one side. He closed his eyes, then grabbed Chris's forearm. "I hear it. Up in the branches—" His body spun, until he was facing a section of trees farther down the trail. "Over there."

Chris bounced on the balls of his feet, biting his lower lip. "I'm on it. I have *so* got this." He shot Celeste a look, narrowing his eyes as his mouth kicked into a grin. "Let's see who the super birder is now, eh?"

Celeste laughed as Chris bounded down the trail, but John's

hands on her waist made her gasp. He guided her until her back hit the trunk of a tree, and then his mouth was on hers, tongue gliding along her lower lip. She opened to him without question, grasping the back of his neck to keep him in place, urging the kiss to go deeper by releasing a moan into his mouth.

When they both came up for air, John leaned his forehead against hers, smiling. "Hey."

Celeste hummed and ran her fingers through his beard. If anything could pull her brain and body into the present, it was kissing John. It was impossible not to be present under the force of his attention and touch.

"Hey yourself." Celeste cleared her throat and looked in the direction Chris had gone. "Did you tell him you heard the bird to get us some privacy?"

John laughed and shook his head. "No, I actually heard it."

Celeste pushed herself off the tree, brushing past John before turning back to him. "Seriously? Then what are we kissing for? We've got to go see it!"

John shrugged. "I thought we could give him a minute to try on his own. Finding that bird will really make his day."

Celeste took a fistful of his shirt, pulling him close to her. "John Maguire. You are such a softy, you know that?"

His eyes darkened as he ran his index finger down her neck. "I'm not always soft. Especially with you."

She slapped his chest, gasping. "Did you just make an erection joke?"

John's lips tilted up as he gently turned her, heading them both down the trail. "You must be a bad influence."

She looped an arm through his, leaning into his shoulder. "No, I am the best influence. I'm so proud right now. I'm gonna put it in my calendar—'John's first erection joke.'" She bumped her shoulder into his. "And since we're alone, this would be a good time to tell me I'm a better birding partner than Chris could ever be."

John smiled as he drew his lips tight, shaking his head. "Not saying a word."

"How about the next time you rub your beard, it means I win. That I'm better than Chris."

"I rub my beard all the time."

"So it's the perfect signal. He'll never know what you're doing. If you'll just throw me a bone"—she giggled after the word—"I'll make it worth your while later. Otherwise, who knows, I might have a headache."

John stopped, pulling Celeste to a halt with him. He reached a hand up, her body shooting to high alert anticipating where his touch might land. But he only touched her with his gaze, hot on her skin where her heartbeat was kicking up in her throat.

His laugh sent shivers across her neck. "A headache, huh?" Just as her legs turned to jelly, John stepped into her body. His mouth brushed hers lightly on the way to her ear, where his whisper was full of gravel.

"You make a better partner than he could. Your enthusiasm is tempered by just the right amount of patience and perseverance." He backed up and rubbed his nose across hers, nipping at her mouth. "Don't you dare say a word to him."

And somehow, bragging to Chris was suddenly the last thing on her mind. "I promise, your secret is safe with me."

Chris came running into view, windmilling his arms and pointing behind him. "The bird," he wheezed. "Oh my god, I saw the fucking bird. I am such a master."

Celeste stepped away from John, pulling out the blue notebook where she kept her list. This was a bird she had to see, and putting a little distance between her and John wouldn't hurt either. Space to remind her that she'd be just fine in nine days.

She stuck her pencil in her mouth and jogged to Chris, giving him a strong pat on the back. "What are you waiting for, master? Show us the fucking bird."

CHAPTER 28

BIRD BINGE, DAY 36 OF 42
BIRD COUNT: 107

Surrounded by the gnarled alligator junipers and soaring white-barked sycamores of the Santa Rita Mountains, John tipped his face toward the sun. When he was a kid, his family had treated these mountains as their personal playground, and being here now with Celeste infused the familiar place with a renewed sense of discovery.

The Santa Ritas, just within the range of the contest, included one of the most diverse birding regions in the world. With Morgan at her dad's house, Celeste and John had taken to the mountains in a mad dash for more birds and a night under the stars.

They'd been exploring the casual—and temporary—parameters of their relationship for the past two weeks, but despite their insistence on the label, things didn't feel casual. The demands of Celeste's life meant John still had plenty of the alone time he craved, yet her toothbrush no longer made its way back into her overnight bag. The night before they'd simply curled up and slept together, fully clothed, after an exhausting day. Texts that started out either as birding plans or midday sexts turned into daily check-ins and quick chats. Celeste had become much more than a bird-watching partner and casual sex buddy—she was his friend.

He didn't know what would happen a week from now. Would they cut off contact altogether? Simply stop with the sex? Would they naturally separate without the bird-watching contest holding them together?

More questions than answers rattled around his head, but voicing them now would spoil their weekend, and he wouldn't squander two days in one of his favorite places on earth. Not when Celeste bounced eagerly on her heels, ready to head out on the trail. And not when he'd have her with him in the tent all night—touching her body in the darkness, testing her limits of keeping quiet with only nylon between them and other campers.

"Obviously my goal today is the trogon." Celeste spoke through the pencil nub held between her teeth, her eyes darting across the pages in her worn notebook. "But I also really want to see the painted redstart, the Montezuma quail, the hairy woodpecker . . ."

A familiar voice caught his attention from behind.

"John Maguire, I should have known I'd see you here."

John didn't have to turn to know the voice belonged to Daniel Winters, one of the most sought-after pro guides in the region. Dan and John had birded together years before, but whereas John had pursued stable office work, Dan had thrown himself full-on into the world of birding. He funded his travels around the world through his nature photography, showing up at conferences and expos as he built a reputation for being both gregarious and brilliant. He'd coauthored one of the authoritative texts on birding in the Southwest. The last John had heard, Dan was working on updates for the next edition.

Breena had always compared John to the Dans of the world—accomplished, acknowledged, showered with honors and respect.

While Dan had redefined bird guiding in their region, John had been fiddling with pieces of wood and spreadsheet formulas.

John mustered a smile and waved at the man, who was laden with binoculars, a camera around his neck, and a thousand-dollar scope in one hand. “Dan, nice to see you.”

“Always great to see you, John.” Dan’s eyes moved to Celeste, who’d looked up from her notebook. “Ah, this must be your new partner. I heard all about her from Linda the other day. Dan Winter.”

Celeste tucked her pencil behind one ear to shake Dan’s hand. “Are you birding in the contest, too?”

He shook his head and laughed. “Oh no, I haven’t participated in that for years. Can’t seem to find the time.”

“Dan is a guide,” John clarified for her. “He’s usually booked months in advance.”

“I’m actually scheduling over a year out now.” Dan beamed. “And trying to finish up edits on the next book and keep up enough of a speaking schedule to stay relevant, you know? But I do miss those days.” He lifted his cap and ran a hand through his short-cropped gray hair. “Say, John, you’d talked about doing some guiding yourself, isn’t that right?”

“Well, eventually.” John shrugged. “I haven’t really—”

“After the contest ends,” Celeste interrupted. “When we win, that will be his jumping-off point.”

“Oh, very strategic, I like it.” Dan nodded, focused on Celeste. “Use that burst of attention to get going. The magazine feature for the winner could really plug the business.”

“Exactly!” Celeste pointed at Dan, smiling. “He needs a website, and he’s still rusty at social media, but I think we’ll get there. John’s ready to make a splash on the local scene.”

This was the Celeste from the park the other week, going on about Instagram as John failed to keep up. He gripped the back of his neck, squeezing tense muscles as Celeste and Dan ping-ponged opinions about his future between them. She talked like his business was a foregone conclusion, with her as conductor of all the things he needed to do.

"The ideas he has are out of this world." Celeste huddled with Dan. "I think this backyard birding thing is really going to take off. I will never look at my yard in the same way again."

"Linda and I have been talking for years about how John could be doing more, really making his mark on the field. I'm excited he's finally moving on it."

"You are *so right* about how much more he could be doing. If he just puts his mind to it, after the contest there's going to be no stopping him."

John's free hand curled the thick pages of his guidebook into a spiral.

"Linda went on and on about you, Celeste," Dan continued. "And now I see why. I think you're just what John needs."

Celeste's laugh was breezy. "Well, I don't know about that. But I do have some ideas about how he can—"

John's ears went fuzzy as an American redstart preened on a branch above them. He should alert Celeste, let her make an ID and scribble it in her poetic mess of a notebook, but she was deep in conversation with Dan.

Since coming together with Celeste in that closet, he'd felt at home in his skin, spending his time just as he wanted—birding, woodworking, and treasuring Celeste's sweet, responsive body with his hands and mouth. Meanwhile, she'd been laying plans for him. For all the ways he could be different.

He needed space and air. The simplicity of looking for birds.

John grabbed his pack and threw it over one arm. "I'm going to head out," he said loudly, motioning to the trailhead that weaved through oaks and junipers from the campsite. "I'll wait for you where the trail meets the streambed."

Celeste's face crinkled as she looked to Dan, then to John again. "Oh. I'll—okay. I need to gather my stuff, but I'll catch up."

"Fine." He was already halfway to the trailhead, nodding a goodbye as he passed Dan. "Nice to see you, Dan. Best of luck."

"Right, same to you." John didn't miss the questioning glance Dan sent to Celeste, but he looked away before he could see her response. He'd taken about as much of their conspiring as he could.

Instead, he focused on the crunch of twigs beneath his boots, the squawking cries of scrub jays in the treetops, and the trail before him, promising solitude.

He enjoyed about two minutes of quiet before Celeste crashed down the path behind him. "Wait up," she called, gasping. "Jesus, John."

He closed his eyes for a breath, coming to a stop and reaching for his binoculars. "We could stop and look around here."

"Hold up." Celeste pushed his binoculars back down, inserting herself between him and the spot he'd been studying on the ground. "What's going on? Why'd you storm off and leave me there?"

He tried to step around her. "I didn't leave you." Celeste wouldn't budge. "I was just down the trail. And I didn't storm."

"I work with teenagers," she huffed. "I know storming when I see it."

"You didn't have to chase after me," John scoffed. "You and Dan seemed to be having a productive conversation."

Her eyes narrowed, face going tight. "Wait, you're mad about what, exactly? Two friends of yours talking about how brilliant and awesome you are?"

"Not how brilliant and awesome I am," he spat back, loathing the whiny tinge in his voice even as he couldn't stop it. He'd never responded like this to Breena, actually telling her how her meddling made him feel. The release was new, but not unwelcome. "How awesome I *could* be, if I just followed your plans. If I spent all my time trying to trend on Instagram, maybe I could be a big deal like Dan."

"I never said you needed to be like Dan. I just believe in what you can do and I want—"

"And you want me to do it your way."

She groaned, tugging at her ponytail. "That is not what I said, John. But is dreaming a little bigger really so bad? Sometimes you have to take risks to get the life you want. You have to be brave."

She'd probably been planning this *you can do it* speech for weeks. "Not everybody is like you, Celeste. Taking on the world, running like you're always in a marathon. And I know your ideas and energy come from a place of caring, but sometimes it can be—"

The words stuck in his throat, but she finished the sentence.

"Too much." She swallowed and blinked and—*shit*—wetness gathered on her lower lids. But the next moment she coughed a harsh laugh and shook her head. "Right."

He'd been angry and hurt, but he'd give anything to swallow those words back down. The bulk of his resentment deflated at the sight of her quivering jaw. "I didn't mean it to come out like that."

She sniffed and nodded, adjusting her pack. "No worries. Nothing I haven't heard before, right?"

"Celeste—"

"Let's just stick to why we're here, okay? We have lots of birds to see. Gotta win that contest so you can think for another few years about starting your business."

And then she was off, her capable legs taking her swiftly ahead of him, leaving behind his dreams of how their day would go, and a reminder that tonight they had only one tent to share.

CHAPTER 29

BIRD BINGE, DAY 36 OF 42
BIRD COUNT: 131

Celeste turned in her sleeping bag again, staring at the same page of the book she'd been looking at for thirty minutes. She didn't need to look behind her to know that John was doing the same. This was what they'd done since climbing into the tent after a silent dinner: stared at their respective books without even bothering to turn the pages.

The day had sucked.

The forest was beautiful, the weather perfect, the mountains divine, the birds plentiful.

But the day sucked. Celeste's argument with John had drained out all the enjoyment they'd always gotten from birding together. Gone were the still moments full of anticipation as they watched a bird shoulder to shoulder, and the amused chuckles and hums from John when Celeste went off on a tangent about something she'd heard on a podcast. Vanished were the quiet high fives when she made a correct ID, and the soft kisses he placed on her brow as she studied her guidebook.

And the flirting and teasing that had come to fill their hours birding together with an eager, hot anticipation of how they'd spend their time afterward? She might have just kissed that goodbye altogether.

Instead, it was caveman birding—pointing and grunting, showing each other the glorious birds of the Santa Rita Mountains with as little actual communication or interaction as possible.

And they did it all damn afternoon.

Behind her, John sighed. She knew he'd regretted that *too much* before the words made it out of his mouth, but it didn't matter. He'd thought those words and felt them. He'd meant them.

And Celeste shouldn't have cared so much. She wasn't for everybody, and she'd never set out to be for John. But hell, all she'd done was agree with that total stranger that John would be an amazing bird guide. Was she supposed to apologize for believing in him?

So she'd kept to herself all day, determined not to be the one to break their self-imposed mutual silence. Her stubborn streak had met a worthy opponent in John Maguire, who was an expert at spending a day alone in complete contentment. By their third hour of near-silent birding, she'd wondered if he preferred it this way. Maybe he'd often wished these past few weeks that she would just shut up.

She dog-eared the page of her book and let it drop beside her, knowing she was being dramatic. John wasn't Peter, or Peter's law colleagues, or any number of the teachers Celeste had caught rolling their eyes behind her back in the teachers' lounge. It was just days before that he'd urged her to talk *more*, begging her to tell him everything she was thinking as he knelt in front of the couch, pushing her knees apart.

Outside, junipers and oaks cast shadows from the full moon. This place was gorgeous, and she should have spent the day pulling stories from John about his childhood. He'd mentioned camping trips and hikes here as a kid, and it was clear from the easy way he moved down the trail, knowing just where to stop for a quiet lunch at a set of boulders perfect for a picnic, that he was in familiar territory.

She should just roll over and talk to the damn man, make him hash it out with her the way she would with Maria or Morgan. She and Dan had somehow hit a nerve with John, one she hadn't realized was so tender. As simple and honest as John was, he could also be hard to predict. Giving in to the wave of thoughts in her head might make him retreat even more.

Her phone buzzed, lighting up in the pocket near her head. Morgan was at Peter's that night, but Celeste always had her phone on her just in case.

But the text wasn't from Morgan.

JOHN: *Hi.*

JOHN: *Sometimes writing what I want to say can give me time to say it like I want. Is it okay if I do that now?*

The knot in her chest started a slow unwinding.

CELESTE: *Of course.*

Behind her, John shifted in his sleeping bag as dots appeared and disappeared on her screen.

JOHN: *I understand you were being supportive earlier. The truth is that I have some baggage around being told how much more I could be doing. But that's for me to deal with, and I shouldn't have responded that way.*

JOHN: *I'm sorry that I hurt you.*

There were more dots then, appearing and disappearing again and again. After a minute without another message, Celeste responded.

CELESTE: *Thank you.*

CELESTE: *Obviously I have baggage, too. And I'm sorry I poked at yours.*

I don't think you need to be more than you are, she typed. *I think you're so fucking great. Smart and kind and sexy and*

And what was she doing, waxing poetic to her birding partner? Yes, they'd enjoyed some benefits, but if anything, today had demonstrated why things couldn't go beyond that. She'd already let herself slip into too-comfortable territory with John, and today it had come back to bite her. She'd found herself imagining birding with him after the contest, teasing and goading him on his couch until he finally picked a name for his business, supporting him in his next steps.

But he obviously didn't want her advice, and she didn't need to make plans for anyone but herself.

It looked like John could be composing a novel on his side of the tent for all the dots on her screen, but when his next message popped up, it was short.

JOHN: *I guess this is why neither of us date.*

She'd been thinking the same thing. So it really shouldn't have stung.

CELESTE: *I guess so. We've both got baggage to unpack.*

CELESTE: *And dry-clean. There's definitely some stuff in my baggage that needs deep cleaning. Or maybe cleansing by fire.*

The chuckle shook his body behind her. She curled her body just enough that their spines touched through the soft give of their sleeping bags.

CELESTE: *Can we talk in person now?*

"Yeah."

They rolled over at the same time, ending up just a few inches from each other. Celeste propped her head up in one hand. "Hey."

"Hi." The moonlight in the tent shone across the small lift of his smile. "Thanks for texting me from six inches away."

"It's not a bad method." Maybe she just needed to text Morgan about college. "Sorry our day sucked. I get really enthusiastic about stuff, but I didn't mean to imply that you're doing anything wrong."

His laugh had an edge she didn't hear much. "Well, maybe I am. I tend to get lost in deliberation."

"Well, sure, but that can be—"

"You know what?" he said, interrupting her, though his voice was gentle. "Let's not do this. I'd rather just move on, if we could." His eyes sought hers out. "If you could. I know I was a jerk."

Celeste cracked a smile. "You were, actually, a little bit, but it was sort of exciting. I didn't know you had it in you."

"I'm not sure I did, either." His smile dropped as he watched her, his eyes drifting across her face and over her neck. "Today wasn't how I imagined being here with you."

"No?" She risked reaching a hand toward him, threading her fingers into his beard. "How did you imagine it?"

John's lids lowered as his tongue made a quick swipe across his lower lip. When he looked back at her, there was heat in his gaze, but uncertainty, too. Just the smallest line of worry in his brow.

She slid her hand behind his neck, playing with the wisp of curls. "Are we— Do you still want to do the benefits part, after today?"

His neck flexed with a swallow. "Do you?"

"I know today was complicated. But this—" She didn't need to say what "this" was, because it was obvious, the inches between them pulled so tight she could barely draw breath. "This doesn't feel complicated."

John must have spent a lot of hours camping in his life, because he was out of his sleeping bag like a magician, then drawing down the zipper of hers and moving into her space. He covered her body with his, pressing his knee between her legs.

He hovered above her on an elbow as his other hand roamed her body, his touch firm and possessive, like he was making up for a day without touching her. She arched into his hands, grinding her hips into where he'd already grown hard for her.

John's hand slipped under her shirt, teasing her nipple with a long, perfect tug. "Nothing complicated about how much I want you." His beard scraped her face as he growled into her ear. "I wasted so much time today."

"We can wake up early," she gasped, grappling to push down the elastic waistband of his shorts. "Do some more birding then."

He groaned into her neck as her hand found him, wrapping her fingers tight. "I wasn't talking about birding."

Then his mouth was on hers, hard and demanding, and the day and all its baggage faded into his touch on her breasts, her hip, her calves, the ache between her legs, until there was only John and the moonlit trees beyond.

CHAPTER 30

BIRD BINGE, DAY 42 OF 42
BIRD COUNT: 169

Birders were everywhere. Mingling near the glass cabinet of finches frozen in taxidermic flight, sipping cocktails in the shadow of the towering skeleton of a Sonorasaurus, chatting over a table demonstrating the watershed of southern Arizona. The Tucson Science Center, home tonight to the annual gala of the Arizona Ornithological Society, was very cool, but Celeste wished they would all sit the hell down. Linda had taken to the mic three entire minutes before to ask people to take their seats, and barely anyone had budged.

Was Celeste the only one who'd been up half the night in anticipation of the announcement? She'd stayed home because Morgan was there, but hadn't realized until she closed her bedroom door that this was it. The next day the winners would be announced. Her time with John would be at an end.

But at least they'd go out with a bang. A win for John wouldn't just validate his knowledge and his work; it would create a path for him to pursue his goals. She wouldn't push him—she'd learned enough that day in the mountains to know he had to take the steps himself. But she sure as hell wanted to open the door.

Then she'd leave. Morgan's art show was already starting a

few miles away, and though the formal ceremony didn't happen until later, Celeste hated to miss any of it. The timing was terrible, but perfect too, giving her the tug she needed to walk away from the gala, from the soothing warmth of John's hand settled on her lower back as they tried to get to their table.

One of her new birding friends waved from across the room, but Celeste veered left, John dutifully at her shoulder as he whispered in her ear, "Watch out, more of your admirers up here."

She'd become acquainted with many of the other birders through the contest, crossing paths at popular birding spots. Celeste loved a good tangential conversation in the shade of a tree as they scanned the branches, but not tonight. Tonight she was on a mission.

John's mouth brushed her ear in the passing tease of a kiss. When she stumbled, his hand held her hip to keep her upright, fingers pressing where she was still tender from his grip two nights before, under much more naked circumstances.

In the days since their complication in the mountains, something small had shifted between them. They were still easy with each other, but she'd rebuilt some of her defenses, and she could tell he had, too. Her tendency to shower people with her planning-prone enthusiasm had clearly rubbed against John's learned defensiveness, exposing rough edges for both of them. And while her instinct that night had been to talk it all out, she'd understood why he'd asked for them to just move on.

They were just birders with benefits, after all, and that didn't come with emotional entanglements.

But it did come with sex, and they'd been having as much of that as they could. In his bed, on his couch, in his woodshop, and, in one particularly exciting encounter, against a tree in an empty corner of a park. And just like they had in the tent that night when John had muffled her cries with his mouth, they'd poured themselves into each other almost desperately, grappling for any time they had.

Their sex drives were rivaled only by their mad dash to find as many birds as they could, with Celeste setting a rigorous schedule. She'd used a few of her cached sick days to make the most of the past week, focusing on adding to their list while ignoring the dwindling number of days they had left together.

And now, on the last day, everything just felt weird. She was tense and excited about the contest results, anxious and thrilled to get to Morgan's show, and fighting constantly against the magnetic pull between her body and John's. When they'd met outside the museum, she'd tried to make a joke about their last fake date, but it hadn't landed. It had just made John look sad, which made her want to make him feel better. But she'd slapped on a smile and ushered them inside instead.

They finally reached their table, which was draped in maroon polyester and decorated with bright sunflowers. Chris—there both for moral support and to admire "the large repository of preserved gastropods"—was chatting to a woman with short blond hair and an expression so rapt it was clear she was fully in his charismatic thrall.

Next to her, John leaned forward on his elbows. His button-down shirt fit perfectly across his wide chest, and he'd added insult to injury by rolling up his shirtsleeves to expose his forearms. He nodded to the crowd. "You're very popular."

"They just like my novelty." Celeste flicked her fingers against a sweating water glass, sending a few drops flying. She'd had a flurry of hobby-hopping after her divorce but had never stayed still long enough to form new relationships. A nagging worry that she was missing something, somewhere, had her always moving on to the next thing. But six weeks of the Bird Binge had landed her in a community that embraced her with open arms, in no small part because they believed she was John's girlfriend. Faking it with him had seemed absurd but acceptable when they'd started, but now, as Linda waved at her from the small stage, it felt a lot like betrayal.

"Feel free to vilify me when you tell them about our breakup," she said with a laugh she wished wasn't so forced.

The smile on John's face faltered, and Celeste moved to smooth his lips back into a curve. But she stalled her hand between them, and diverted to a sunflower instead, adjusting it in its vase.

She was doing them a favor by weaning them from the habit of small touches, ignoring the store of knowledge she'd acquired about John's body. Like how he would laugh if she poked him in just the right spot on his cheek, or how his gaze turned to glass when she scraped her nails under his jaw.

"Celeste!" Chris called to her across John as his fingers drummed on the tabletop. "Have you seen the gastropods yet? I can walk you through the collection later if you want. It'll blow your mind."

"I can't," she answered glumly. Chris's enthusiasm about snails was oddly contagious. She was going to miss the guy. "I've got to go right away to my daughter's art show."

"Oh, yeah." Chris glanced to John as he swallowed. "I remember John mentioning that." He cleared his throat as the three sat in a heavy silence that left Celeste to wonder what else John had mentioned. "Well, we'll have to come back, okay?" Chris said with strained cheer in his voice. "The exhibit is not to be missed."

"Okay." She nodded, grabbing for her ponytail before remembering she'd left her hair down. "I'll make sure to see it."

Rolling her neck, Celeste studied the giant fish model hanging from wires over their heads, its pale underbelly and gaping gills out of place in midair. As John and Chris conferred quietly beside her, she tapped out a message to Morgan, assuring her she'd be there soon. Morgan quickly responded with a thumbs-up and *Did you win yet???????*

Celeste stowed the phone with a small sigh as her right leg started a fast up-and-down. "Would they get on with it?" she mumbled.

John's palm covered her knee, stilling her movement. "You okay?"

"I'm totally fine." She should move away from his touch, but her system was relieved to absorb John's steadiness through her kneecap in some kind of energy osmosis. "Just excited. Hope you're ready for your magazine spread."

"You don't know that we're going to—"

"I don't know, but I believe." She hit the table too hard, rattling all the silverware. "We're just two short of your count from last year, with you-know-who." After Breena's swipe at Celeste during the Instagram scavenger hunt, she'd stopped using her name. It was totally immature but felt great. You-know-who was across the lobby now, shooting a surprisingly low number of furtive glances their way.

Probably because John had shown her just what he could do Breena-free. They'd spotted 169 different species of birds. Yes, Celeste had been there, but it was obvious she was along for the ride. This was John's list, and John's impending victory. And although she had to leave before his victory lap, she hoped he would eat it up.

"Good evening, fine people!" Linda cheered from the stage, beaming like a proud mom at the assembled birders.

"Thank fucking God." Celeste settled her hand over John's. Not ideal, but better than knocking over her water with her jittery energy. His fingers flexed under her palm, squeezing her knee.

Celeste was ready for the main event, but Linda had the audacity to embark on a long series of talking points about the association's work toward conservation and future goals for the organization.

As John's thumb stroked her knee again, Celeste picked through the phrases she'd parsed to say goodbye. She'd stared at her mirror while she got ready at home, her face surrounded by the halo of colorful notes as she practiced her delivery.

John, I wish you all the best.

Or, less formal: *I appreciate all the orgasms, good luck with the birding.*

Nothing was quite right. She'd have to settle for something between *thank you* and *goodbye*.

As Linda completed her mini–TED Talk, a slide show began on-screen behind her. First were pictures from the opening day, when Celeste had shown up as a girlfriend and left a new birder, then shots of birds the participants had captured in stunning photos, many of which she actually recognized, because apparently she was a bird-watcher now. She laughed at a shot she hadn't seen yet—of her and John at the bar, Celeste's arms raised in victory after saving the day with Emily Dickinson. Just on the edge of the picture, Breena frowned.

Finally, the slide show moved through the team selfies participants had posted. Chris whooped and whistled when John and Celeste's photo appeared, but Celeste barely had to look up to know just how the creases of John's cheeks held his smile, or how the dappled sun made her skin look pink. She'd studied the picture enough on John's Instagram.

Tonight when she got home, she'd unfollow him so her thumbs couldn't find that photo in weaker moments.

"I'm thrilled to tell you that this was our biggest year yet," Linda declared, beaming. "We had more teams than ever before. And we know what you're all waiting for, so I'll get to it!"

Linda inched open an envelope like an Oscar presenter, as if she wasn't the person who'd put the paper there in the first place. Under the table, Celeste slipped her hand under John's, rubbing at his calluses with her fingertips. These she would miss most of all. Chris flashed a toothy smile and a thumbs-up as the birders sat rapt, stuffed specimens watching with glass eyes all around them.

Linda cleared her throat.

"The winner of this year's annual Arizona Ornithological Society Bird Binge . . ."

Celeste held her breath, squeezing John's hand.

". . . with an amazing total of one hundred seventy-eight birds . . ."

Her heart dropped into her stomach.

Linda's arms went wide in celebration.

"Francine and Jose Castaneda!"

CHAPTER 31

BIRD BINGE, DAY 42 OF 42

BIRD COUNT: 169

John knew exactly what to expect from Celeste if they won the Bird Binge. There would be jumping and screaming, probably high-fiving of everyone in the place. Thinking about the pure joy she'd be sure to display had kept him focused on the birds in those final days, even as Celeste flitted ahead of him on the trail, her hips begging for his hands. He knew he should want to win for himself, and for the publicity and validation it would give him. But as soon as Celeste had spotted that first bird in the blooming palo verde six weeks before, he'd wanted to win for her.

He'd never even thought about how she would react if they lost.

Beside him, Celeste was quiet and still, shoulders folding inward as Francine and Jose took the stage. She blinked rapidly, as though waking from a disorienting dream.

Her daze only lasted a few seconds before she released his hand and clapped appropriately, a perfect smile draped on her lips. Reluctantly, he lifted his hand from her knee to clap as well.

John waited for a pull of regret as he contemplated how things could have gone differently. He could have stayed out of the contest altogether, as he'd been inclined to do. Or pursued an expert partner, all but guaranteeing a win. He could have taken more control of his outings with Celeste, speeding them up and focusing on the count instead of on discovery.

But the regret didn't come. The Bird Binge had been not just a wonderful time but a profound reckoning, reminding him why he wanted to guide in the first place, and a real-life boot camp in bringing someone new into the hobby.

And as Francine and Jose stepped onto the stage, Jose waving like royalty, relief unspooled in John's chest that it wasn't him up there. He'd never liked the spotlight.

Francine grappled for the mic as Jose laughed beside her. But next to him, Celeste pushed back her chair and stood. When John caught her wrist, she stared at his hand, then his face, and shook her head slightly. Leaning into him, she whispered, "I'm just getting some air. It's stuffy in here. I'm not leaving. I'll—" Her swallow was practically audible. "I'll make sure to say goodbye before I go."

As she slipped away, John caught a glimpse of her sandaled feet—toes a bright azure blue tonight—heading up the stairs to the second floor of the museum.

An elbow to the side from Chris brought him face-to-face with his friend, eyebrows drawn in.

"She's just getting some air," John said quietly as the program onstage drew to a close.

"You okay, buddy?" Chris pushed his shoulder into John, his face softening.

"Yeah." Around them, people left their tables to raid the buffets of snackable foods. "You can't ever predict the numbers."

Chris laid a hand on John's forearm, leaning in. "That's not what I mean. I know Celeste cared a lot more about winning than you did. I'm asking if you're okay about"—he glanced to the stairs where Celeste had fled—"that. This is supposed to be the end of the casual thing, right?"

"Right." John studied the empty staircase as Chris's fingers drummed on his arm. Often, when the world around him was noisy, John's mind was a refuge where his thoughts moved at their own pace. He liked to sit in the calm where he could study them as he would a block of wood in his shop or a bird in a tree.

But tonight nothing quite made sense. He wanted to hover near Celeste as much as he knew he should walk away from her, wanted to push them past the boundaries they'd drawn as much as he wanted to retreat and settle into the known space he was building for himself.

"Right," he said again, rubbing one hand across his beard.

"Seems an awful waste." Chris's voice held none of his normal teasing or bravado. "To throw away something like this because of an agreement you made weeks ago."

"It's not throwing away. It's—" He sighed. It was letting go. The "something like this" they'd had was a thrilling, lusty thing. It had been fun and stimulating and much, much more than he'd expected. But it was always meant to be like that—a firework they both needed to ignite. He didn't know how to capture that and make it real, not without asking them both to take the risk of being burdened with all that old baggage.

Chris eased back, watching John carefully. "Your brain's really going, huh?" When John only nodded, Chris motioned back to the stairs. "She looked sad. Maybe she needs a friend." A smirk rose on his lips. "Should I go check on her?"

John knew just what he was doing, and it worked like a charm. "No," he said firmly. "I'll go."

But just as he stood, Breena appeared at their table, her fingers twisted together in front of her stomach.

She shrugged, forcing a smile. “Hey, at least we both lost, right?”

When John and Chris just stared at her, Breena inflated her cheeks and blew out, tipping back on the heels of her black boots. “I wanted to talk to you for a minute, if that’s okay. I’m going to therapy and trying to be . . . happier. And coming to terms with some stuff, and so . . .”

Her eyes shifted back to the ground.

Chris, now standing beside John, made a choking sound, half gasp and half laugh. “Whoa. Should I leave you guys alone?”

Breena’s shoulders slumped slightly before she looked back, dark eyes tracking from John to Chris and back again. “You’ll probably enjoy witnessing this, and my behavior affected all of us, so . . .” She only shrugged. Chris, never one to miss a dramatic moment, crossed his arms over his chest and stayed put.

She looked back to John, taking a big breath. “I’m sorry.”

John raised a hand to his beard, tempted to look behind him, to whomever she was talking to. “Okay.”

Breena never apologized. It was something he’d found intriguing when they’d met. She carried confidence like no one he’d ever known, and he’d wanted to see inside her to see how it worked. It had occurred to him only recently, seeing Breena react to Celeste, that her confidence might be at least in part simply bravado.

Breena sighed. “Are you going to ask what for?”

John shrugged. A long time had passed since he’d expected anything from Breena other than frustrated disapproval. But tonight there was a crack in her armor he’d never seen before, so he asked, “What for?”

“I’m sorry for kissing someone else; that was wrong. And I know after that you didn’t trust me, and maybe you didn’t believe. . . ." She looked up from the ground and caught his eye. "But nothing else ever happened. With him or anyone else. I messed up, I know that. But I wouldn't have messed up that bad."

He'd stopped asking himself those questions months ago, but the answer loosened something in the back of his brain. "Okay."

Chris shifted next to him but stayed silent. John watched the staircase again, hoping to catch sight of Celeste. Morgan's show was underway; Celeste wouldn't stay much longer. And she'd promised to say goodbye.

"Also"—Breena cleared her throat—"I know when we were together, I wasn't always very nice. I know, as a person, I can seem cold."

She pulled nervously at her cuticles, just like she used to before a big exam.

Her words poured out like they'd been rehearsed more than once. "I know I put pressure on you when we were together. Bugged you about school and work and everything. And I wanted to tell you that I think sometimes my attitude toward you was just insecurity on my part. Like, when you didn't want the same things I wanted—to do the doctorate, to publish, to get noticed like that in your field—I felt bad and greedy for wanting it so much. Like there was something wrong with my ambition."

"Breena—" John moved to interrupt. They'd always had different visions for what they wanted, but that hadn't been her fault. Yes, she was serious, focused, intense, and wildly ambitious. But there was also a fire and an energy to Breena that were contagious. It wasn't something to be ashamed of.

"I know that was never your intention," she went on. "I know you supported me, but I just felt so insecure that I ended up lashing out at you about it and acting like you should want something other than what you did. And I'm sorry I did that."

For months after John had asked Breena to move out, he'd wanted these words from her. Hiking for hours, he'd poked and prodded at the nagging need to hear her take blame, for anything at all.

So it was a shock to realize he didn't need it anymore. Somewhere in his woodshop or on the trail in these past weeks and months, he'd recovered a part of himself she'd made smaller, until her opinion of him now barely registered at all. And in some of that space he'd taken back, he found himself with room to see her more fully, even if just a little.

Chris blew out a loud sigh, reminding John he was there. "Holy fuck, B." He scrubbed at his hair. "That's some therapist."

Breena laughed, her brown eyes catching a flash of the museum's fluorescents. Chris and Breena had been close once, their big personalities playing off each other like a comedy act, before Chris had sworn loyalty to John after the breakup.

John took a risk and reached for her hand. They hadn't touched in over a year, but the shape of her hand in his was familiar. "Thank you." Her lips parted, but she didn't pull back, so he gave her hand a squeeze. "You're brilliant and ambitious, and those are great things about you. I never meant to make you feel like those weren't good qualities. I just didn't always share them. I think"—he squeezed her hand again before releasing her—"we just weren't a good match, and we didn't know how to let it go."

Breena cleared her throat, blinking fast. "I'm sorry I was sort of a bitch about Celeste. I knew you'd move on someday, but I didn't expect it to be so in my face, and . . . someone so cheerful brings out something different in you." She closed her mouth, shaking her head, but then continued. "And if I could give you a little unsolicited advice, from someone who's been there?

Sometimes people need to hear you, John. What you want and what you need, and when something is wrong. Don't expect Celeste to be a mind reader, okay?"

John nodded numbly, suddenly heavy with guilt about the game he'd played, letting Breena think Celeste was his girlfriend. He opened his mouth to tell her the truth, but what could he say? He couldn't honestly say that none of it was real. And if it was all ending tonight anyway, it hardly mattered.

But he knew one thing for sure. He'd rather be with Celeste than hashing out the past with Breena. "Thanks, B. I'll keep that in mind."

He made a move for the stairs but turned back to Chris and Breena, who were standing awkwardly side by side, looking down at their hands. "You two should be friends again," he blurted. "You were close once and —" He looked at Chris, who was still struggling to fit himself into the mold of academia. "Chris could use a real friend on campus, somebody who gets him."

Chris struck a sassy hands-on-hips pose, but he was smiling. "Who even says I want to be her friend again?"

John shook his head with a chuckle. "You want to be everyone's friend." And since Breena hadn't walked away, he thought there might be hope for the two of them to rebuild the connection they'd once had.

But that would be up to them. Meanwhile, a tug in his chest pulled him toward the staircase, and he headed up to find Celeste.

CHAPTER 32

BIRD BINGE, DAY 42 OF 42
BIRD COUNT: 169

A tiny blue butterfly floated to a stop on Celeste's knee. Another rested in the hammock of her dress, its iridescent wings opening and closing languidly. Yet another, yellow and black, sailed past her face on its way to a broad green leaf.

She hadn't had a destination when she headed upstairs, but when she'd skidded into the education room and seen the netted structure in one corner with a hand-drawn sign proclaiming the place *Butterfly Land*, she'd unzipped the door and ducked inside.

And she'd sat in silence with the butterflies, hoping the leaves and flowers would absorb her bad mood so she could stand up, put a smile on her face, and get the hell out of there. It would mean finding some way to face John, to answer for their loss, and to say goodbye.

Any minute now, she'd be ready.

The loud zip of the door drew Celeste's eyes from the butterfly to John, ducking inside and lowering himself to sit next to her.

"Hey." His voice was so soft among the plants and the butterflies. He was so nice, his smile gentle and worried at the edges. "You okay?"

She slipped a finger under the butterfly on her knee, letting its featherlight insect feet grip her skin. "What's a group of butterflies called?" She lifted her hand slowly, bringing the little creature just before her eyes.

He smiled in the background, unfocused behind the blue wings. "A kaleidoscope."

She didn't have a response to that. It was just too lovely.

Instead she sighed, scaring the butterfly off. "I'm sorry you got stuck with me and lost the contest." She looked from butterfly to butterfly, avoiding John's eyes. "I know you were counting on this. Without me slowing you down you could have worked faster, you could have—"

"Hey." His hand squeezed her shoulder and his thumb drew steady lines back and forth at the base of her neck. "Stop."

Maria was already at the show, texting her that the art was *so fucking amazing*. But for a minute she let herself look at John, at the brown-green swirl of his eyes and the cinnamon sugar of his beard.

"It's bird-watching, Celeste." His fingers kept stroking her neck. "It could have been the difference in the time of day, or a breeze, or anything. You can't always predict this stuff, no matter how hard you try. There is no reason to blame yourself."

She shook her head. "But that magazine piece would have helped you, I know you don't want to go forward in your business without this boost."

He squeezed her shoulder again, running his hand down her arm. "We both know I was using that as an excuse, one more reason to stand still. If I'm actually ready to try, the contest shouldn't matter."

"Okay." She hoped he could believe in himself even half as much as she did.

John reached into the small backpack he'd been toting around all evening and pulled out something wooden. He held the object between them for a long, quiet moment before Celeste reached out. Her arms dipped with the weight when John transferred it to her, and she turned it over in her hands, eyes narrowed.

He cleared his throat. "I wanted you to have this, no matter what happened with the contest. You deserve it."

The wood was pale, almost silver, with streaks of grain in tan and chocolate, smooth under her fingers. It was shaped like a teardrop, or maybe a leaf, and was flat on one end, like it could balance on a level surface. One side of it was slightly concave, and two lines of text crossed the center:

Celeste Johanssen
Most Improved Birder

Celeste rubbed at the words with her fingers, tracing each one. The burned-in type was a rich brown, each letter etched precisely into the plaque.

"You made this?" Her voice shook.

He nodded, his bottom lip drawn in, looking nervous. "Yeah. It's not perfect, but I think—"

"John," Celeste said, cutting him off, still gazing at the award. The one he'd made especially for her. "It's so beautiful."

A single tear fell, and she wiped it off quickly, noting the shine it left on the wood. She was digging herself out of the disappointment and guilt of the loss and swinging into something else as light and colorful as the butterflies around them.

She turned the award over in her hands again, laughing at the inscription. After a moment, a cheek-aching smile rose up her face. "I am definitely the most improved birder, huh? From not recognizing a house sparrow to hobnobbing with the elite members of the Arizona Ornithological Society."

As the two of them laughed, a small yellow butterfly landed on the award. Its wings opened and closed slowly, hypnotizing her for a moment. When she looked back up at John, he was watching her, jaw clenched.

He was beautiful, kind lines around hazel eyes, a leaf bobbing just over his head. And he'd placed the evidence of his caring right into her hands, the hours of his time evident in the smooth curve of the wood.

Putting the award down gently so it balanced upright, she rose on her knees and scooted to him. She was meant to be drawing herself away from John tonight, but she had to thank him, didn't she? So she leaned down and, brushing her hand against his cheek to tip his face up, lowered her lips to his.

"Thank you." She whispered it against his lips, past his cheek, then into his mouth, the tips of their tongues just barely touching.

"Thank *you*." He gave the words back.

Their kiss was as slow and light as the butterflies, until John's hands molded around Celeste's hips. She imagined his fingers closing on the award he'd made her, just like he was holding on to her now, and groaned into his mouth. John deepened their kiss and pulled her across his thighs so that her ass nestled in the basket of his legs. Their bodies clicked together. It was so easy.

"Without you, I wouldn't have had a partner." John spoke into her hair. "You were brave to say yes."

She chuckled against his ear. "You were brave taking me on, even if you didn't know it at the time."

He just laughed and kissed her harder. She knew he'd wanted this all night just like she had—their connection made firm, the current between them flowing one more time. He slid his hands under her ass and pulled her tight against where he was growing hard. They rocked together, Celeste kissing him hungrily, taking every moment she could. John's hands moved up her thighs and slid beneath her dress, fingers hot on her skin.

But despite the firm grip of his fingers, and the way she rocked against him just right, the ticking clock in Celeste's head wouldn't be silenced. She willed time to slow, to drag like the lazy beating of the butterfly wings around them, but it was useless.

Celeste slowed her movement, lifting her mouth from John's and leaning her forehead against his. "I have to go."

John's face fell for a moment, but he nodded quickly, pulling his face back and rubbing his beard. "Right, of course. You need to get to the show, and—"

And the contest was over. This was when they were supposed to walk away.

The butterfly house lit up, glowing amber with evening light threading through the upper-story windows.

The contest was over, but the day wasn't. A technicality, sure, but Celeste would take it. There were still some grains of sand in that hourglass, and she was going to use every last one.

"You should come."

He blinked, brows pulling together. "Come with you? To Morgan's show?"

"Yes." She lifted off his lap, kneeling in front of him again. "Unless you want to stay here, with all your people, which I would understand. But the show is nearby anyway, and I love showing off my daughter, and it would be a better way to end the day than losing and—"

And I can't walk away, not yet.

His hand brushed her cheek, fingers trapping her nervous lips. "Celeste, I'd love to come."

CHAPTER 33

BIRD BINGE: COMPLETE

John spotted Morgan right away across the large warehouse turned art space. She was an inch or so taller than her mom, with the same sun-kissed face, and sandy hair sporting a blue streak. And when she smiled, her mother was there in the bright eyes, the warmth and the openness.

“So, there’s Morgan. We should go say hi.” Celeste nibbled on her lower lip, and John hoped, again, he was right to be there. She’d been enthusiastic in her invitation, but it had been in an *enthusiastic* moment, their bodies flush together and surrounded by butterflies.

He’d answered without hesitation. Not just because he was interested in seeing Morgan’s art, though he was. And not because he worried about Celeste dipping back into sadness after the contest loss, though he did.

He was there because she had asked him to come.

Celeste broke into a faster walk as they reached Morgan, pulling her daughter into a tight hug.

“Hi, Mom.” Morgan’s voice was muffled as she squirmed out of the embrace.

Celeste beamed. "I'm finally here!"

"You didn't miss much, just a lot of standing around." Morgan glanced at John, her eyebrows shooting up in a look of intrigue that was quintessentially Celeste. "I didn't know you were bringing the bird guy."

"I didn't bring him," Celeste said quickly. "We drove separately. And you know he has a name."

Morgan smirked and nodded toward him. "Hi, John. Thanks for coming."

"It's a pleasure."

"How was the dinner?" Morgan looked between them. "Did you guys win the—"

Celeste cut her off with a quick "No."

Morgan tilted her head, watching her mom, as she tugged on a strand of her blue hair. "Oh fuck, really?"

"Language, Morgan."

Morgan's answering groan prompted a smile from Celeste, one that grew as Maria skidded to a stop next to them.

"Cel, thank God you're finally here. Did you know they're only serving juice? My first night out on the town without my baby and there's no alcohol." She shook a small plastic cup full of the unsatisfactory liquid.

Celeste laughed. "It *is* an art show for high schoolers."

"And those high schoolers don't have parents? Or wonderful aunt-type role models who left their baby at home and just want a glass of fuc—" Her gaze hit John. "Well, hello! I didn't expect to see you here." She looked back to Celeste, eyebrows high.

"I thought he'd like to see the show," Celeste answered, the smile on her face wobbling.

"I'm sure he would." Maria downed her juice in one gulp. "So, are you celebrating after the big win?"

Celeste tipped her head back. "This is what I get for being overconfident. A night of being reminded I lost."

Maria frowned. "Oh fuck, really?"

Celeste and Morgan laughed, the echoed tones twisting together. "Well," Celeste said, clapping her hands. "At least there's consensus."

Morgan pulled her phone from her jeans pocket and showed the lit-up screen to Celeste. "I really have to do this?"

"Yes. He is your father and he wants to see your show." She reached for a strand of Morgan's hair, rubbing it between her fingers before tucking it behind her ear. "Just give him the tour. You can make it fast."

"Fine." She pressed something on her phone and walked away, heading toward one of the gallery walls.

"You convinced him to do it?" Maria asked once Morgan was out of earshot.

John remembered Celeste's phone call with Peter—her request and his response that she was overboard. It seemed ages ago, that evening she'd come into his workshop and swiped her finger along his worktable. Since then, he'd had her largely to himself, either at his house or outside looking for birds. But as she huddled with Maria, her eyes following her daughter as she walked the phone around the room, he realized how much of her life he hadn't seen, how much of herself she'd kept on the other side of their agreement.

"Well . . ." Maria cleared her throat and looked at John again, then to Celeste. "There might not be wine, but there are adults without spit-up on their clothes, so I'm going to go mingle."

With a little wave, she was gone, leaving Celeste and John alone. John pulled awkwardly at the sleeves of his button-down. "Are you sure it's okay that I'm—"

"Oh gosh, I just remembered." Celeste glanced around the room. "They wanted to check in with all the parents about permission for a news story." She bit her lower lip slightly as she addressed John. "You okay to look around for a bit?"

He nodded, twisting his hands together to keep them reaching for her. "Of course. Go do your thing. I'll be here."

A few minutes later, he was looking at Celeste's back. It was drawn in pencil, filled in with bright colors that captured the ephemeral light from the window in the bright morning hours. In the drawing, she was leaning her palms against the kitchen counter, looking outside.

Morgan's pieces were grouped together along a cream-colored wall. One showed a detailed black-and-white sketch of a pair of high-top Converse standing on a skateboard. Another depicted saguaros scattered along a steep mountain slope. And then there was this—Celeste, awash in color, her hands curved over the edge of the yellow countertop. Her hair was up in a ponytail, like always, and Morgan had even managed to capture the unruly wisps along her neck.

"You've been looking at this one a long time. You might be my biggest fan."

Morgan smirked from where she'd appeared at his side. The familiarity of her expression put him at ease, even if he didn't have a lot of experience with teenagers.

"Your mom holds that title."

"Mom takes support to a whole new level. I honestly worried she'd show up in a special T-shirt." But even as she rolled her eyes, Morgan smiled.

John nodded to the drawing. "It's hard to believe you can do so much with just pencils."

Morgan hummed, eyes on her work on the walls. "That's

kinda been my thing, I guess. I'm excited to try some new stuff when I'm—" She stopped abruptly, combing her fingers through her hair. She cleared her throat and nodded toward the drawing of Celeste looking out the window. "This one was, like, a miracle."

"How so?"

"She never stands still like that, like ever. She looked so cool with the light coming in, I wanted to get it, but I was sure she'd start bustling around again before I was done. But she just stayed there. I threw it into the show at the last minute."

John realized why the sketch had absorbed him so thoroughly. He'd heard about it, from Celeste. "She was looking at a bird."

Morgan turned from the wall of art to face John. "What?"

"She told me about it later that day. She saw a bird fly into the yard, and she was trying to identify it. And then"—John looked around the room for Celeste, his eyes landing on her not far away, chatting with Maria—"she heard you drawing."

Morgan's brow furrowed, and he continued. "She heard your pencil, so she didn't move. She said it had been a while since you'd drawn her, and"—there was something in the anticipation in Morgan's eyes that made him keep going—"she was happy you were doing that, so she stayed still. After the bird flew away."

She stared at the drawing again, tilting her head back and forth. A screech of microphone feedback made them both turn toward a man across the room, standing at a drab podium.

"If everyone could gather over here, please, we'd like to honor the artists."

John and Morgan walked together toward a group of folding plastic chairs, where Morgan peeled off to sit with a friend. Celeste herself was waving at him from a place near the front, and as he approached she patted the empty plastic chair beside her.

"Sorry I disappeared. Too many people to say hi to. I saw you talking to Morgan. What did you two talk about?"

"Just art." He shrugged, knowing it would elicit a frustrated sigh. But he wasn't ready to hand over his quiet moment with Morgan just yet. Before Celeste could begin an interrogation, the event organizer began reading off a few announcements and then launched into short bios of each student.

John enjoyed hearing the little snippets—some kids had grown up with art, while others had started more recently. Most were heading to college the following year in Arizona, like Morgan, while some were setting out around the country.

"Morgan Johanssen-Davis, Tucson High."

Celeste's knee shook fast next to John's leg as Morgan's name was read.

"Morgan is a senior at Tucson High, where she has participated in art club, yearbook, and the LGBTQ club. She has been an artist for as long as she can remember, and her favorite place to draw is at the kitchen table in her mother's house."

A strangled sigh escaped Celeste, and when John glanced at her, her bottom lip was shaking. Slowly, she slid a hand onto his thigh, and he covered it with his own, rubbing gently over her knuckles.

"Morgan's preferred medium is pencil, though she has recently experimented with chalk, charcoal, and pastels. She would like to thank her parents and Em for their support. In August, Morgan will move to Los Angeles, where she plans to hone her craft while experiencing the vibrant art culture of Southern California."

Celeste's hand froze on John's knee as his own brow furrowed, mirroring hers. Celeste had told him weeks ago that Morgan was bound for college in northern Arizona, quizzing John about his younger brother Jared's balance of lifetime interest in art while also holding down a “real” job. He wondered why she hadn’t mentioned Morgan’s change of plans.

But as Celeste gasped, it became clear she hadn’t known herself. Her eyes went wide, and then her voice reached well above the volume of the golf clap following the reading of Morgan’s bio.

“Excuse me.” All heads swiveled her way. “But what the hell did you just say?”

CHAPTER 34

"Mom, God, calm down!"

They were squared off in the parking lot, Morgan's chest heaving in big breaths, her hands in tight fists at her sides. She'd stormed out after Celeste's outburst, and Celeste had quickly followed. Em had slipped out the door right after that, and maybe some others. Celeste didn't look back to see. Nothing mattered right now except understanding what the hell her daughter was up to.

"You didn't tell your mom, Morgs?" Em passed a hand gently down Morgan's spine before tangling their fingers with hers.

Celeste stared at the intimate gesture.

Em was going to UCLA. In Los Angeles.

"Are you two—" Morgan's cagey behavior, her hours spent away from home, it all finally made sense. "Why didn't you tell me?"

Celeste and Morgan had always shared secrets, but apparently not all of them. Secrets like Morgan dating her best friend. And forgoing college for a move to—

"LA, Morgan? What was that about? You're not going to LA, you're going up to Flagstaff, to NAU."

Her finger was pointed straight at her daughter. When had she become a finger-wagger? She lowered her hand but kept her gaze hard on Morgan. This was what she got for not pushing her these last weeks, not reviewing their plan and getting Morgan excited about college. She'd been so damn distracted, and now her daughter was talking nonsense.

"I'm not, Mom. I tried to tell you a million times, but you wouldn't listen. I don't want to go up there next year. It's not right for me."

"Of course it is, honey." Celeste tried to modulate her voice, to cut out the angry edge, but it wasn't working. "We talked about this. They have a great art department but you can still focus on other academics. Get in-state tuition. Keep your options open if your art doesn't work out."

"No, *you* talked about it, Mom. And talked and talked. It was never my plan. It was always yours. I want to go to LA. Em and I can stay in the basement apartment at their aunt's house and—"

Celeste's knees faltered for a moment. Living together? "Oh no. You are not skipping college to go live in a basement with someone you're dating!" Celeste looked at Em, whom she'd known since they were ten. "No offense, Em. Under any other circumstances I would be thrilled about you and Morgan. You know I love you."

Em kicked the ground. "I know, Ms. J. It's cool."

"It's not cool!" Morgan was yelling now, her face gone red in the hazy parking lot lighting. "You should be thrilled *now*! I love Em and we're going to California together!"

Celeste resisted an eye roll, but just barely. "Morgan, you can't be serious." She wiped a hand across her face, searching for calm. "Honey. Think about this. Em is going to be in college. Taking classes, meeting new people. What are you going to do?"

"I already called an art school there. I can take classes for trade if I help out." Morgan raised her eyebrows triumphantly. "I have a plan, Mom. It's just not your plan."

A plan to follow Em to California and take out the trash at some art school? "Honey, if you want to take a gap year before you go to college, we can talk about that. But following someone just because you're dating, giving your life over to that, is no way to make decisions."

Morgan groaned, shaking her head. She looked at Em with a look like, *You see this?*

"This is why I didn't tell you about Em!" Morgan let go of Em's hand and stepped in front of them in a protective stance. "This is exactly why! Because you're so fucking jaded! I know you're on some pathetic self-imposed path of discovery, Mom, but some of us *want* to be in love, okay? I'm happy, doesn't that matter to you?"

In love. Her daughter. Her little girl. What would happen to her? How could she risk so much—her future, the start of her own life after high school—for something so fragile?

"Moo, you're too young for this, baby. When you're in love, everything else falls to the side." Celeste knew that all too well, and was still digging herself out of that hole. "Don't you see yourself doing that already? Giving up your chance for college, following Em to California?"

"I'm not giving up anything!" Morgan shouted. "Just because that's how love feels to you doesn't mean that's how it is for me!"

Celeste took a breath. "Is this about me? Is this your way of getting back at me? For divorcing your dad?"

Morgan groaned as she looked at the dark sky. "Oh my god, Mom. Not everything is about you. Jesus." She let out a harsh, angry laugh. It wasn't a sound Celeste had ever heard from her daughter, and the edges of it sliced at her. "What's funny is, I thought you'd be proud of me. Seriously. What about all your little mantras? *Be bold! Say yes!*" She held her hands up in the air. "That's what I'm doing! But I guess that only applies to you, huh? It's the story you tell yourself to make it okay to split up your family, jump from hobby to hobby like a kid on a sugar high. You do whatever you want as long as it fits your stupid plan. But what about me? What about what I want?"

"You don't know what you want!" *Split up your family. You do whatever you want.* Morgan knew just what to say to cut deeper. But Celeste pushed back, all fight. "You think you know, but you don't know a thing, Morgan. You have no idea what you're doing."

"Fuck you, Mom!"

Morgan faltered, her face falling for just a second before her shield shot back up. "I'm leaving." Morgan stepped back and tucked an arm protectively around Em's waist. "I'm going to stay at Em's tonight."

Celeste shook her head. "No."

Em cleared their throat and muttered something to Morgan, who rolled her eyes but nodded. "I'll stay in the guest room, okay? Em's mom will text you later." She glared at Celeste, obviously furious to have made a small concession. "Okay?"

Celeste knew her hurt feelings were brewing into something terrible, and she didn't want to see that come out directed at Morgan. They would talk about all of it. But not tonight.

So she nodded, jaw tight. "This conversation isn't over."

But Morgan was already walking away with Em.

Celeste was ready to collapse in a ball where she stood. It wasn't the yelling so much as all the rest—the secrets, and the piles of resentments, with Celeste herself at the source. *Some pathetic self-imposed path of discovery*. If she hadn't felt so broken, she would have laughed.

Woozy, Celeste swayed on her feet, but her back was steadied by a hand. Maria's familiar voice said, "John's going to take you home, okay? We don't want you driving right now. I'll bring you back over to get your car in the morning."

Celeste looked at Maria, her friend's face scrunched in concern as she pulled Celeste into a tight hug.

"Oh god." Celeste melted into Maria. "Did you both see all of that?"

"We did." Maria's hand rubbed up and down Celeste's back. "But that's good. It means you don't have to summarize it for anyone." She pulled back, catching Celeste's eyes with her own. "She's a teenager, Celeste. This is what they do. I know it's not usually what you and Morgan do, but it is normal."

Celeste nodded, feeling like a zombie. "The things she said, Maria."

"I know, honey. I know." She leaned in close, lowering her voice. "You going to be okay with John? Can he handle this sort of thing? I could get home and pump some milk for Xavi and come over."

She glanced behind her to John, his eyes heavy on her. He could build a bed, ID a bird from sound alone, pull Celeste out of the doldrums with a silly and sincere award he made by hand.

Comforting her after a public fight with her rash, emotional, judgment-impaired daughter wasn't really in the birders-with-benefits job description. She'd invited him to the show because her body had been in a mixed-up state between sadness and excitement, and she hadn't wanted to say goodbye like *that*.

But mostly, she'd wanted him there.

Just like she really wanted to let him take her home.

"Yeah, I think it'll be okay. I'll call you in the morning."

A few blurry minutes later, she was in John's car as he piloted them toward her house. The night's events—the crash of losing the contest, the wood of the award beneath her fingers, John's hand on her thighs, the way he'd greeted Morgan so naturally, and Morgan herself, her sweet baby, all anger and resentment—poured through Celeste in a jumble, leaving her surprisingly blank. But John simply drove as Celeste stared out the window, counting the streetlights as they blurred past. She hardly noticed when he went off course, and only looked over when they turned into an unfamiliar parking lot.

"What are we doing?" It was the first she'd spoken to him, and she was surprised at the raw, scratchy sound of her voice.

"We're getting fries."

He ordered, and soon she had a steaming bag of crunchy, greasy fries in her lap.

"I love fries," she choked out, just above a whisper.

He gave her another weak smile before pulling back out onto the street, heading toward her house. "I know."

She lifted a fry to her mouth. The salt hit her tongue first, then the heat of the steaming center, then the sweet comfort of grease. She closed her lips around it and, finally, she started to cry.

CHAPTER 35

The bath was everything. It was hurts-to-step-into hot, the kind of bath that turned her skin pink and called for a cold washcloth on her face. The heat leached out all the negativity and worry, if only for an hour.

Her head was still spinning as she put together the pieces she'd been missing in her conversations with Morgan and reckoned with the words her daughter had thrown at her. Celeste knew Morgan had been speaking in anger and defensiveness, but she'd managed the sinister teen magic of getting straight at Celeste's deepest fears and yanking them out to shake in her mother's face.

Had she been selfish? *Had* Celeste made her postdivorce life about only herself? And if she had, could anyone really blame her? She was over forty, her life half done. If she couldn't be selfish now, then when?

She shook away the thought and sipped at the tea John had handed her. She hadn't asked him to stay, but she also hadn't asked him to leave, and his presence was a comfort.

If Maria had come over instead, Celeste would be three glasses of wine deep and sobbing on the couch, reliving every moment of her fight with Morgan and questioning every decision she'd made in the past two years. And that would have been fine. But this was fine, too. In fact, crying in the car with John's hand on her knee and then sharing a puddle of ketchup as they ate their fries at her kitchen table was so much more than fine that Celeste almost wished he'd hadn't come at all.

Almost, but not quite.

She just needed to soak, and think, and gather herself for whatever was to come with Morgan. She knew that no matter what sense she tried to talk into her in the weeks between then and August, that Morgan would go to LA. She'd recognized the determination in her daughter's voice, because it echoed her own.

Morgan was creative and daring and brave, with the confidence and sense of adventure and belief in herself that Celeste had raised her to possess. She was everything Celeste could have hoped for, and more.

But she was also seventeen, and naive, and letting her heart take over the rest of her life. Next thing she knew, she'd be blinking awake in her late thirties, wondering where she'd gone.

Wouldn't she?

She rose with a sigh, water streaming down her body. Her hazy outline stared at her from the bathroom mirror and she stepped closer, the thick weave of the bath mat soft under her toes, her array of notes spread out and curling before her on the fogged mirror.

So many messages.

What about all your little mantras? Morgan had asked.

What about them, indeed? She'd started collecting them for answers, but sometimes there were so many voices in her head that she couldn't sort out her own. Was she supposed to *Find happiness alone* or *Grab life by the horns*? Was it better to *Seek joy* or *Relish safety*? What happened when doing one meant turning her back on another?

Lecture Morgan all she wanted, it had taken Celeste only a few weeks with John to start wavering about the plans she'd made for herself.

Yes, it would be easy to fall into real relationship territory with John. But it had been easy with Peter. Easy to fall, harder to climb back up, and more difficult still to grow once out of that shadow.

There were times with John, especially with their bodies pressed together in the dark, when she believed altering her course was worth the risk. But then daylight would come, and she didn't know. Didn't know when she was being controlled by emotion, or lust, or logic.

She was as lost as she'd ever been. She'd spent two years trying to lay the foundation for her second life, and she was no closer to finding it than when she'd started.

When at last she opened the door to her bedroom, John was in her reading chair, those sexy-as-hell glasses perched on his nose. It was her favorite spot to read in, though lately she'd spent more time there simply looking out the window, waiting for birds. Seeing John there, surrounded by the small intimacies of her bedroom, squeezed her lungs. They'd never explicitly agreed to keep their activities to his house, but she'd never invited him back to hers after their birding session in her yard. Somehow it had felt safer to keep him far removed from these parts of her.

John brought two fingers to his mouth, flicking his tongue against them before sliding a page between his fingertips.

"Hey." Her voice was raspy in the aftermath of the cry she'd had.

His eyes shot up to her as he slid the glasses off his nose. "Hey, how are you feeling?"

She fiddled with the belt of her robe, watching his hands on the book. “I’m all right for now. Thank you for the fries.”

“Of course.” He stood, dropping the book onto the chair and slipping his glasses into his back pocket before tugging at his folded sleeve. “I can go.” His eyes looked to her bedroom door. “I should probably—”

“Stay.” She wasn’t ready to lose the sight of him in her bedroom. “Maybe you could stay?”

“Sure.” He swallowed. “If you need me to.”

A little dizzy from the heat of her bath, Celeste tugged at the neckline of her robe, pulling it loose over one shoulder. John’s gaze drifted across her exposed skin until he seemed to catch himself, bouncing his attention back to her face.

But that had been enough to wake her up. Just one minute under John’s careful attention and she was lighter. This was what she needed. To be out of her messy brain and fully in her body, to lose herself in the give-and-take she and John did so well together.

One tug on the belt undid her robe. A shrug of her shoulders sent it to the floor.

John blinked but didn’t look away. Instead, he took his fill of her, as he always did. But he left the space between them. “I can stay without sex, Celeste. You’ve had a tough night, and—”

“And I want to feel good. Please, John, let’s feel good.”

CHAPTER 36

John should go. Get to his house, turn on the work lights in his shop and build something. He should help Celeste by giving her what she needed—time and space to be alone.

But instead he took a long, selfish moment to look at her, bare before him. Brightly painted toes, the smooth curve of her calf, the small white scar on the underside of her knee, the strong thickening of her thigh. Then the sweet pale crease where her thigh met her hip, the indent where his thumbs fit just right. Up across the plane of her stomach, the stretch marks that painted her abdomen like tiger stripes, then the hard ridges of her ribs. He loved to trace those lines with his teeth and tongue, teasing her relentlessly until reaching the small lift of her breasts, the rosy peaks of her nipples, and the strong ridge of her collarbone.

She didn't come closer, leaving him the choice. But it was no choice at all.

It took him two steps to put them face-to-face, and one more to press his body against hers. Heat radiated off her skin, warming him even through his clothes.

They shared one long breath before coming together, just long enough for him to wonder what this might mean for them and push aside the thought, bringing his mouth to hers until all his senses were simply *Celeste*.

That guidebook he'd once created in his mind had grown into a hefty thing. It didn't just catalog her swinging earrings, or that freckle behind her ear he'd first noticed at the bowling alley. Now it held the details of how she woke in the morning (cheerfully, sitting up to look out the window before saying a word), the way she drank a beer (sprinkling a slice of lime with salt before squeezing it in), and the exact force with which she liked him to tug her hair (harder than he would have tried if she hadn't kept urging him on). The margins had scribbled annotations like his bird book, special notes and observations. But it still held blank pages waiting for more discovery.

The kiss started slow and searching, her fingers combing through his beard. He stroked up her back, then down, flattening his hand to scrape his rough palms against the soft curve of her ass.

"I liked this shirt until right now," she whined against his mouth, fumbling with his buttons. John took over, and soon they had him stripped, his clothes landing in a pile next to Celeste's robe.

Her fingers wrapped around his erection, pulling with just the right, tight pressure he loved. She licked and groaned into his mouth as they stumbled the few feet to the bed. The mattress hit the backs of John's knees and Celeste pushed, sending him onto his back and crawling over him. Her legs spread over him, grazing his cock where she was hot and wet.

It was tempting, so tempting, to lie back as she lowered herself onto him. But he'd learned that sometimes Celeste needed help to slow down. So he rolled her, pinning her to the mattress and covering one nipple, then the other, with his mouth. He licked and nipped until she was writhing beneath him, gasping pleas. Only when she seemed boneless did he hook his hands beneath her knees and tug her to the edge of the bed. His own knees hit the floor as he pushed apart her thighs.

She spread her legs and accepted his worship. He groaned into her at the first taste, licking with the stroke and pressure he knew she craved. Because he'd learned that when Celeste was the loudest, and asking for the most, was when she was the most vulnerable. He knew just what she needed tonight.

She needed to be pulled out of her thoughts.

She tugged hard on his hair as he doubled his efforts, circling his tongue on her as he slipped one, then two fingers inside. Celeste arched her back and groaned his name, moving her hips against his hand and mouth. When her thighs trembled and her breath caught, he knew she was close.

So he went still, curling with his fingers but easing the pressure of his mouth.

"John . . ." It was a long whine, beautiful in its neediness.

"Just wait," he said against her inner thigh. "It's okay."

Then he returned. Slower now, taking his time to build her back up. Her fingers left his hair and he knew from her long, throaty moan that she was touching her nipples.

Her heels dug into his back and he pressed harder with his tongue, taking her back up. His name on her lips evaporated after the first hard *J*, until her only sound was the desperate breathing that came just *before*.

John forced himself to pull away, standing up to gaze at her.

Celeste was flushed, lips parted and eyes wide open, with her hands cupping each breast. "Oh my god, John, *please*."

He latched his hands onto her hips, notched his cock at her entrance, and thrust inside her. Their groans held the same note of satisfaction. He moved fast and hard, all the while watching her as she bit her lip and nodded, whispering "yes" again and again. Then her *yes* morphed to *please*, and he couldn't hold back any longer.

He withdrew and climbed to the bed, pulling her up the mattress, then urged her on top, as they'd started. She stroked his slick cock and licked her lips, then slid onto him with a hearty moan. When he put his hand between them, holding his thumb so she hit it with every movement of her hips, she sighed and laughed and groaned all at once.

"Do not. Move. This hand."

She braced her hands on his chest and rode him, his thumb a tool for her pleasure that she knew exactly how to use. His free hand toured the familiar terrain of her body, plucking at her nipples and stroking her neck where her pulse raced. When her movements got sloppy as she ground down on his thumb, John met her with his own thrusts, studying her face as she brought herself back to the edge.

She folded over him, kissing him hard. They came together like that—her body tightening around him as he moaned her name and drove his hips into her hard, coming undone as their tongues and lips tangled. The long crest of her orgasm gripped them both, followed by the slow melt after.

Breathing hard, she pulled away and looked at him. Flushed and messy, brown hair falling in sheets across her face.

Christ, she was beautiful.

Celeste blinked and rolled off him, landing on her back and staring at the ceiling. The room was quiet but for their breathing and the whir of a car passing outside.

Usually Celeste ended sex with some sort of joke or dirty compliment that brought laughter into the postcoital haze. But she was silent now, hands resting on her abdomen as it rose and fell with her breath.

"I'm just gonna . . ." John started, climbing off the bed. The need that had driven them together was slackened now, and it invited questions he didn't know how to ask. He retreated to the bathroom for a splash of water on his face.

Though he'd never been in her bathroom, the room was familiar because it was hers. Necklaces and earrings hung like decorations from nails and hooks on the wine-red wall. A snippet of a Mary Oliver poem was tacked above the light switch, and another by Nikki Giovanni above the toilet.

And then there was her mirror. A kaleidoscope of notes, as colorful as the butterflies that had surrounded them just a few hours before, paper edges curling like wings.

John's eyes drifted up the mirror, taking in the wide rainbow of advice.

We're all works in progress.

Walk boldly.

Seize the day.

It was a display of Celeste's bravery and sense of adventure, the way she sought out joy and faced risks and challenges.

Better off alone.

Don't lose yourself.

This was the Celeste who had sworn off dating and set an end date to their arrangement. Who had yelled at Morgan in the parking lot about how love would push everything else aside. The one who'd stopped them in the closet that day, making sure he knew she wasn't looking for a relationship.

The discovery she was seeking was of herself, by herself.

John was dimly aware of the rise and fall of his chest, still damp with sweat from his lovemaking with Celeste.

Lovemaking.

God, he was a fucking fool. Celeste had laid out just what she wanted, and what she didn't. From that very first morning, pastries in hand, she'd been clear about not wanting a relationship, and she'd never wavered. A relationship was something that would hold her back. Love was something dangerous.

And he'd started on the same page. But between helping Celeste see that first bird and buying her those french fries, something within him had shifted.

It wasn't Celeste's fault. But damn, it still hurt.

His heart raced, propelling his body out of the bathroom and back into Celeste's room, where he bent for his clothes.

He made the mistake of glancing at Celeste. She was on her back, propped up on her elbows, her entire body on view for him, flushed and beautiful.

Her nose wrinkled as John quickly stepped into his boxers, then his pants. He could barely pull up the zipper for his shaking hands.

As he yanked his shirt over his shoulders, Celeste sat up and pulled a corner of the comforter over her body. "Are you— You can stay tonight."

John shook his head. "I can't." He picked up her robe and laid it across the bed, avoiding her eyes. "I shouldn't, it's—" Exhaling a long, grueling breath, he looked at her. She was tugging at the tendrils of hair falling around her face.

He swallowed. "The contest is over, right? This was our last day. I don't think we should push it past what we agreed."

"Oh." She reached for the robe, using it to cover her body. "Right."

Silence fell between them again as he pulled on a sock.

"Maybe . . ." Celeste cleared her throat. "This seems to be working, right? Maybe we should keep doing this."

His heart gave a hopeful lurch, ready for any justification to crawl back into bed with her and wipe that frown off her face for the rest of the night. And longer. "Doing what?"

"What we've been doing. The birders-with-benefits thing. It's working, right? It's fun, and easy, and—"

He almost said yes. But Breena's words from earlier cycled through his head. She hadn't known the whole context of John's time with Celeste, but that didn't matter. She'd seen something between them, something true, even when John was trying to pretend it wasn't there. And so had Chris. And Jared.

And dammit, so had John.

He stopped, stood straight, and looked at Celeste. "No, I don't want to do that anymore."

She tugged the robe up to her chin, frowning. "But why?"

"Because I'm falling in love with you."

CHAPTER 37

Once, when Celeste was birding with John, a Cooper's hawk had slowed to land on a branch just above her, so close she could see the shine of its talons. Both then and now had brought a sense of wonder—seeing something beautiful and dangerous all at once. Then, she'd just whispered "wow." Now, she said nothing at all.

After a moment, John bent for his other sock, then turned his back and made his way to the living room.

The sight of him disappearing through the doorway shocked her into action. She threw on her robe and bolted to catch him in the living room. "Wait up. Whoa. John, hold up!"

John had one hand pressed tight to his nape, his tense back to her as his shoulder blades pushed against his shirt with each breath.

He was quiet a lot of the time, but this was different. This silence made her bones ache. It was heavy with questions she was afraid to ask, like *why* and *when* and *what now?*

John sank onto the couch and rested his elbows on his knees, fingers entwined. Celeste took a seat in the worn wingback chair facing him. "Can you tell me what's going on?"

Finally, he looked up and met her eyes. "You were clear from the start about the dating stuff, and I thought I was too. I was excited to try this with you, to have something uncomplicated." He picked up a pencil off the table and rolled it between his fingers. "But something changed for me along the way. I don't know where or when exactly, but I'm not where I started."

"Okay."

An eloquent response for a woman who talked to students all day about the power of words. But what else could she say? She wasn't where they'd started either. Now she didn't know where she was at all.

Behind her, the clock marked each passing second.

"With Breena"—his eyes stayed on the pencil as he passed it between his hands—"I spent too long trying to be what I thought she wanted, and never feeling like enough. I'm done doing that. That's why I can't keep going like we have been, pretending it's casual. I want more than casual with you, Celeste. Do you . . ." He raised his eyes to hers. "Is that something you could be open to?"

She was so proud of him, even as her stomach twisted. He was making a move, saying what he wanted, changing up the status quo.

But she was also so fucking scared.

She cleared her throat, forcing out some words. "There were reasons I didn't want to date for real, and you were on board with that. I've made promises to myself, John. Plans. I'm just starting to *see* myself again, and I can't just flip a switch and know exactly how to change course."

He dropped the pencil to the table, then rubbed at the tight line on his forehead. "I'm not asking you to. I'm not asking for any promises, just . . . openness." If Celeste leaned forward, she could reach him over the corner of the table. Instead, she drew up her knees and hugged them tight.

"I want us to keep seeing each other, Celeste. But if we did," he continued, "I would need to know you're open to having bigger feelings for me. That if you start to fall in love with me you'll let yourself. Because I'm halfway there already."

Celeste cradled her face in her hands, pushing hard at her cheeks. She wanted to crawl into John's lap, curl up under his callused hands, and ask him to tell her more about what "halfway" meant.

But alarm bells clanged as her old armor clicked into place.

"I'm scared," she said finally. The confession barely made it through the slats between her fingers.

"I know." And then John was crouching in front of her, pulling her palms away to look at her. "I'm not Peter, Celeste."

And she laughed. Because it was either that or cry. Of course John wasn't Peter. He was quiet, soft-spoken with his competence, generous to a fault. And he wasn't the problem.

"I know you're not." She cupped his face, stroking his beard once before sitting up straight and pulling her hands back into her lap. "But I'm still me. And that's what scares me. I'm the one who let myself get lost, who let myself get smaller. I'm the one who was so eager to make everything okay that I never asked for more of what I needed. And I can't trust myself not to go there again. I'm just now growing into my own space. Figuring out my own shape, you know?"

"Okay." John tucked a strand of her hair behind her ear and let his hand linger at her face. "I understand." He stood. "I'm sorry this is happening now, after your argument with Morgan. Do you want to call Maria? She could come over."

She didn't look up, just watched her hands as they twisted together. "I'm okay alone, but thank you."

Alone was what she wanted, wasn't it?

He touched her cheek again, and Celeste recorded the memory, the way the softness of his hands, calluses and all, always surprised her.

Then his fingers were gone, and so was he.

CHAPTER 38

"So, how were your Lonely Days?"

Chris gathered up the crumpled paper remains of their burrito wrappers and tossed them one by one into the nearby garbage can basketball-style, murmuring, "Two points!" with every successful basket, then turned to John for his answer.

When John went radio silent after Breena kissed the stupid genius, Chris had instituted the Lonely Days rule. When working through something, John was allowed three days all alone, after which he was expected to check in with his friend.

Which was what had brought him to campus with burritos from their favorite shop.

This set of Lonely Days had been spent either in his workshop or outside, feet pounding familiar trails as sweat soaked his back. He'd slept in his shop for two nights after tossing and turning in his bed and then on the couch. Celeste's imprint was on every surface, her greedy sighs trapped in his sheets.

Chris's *It's time* text had actually come as a relief.

They'd eaten in silence, watching university students passing on the crisscross of sidewalks that weaved between redbrick buildings.

But Chris watched him now, eyebrows up in expectation. "You want to tell me what happened?"

John sipped his iced tea, shaking the ice around in the cup.

Sighing, Chris pulled his phone from the back pocket of his tattered black jeans. "Let's see what we can do with two minutes, okay?" He smiled as he held up his phone, displaying the timer on the screen. If John was being specifically cagey about a subject that would probably feel good to talk about, Chris set a timer and encouraged his friend to force some words out of his mouth until the alarm went off.

A swallowtail butterfly landed on a wildflower across the sidewalk, so John decided to start there. Soon he was telling Chris about the butterfly house, the art show, and Celeste's consequent fight with Morgan. When he got to talking about the time at her house and his confession to her about his feelings, he was soft on details, but Chris followed along, nodding as he listened.

John watched the last few seconds tick by on the phone. "And I've just been working ever since."

"Okay." Chris silenced the timer and then turned to John, his eyes warm. "Saying what you wanted like that—hell, even really knowing what you wanted . . . I'm proud of you, John."

John was proud of himself too, despite having spent plenty of moments regretting it all and wishing he'd taken anything Celeste wanted to give. But those regrets hadn't lasted. He cared too much for Celeste to hide his true feelings, and too much for himself to fall into old habits.

"I thought she might be open to it," he admitted, the confession stinging. "She's always so excited about discovery, and I hoped maybe . . ."

Celeste had shown up at a park to be a fake girlfriend to a total stranger, gone headfirst into a contest she knew nothing about and actually almost won it with him, jumped into mountain pools, and formed friendships with frogs. She opened herself to the whole world—but not to him.

Chris stretched an arm along the back of the bench, flicking John with his thumb and forefinger. “I can hear your thoughts, John. Don’t get broody thinking you’re not enough for her. This is a Celeste thing, not a you thing.”

“But what if it *is* a me thing, just a little? What if I’m not built to be the kind of person someone wants?”

Chris’s arms flew into the air, sending a white-winged dove fleeing from the branches over them. “Well, Jesus, fuck them, then!” He groaned and took a breath. “Truth is, you’ve had serious relationship experience with one person and that ended badly. Honestly, there’s a lot about Breena that I liked once upon a time, and I’m open to liking her again. But current therapy or not, she wasn’t it, man. She saw your potential but never celebrated *you*.” He leveled his blue eyes at John. “Thinking you wouldn’t be what someone wants? That was Breena’s shit, not yours, so let it go.”

Chris leaned forward. “And another thing.” John knew there was no stopping him once he got going, and Chris’s analysis was a welcome distraction from his own thoughts, which had only grown muddier over his days alone. “You may be aware of this fact, Johnny boy, but you can be a hard person to get to know. I managed out of sheer determination, and it was well worth it. And when I watched you and Celeste together, I could tell—she *knows* you. And whatever’s going on in there for you”—he thumped John’s chest, hard—“it’s happening to her, too. Whatever reason she has for not wanting to go there is all about her.”

She’d said as much that night, and John had played back their short conversation over and over, wondering whether if he'd picked different words, they could have found a different outcome. But she'd been resolute. Scared, but resolute. The only thing he could do was give her the space she'd told him she needed all along.

"I didn't think you were really built for casual sex," Chris said after a moment. "But I was excited you were trying something new and I was just happy you were getting laid. And Celeste is so damn cool. I'm sorry if I should have raised some flags along the way."

"I saw the flags," John assured him. "I just ignored them." And despite the hurt he was feeling now, he wouldn't have changed a thing. "I'm just not sure what to do now, if anything."

Chris pulled up his feet to sit cross-legged on the bench, resting his palms on his knees. "You know how I've been hating my job lately? Well, I listened to a few podcasts that . . . someone told me about."

"You can say her name." Celeste had told him about the Help Chris Love His Work Again playlist she'd curated after listening to his job complaints on their birding outing together.

"All right." Chris sighed. "Celeste gave me some things to listen to, self-help shit and all of that. It turns out, that stuff *actually* helps. And I realized I've been thinking about things wrong. I've been waiting for me to fit into this job instead of making this job fit me, making it about who I am and what I can do. There's a balance between what's expected of me here and what I want. It's going to take some time to figure out what that looks like, but I'm up for the challenge."

Chris shifted, pulling his knees up and hugging them to his chest. "I want that for you. Not *here*, obviously." He motioned to the campus around them. "This place wasn't right for you. You move at a different pace, buddy. And I know sometimes people, even me, push you to move faster. But there's a speed between running and sitting still, even for you."

A group of students walked past, giggling as they leaned together over something playing on a phone.

"And I want you to know you have everything it takes to get what you want, whether it's from work or life or a relationship. Maybe that will be with Celeste or maybe it won't, but you can find something different than what you had with Breena, if you want it. Something that fits you. You deserve to believe that."

John's gaze drifted into the mesquite fanned above them, where a verdin buried its face in the cluster of newly bloomed yellow flowers. For as long as he could remember, he had looked into trees and seen possibility—the birds and critters that could be there, the leaves that would unfurl each spring, even the shade the tree would offer as the sun moved across the sky.

Somewhere along the way, he'd lost that sense of possibility for himself. Instead, he'd focused on what he didn't have—multiple degrees, published articles, the swagger and gusto of professional guides and scientists. He'd heard encouragement as judgment and let his small dreams fade before they even began.

But with Celeste at his side these past few weeks, he'd reacquainted himself with the thrill of discovery. And regardless of what she might want or need now, he'd learned something from being along for part of her journey. Sometimes you just had to *Say yes*, even if it was only to yourself.

"Tell you what." He rubbed at his beard and watched Chris raise his eyebrows. "How about we both try to make some changes?"

Chris lowered his legs and sat up tall. "I'm listening."

"Good." John nodded, a familiar, beloved buzz moving up his spine. "Because I think I'm going to need your help." He slipped his phone from his pocket. "How the hell do I use Instagram?"

CHAPTER 39

"Maria, this absolutely sucks. Please tell me we're almost done."

Celeste and Maria were on their fifth lap around the high school track, power walking as Maria pushed Xavier in the stroller. The early morning sun was already scorching, and Celeste's back was soaked with sweat.

"We're exercising, Celeste," Maria huffed. "You like exercise."

"Wrong. I like activity. Ultimate Frisbee, hiking, synchronized swimming on occasion. This"—she motioned to the track—"is horrible." She shook her head and smiled. "But I love it, if it means being with you, of course."

"We should all be so lucky to have such dedicated friends. And thank you for making time for me in your busy schedule." The exaggerated roll of Maria's eyes told Celeste exactly what she thought of her busy schedule.

So maybe her days were a little full. She was dropping into pottery classes three days a week after work, co-teaching an after-school program the other two, and had insisted on babysitting Xavier twice in a week's time.

And it had nothing to do with the fact that it had been eight days since John walked out of her house.

She'd ended up sleeping on the couch that night, unable to return to her bed after having shared it with John so recently. When Maria called the morning after John had left about retrieving Celeste's car, she'd known something was wrong and had arrived ASAP with iced lattes and warm, flaky pastries.

She hadn't grilled Celeste for details that morning, but she'd been grasping for them bit by bit ever since, and Celeste recognized the morning walk for what it was: an interrogation.

"So, while we're out enjoying this beautiful Arizona morning, I'm going to ask you a few questions about what happened with John that has you spamming me with babysitting requests. This is what I know so far: after your fight with Morgan, John bought you fries, then you had great sex. He told you that he was a little bit in love with you, and you panicked."

Celeste shook her head. "No. He said 'halfway there,' about the love stuff. And I didn't panic. I stuck to my plan."

"To be alone."

"To be with *myself*, Maria. Being alone is just a side effect."

Maria tsked, pushing the stroller along the turn. "And being with yourself and opening up to whatever could happen with John are mutually exclusive? Is it impossible to be both an individual and someone in a relationship? Because I didn't get the memo that I gave up my personhood to be with my partner."

Celeste glared at Maria even as she gasped for breath. Speed walking was awful. "You're being purposefully argumentative. Of course you didn't give up your personhood." Maria was talking about *her* life, *her*self. It wasn't the same. Celeste did her best to outpace the argument, pumping her arms hard.

This was easier, anyway. The stuff with John was over and she could return to her plan without any distractions. And the next time she met a charming, quiet, sexy, kind, captivating librarian lumberjack, she would definitely not offer to be his fake girlfriend.

Maria caught up, nudging Celeste with a shoulder. Celeste knew better than to try to outrun Maria—her friend showed up, no matter what.

"I don't know why you're being so hard on me," she said, sucking air. "He's the one who left, Maria. He's the one who walked away."

"Sorry, honey, but it sounds like he laid it out there and you failed to pick it up. You just happened to be at home, so he had to do the leaving. Listen, it's okay to not know exactly what you want, Celeste. And it's okay to be scared. But you like John, I know you do!"

"Of course I like him." How could she not? He'd read every Barbara Kingsolver book in print and could make a bird feeder while she whispered dirty words in his ear.

"So. He likes you, you like him. That's all you need to start. Don't be so damn stubborn."

Celeste scoffed. "It's so much more complicated than that."

Maria stopped, leaning onto the handlebar of her stroller and breathing hard. She grabbed her water bottle out of the cupholder and took a long swig. "We can either speed walk or argue about John, but I can't do both simultaneously. I'm not even three months postpartum, for Christ's sake. Stop trying to kill me."

Celeste laughed and grabbed her own water from where she'd stashed it under Xavier's stroller. He snoozed in his shaded seat, chubby and content. Maria lowered herself to the ground, reaching for her toes.

The heat of the track warmed her butt and thighs as she

joined Maria. They stretched in silence for a moment as Celeste waited. No way was Maria through with her yet.

But when Maria spoke, her voice was light. "Actually, I could use some advice."

Celeste perked up. "All right. Is this about David? Has the sex stuff been all right?"

"Girl." Maria lowered her voice, as if Xavi might eavesdrop. "The sex stuff is great. Once I got over that hump, we got back into it. Way less frequently than before, but definitely storing up for when my mom gets here and the well runs dry. Thanks for the encouragement."

Maria lay down and closed her eyes, smiling into the sunshine. "It's actually about another thing. I met this guy that I really like a lot. He's super smart and extremely good in bed."

"Wait, what?" Celeste rose to her elbows, but Maria continued serenely at her side.

"And I had the major hots for him, basically right away. But I'm also on this self-proclaimed path to always be alone because I think all relationships are bound to take over my life. Because my ex-husband turned out to be a bit of a dickhead."

"Maria."

"So I made this perfect plan to just hook up with this guy for a few weeks, friends-with-benefits-style."

"What are you—"

"But here's the thing." Maria's eyes stayed closed, but her finger pointed in the air. "He caught feelings. And . . ." God, she was enjoying this too much. "And this is really hard for me to admit, but I caught feelings, too. When I look at him my whole body feels like one of those emojis with the big heart eyes."

"Okay, that's a little much—"

"But I ran scared, because it doesn't fit with what I thought I needed. And I'm not sure I did the right thing."

Maria's eyes opened, dark brown and sparkling, as her mouth turned up into a grin. "I'd love your advice on what I should do."

Celeste scoffed, even as Maria's words bounced in her head. "You're being an asshole."

"Me?" Maria gasped. "I'm just a person in need. And I'm coming to my best friend, the woman who gives the best advice and makes the best plans in the world. The person who pours her heart into me, and gives me strength, and amazes me every day. I'm asking her because I trust her."

Celeste's eyes flooded. "Don't do this."

"Don't do what?" Maria sat up. "Ask you to give yourself half the trust and friendship you give me? Well, I'm going to. Because I'm that bitch, Celeste. I love you, and I would be doing you a disservice if I didn't push you right now. You're being stupid."

Celeste shook with laughter even as she wiped hot tears from her cheeks.

Maria took her hands in hers, rubbing her thumb over Celeste's knuckles. "Just try. Try to be your own friend."

Celeste closed her eyes. The wetness on her cheeks vanished quickly under the heating sun. "Well." She took a deep breath to steady her voice. "If I was talking to someone with this problem, I would probably ask her what she's afraid of."

"Okay. And how do you think she'd answer?"

Celeste sniffed. The world was all yellows and oranges behind her closed eyes. "Maybe she'd say that she's afraid she got lost a long time ago, and that she won't know when she's found again."

Maria squeezed her hands. "What else?"

"She might say that sometimes she runs around because she's

afraid to stand still. Because if she stops, she's not sure what will be there."

"Okay. And what advice would you give that friend?"

Celeste opened her eyes to find Maria watching, a gentle lift in her lips.

"I think I would tell her that we're all works in progress. That she isn't a destination, but a process. That she's always a discovery. And that . . ." She swallowed hard, shaking her head. "That she should trust herself more. That she's in control of keeping herself in the sun, and that what happened in her past doesn't define her future."

Their look held for a moment, and then Maria raised her hands to the sky. "Hallelujah! I am so fucking good."

"Yeah, yeah. If you ever get tired of math, you could be a guidance counselor. Now shush, you're going to wake up Xavi." Celeste laughed.

"Let him wake up. I'll tell him that his aunt Celeste is going through something and his mom is working wonders. I honestly don't care what you do about John. Maybe this isn't the right time for you to start something new. But that's for *you* to decide. The Celeste of this moment, in this life. The question is, do you trust her? The woman you are today?"

Celeste remembered that flower. The one in the sidewalk crack searching for the sun. Reaching for possibility. All it had to do was let itself grow. "I think I do."

CHAPTER 40

The call-and-response of Celeste's cardinals poured through her kitchen window, mocking her with their easy devotion.

"Sure, guys," she muttered. "Rub it in."

Not that it was their fault she was stuck in some angsty no-woman's-land territory, trying to trust herself without understanding just where it had gotten her. As far as she could tell, trusting her instincts meant taking a lot of very hot baths and writing texts to John she didn't send. Texts about the cardinals in her yard, about a black phoebe she'd IDed without even cracking open her guidebook, about a story on the radio examining the potential for large-scale desalinization to address the inevitable water crisis. Hell, she'd even written a text about her switch to oat milk in her coffee.

None of which was what she really wanted to say to John.

The problem was figuring out what she *did* want to say. What she wanted at all. She'd leaned so hard into her postdivorce fly-solo plan, she wasn't sure she could find solid ground without it.

And she and Morgan were still dealing with the fallout from their argument, now two weeks old. They'd settled into a cold war that had lasted days, full of vacant stares in the kitchen and short texts from Morgan informing Celeste she'd be spending the night at her dad's.

Instead of driving John from her mind, the tension with Morgan made her miss him even more. He had a gift for helping her settle, a subtle way of calming her with a simple touch or a small smile. But she couldn't reach for that comfort without being sure of what she could offer. He'd made that much clear the night he left. And he deserved that, and more.

And she was a mom first, plain and simple. Maybe it wouldn't always be that way. Morgan was growing up and away from her exactly as she should, but for now Celeste wanted to travel back two weeks and somehow stop their blowup. Shit, she wanted to travel back years and hold little Morgan in her arms.

But all they could do was grow.

"Hey, Mom."

Morgan appeared in the kitchen doorway, hair piled on her head. A simple "hey" was friendlier than she'd been for days.

"Hey." Celeste put down the coffee that had been cooling in her hands, oat milk and all.

"Um, so, Em's aunt, you know with the house in LA, she's going to be in town next weekend and we thought it would be good to meet with all the parents."

"Oh. Well—"

"Mom." Morgan's tone was short. "Please don't start. This isn't an invitation to tell me not to go."

"I know, honey." Celeste sighed. "I know. And I'm still not thrilled, but I'm . . . resigned." It was obvious Morgan was determined to go, and Celeste didn't want to alienate her even further. And the plan to meet up with the aunt was a good one. "And I would, of course, love to meet Em's aunt. Will the mysterious Em be there as well?"

"Em's not mysterious, Mom." Morgan rolled her eyes. "You've known them since they were ten."

"Sure I have, but not like this. Not as my daughter's . . ." Celeste paused, unsure of what word to land on.

"Person," Morgan offered, a blush rising in her cheeks. "I just call them my person."

Seeing the hearts fly out of Morgan's eyes didn't raise Celeste's hackles as much as she'd expected. Instead, she felt proud of Morgan and Em for carving out space for themselves when outdated labels didn't fit.

"Can your person come over for dinner next week?" Morgan bit her lip, but Celeste kept going. "It's not a trap, Morgan. I promise no LA talk unless it's researching museums, okay? I just want to spend time with you both."

Morgan looked unconvinced, but she nodded. "Okay."

Morgan tugged at her hair and glanced out of the room. "Um, can I borrow the lip gloss you have? The shiny stuff?"

"Of course." First a "hey," now lip-gloss borrowing? This was incredible progress. "You know where it is."

Morgan cleared her throat. "Well, I looked and I couldn't find it. Could you look, maybe? For me?"

"All right." Celeste shrugged and headed toward her bathroom. She kept all her rarely used cosmetics in the same drawer, so she wasn't sure why Morgan couldn't find it. Once in her bathroom, she opened the drawer and pulled it right out, but when she straightened up again she caught sight of the mirror.

All her notes were gone, the mirror clean and shiny.

All the notes but two, written in Morgan's handwriting.

She turned to look for her daughter, but Morgan was already there, smiling and leaning against the doorway. She slid her hands into the back pockets of her cutoffs and shrugged. "I wanted to say sorry for the whole 'fuck you' thing. And for not telling you earlier about the LA stuff." She looked down, pursing her lips. "And also for—well, Em thought maybe I was a little harsh when I railed on you about splitting up the family. And they're smart and"—she swallowed—"right, in this case. Anyway, I wanted to do something nice, so I made you some new mantras that I thought you might need."

"Hon." Celeste glanced back at the new notes, her throat tightening, before turning her attention to Morgan. "Thank you. I accept your apology." She sat against the counter, taking a breath. "But I did split up our family. I didn't do it out of spite, or wanting to hurt anyone, but a fact's a fact. And I regret causing people pain, especially you, but I wouldn't do it differently. And you're allowed to feel about it however you feel about it, okay?"

Morgan nodded and gave a little sniff but kept her eyes on the ground. "Okay."

"But, honey"—Celeste reached a hand out to tip Morgan's chin up—"don't you ever say 'fuck you' to me again, do you understand? I expect more creativity from you."

Her daughter smirked and rolled her eyes. "I'll try harder next time."

"Lord help me," Celeste groaned, turning back to the mirror. "You want to tell me about these?"

Morgan leaned forward and pulled a pink Post-it note off the mirror and handed it to Celeste.

Listen to yourself.

"I was just thinking," Morgan said, "that you had all this advice up here like you actually needed it. But you're smart and confident and really good at helping everybody get their shit together, even if you're too bossy about it sometimes, and I think you can do that for yourself, too. If you give yourself a chance."

Celeste turned the note around in her hand. "Have you been talking to Maria?"

"Uh, no. Why?"

"It's just . . ." Celeste read the note again. "She said something similar."

Morgan's smile cracked a little wider. "Maybe it's because we both know you best."

They really did. And Celeste could hardly believe her luck. "Moo."

Morgan's eyes went wide. "Do not cry, Mom. Seriously."

"Oh honey." Celeste scooped Morgan into her arms, hugging her tight. "Of course I'm going to cry."

And she did, shedding tears onto Morgan's shoulder as her daughter finally wrapped her arms around her, squeezing her back. After a long moment Celeste pulled away and held Morgan by the shoulders.

She looked at her daughter with amazement, marveling at how far they'd both come. This was the little girl who'd hiked three miles with a bleeding knee because she was determined to draw the view from the top of the mountain, the girl who'd pushed a boy into his locker when he'd purposely misgendered Em, the girl who worked her pencils to nubs to understand a new technique.

The young woman who'd seen the path everyone expected her to take and had decided on something else, something that would feed her passion.

"I am so proud of you, baby. And I'm not going to pretend I like the LA plan, but I really am proud of you for setting your own course. You amaze me every single day."

Morgan nodded as tears spilled out of her own eyes. She quickly wiped them away with the back of her hand and nodded toward the mirror. "There's one more."

Celeste glanced at the second note, shaking her head.

Call John.

"What would you know about me needing to call John?"

"Oh, let's think," Morgan scoffed, giving a final sniff. "You were seeing John a bunch and you were super cheerful, like all the time. Now he's disappeared and you're listening to your sad-lady music anytime you're at home, which is barely at all. Plus, I've been waiting for you to bug me to go to his birding thing tomorrow, but you haven't even mentioned it, so I'm pretty sure you guys aren't talking."

Celeste was about to take offense at "sad-lady music" when her brain caught up. "What birding thing?"

Morgan cocked her head, then pulled her phone out of her pocket and did some swiping. "This birding thing."

She held out the phone to Celeste, an Instagram post up on the screen. It was a logo—blue mountains and cacti in the background, with the outlines of birds in the sky and illustrated streaks of sun against blue. The foreground contained a pair of binoculars leaning against some hiking boots, with words in bold cutting across:

Wings of Discovery

Guided bird-watching for the beginning birder

This wasn't the personal account he'd begrudgingly started. The description announced a free walk the next morning guided by "local birder John Maguire." It was smart—give people a taste of what it was like to bird with John, and they'd come back clamoring for more.

"He's doing it." A smile grew on her still-wet face. "He's really doing it."

But Morgan yanked the phone away, eyeing Celeste seriously. "So what happened there, Mom?"

Celeste just shook her head. She and Morgan had had enough drama. "Nothing you need to worry about, honey."

"If you tell me, I'll do one dinner-and-movie night with you every week until I move."

"All summer?" Celeste clarified, and Morgan nodded.

But Celeste hesitated, pulling at her hair. "You're sure this is okay to talk about with you? It doesn't make you uncomfortable?"

"What makes me uncomfortable is Joni Mitchell blaring every time you take a shower. If I hear 'A Case of You' one more time, I will perish on the spot. Please, just spill."

Celeste laughed as she lifted herself to a seat on the bathroom counter. "John and I were friends, and"—she cleared her throat—"and a little bit more. And he said he had feelings for me."

Morgan nodded, her arms crossed against her chest, a smile playing on her face. "And what did you say?"

Celeste blushed. "I said no."

Morgan stared at her for a beat. "Okay. But you like him?"

Celeste sighed, peeling the *Call John* note off the mirror and rubbing it with her fingers. "Yeah. I really, really do. But, hon, I never wanted you to think you weren't my top priority, and—"

"Seriously, Mom. I would *love* to not be your top priority."

Celeste laughed and pulled a tissue out of the box on her counter for a hearty blow.

"If you're scared of something," Morgan continued, "don't make it about me. And don't make it about him. This is on you."

Celeste blinked, floored by Morgan's simple wisdom. If she were talking to herself as a friend right now, she'd say she'd done a fucking awesome job raising this kid.

"You can really be a know-it-all."

Morgan spread her arms wide, eyebrows up. "I learned from the best."

Celeste hopped off the counter and wrapped an arm around Morgan's waist, turning them both to face the mirror. Looking at herself, side by side with her daughter, she had never felt more beautiful.

And it was a hell of a lot easier to see herself without all those damn notes in the way.

Celeste caught Morgan's eye in the reflection and grinned. "I'd like to do more than just call him, I think. I'd like to make a statement. Something he deserves. You seem pretty good at this stuff. Do you have any advice?"

Morgan was still for a moment, then her mouth curved up.

"I have an idea, but we need supplies. You order a pizza and I'll call Em." She turned to Celeste, her smile sky-high. "This is going to be so much fun."

CHAPTER 41

"So how would this work, exactly? If we wanted to do a little more bird-watching?"

John did a double take, making sure the red-faced man in the floppy hat was talking to him. When he'd thrown together the plan for the free guided walk under the banner of Wings of Discovery, he'd hoped to gather some interest for his private guiding services.

But now that he was faced with that very interest, he just stared and swallowed.

Chris's elbow hit him hard in the ribs. "John. This nice man is asking about birding."

John shook his head and cleared his throat, reminding himself to smile as he pulled a business card out of his back pocket. It showed the logo he'd sketched out with Chris and sent to his brother Jared for a more formal rendering, along with his phone number and brand-new website.

"You can contact me here and we can set up a time to go out and get started. I work in thirty-minute increments, so we can plan for whatever you think will work for you—from thirty minutes up to three hours." The man looked over the card before tucking it into his pocket. "And you don't need to worry about binoculars or anything," John added. "I can provide all of that."

The man turned to his companion, a lanky Black fellow with a white beard and wire-rimmed glasses, and raised his eyebrows. "Could be fun."

"Definitely," the other answered. He offered a hand for John to shake. "Great to meet you; we'll be in touch."

John shook his hand quickly as Chris bounced beside him. The two men drifted away, still looking around at the trees and across the small pond that served as the centerpiece of Rivera Park.

As soon as there was some distance between them and the budding birders, Chris shoved John hard in the shoulder. "Look at that! Fuck yeah, John. Clients are lining up."

"It was one client." Still, John couldn't repress his smile. For an event thrown together so quickly, it had been a success. It might have made sense to spend more time planning, but he couldn't risk losing his momentum or letting his old doubts retake their space in his brain. So he'd decided to just get the hell started.

Chris ripped open a granola bar and took a big bite, looking content. He'd been eager to join John as his assistant and had been great at chatting with the people who'd come for a taste of bird-watching. "Two clients, actually. And ten other people at the walk, who all got a card from me as they were heading out. And I bet more than half of them will call you, if not more. They were entranced, dude. You have a gift."

Celeste had said something similar, and he was on the path to letting himself believe it. He'd stopped himself from sending her the information about the walk, which was at the park where their concocted first meeting had taken place. But this step was about John, not about proving anything to Celeste or finding excuses to reach out to her, as much as he wanted to. If Celeste was going to reach a place of openness to their being together, he knew she had to get there on her own.

Chris swung his backpack over his shoulder. "I've got to shower before my board meeting. You all good here?"

Chris had joined the board of a local nonprofit that focused on watershed advocacy and restoration, a big step in the "Help Myself" plan he'd drawn up.

"Yeah, I'm good. Board stuff still going well?"

Chris's face lit up. "It's so cool, John. Really digging it. We're planning this community event where kids come and learn all about the watershed, and they said I could bring some snails! I can't wait."

As John turned to gather his things, he spotted the two men he'd just talked to. They were shading their eyes and peering across the pond.

Unable to resist the urge to help someone spot a bird, he joined them, pulling a pair of binoculars out of his pack and passing them over. "See something over there?"

One took the binoculars and adjusted them at his eyes. "What is she doing?" He passed the binoculars to his companion.

"She's holding some kind of sign? It says 'Hi.' What in the world?"

John heard Chris gasp and turn, jogging to reach John's side.

John brought his binoculars to his face and focused. Celeste was standing in her turquoise dress, the one she'd worn the last night he'd seen her. In her hands was a big white poster board with designs swirling around its edges and a single word written in the middle.

HI.

She laid the poster board on the ground in front of her and picked up another from beside her, holding it up next.

CAN WE TALK?

"Can we talk?" The man with the floppy hat passed the binoculars back to his friend. "Who does she want to talk to? You?"

Their voices were like birdsong filtering through John's head as he kept his eyes trained on Celeste while she reached for the next sign.

I'M HALFWAY THERE, TOO.

"Halfway to what?" Chris was right next to him, his own binoculars back up and at his face. "Where's she halfway to?"

A great blue heron lifted from its post at the edge of the pond and took flight. As it passed over her, Celeste lifted her chin to watch it fly.

John had never been so happy to have splurged on an expensive pair of binoculars. He could see each escaped strand of Celeste's ponytail waving around her face in the breeze.

His phone buzzed in his pocket, and he pulled it out to see an incoming call from Celeste. He showed the screen to Chris, who was beaming. "I'm gonna take this. Have a good meeting, buddy, thanks for coming."

John raised the binoculars back to his face, training them on Celeste again as he answered the call. "Hi."

She smiled and bit her lower lip, holding her phone in one hand and still gripping the sign in the other.

"Hi." Then she laughed into the phone. "Looks like Chris is giving us some privacy."

John turned to see Chris walking away with an arm around each of the straggling new birders, talking to them enthusiastically as he directed them toward the parking lot. John heard the words *snail* and *watershed* and imagined they were halfway through a lecture about snail ecology already.

He turned back to look at Celeste. "Stay where you are. I'll come over."

She shook her head, toying with the hem of her dress. "No, we'll meet in the middle. You head left and I'll go right."

A minute later, John turned the corner on the path and saw her as she gasped and skidded to a halt in the loose gravel of the trail, her face flushed. She gripped her posters in one hand, her backpack hanging from her shoulders.

The last few feet between them felt like a mile. She'd shown up, posters and all, but John was still afraid she might flee at any minute. Her feet crunched on the path as she closed the distance between them, stopping just close enough for him to reach out and touch her, if he dared.

He kept his arms at his sides for now. "How did you know I'd be here?"

"Morgan told me." Her voice was quiet, more timid than he'd heard her before. "She saw it on Instagram." A smile cracked on her face. "The walk was a great idea. How'd it go?"

"It was good." Great, actually. But not exactly what he wanted to talk about. He cocked his head. "Morgan told you I'd be here? So you two are okay?"

Celeste shrugged, but she was smiling. "Yeah. Not perfect, but okay for sure. She helped me with the signs."

She held one up briefly, and he got a better look at the designs that bordered the edges. Vines and flowers, intricately drawn, interspersed with hearts and hand-drawn emojis. John laughed at a particularly enthusiastic yellow face with red heart eyes.

"Em helped, too," Celeste said, following his gaze.

Seeing her mouth upturned and hearing the laugh like music from her lips was almost more than he could take.

"Could you," he forced out, "tell me why you're here?" The signs seemed clear, but he had to hear it from her.

Celeste leaned the posters against a tree and took one step closer. "I'm here because one morning on my porch you told me I was brave, and I'm trying to be brave again." Another step. "I had this story in my head of what it meant for me to . . ." She swallowed. "Fall in love. And it's hard for me to let that go, but I'm trying."

She took another step and reached for his hand, twisting her fingers with his. "You asked if I could be open to this. I am."

John closed the distance between them and cradled her face in his hand. "Yeah?"

She nodded and swiped her bottom lip with her tongue. "Yeah." Her pulse thumped against his thumb where it rubbed just under her jaw. "I'm open to finding something that fits us and what we need, even if we don't know exactly what it looks like yet. But it's scary."

"I know. I'm scared, too." Celeste made him want things he'd given up on, and made him aware that the world was even bigger than he'd imagined. "From the start, you've been a whirlwind, and I don't want to slow any of that down. You aren't too much for me, Celeste."

She sighed, leaning into him. "I know that. But, I might need reminders sometimes." Her hands pressed against his chest, fingers curling into his T-shirt. "And you need to talk to me, tell me when I push too hard."

"I will." John kissed her jaw, inhaling deep to catch the sweet, familiar tang of peppermint.

"Wait." She breathed hard. "There's one more part of my plan. After the signs and the talking."

"I think we need privacy for that," he murmured against her skin, wrapping an arm around her waist.

She giggled and pushed him away. "Not *that*, you dirty man! I mean, yes that. But this first."

Celeste reached a hand to her ponytail, pulling it through her fingers, then smiled at him. "I wanted to ask you, officially, if you'll be my person."

"Your person?"

She nodded, looking so sweetly shy he could melt. "'Boyfriend' doesn't seem right for you. But I heard someone just use 'person' and I liked it. So, do you? Want to be?"

Her nervousness was as endearing as it was ridiculous. Who wouldn't want to be this woman's person? She could hike eight miles without blinking and talk for hours about different adaptations of *Pride and Prejudice*. Everything she did—from parenting to birding—was done with passion and dedication.

He cupped her face with both hands. "Do you want to be *my* person?"

She nodded, her lips parting.

"Then we're people, together." His mouth landed on hers, smiling and open. Kissing Celeste was falling underwater and losing all sense of direction. It was the vast Arizona sky with no up or down.

Eventually they separated to gasp a few deep breaths, but Celeste kept her arms wrapped tight around John's neck. He walked her back until she was pressed against the rough bark of a cottonwood as his hand slid from her back around the front of her body, gripping her hip bone.

He smiled against her mouth, then kissed her again, harder this time, pressing his body against hers.

"Oh, John," she gasped and laughed into his mouth. "Did you bring some wood from your shop, or are you just happy to see me?"

His laugh filled the space around them, free and open. He pecked at her lips, shaking his head. "I missed you. I really did."

Speaking the truth about how he felt with her, and without her, left him feeling as light as the air around them.

Celeste traced his smile with her fingers. "I missed you, too."

They locked eyes as her fingers trailed down his cheek. John knew what Celeste was giving him with just a simple statement, and how vulnerable it must make her feel.

It made him want to repay her gesture tenfold, to shower her with his trust and gratitude until she was writhing beneath him, moaning his name.

"Maybe we should go." His mouth moved along her jaw. "Spend some time at my place."

Celeste caught his mouth with hers, kissing him deeply. When they broke apart again, breathing hard, she was smirking. "First, can we—can we walk around a little? Go birding? I've missed it, and soon you're going to be busy with all these new clients."

"You know a perk of running my own business?" John tucked a wisp of hair behind her ear. "I can be as busy or not busy as I want. And I'll never be too busy to go birding with you."

Celeste leaned into his hand, all but purring. "I'm glad to hear that, because you wouldn't want to lose me as a partner. I don't know if you heard, but I was the most improved birder in this year's Arizona Ornithological Society contest. I have an award to prove it and everything."

"Do you?"

She nodded, looking haughty and cute as hell. "And speaking of contests, I thought maybe we could have one of our own?"

John buzzed with the energy that came from being near Celeste, like anything might happen.

"First to see five birds wins," she said. "The loser is the first to get naked back at my house."

He drew in a long breath. "It sounds like no matter what, we both win."

The playful, heated look on her face said it all. "That's the point. You in?"

John stepped back into Celeste, crowding her against the tree. The sun streaked through the branches, shining against the chestnut sheen of her hair as a red-winged blackbird trilled from the reeds along the nearby pond. His mouth brushed hers softly before he pulled her bottom lip between his teeth, tugging just like he knew she liked it. "You're on."

AUTHOR'S NOTE— OR, WHY I WROTE A ROMANCE ABOUT BIRDING

Many Sunday mornings of my childhood were spent on trails outside Tucson with my dad, naming the birds and plants we knew as we walked. What we lacked in gear and knowledge we made up for in sheer enthusiasm, always willing to pause on a dusty trail to watch a red-tailed hawk circle in the sky above.

Fast-forward twenty-five years. I'd left for a while, but I was back in Tucson as an adult. My second child was an infant when I found myself in an evening class called "Birds and Poems." The class was a serendipitous combination of things I loved: a lens through which to look at the natural world, a meditation on the desert Southwest that I call home, a deep dive into words and language, and a place to write with abandon. And it made me a birder.

For a long time, I hesitated to call myself a birder, just as I still shy away from claiming the label of *writer*. Both feel too official, like titles too venerated to describe what I'm actually usually doing: fumbling along, looking up as I walk, seeking a story as I go. But really, both titles ask nothing more of us than intention and practice.

Most of my birding happens in my own habitat, where the birds I know best share a space with me. The sprawled mesquite trees and spiky palo verdes of my yard host Gila woodpeckers, verdins, broad-billed hummingbirds, white-winged doves, lesser goldfinches, and so many more. Occasionally, they all cry out at once, and I know when I look, I'll find a Cooper's hawk, stripes of copper across its compact chest, scanning the ground for anyone who might not be paying proper attention.

In 2020, during the pandemic, I was at home managing three kids through virtual schooling while embarking on graduate school myself. It should have been a hard time, and in truth it probably was, but I remember it like this: all of us in solidarity and shared unknowing, my own thinking expanding into new places, and watching a lot of birds in the yard. It was during this time that I was assigned to read a romance novel in a grad school class, and from there I was off, reading every happy ending I could get my hands on.

I consume romance novels for the same reason I watch birds—for the sparks of joy, because I prefer to be happy when the world gives us so many reasons to be sad. So when I, as so many others did, started writing that year, it seemed only natural that the romance I wrote should include birding. After all, what is love if not the thrill of discovery, the willingness to learn something new, and the desire to find magic in the world around us?

If you came to this book as a birder, I hope you leave a fan of romance. And if you came as a romance reader, I hope you leave a birder. My website (www.SarahTDubb.com) has resources for those looking to start bird-watching, including some of my favorite books and advocacy organizations. You don't need anything to become a birder—just intention and practice, and a willingness to look around. And when all else fails, remember John's advice: *Start with discovery, and go from there.*

ACKNOWLEDGMENTS

Before I ever tried writing a book, I imagined the author's journey as one that happens alone, each writer sitting at a desk and crafting a book with their bare hands. But I have learned that a finished book is actually touched, molded, held, and shaped by many, many hands. So I must begin with my deepest apologies for not being able to name everyone here, because an attempt to do so would leave this section of the book as long as my sex scenes, and not nearly as entertaining.

It's no exaggeration to say that every word I write goes back to my mom, a free spirit who had piles of paperback romances on her end table. If she could read this book, she wouldn't just love it, but would yell about it in the streets. If nothing else comes out of this publishing thing, knowing that is enough.

Enormous thanks to my agent, Amy Giuffrida, who saw something to believe in back in 2020 and has held me up ever since. Amy is an advocate, a bulldog, a sassy pants, and a friend, and I couldn't ask for a better partner on this journey.

To Abby Zidle, my incredible editor, who plucked me out when I was close to saying goodbye to this book: working with you is an actual dream come true. Many thanks to Frankie Yackel, the intrepid assistant editor keeping us all in line, and to Sarah

Horgan, whose cover art is actual Arizona-inspired perfection. Polly Watson is a true artist of a copy editor (and very fun in her comments to boot), and Hope Herr-Cardillo worked their design magic to make the book come even more alive on the page. Additionally, enthusiastic thanks to production editor Nancy Tonik, marketer Tyrinne Lewis, publicist Julia McGarry, and the rest of the wonderful Gallery team.

To my critique partners, Livy Hart, Laya Brusi, and Jessica Joyce: you have held and loved this book in its many forms and iterations, just as you have held and loved me through my many forms and iterations. A thank-you will never be enough. I look forward to years of more books together.

Enormous thank-yous and love also to: Ambriel McIntyre, my ride-or-die friend and biggest fan—I'm so glad writing romance brought us together; Jess Hardy for always keeping it real, making me laugh, and inspiring me to write what I love; Erin Langston for helping me be a silly goose; and Maggie North for helping me sort out feelings about publishing as I ramble into my phone while I feed the chickens.

I owe so much spirit to the community of writers who have held me up: the OG crew of Hopefully Writing; the Bananas, one and all; the dreamers and schemers of Smutfest; my amazing and resilient agent siblings on the A-Team; and my boisterous buddies in the Tucson writing group and Romance Book Club, especially Jen DeLuca, whose generous spirit and wealth of advice kept me going to the finish line.

Kudos, appreciation, and affection to my colleagues and friends in the Pima County Public Library system who do amazing work every day. Special thanks to Jeff McWhorter, who cheered me on when I texted "I think I'll write a book," and a standing ovation to Jessica Pryde, librarian extraordinaire, whose advocacy for diverse romance is not only a gift to our library system but an absolute necessity to the world at large.

This book is rooted in a love of birding, for which I thank the amazing naturalists and poets Eric Magrane and Simmons Buntin, whose "Birds and Poems" class planted a seed that blooms among these pages. Gratitude also to Luke Safford at the Tucson Audubon Society for his advice regarding bird counts, and the organization at large for its work to advocate for our winged friends.

I rediscovered romance in a readers' advisory course in library school, and so I must thank Debe Morena for encouraging (nay, assigning) us to read popular fiction to better understand the tastes of library patrons. To think that my book may fall into someone's hands through serendipitous discovery at a library is more than I ever could have hoped for.

To my family (through blood, marriage, and the sheer passage of time) who have cheered me on: thank you for always supporting me in all my stages and phases. If you actually read the book, let's just agree to not talk about some of the scenes, okay?

The McDonald women—Kate, Colleen, and Connie. You are my second family. Thank you not only for always holding me up but for keeping the memory of my mom close throughout this journey. So many of these words were written in your beautiful home away from home, Connie, and I only hope they do it justice.

It really does take a village to write a book, so I must give all my love to mine—Ellie, Becca, Katy, and Lila. In many ways, we've raised each other as we've raised our kids together. Even when you didn't know I was writing, you were supporting my work through your friendship (and childcare!), and I hope the mothering in this book honors us all. We are all works in progress, and we all deserve our own friendship. Additional huge hugs and thanks to Rachel, an amazing friend and the very first person to read Celeste and John on the page, and to Mike, who has been a rock-solid support throughout this journey.

Endless, bottomless, gooiest, and mushiest love to Rob, for being my rock when I need to be steady and my wings when I need to fly. You are my blueprint for every happily ever after.

And finally, to Carter, Hazel, and Emery—I want to go into full-cringe mode right now, but instead I'll just say: I love you, and I am honored to be your mom as you bloom into your amazing selves. Thank you for always believing in me, and I promise to always believe in you. I'll try to write something you can read one of these days.

BIRDING WITH BENEFITS

SARAH T. DUBB

This reading group guide for Birding with Benefits *includes an introduction, discussion questions, and ideas for enhancing your book club. The suggested questions are intended to help your reading group find new and interesting angles and topics for your discussion. We hope that these ideas will enrich your conversation and increase your enjoyment of the book.*

INTRODUCTION

Newly divorced, almost empty nester Celeste is finally seeking adventure and putting herself first, clichés be damned. So when a friend asks her to "partner" with his buddy John for an event, Celeste throws herself into the role of his temporary girlfriend. But John isn't looking for love, just birds—he needs a partner for Tucson's biggest bird-watching contest if he's ever going to launch his own bird-guiding business. By the time they untangle their crossed signals, they've become teammates . . . and thanks to his meddling friends, a fake couple.

As the two spend more time together, they end up doing more than watching birds, and their chemistry becomes undeniable. Since they're both committed to the single life, Celeste suggests a status upgrade: birders with benefits, just until the contest is over. But as their bird count goes up and their time together ticks down, John and Celeste will have to decide if their benefits can last a lifetime, or if this love affair is for the birds.

TOPICS & QUESTIONS FOR DISCUSSION

1. Celeste is in an era of adventure throughout this book. If you followed in her footsteps and started a year of adventure tomorrow, what is the first hobby or activity you would pick up? Would you pursue any of Celeste's hobbies?

2. This book is packed with vibrant descriptions and imagery, both of nature and of Celeste's and John's feelings. What are some of your favorite descriptive lines, and why did they stick out to you?

3. A major theme of this book is self-discovery. What part of the story do you think had the most impact on Celeste's journey of self-discovery? What about John's journey?

4. John and Celeste both enter the story with their own relationship traumas and complicated histories. While we watched how those experiences challenged them, what do you think were the positive influences that those histories had on their love story, if any?

5. Humor plays a major role in this story. What funny moments stuck out to you the most, and why? How do you think humor affected Celeste and John's love story?

6. If you had to list three attributes that describe Celeste, what would they be? What aspects of her character, or moments in the story, made you choose the ones you did?

7. While John's character could be described as a "cinnamon roll" (gooey, soft, and warm on the inside), he is also quiet for a romance hero. How does John's characterization work within the romance, and what heroic tropes does he embody?

8. Friendship is another theme that pops up often throughout the book. How do you think Celeste's and John's friendships with the other characters develop the story? Are there aspects of these friendships that you admire, or that surprised you?

9. While John and Celeste were both on paths to self-discovery throughout the book, Celeste was navigating another journey: parenthood. How do you think Celeste's experiences and challenges as a mother affected her love story with John?

10. One of Celeste's best qualities is her ability to tap into emotion. What emotions did this book bring out in you? What moments in the story made you feel the strongest positive or negative emotions?

11. Often parts of the stories we love stay with us long after we've read them. What lessons, pieces of advice, or other impactful moments will you take away from Celeste and John's story?

12. This book has a beautiful dedication to "all who facilitate discovery." The author then lists those who facilitate discovery in her life. Who facilitates discovery in your life? Who would you include on that list? How do your answers compare with those of the author's?

ENHANCE YOUR BOOK CLUB

1. One group activity that Celeste and John participate in is trivia. Gather your group, make a list of questions (including, especially, any fun birding facts), and spend some time playing a killer game of trivia.
2. Celeste falls in love with birding throughout the story—so why not try it out? Weather permitting, take some time to head outside and see what you can find. If that's not an option, hop online and find out what kind of birds are native to your area so you can search for and spot them in warmer weather.
3. When you fall in love with a book, you never want it to end. If you could request an extra epilogue set at any point in Celeste and John's future, what moment in time would you pick? Get together with your group and plot out where you think Celeste and John would be, or what they'd be doing, in your dream epilogue. You can even share your ideas with the author via the contact option on her website, www.sarahtdubb.com!

TURN THE PAGE FOR A SNEAK PEEK AT
SARAH T. DUBB'S NEXT LAUGH-OUT-LOUD ROMANCE!

COMING FROM GALLERY BOOKS IN 2025

"The question at hand is: When exactly would a midlife crisis commence?"

Pushing a wave of floppy hair off his forehead and training his eyes on the tank, Chris stared until his vision blurred. Tiny whirls of tan, like coffee and cream, spotted the glass, some so small they'd get lost on a pencil eraser.

His life's work.

"If we think about the average human lifespan, which for a cis man in the US like me is seventy-seven years, the actual middle of life would hit at thirty-eight. Which would mean that, at thirty-four, I'm a little young for this. If that's what 'this' is."

A frustrated raspberry fogged up the glass, but his little treasures didn't stir. They'd been living their small, shelled lives since the Cambrian period, and weren't ones to be bothered by a wildlife biologist having a bad day.

"Or a bad year," he mumbled, standing and tugging at the hem of his shirt, trying to catch some air. His well-loved Pogues T-shirt had enough threadbare sections to act as ventilation, but his basement lab was still stuffy as hell.

"Talking to the snails again?"

Chris laughed as he spun to face Vita, his star grad student, leaning through an open doorway with a smirk on their face.

"They're great listeners," Chris admitted, glancing at the old clock on the wall. "Didn't mean to steal your lab time."

Because the space was so cramped, they'd worked out a schedule so that they were usually down there one at a time. Tuesday and Thursday mornings were for Vita to take routine measurements concerning water quality and other variables in the tanks in order to learn how to support the snails' ability to survive in a changing world. It was research Chris himself had started years before. Work he thought he'd do forever, because that was the plan he and his parents had built for him when he was fourteen.

Well, they hadn't picked the snails. That had been all him. But if it came with a PhD, his name in research publications, and accolades at conferences, snails would do.

"It's cool." Vita strode into the room, crisply dressed as always in a button-down shirt and slacks, their dark brown hair cropped short to reveal half-inch plugs in each earlobe. "I came in a little early because I've got a coffee date later. Snails offer you any insight, Professor?"

Chris groaned, drawing a knowing chuckle from his companion. The first day Chris had taken his new grad student under his wing, he'd made it clear that "Professor" was a title reserved for his father, especially since Vita had already collected their first PhD in evolutionary biology. But it had still taken him a full year—and several pints of beer—to convince them to call him Chris.

"Surprisingly, they offered no commentary." Chris sighed as a phone notification pinged in the back pocket of his jeans, tempting him to dunk the technological wonder into one of the tanks.

"More of your adoring fans?" Vita dragged a stool over and pulled a laptop out of their shoulder bag. "When I asked you to be my advisor, I didn't know I was getting a celebrity."

Chris only rolled his eyes, swiping his phone open to TikTok, where dozens of notifications signaled that his last video had been a hit.

He'd posted his first video six months earlier at the urging of his big sister, Lu, who'd told him to"share your brilliance with the masses, not just with us." Chris has gotten into the habit of recording little tidbits for his niblings in DC—special facts about his snails and his research, or cool details about other animals in the Southwest, where he'd settled during graduate school. It had been one of several strategies in an attempt to reengage with his work, and had the great side effect of strengthening the long-distance connection between him and his big sister and her awesome kids.

It seemed easy enough to step up the videos he was making anyway for Dylan and Jules. And so, @thesnailguy was born.

But he'd never expected the response.

Apparently, there was an ample audience for a scientist who looked like a washed-up musician and smiled a lot while sharing nature facts.

Did it help that Chris had eaten up the flood of attention, staying up late to respond to comments? It sure didn't hurt.

And now there were people all over the world learning from him. It was exciting, but it was also . . . a lot. Now he had a new group of people to keep happy, which was a seriously weird thing to feel so stressed about.

Yesterday he'd posted his most recent video, ninety seconds about earthworm adaptations, and the comments were streaming in.

I'll never stomp on one again!

Oh, look at those wriggly little sweeties!

I remember always going out in the rain looking for worms as a kid!

Is that a skeleton tattoo peeking out from @thesnailguy's shirt? 😳

Shirtless vids, please!

Wouldn't *that* be something. The viewers would see a lot more than that skeleton and the full-sleeve tattoos on both arms. What might they think of the sloppy Casper the Friendly Ghost he'd gotten on one pec to impress a boy in college, or the Scorpio constellation over his right hip he'd gotten to impress the boy's sister the following year?

"Is that a grimace I see?" Vita nudged Chris's elbow. "Does the university's hottest biology professor tire of his fame? I'd think it would take your hookup game to the next level."

"You dare talk to your advisor that way?" Chris scoffed, even as Vita chuckled in response. The two were almost the same age, and with their mutual love of mollusks and watershed ecology as a great equalizer, Vita enjoyed ribbing Chris about his active social life.

Chris wasn't ashamed of it. Hell, he loved nights of fun, snippets of intimacy with strangers, casual mornings after that didn't ask for anything more. There was a brief infusion of joy in those encounters, a deep knowing of another person, even if just for a few hours. For a long time, they'd been exactly what he wanted. They'd been enough.

He glanced back at his phone, a practiced smile plastered on his face that probably didn't fool Vita, even if it worked on almost everyone else. Managing the account was taking up hours of time when he was already struggling to dedicate himself to his path at the university, and it was one more place where he was expected to be . . . well, himself.

Chris was nice, Chris was easy, Chris was *fun*. That was his thing, and he liked it.

Didn't he?

"Why am I asking snails about midlife crises?" he said aloud.

"Probably because you're in one," Vita said simply, folding their laptop and swiveling to face Chris. "I have mad respect for you, and you're basically my snail hero, but you know you've been phoning it in this semester, right? Last year I had to actually drag you out of lectures on the days you talked about land snail resilience after forest fires, but now—"

"I know." Boy, did he know. He should have applied for tenure last year, a fact that his father, the actual Professor Andersen, missed no opportunity to mention.

You're thirty-four, Christopher. Are you going to be an adjunct forever? You know you're better than that.

He stood and ran a hand through his hair, shaking off the memory of his last disastrous trip home to Illinois. With two parents as academics, he'd actually thought they might have insight about his particular crossroads: he was passionate about his work but weary of the red tape and myriad expectations that involved neither a classroom nor his research, and hesitant to dig himself even deeper. But they'd rolled their eyes at his concerns and begged off viewing any of the videos of what they called "his distraction."

Nope, clarity wouldn't come from good old Mom and Dad. He needed something *else* . . . he just didn't know what it was.

"I'll leave you to it," he said to Vita. "You treat our babies right."

Vita narrowed their eyes for a moment but just nodded. "I always do. Get some sunshine, yeah? Touch grass?"

"Grass in Tucson in the summer? Unlikely, but maybe I'll go touch cactus."

Outside, in the shadows of the redbrick biology building, Chris slipped in his earbuds and dialed his sister's number. He pushed an index finger against the white spine of a saguaro, pressing just enough to indent his skin without piercing it, as he hoped Lu would pick up.

"What's up, nerd?" At the sound of Lu's typical greeting, Chris's shoulders relaxed. His big sister always made him feel better. "You okay?"

He hadn't said a word, but her "sister sense" was clearly activated. She was one of the few people who could see through Chris's smiles, her expertise built through years of looking out for her super-skinny, too-smart, probably-queer little brother. He really should grow the hell up and not expect Lu to always take care of him.

Any day now.

"All good, just wanted to say hi."

"Mm-hmm. I buy that a hundred percent." Behind Lu's voice, the bustle of her household hummed. "Did you see that someone proposed marriage in your last comments? Among other things that made my eyes bleed."

"I haven't looked closely." He'd need to, later, so he could respond and express gratitude. "How are things there?"

"No! Jules, do not—" Lu sighed. "Sorry. Things are good, but we're scrambling. I can't really talk for long, because we're dealing with this child-care disaster."

Chris traced the waxy ridge of cactus between spines. "Is everybody okay?"

"Yes, everybody's fine, sorry. That was hyperbole. But Maggie's got this big training coming up, you know? In Minneapolis?"

"Yeah, for the super teachers." Lu's wife, Maggie, was a school administrator, but had spent years as an exceptional teacher and had planned a summer retreat and training for teachers from around the country. "What happened?"

"Her assistant, who basically holds Mags together during this shit, has to stay home because of a family emergency. So now—" There was the slamming of a cupboard and mumbling in the background. "No, I'll be right there. It's Chris on the phone, just give me a minute." She cleared her throat. "Anyway. Maggie has to be there in three days and we're trying to figure out if I can go. I could help everything run smoothly and work on my own stuff in the evenings. But that's two weeks we'd need someone here with the kids."

"Two weeks? Wow, that's tough." He walked a few steps to settle on a bench, leaning forward between spread knees. "Can they stay alone?"

"Chris. Dylan is thirteen. I'm not leaving him home to take care of his little sister."

"You did it." It hadn't happened all the time, but from time to time Chris and Lu's parents had decided to head to an academic conference together, and teenage Lu had been in charge of the house.

She groaned. "That was shitty. We managed, but you know it was wrong of Mom and Dad to leave us alone at that age, right?"

"Hey, we had fun." Of course he knew it hadn't been great of their parents, but it was still time he'd valued with his sister. Then and now, she managed to be enough family for him. Watching her build her own family and give her kids that love and support was a fucking joy. His heart ached that their adult lives had been spent with a whole country between them. But Lu and Maggie had met in college in DC and loved the city so much that they'd never left, and his snails were here. "So what are you going to do?"

Lu sighed, a rare sign of exhaustion from his sister, who could do it all. "I don't know. It's not easy to find someone who can drop everything and come run our lives for two weeks, you know? It's not just staying here and keeping the house intact; it's all of Jules's practices and the lessons Dylan does for . . ."

But her last words were lost in the swirl of Chris's thoughts. *Not just anyone could drop everything for two weeks.*

But Chris wasn't just anyone. He was Lu's little brother, the one she'd been there for again and again. His classes for the semester were wrapped up, grades turned in, and Vita was more than capable of running the lab for a couple of weeks. Hell, they'd probably love having Chris out from underfoot.

"So anyway," Lu continued, "obviously I'm not asking Mom and Dad, and Maggie's mom isn't in the best health, but she's going to check with Frankie—"

"Frankie?" He choked out, stepping into the sun to let the heat push out the intrusion in his thoughts—dark hair streaked like wood, lips almost always teasing a scowl. "Why would she call Frankie?"

"Uh, because she's Maggie's sister? And pretty good at handling tough situations."

"Right." He bit back a laugh. Chris had seen himself how well she'd handled the situation of slipping up with him one night five years ago—by never speaking of it again.

"You don't need Frankie," he rushed to say before traveling further down memory lane. This was about Lu. "I'll come. I'll come stay with Dylan and Jules. I'll get a ticket tonight."

When Lu spoke, her tone was measured. "That is such a sweet offer. But . . ."

Chris strode back toward the bio building, which held his small office upstairs. Why wait till tonight to book his ticket?

"But what?"

"You've never exactly watched kids, like, on your own."

"Technically that's true. But I'm responsible! You know I have two master's degrees and a PhD, right? And I run one of the most noted labs in the country."

"For snails, little brother. Not to knock your little mollusks, but my children are humans."

He pushed through the heavy metal doors and bounded up the stairs to the third floor. "I can do this, Lu! I'm their uncle!"

"You're their *fun* uncle! The guy who throws them over his shoulder and teaches them guitar riffs and lets them stay up too late watching movies. This is volleyball practice, dirty dishes, and brooding adolescents. It's not what you're used to."

"Exactly!" He paused at the top of the stairs, breathing hard. "Believe me, not what I'm used to is exactly what I want right now."

He heard her exhale, then let out a resigned sigh. "I don't know, buddy."

"Luckily, I do. We're not going to debate it anymore. Tell those niblings of mine to get ready, because I'm coming to Washington."